# The Spirit Bird

*Drue Heinz Literature Prize 2014*

# THE
# SPIRIT BIRD

Kent Nelson

*University of Pittsburgh Press*

Published by the University of Pittsburgh Press, Pittsburgh, Pa., 15260
Manufactured in the United States of America
Printed on acid-free paper
10 9 8 7 6 5 4 3 2 1

Library of Congress Cataloging-in-Publication Data

Nelson, Kent, 1943–
[Short stories. Selections]
*The Spirit Bird: Stories* / Kent Nelson.
        pages cm. — (Drue Heinz Literature Prize)
Summary: "The flight path of *The Spirit Bird* traces many landscapes and
different transitory lives. A young man scratches out a living from the
desert; a woman follows a rarely seen bird in the far reaches of Alaska;
a poor single mother sorts out her life in a fancy mountain town. Other
protagonists yearn to cross a racial divide, keep developers from a local
island, explore their sexuality, and mourn a lost loved one. The characters
in this collection are compelled to seek beyond their own horizons, and as
the stories unfold, the search becomes the expression of their desires. The
elusive spirit bird is a metaphor for what we've lost, for what we hope for,
and what we don't know about ourselves." —Provided by publisher.
ISBN 978-0-8229-4436-2 (hardback: acid-free paper)
I. Title.
PS3564.E467A6 2014
813'.54—dc23                                    2014029621

*For Lulu, always.*

# CONTENTS

The Spirit Bird

# ALBA

ÚLTIMO VARGAS HAD BEEN IN HATCH, New Mexico, only six months, since March, and already he owned his own business to compete with Netflix, delivering compact disc movies and video games to ranchers and people who lived within twenty miles of town. He had worked out a deal with Señora Gaspar, who owned the video store, to pay him 90 percent of the delivery fee, and if he took out more than fifty videos in a week, a premium on the extras.

Último had a moped, which made it feasible. Gas prices were high, and the delivery fee saved customers money. Also, it was convenient—they didn't have to wait till they had an errand in town. Most of the customers were Mexican families who worked the land for Anglos, or Anglos who owned cattle or pecan groves. Último organized his schedule by time and direction to avoid random trips. It was a lot of riding on the moped, but he liked the terrain—the low hills, the bare mountains, pale blue in the day and silhouetted in the evenings, the vast sky. He liked seeing the fields of onions and chiles, the pecan trees, the alfalfa growing, the cattle grazing. He saw hawks, antelope, badgers, deer, and learned their habits.

In a few weeks he knew most of his customers—the Gallegos family out Castenada Road, who grew green chiles, the Brubakers farther on, the widow woman, Señora Obregón, who still ran the Bar SW. The Michaels family was a mile east, the Garcias were on the other side of Interstate 25—they owned the bakery—and Tom Martinez lived in the turquoise trailer a mile past. Many of the families grew chiles—that's what Hatch was famous for—and marketed them to the co-op in Albuquerque or along the town highway, pickled or fresh, or in jellies, or as *ristras*. Everyone knew Último, too, the *chico loco* on his moped.

The more people knew him, of course, the more people knew about his business. He was strong, had a good smile, and was a natural salesman. He talked to the Mexican families in Spanish, asked where their relatives came from, who was left in Hermosillo or Juárez or Oaxaca. He talked to the Anglos to improve his English and to show he was a serious businessman. He expected great things of himself one day.

Último's English was passable because he'd worked almost a year in Deming before he came to Hatch. He'd washed dishes at Si Señorita from six to two, and at four he mopped floors at the elementary school. In between he spent his off hours at the Broken Spoke, where he met people, even some women, like Brenda, who was a hairdresser, then unemployed. One night Último was walking home to his trailer at eleven p.m., and Brenda stopped in her Trans Am with the muffler dragging. She gave him a ride, and one thing led to another. He fixed Brenda's muffler and relined the brakes, and she fucked him like there was no tomorrow. After a month Brenda wanted to get married—she was pregnant, she said—and Último said why not. Two weeks after the wedding, when he found out there was no baby, Brenda ran off to California with a wine salesman.

To pay off Brenda's debts, Último used his meager savings and took a third job unloading freight at the train yard, though he still wasn't making enough money, or sleeping enough, either. One evening, after he had been threatened with eviction from Brenda's apartment, his boss at the school found him dozing at a teacher's desk. He was finished in Deming and he walked north with his thumb out, but no one picked him up. In two days, forty-six miles later, with nothing but the clothes he wore and a blanket he'd brought from home, he staggered past Las Uvas Valley Dairy and a few broken-down adobe houses and into Hatch, where he saw a HELP WANTED sign in the window of the Frontera Mercado. He went in and got a job stocking groceries.

Hatch was in the fertile cottonwood corridor along the banks of the Rio Grande, the interstate to the east, and open country in every other direction—ranches, pasture, rangeland. The days were getting warmer by then, and he slept in the brush along the river, shaved and washed himself there, ate for breakfast whatever he had scavenged from the *mercado* the day before. If he wasn't working, he spent sunny mornings in the park and rainy ones in the library. Then Señora Gaspar hired him to work the morning shift at the video store, checking in rentals, cleaning, replenishing the stock of candy bars and popcorn. He established a more efficient check-in, organized a better window display, and built a new sign from construction waste: GASPAR'S MOVIES, and in smaller letters, Pregunte sobre nuestro servicio de mensajeria.

"What delivery?" Señora Gaspar asked.

"Our delivery," Último said. "I have bought a moped from Tom Martinez."

Some of his customers ordered movies for the company Último gave them. Señora Obregón, fifty-five years old, had lost her husband and wanted someone to talk to. She reminded Último of his abuelita in Mexico, and he often made the ranch his last stop of the evening so he had time to sit on her porch and listen to her stories. Her husband had been killed two winters before when, as he was feeding the cattle in a blizzard, a fifteen-hundred-pound bull slipped on a patch of ice and crushed him. They'd lost a hundred head in that storm. Her children were in Wichita, Denver, and Salt Lake City, two sons and a daughter, and none of them wanted anything to do with the ranch. Señora Obregón dressed well, as if Último's presence meant something, and she offered him steak and potatoes and always leftovers to take with him afterward.

Another person who ordered movies but didn't watch them was the Garcia's daughter, Isabel. She was seventeen, had bronzed skin, short black hair, and a good body. One day in June, she called the store and ordered *Babel*, "Pronto," she said. Último was alone, so he put a CERRADO sign in the window and took off on his moped. Isabel came to the door in a tank top. "Let me find the money," she said. She didn't invite him in, but she paraded around the room pretending to look so Último could see the sunlight on her body. She found the money and came back to the door. "Come again," she said and handed him a five-dollar bill.

Elena Rivera also ordered movies. She had lived all her life in Hatch—her family owned a small dairy that competed with Las Uvas—and she was married to a village trustee, Manuel, who grew chiles. Manuel was often there when Último came by, as was their son, Aparicio, twelve years old, who was sick. Elena Rivera thought it was good for the boy to see other people, and Último obliged her by playing games with Aparicio and telling him jokes. The more time Último spent with Aparicio, the more movies the Riveras ordered.

Último was born in the village of Ricardo Flores Magón and raised there with two older sisters without being much aware of the wider world. Growing up, he thought of his father, Fidel, as already old. He slouched, his face was wrinkled, and he wore a straw hat with the brim coming apart. The hat had a blue-gray heron's feather tucked into the sweaty red band. "This hat keeps me alive," his father told Último. "You don't know." His mother kept goats and chickens and a small garden, watered by hand, and made baskets from yucca fiber and marketed them in Chihuahua. Then his father disappeared, no one knew where, and money arrived from different places Último had never heard of. His mother said in the States money grew in the gardens like squash and beans.

Último was an altar boy—every boy was—but he had doubts about God. Último had been to Chihuahua with his mother once and felt the energy of the city, had seen the lights and the cars, the radios and TVs, the clothes, soaps, and a thousand other things, and why would God make such things that belonged to so few?

Último did well in school without much effort, and girls were kind to him, especially his sisters' friends who came over to their house all the time. When Último was fourteen, the padre warned him of sins Último had never thought of, and when he inquired of his sisters' friends, they laughed and kissed him and showed him what pleasure a boy might receive from their hands and mouths. Último was troubled that God should not want him to do what felt so joyful.

So he passed his days playing, reading, and learning from the girls and playing soccer. When he was seventeen, his father came home for several months. He had a car and nice clothes and wore a hat that was useless against the sun. He told stories of Fresno and cotton picking, of Castroville, where artichokes grew, and Yakima, Washington, where apples were heavy on the trees. If a man was willing to work, he said, there was money everywhere.

His father wanted to take Último back with him to California, but Marta, the older sister, was pregnant in Buenaventura and needed help and the younger sister, Lorena, couldn't be left alone. Most of the day she sat with their abuelita under the thatched awning, but sometimes without warning she screamed at a lizard or a bird, and once she'd torn off her shirt and run through the village crying out "God is chasing me." Another time she took the knife she was slicing papayas with and stabbed herself in her arm. The abuelita was too old to do what was necessary for Lorena, so when his father went back to the States Último had to stay longer in Ricardo Flores.

Elena Rivera appreciated how good Último was with Aparicio and saw no reason not to help a tall, good-looking boy who had gotten himself to the United States. That's what she told Último one afternoon in September when he brought over a video of *Abu and the Giraffe* for her son. "What will you do when it gets cold?" she asked. "You can't sleep at the river all winter."

"Maybe I will rent from Hector Lopez when his pickers are gone."

"My parents have a vacant house at the edge of town," Elena Rivera said. "There is a spell on it, because a child was killed by a rattlesnake."

"The place by the dry arroyo?" Último asked. "It has tires holding down the tin roof."

"That's it," Elena said. "The windows are broken, and who knows what else is wrong with it. You'd have to do some repairs. Are you afraid of snakes?"

"Yes and no," Último said.

"Which?"

"No," Último said.

"Then, if you're interested, I will ask my parents about it."

At the end of his days in Ricardo Flores, Último had a girl-friend, Alba, three years older, a friend of Marta's, whom his mother had gone to help. Alba was devout and shy, and she went to Mass every day with her mother. She wasn't one of his sisters' friends who'd shown him what pleasure was, and he knew better than to coax her or to try to kiss her. Instead, he asked to see her naked body.

"Once," he said. "I want to remember you when I'm gone."

"You can remember me with my clothes on," she said.

"I promise I won't touch you."

"You will look at me with lust. That's a sin."

"I might look at you with lust," Último said. "That will be my problem, not yours."

"Why would you ask this," she said, "when you know I cannot do such a thing?"

"There is no cost for a question."

The next day, as they walked outside the village, Último asked again.

"I have already answered you," Alba said.

"You might have changed your mind," Último said. "You might have decided there could be no harm in it because I will go to the States."

"When are you going?"

"Soon," Último said. "When my mother comes back from Buenaventura."

"In any case, where do you think we could do such a thing? Lorena and abuelita are at your house, and my mother is at mine."

"In the church," Último said. "There's a room behind the altar where we used to wait before Mass. No one is there in the afternoon."

She laughed "You're as crazy as your sister."

"Only once," Último said. "I want to walk all the way around you so, when I am in the States, I will remember clearly your whole body."

"Without touching?" Alba said.

"Yes."

"It won't happen."

A week passed. Último tended Lorena, who was seeing the Virgin Mary in the clouds. He humored her, sang to her, told her she would live to be one hundred and three years old. They threw stones into the ravine. Último read her stories from a magazine.

Their mother returned, grieving for a lost granddaughter. "It was God's will," she said. "The child was never well, but did it have to die?"

"God's will," Último said, "what is that?"

A few days later, Último filled two plastic bottles with water and loaded his backpack with food that wouldn't spoil—peanut butter, bread, cans of stew—and said goodbye to Alba at the *tienda* where she worked. "I am leaving tomorrow before daylight," he said. "I am going alone so I won't get caught. I promise I'll write."

"How will you find your way?"

"I am destined for great things," Último said.

"I have changed my mind," Alba said. "I will do what you asked."

Último said nothing.

"At two o'clock I have a break," Alba said. "I will meet you at the church."

"Promise?" he asked.

At two o'clock that afternoon, Alba appeared at the church as she said she would. The room Último remembered was behind the altar, though he had forgotten how barren and simple it was. There was only one square window high up in the wall, and light fanned down onto the plaster of the wall opposite.

"You have to turn around," Alba said.

Último turned around and stared up at the light. He heard the swishing of clothes, a dress fall to the floor, then quiet.

"Now," Alba said.

He turned back slowly and saw her body, her small, dark-tipped breasts, her long black hair over one shoulder. She did not hide herself with her hands, but she lowered her eyes. He was aware of her face, the expression of chasteness, but of joy, too, as if she were both ashamed and glad of the moment. Último walked all the way around her so that, for a few seconds, his shadow fell across her body and then her body returned to light.

Elena Rivera's parents agreed to let him have the house in return for his labor fixing it up. An abandoned shack was what it was, with waist-high weeds in the yard. The door was padlocked, but Último looked through the jagged glass of the broken windows. Swallows had nested on the rafters, and the stuccoed walls were covered with graffiti—

VENCEREMOS! VIVA ZAPATA! ANGLOS SUCK EGGS. There were three rooms, one with a sink, but no running water. The outhouse in back was functional, but it leaned two feet toward the dry arroyo where cottonwoods grew. A barrel stove had heated the place, but the barrel was in the yard, and the stovepipe was gone. Último tried the outdoor pump and gave thirty pulls on the long, curved handle. Dirty water came out, but in another thirty pulls the water came clear.

Early mornings in October, before he went to the video store, Último cleared the weeds and burned them. He borrowed tools from the Riveras—hammer, saw, chisel, level, tape measure—and bought plaster, nails, window glass, glazing compound, and a stovepipe. At night he scavenged for plywood, bent two-by-fours, one-by-fours with nails still in them. He fixed the hole in the floor, repaired the damage to clapboard outside, filled rocks into the holes raccoons had made under the house. He scraped away the swallows' mud nests, covered over the graffiti with fresh plaster, moved the barrel inside and cut the stovepipe to fit. He propped two fallen cottonwood branches against the outhouse to make it stand straight. The electricity was turned on. From his customers he cadged two lamps, two chairs, a mattress, and a card table. He saw no rattlesnakes—it was getting cold.

October 25 he moved in and not long after, an unusual thing: one evening he stayed for steak and green chiles at the widow Obregón's and drove home late on his moped. It was windy and dark, and when he pulled up to his shack he was chilled. The moon illuminated the tin roof with the tires on it, and the stones in the yard were silver. When he opened the door to his house, the moonlight came in with him, and there was Alba in the kitchen. She had on shorts and a pale blouse—he couldn't see what color in the dark—and her face was calm but conflicted with desire. "Let me make a fire," he said. "You must be cold." He turned on the light, but no one was there.

Último knew people claimed they'd seen Mary Magdalene and the Virgin Mary and even Jesus Christ, but this was Alba, an ordinary girl from Ricardo Flores. Despite the promise he'd made, he hadn't thought much about Alba. In Deming he'd written her several letters scrawled on torn paper, and he'd received three from her, written on a lined school tablet, the last of which offered him more of her if he came home. But he was with Brenda, and he hadn't written back.

The night after Último saw Alba, he came home from his last delivery with a keen anticipation of seeing her again. Perhaps she'd be at the table or lying in bed, or she'd be at the window looking west into the moonlight, but when he opened the door, the house was empty. He thought it might have been a difference in the clouds or the moon's waning by a single day. Several weeks went by, each night getting longer and colder, and he got over his disappointment and wondered whether he'd ever seen Alba at all.

It rained. At the Goodwill he bought a coat and hat and gloves. With the winnowing light, people had longer evenings to fill up, and he hustled videos even harder because Señora Gaspar was always getting in new movies and his premiums were good money. But with the cold and the early dark, deliveries were more of a burden. Yes, he was familiar with the signs, the location of the poorly banked curve on the Canal Road, the washboard gravel by Jaime Delgado's adobe house where seven people lived, but Último couldn't see the blue hills in the distance or the hawks circling or the silhouettes of the mountains, except as a jagged black line against the stars.

His solace was his house. Each day he became more used to it, more comfortable. The barrel stove was smoky, but it heated the rooms. He had built a platform for his mattress, and he slept well. For a couple of months, he sent money home to his mother and Lorena.

In December, Elena Rivera's parents asked for rent, starting the new year. "You've lived there for free," Elena Rivera said. "What you spent for labor and materials has been accounted for."

"How much?" Último wanted to know.

"Two hundred a month. I've argued your case, but the dairy business is not going well, and my parents want what's fair."

"There's no heat," Último said. "No running water. I'm already paying the electric."

"That's why it's not four hundred," Elena said.

"I understand," Último said. "I will pay the rent."

At Christmas, Señora Gaspar went to Albuquerque to visit her son, and Último was left in charge. He opened the store, answered the phone, logged in the returned videos. He called the people whose DVDs were overdue and offered pickup service. Of course, Señora Gaspar needed someone in the store when Último was making deliveries, so at three her niece, Rosa, came in with a four-pack of wine coolers. When Último returned half-frozen from his pickups and deliveries, Rosa was sitting on the stool with a space heater under her reading comic books.

The next morning the till was short twenty-two dollars. To avoid suspicion, Último made up the difference from his own pocket. The next morning, another fifteen dollars were missing. He didn't know what to do. Señora Gaspar would be gone another eleven days.

Último was saved from one despair by another, because the next night when Rosa closed the store, she left the space heater on, and too close to the wastebasket. It melted the plastic and set fire to the computer tear-offs and then to the desk. It was three in the morning, and by the time the volunteer fire department arrived, the building was ablaze, the inventory destroyed, and Último's livelihood gone up in flames.

For several weeks after the fire, Último sat by the barrel stove and looked out the window at the gray sky. He bought a cheap bottle of red wine and drank it but felt no better. He slept. Only a week before the fire, he had sent money home, so when he paid rent, he had no money left. His only possession to sell was his moped, but it was a mile to town.

He might have looked for his father in California, but where? Or, of course, he could have gone home, but in Ricardo Flores he could not do the great things he expected of himself. Then, on a dark morning, he was lying in bed, dozing, waking, pondering, when Alba came again. She was in the doorway to his bedroom, embracing the wooden jamb, hiding her breasts from view. He sat up and pulled his blanket up to cover his chest and shoulders. Alba's expression was no longer conflicted, but wanton and eager. Último called to her softly. She wouldn't come closer, so he stood up to go to her, and she disappeared.

He interpreted this vision of Alba as a sign to stop moping, and that afternoon he asked Señor Garcia for a job in the bakery. Último had to go in at four a.m., and each day he understood his mother's desperation. How had she endured the long journey to Chihuahua to sell baskets? What had she thought, leaving her children behind?

One of the Garcias was there, Mercedes or Alfonso, and Último helped prepare the dough, knead it, and put it into pans. He learned to make dulces and churros and cinnamon rolls, and at six, they opened the store. Último brewed the coffee. There were three tables for sitting inside.

At eleven, Mercedes or Alfonso, whoever was there, took a break for lunch and left Último alone for an hour. He was not allowed to sit at the tables, but he might drink coffee in the back room, from which he could watch the store. One day, as he was behind the counter gazing at the street, Isabel touched his shoulder, and he jumped. She had come in through the back door from the alley.

"Are you alone?" she asked.

"I'm here where I'm supposed to be," he said.

"They say you're a good worker and do what you're asked. Would you obey me, too?"

"That depends," Último said.

Isabel slid past him, and he smelled her scent. "You don't come to see me anymore."

"I never came to see you. I delivered the movies you ordered."

"Hatch is the end of the world," she said. "I can't wait to leave."

"For me it is the beginning of the world. What should I do?"

She took a bite of a churro. "I'll think of something," she said. "Be ready."

On the day Último left Ricardo Flores he had said goodbye to his abuelita who was old, but not to his mother, and hitchhiked to Buenaventura, where he got a ride north to Las Palomas. In the evening he hiked west into the desert, and a three-quarter moon led him into the mountains. In the morning he hid in a cave, and the next night he walked again. He followed animal trails, and in the morning he was in the United States, at the edge of an encampment of RVs. All that day he watched what the people did there, who was leaving, and at mid-morning of the second day, he saw a couple on their way out stop their motor home at the restroom. Último ran from his hiding place, climbed the ladder to the roof, and lay down.

The ride was easy. He held on to a vent to keep from rolling off on the turns. Most of the time he lay on his back and looked at the sky, the same one that arched over Ricardo Flores, and he daydreamed of Alba—her bronze skin, her black hair, the shame and joy on her face as she revealed herself to him. Several times he raised his head to see where he was, but everywhere around him was desert and mountains.

Once they stopped for no reason Último could see, and he heard voices—questions and answers. Someone opened the back of the camper. Último didn't move. If he couldn't see anyone on the ground, no one on the ground could see him. Then the RV gathered speed again and kept going. A half hour farther on was a town with stop lights, where the couple pulled into a gas station. Último climbed down from the roof and ran.

One afternoon after work in the bakery, Último was in bed but hadn't gone to sleep yet. He'd got a raise of fifty cents an hour and was calculating how much he could send home when he heard the door open in the living room. For a minute he didn't hear anything more. Maybe it had been the wind, maybe Alba. Then the floor creaked. He opened his eyes, and Isabel Garcia came into the room.

"I thought of something to ask," she said. "Do you want to make love?" She walked to the bed and pulled her shirt up over her head. "Move over."

He moved over—he had no choice—and she slid in beside him.

Isabel visited every few days, and it wasn't punishment to feel her hands on him, her mouth, the weight of her body. He liked her sighs, the notes of pleasure she sang to him, the urgency she felt, but he didn't feel love. He felt an uneasy peace, and he slept after, but he worried about who had seen her car there, who might talk, and he knew his days at the bakery were numbered.

He went to talk to Elena Rivera. "I want to grow chiles," he said.

"Everyone in Hatch grows chiles," she said.

"That's the idea," Último said. "I want to be everyone. But I will grow the best ones."

"Do you know anything about growing chiles?"

"I will learn."

"And where will you grow them?"

"On the land around the house that has tires on the roof, on my land."

"You want to buy it?" Elena Rivera asked. "I laugh at you. My parents will laugh at you. But in case they don't, how much are you intending to pay?"

"Ten thousand dollars," Último said. "The house is barely a house, and there are rattlesnakes. Two thousand now, and a little at a time over five years."

"Will you be here in five years?"

"If I get the land."

"The land is full of stones," Elena Rivera said, "and the creek is dry."

"More reasons for your parents to sell."

"But how will you grow chiles there?"

"Magic," Último said. "I am destined for great things."

A week after he talked to Elena Rivera about the land, she came into the bakery. She bought two cinnamon rolls. "Aparicio likes to eat these," she said. "I'll tell him you made them."

"I did," Último said, "only for him."

"I talked my parents into selling," she said. "Who else, I said, would buy a house like that in a field of stones with tires holding down the roof?"

"Others like me," Último said.

"There are no others like you. They want fifteen thousand, three thousand now, and the rest in four years. They will charge no interest."

"Give me two weeks," Último said. "I will find three thousand dollars."

But he had no idea how he would get the money. He tried the bank, but, as he thought, he had no assets and no credit, and even Elena Rivera's recommendation got him nowhere. He thought of asking the widow Obregón for a loan, but that would change their friendship. He had only one other idea, and on a Thursday after work at the bakery, he drove his moped to Deming.

He went first to the Broken Spoke, where the bartender remembered him. "Your hair is longer," the bartender said.

"You've gained weight and look prosperous," said Larry Munzer, sitting on the same barstool he had been on a year ago.

"I am almost a chile grower," Último said. "Do you understand what that means?"

"You're almost a man," the bartender said.

"I'm looking for Brenda," Último said. "We're still married."

"She's back in town," Larry Munzer said. "She's started

up the Hair You Are Salon. She married a nice guy from California."

"All the better," Último said.

Brenda was surprised and not at all happy to see him. The upshot was, in return for three thousand dollars, he offered her a divorce, silence, and forgiveness of the money he'd paid on her debts. She siphoned the money from her loan. It took a few days — Último had to ride back to Deming another time — but he signed the contract to buy his house and the land around it.

Before offering to buy the property, Último had examined what he was doing. The cottonwoods along the arroyo were healthy, and, though the arroyo was dry, the well in the yard was good. Último disassembled the hand pump and measured the well casing — fifteen feet, not very deep. He borrowed an electric pump from Tom Martinez and ran an extension cord to the house. Whether there was a stream underground or a reservoir Último didn't know, but the pump produced five cubic feet per second, which was plenty to irrigate five acres of chiles.

Then Último eyeballed the highest point on his property, figured out how he would get water to it, and traded away his moped to Alex Tomar for the use of his tractor. On Sunday, when the bakery was closed, he plowed up the stones. The plow blade broke, and Último welded it. It broke again, and he welded it again, and he finished plowing in the dark. On Monday, surveying the field of loose stones, Último had more work than ever.

For the next two weeks, every spare minute, he carried stones. Aparicio helped. They gathered the stones into a pile, loaded them into a wheelbarrow, and wheeled them across a plywood trail laid out over the broken ground. The wheelbarrow was too heavy to dump, so Último turned it on its side, and they heaved stones into the arroyo.

After work, Último had no time for siestas and no time for Isabel. He loaded and unloaded the wheelbarrow hundreds of times, each day creating more arable ground. Then one day when he came home Isabel was there and asked her usual question.

"I can't now," Último said. "Come back when it is too dark to work."

"You'll be too tired."

"I'm too tired now."

"Would you want me to tell my father about us?"

"What have I done but what you wanted?" Último asked. "What kind of love is it if you force me?"

"Better than nothing," Isabel said. "Come inside, Último. I need you now."

When the stones had been carried away, Último broke apart the big clumps of earth with a hoe. That took another week. Then he borrowed back his moped and visited the widow Obregón and asked to buy manure.

"You can't buy it," she said. "I will give it to you."

"Can I rent one of your trucks to haul it?"

"I will lend you the truck."

"Thank you," he said, and he listened to her complain about her son in Wichita who worked for Cessna but never came to visit her.

Último spread the manure with a shovel, fifteen loads over ten days. He hoed furrows three feet apart and arranged a flexible plastic pipe to the highest point in the field north of the house and irrigated the dry ground so it could get used to moisture it had never experienced except as rain. He did the same thing from the highest point to the south.

He spoke to other chile growers he'd met when he delivered movies—the Gallegoses who marketed their chiles to Safeway; to Arnie Yellen, who grew chiles on an acre behind his house and sold them on the highway; to Alfred Saenz, who was the biggest grower in the Hatch Valley. He talked to Ned Cruz, the owner of The Chile Store, who sold chiles year round as paste and in powder form, dried, fresh, and frozen. In the library he read in Spanish and English about green chiles and red chiles, their growing seasons, the ways to keep insects off the plants, how to make sure the chiles flowered. He called the agricultural extension agent of Doña Ana County for recommendations and learned that the less water chiles had, the hotter they were.

As the weather warmed, the bakery became busier. Locals shed their winter isolation and moved around outside. Motels were full of spring travelers, and these people wanted dulces and coffee for the road. Último came in at three a.m. to make more bread, more cinnamon rolls, more churros. Even Isabel helped. She was at the cash register before school and came back for an hour at noon and complained the whole time.

Still, Último labored every afternoon on his land. He had carried the stones away but continued to find new ones; he broke clumps of earth smaller and smaller; he irrigated the ground. Then, finally, in April, he was ready to buy seeds.

There were too many choices—sweet or mild, hot, super hot. A habanero was fifty times hotter than a jalapeño. There were bird chiles, Bolivian chiles, Peruvian chiles, all undomesticated, plus bell chiles, Cherrytime, Hungarian Hot Wax, Hot Cherry, red, cayenne, and serrano. And there were specialized versions of these, too, like Cherry Bombs, Marbles, and Bulgarian Carrot, as well as hybrids like Ancho 211, Thai Dragon, Conchos Jalpeño, and Serrano del Sol.

He was pondering what to buy when Isabel came over and asked him to go with her to Las Cruces to find an apartment. "I'm moving as soon as school's finished," she said.

"Is it all right with your parents?"

"I'm not asking."

"When do you want to go?"

"Now," she said, "right after you fuck me."

Isabel had read a newspaper ahead of time and had marked the ads, and by three o'clock she'd found a one-bedroom not far from the university. The manager of the building wanted a month's rent in advance, which Isabel supplied. "You can visit me anytime," she said to Último, "and you'd better."

"Since we're here," he said, "do you mind if I run an errand? I want to buy a hat."

They found a hat store in the Yellow Pages, and Isabel drove him there and waited in the car. He bought a straw hat with a brim to keep the sun from his face.

"You look silly," Isabel said.

"It's a hat like my father's," Último said. "Now I have to go to the university."

"I have a friend there," Isabelle said. "I'll see if he's home."

Isabel let him off on the corner of Espina and Frenger, and Último found the Chile Pepper Institute of New Mexico State. He asked to see the director, and after a short wait was ushered into a small office and sat down across the desk from a young woman. "I am going to grow chiles in Hatch," he said. "I need magic."

He set seeds in the ground in rows three feet apart, each seed eighteen inches from the one he'd planted before. He marked every seed, fertilized it, and watered it by hand from a bucket he carried along. He moved on his knees from one planting to the next like a pilgrim crawling for miles to atone for his sins. It took him three days to plant the seeds—the experimental ones the institute was paying him to grow.

Then he waited.

So the water wouldn't evaporate in the heat of the day, he irrigated after sundown, again at midnight, and a third time when he got up to go to the bakery. On his break at nine a.m., he ran home and turned off the pump.

One afternoon he came home and saw two trucks parked along the arroyo, an old one and a new Dodge. He recognized Señora Obregón sitting in the shade with her hired man, Paco. Último came up, and they all shook hands.

"It was my turn to visit you," Señora Obregón said. "I see how hard you've worked."

"I have planted chiles," Último said. "I can offer you a drink of water. It is a humble house."

"I would like you to bring me chiles from the harvest," Señora Obregón said

"I will be glad to," Último said, "but the harvest is far away."

"Closer than you think," Señora Obregón said. "That's why I'm here. How would you bring me chiles without a truck?" She nodded toward the old truck. "The tires are worn, and it has a hundred thousand miles of use. But it's a Toyota and has lived well."

"I am honored," Último said.

"The title is on the seat," Señora Obregón said. "Here's the key. Now you can visit me again."

May 21, a long day. Último had hardly slept because at two in the morning, something had made an eerie, quavering sound in the cottonwoods. He stepped outside with a flashlight and heard the unmistakable buzzing of a rattlesnake. He found the snake in the beam of the flashlight, coiled, with its head raised, its tongue flashing. Último got to his knees and shone the light into the snake's eyes. "I will leave you alone," he said, "if you will leave me alone."

The snake didn't answer, but Último believed they had made a deal.

He heard the quavering again—like a saw blade being played—and he skirted the snake and walked to the arroyo. The sound came from upstream in dark billowy trees, but each time he reached the place he thought it was it moved farther away.

The night was cool, but the stars were out, and as Último waited to hear the sound again, he urinated into the arroyo. Like every man in history who had done the same thing, Último felt the enormity of the sky, the deepness of space, and his own tiny greatness in the effort he had made in his field. Then the quavering came again from the trees nearby.

Último shone his light back and forth into the leaves until he found the shining eyes of a small owl. It was thirty feet away and a little above where Último stood, and Último made a deal with the owl, too, never to die.

Último lowered the light, and the bird flew deeper into the trees.

He set water and went back to bed, but still couldn't sleep because he felt the air move though the house, sweet air, humid with the earth's smell. He got up when it was still dark and went to bake bread.

At nine o'clock he drove his new old truck home and cut off the pump and sat for a minute on the smooth stone he had put down as a step to his door. He was wearing his straw hat against the sun. The snake's path was carved in the dust in the direction of the arroyo, and cottonwoods tattered in the breeze. Because he hadn't slept, Último felt part of everything that lived nearby. He remembered his mother and Lorena in Ricardo Flores, Marta in Buenaventura, his father in California, wherever he was, and wished they all could see him at that moment, tired and exultant.

He closed his eyes for a moment and leaned back against the door, and when he opened this eyes again, he saw tiny sprigs of green coming up through the soil. He stood up and ran into the field. The chiles were coming up, three feet apart in the rows and eighteen inches one plant from another. He knelt down in a wet furrow between two rows and kissed the ground, and when he looked up again, Alba was a few feet away, gazing at him. She wore jeans and a white blouse, and her expression was dreamlike, as if she had believed in him all along and was answering his call.

# THE SPIRIT BIRD

THE TURBOPROP KING AIR DESCENDS from the clouds and cants low over the sea, around the snowy block of Sevuokuk Mountain—the sacred place—and there's the town of Gambell: lines of shacks strung out on a stark gravel bar, with the lake behind, still frozen at the end of May. Some of the shacks have red roofs, some blue, some shiny tin, and each house has a four-wheeler beside it. There are no trees. I see only one large building, the aluminum-sided school at the edge of town toward the mountain, but otherwise, no brick post office, no granite courthouse, no white-painted town hall—no center. The plane circles the point, where offshore ice stretches away into the clouds forty miles to Siberia, and makes for the runway between the ocean's shoreline and the frozen lake. It's mid-afternoon, but time doesn't matter here because, this far north, it's daylight forever.

On the ground, the eight of us birders, strangers to one another except for a mother and her college-aged son, are ferried by ATV to the hotel, such as it is, a modular structure with ten rooms along one hallway, a kitchen in the lobby, and a room for eating and watching television. I'm in number five with Janet Moreland, a forty-year-old widow from Minneapolis, and I unpack my sweat clothes, heavy socks,

slippers—I didn't bring makeup or my hair dryer—and then
we assemble in the TV room and are reminded of the param-
eters of our visit. We have five-day permits to be on the road
around the lake and in the boneyards and along the shore to
the northwest point. If we want to search the tundra or the
mountain—if we want to look for the Eurasian Dotterel—
we'll need a native guide. No alcohol is allowed. No noise
in the hotel after eleven p.m. We will monitor channel 6.1
on our two-way radios. As part of the package, our group
has rented five ATVs, and whether or not we stay with our
guides, Heather and Larry, or go off on our own is up to us,
but we should pace ourselves. The days of long light can be
wearying. Get some sleep. Most birds are not one-minute
wonders; they stay a day or two.

Within an hour we're dressed in parkas and wind pants
and are out with the guides in the Near Boneyard searching for thrushes blown off course from Asia, sandpipers
and plovers that breed in the far north, pipits, Bluethroats,
buntings, not one of which my friends in New Hampshire
would ever have heard of. The boneyard is a dug-up expanse of what looks like a battlefield—holes ten feet deep,
some with water or ice in the bottom, bones strewn everywhere. In decades and centuries past, the Yupiks buried
the corpses of seals and walruses near the town. In the last
fifty years, as walruses diminished and ivory carving became sought after, the walrus tusks had a new value, and
the digging began. Birds hunker down in these holes out of
the wind.

We walk through stealthily, in as much of a line as we can,
Janet Moreland on my left, and the college kid, Eric, on my
right. Heather calls out redpolls, Lapland Longspurs, Snow
Buntings—all common birds here. Janet is a serious lister

and eager for a Brambling or Eye-browed Thrush. She has on a black parka with a hood and holds her Zeiss binoculars with both hands. I imagine her a store manager, setting up quotas for the sales force, or maybe an accountant. The boy, too, has all the gear—blue knit cap pulled low, gloves, red windbreaker, Swarovski glasses—but he's not looking as the rest of us are. He pauses and stares out beyond the shacks to the beach, where, following his gaze, I see seal meat drying on racks and the skeleton of a whale. On his face is an expression of wonder, as if he were fleshing the bones of the whale and seeing it alive.

"You're not a birder?" I ask him.

"My mother made me come," he says.

"From?"

"Houston."

"Good birding territory."

"I know a little," he says. "I've done High Island and Big Bend and the Lower Valley. My mother takes me to corroborate what she sees."

"But you're not a lister?"

"I know everyone else is. How many do you have?"

"Seven hundred and sixteen in North America. What would you be doing otherwise, I mean, at home?"

"Screwing around."

"Literally or figuratively?"

He smiles, as if surprised by the intrusive familiarity of the question from someone my age. "What would *you* be doing?" he asks.

"I'm a professor from New Hampshire," I say. "I'd be reading."

He looks past the shacks again. "How do they kill the whales?" he asks. "Do they use rifles or spears?"

"They ride ATVs and snowmobiles," I say. "I suppose they use rifles."

He ponders this. His face bears into the wind, and long-ish hair spills from beneath his knit cap. His eyes are brown, his chin bristly. He reminds me of my own son I never had, an invisible son, one I imagine.

Then a Bluethroat appears in a hole in front of us. It hops to the edge and struts among the bones—smaller than a robin, rusty tail. "Bluethroat," Janet calls out, and the line of birders breaks and runs toward the bird.

The next morning the weather is foggy, with a cold wind from the east. For passerine vagrants, we want a west wind, but there are still migrating seabirds. Heather and Larry set up scopes on the gravel spit at the northwest point of the island, where the ice pack is a few hundred feet offshore. We collect shreds of cardboard boxes, pieces of plywood, even a smashed Clorox bottle to sit on because an inch under the gravel is solid ice. Hundreds of thousands of auklets and murres fly past, scores of puffins, loons, and eiders. Kittiwakes and gulls weave sinuous lines higher in the air. Now and then someone calls out "Emperor Goose" or "Arctic Loon," and we all find the bird and follow it with our binoculars.

Eric's mother is small and round-looking in her layers of clothes and has on a knit cap like his. Over the course of a half hour, she circles closer to me, then paces nearby. Finally she says, "You're the one Eric likes."

I'm watching a string of Horned Puffins pass by and lower the glasses. "Are you talking to me?"

"You're Lauren from New Hampshire. The professor. Eric has an awareness of people."

"He seems like a good kid," I say.

"I'm Eve Harrison," she says. "Eric's not so good as you imagine. I wanted to get him away from Houston for a while."

I train my binoculars out to the shelf ice where gulls are loafing. "He says he's not much of a birder."

"Oh, he's good. He knows more than I do. But if I'd let him stay home, I wasn't sure what he'd do."

She breaks off and turns away. Again I lower my glasses.

"I wish you'd talk to him," Eve says.

"About what?"

"About whatever. He lost his father recently—the man lived in California, we were divorced, a real bastard, but Eric doesn't know that."

"I'm sure you haven't told him."

"Please," she says. "Eric needs friends."

I look around the group. "Where is he?" I ask.

"I don't know," Eve says. "He's a loner. When I woke up this morning, he was gone."

Eric doesn't show up at the hotel for lunch, and all afternoon as I trudge with the group though the Far Boneyard at the foot of the mountain I wonder where he is. There's nowhere to go except along the coast or around the frozen lake. I imagine him in a Yupik shack talking to children, tutoring, maybe—there's something childlike about him. Or taking drugs. That's possible, too. Is that what Eve meant when she said he wasn't as good as he seemed?

Snowmelt runs off the slope of the mountain and alongside the boneyard. Where there's no snow, grass grows among the rocks. We find a Northern Wheatear and a Yellow Wagtail, though we've already seen these birds on an excursion around Nome. The wind is chilling and incessant, and several of the group have gone back to the hotel, though not Janet, not Eve. They doggedly follow the guides, checking each hole in the ground, scanning the hillside, looking into the sky.

Why am I the one he claims as a friend? I'm no one he knows. I've been a comp lit professor at UNH for fifteen years, never married and never needed to be. From early on I had an intellectual bent. I read; I considered alternatives; I stayed aloof. Growing up, I engaged the nearby terrain—Maine, Plum Island and Newburyport, the White Mountains—and in doing so found an affinity for birds. As I learned more, I was led farther afield to the arid mountains of southeast Arizona, the humid river bottoms of Texas, the Florida Keys, even the islands off California. Birding drew me to the wider world, though my friends claimed the opposite—it made me sacrifice myself to a quest with no meaning. What was to be gained by counting species? What does seeing a bird mean? When the spirit is always on the move, how can it settle?

Heather flushes a Brambling from one of the holes, though none of us has a good look at it before it darts into another bone pit. As we pursue it, I see Eric in his red windbreaker coming up the road from the far end of the lake. I put my binoculars on him, and in that crisp circle he is defined by fog, shrouded in grainy imperfection. He looks up at the mountain with the same expression of wonder I saw earlier, as if he's seeing through whatever he's looking at. He doesn't look at us.

I expect to see Eric at dinner, but he isn't there. I eat with Larry, who teaches ornithology at UCLA, and two men from Ohio who've never been to Alaska. From walking and being in the wind, we're all hungry for the chicken and mashed potatoes.

In the middle of the meal Larry leaves for a phone call, and Eve sits down. "I saw him walking back from the lake," I tell her. "Is he in your room now?"

"He brought cheese and crackers and chocolate bars," Eve says. "If he doesn't eat with us, it's his decision. I gave up telling him what to do a long time ago."

"You made him come on this trip."

"Is that what he told you?"

"He said you wanted him to see the birds, as a witness."

Eve laughs. "People like to be believed," she says, "but my list is my list. A witness doesn't change what I see."

Larry returns, and Eve gets up. "Talk to him," she says.

Eve sits in front of the TV. She's right—it's what you see yourself that matters. When I finish eating, I find a Ziploc bag and pack Eric chicken and potatoes and niblet corn, but when I knock on the door to their room, there's no answer.

The whale skeletons on the beach are draped with rotting flesh. Dilapidated scaffolding holds the whale carcasses, and at the same time falls down around the bones. It's almost eleven o'clock at night, and though the sun is under clouds, it's still light out. I'm walking to escape my room, or, really, Janet, who talks nonstop about birds. Partly, though, it's to feel the place at this hour. In New Hampshire it would be dark, people in bed on a Wednesday night, but here several young girls loiter at the airport runway, some riding bicycles on the only pavement. Two boys race a rattletrap ATV across the humps of pebbles on the beach and pass me without waving. The wind hides the sound of the motor, and then there's nothing but the swirling clouds low over the ice. There's an urgency to things here—people who hunt seals and whales and pick greens from the wild must know in their blood and bones where they are on the planet.

I never did. As a teenager and through college I felt on the outside of things. I had friends, of course, men and women both, lovers, but I didn't know what to do with them, whether to embrace them or push them away. Gina and Ray—two random people—Gina, the year after college when I'd gone to Guatemala to build houses for the poor, and Ray, a welder I met during graduate school. Gina was five feet six, my height exactly, and dark-haired, from Rochester. We shared a room with two beds in a cinder-block building, but after a few days, even in the heat, we slept in one. When our time in Guatemala was nearing its end, Gina wanted to know what was next for us, what we'd do together when we got back to the States. I was going to graduate school. Where, she wanted to know. Should she move? For me such a question had no answer. I didn't want her to go home to Rochester, but I didn't want her to live with me, either.

It was the same with Ray. He had a welding shop next to the repair place I took my Camry, and he drank coffee with his mechanic friends. We had dinner at a café and, a week later, slept together. He was a kind, gentle man with a good sense of humor. He enjoyed his work and talking with his friends. For money he welded car parts, but his real calling was making sculptures from discarded pieces of metal. I went to his duplex on Fridays and left at eleven. Then it was Friday and Sunday and Wednesday. He said I might as well live with him—why did I want to leave? I told him I had reading to do. "Reading?" he said. Two weeks later we broke up. Ray wasn't getting enough from me. He said, "You're not with me." I said, "I'm not against you." He said, "You know what I mean."

So it went. I finished my doctorate, got a job and did research, and absorbed myself in birds.

Eric is alone at the northwest point. His binoculars are trained on the ice, and even though it takes ten minutes' walking on the loose pebbles to reach him, he never alters his attention. When I'm close enough, I follow where I think he's looking, and a whale rises from the sea, bends its ridged back, and dives again.

Finally he lowers his glasses and waves at me. "Did you see it?" he asks.

"Your mother's been worried," I say.

"The nubbly back? It was a bowhead." He looks back into the mist where the whale has disappeared.

A moment passes, and I come up next to him.

"I saw the dead," he says.

I turn toward the ice and raise my binoculars, not knowing what to say. The ice is jagged white, crevassed, stretching out into the mist.

"The ground is frozen, so they put them in coffins and set them in the rocks."

I lower my glasses again. "You saw them?"

"The weather breaks the coffins apart, and the bones disperse. . . ." He turns to me. "I know we aren't supposed to go up there, but at the end of the lake the slough was frozen, and there were no birds, so I climbed to the saddle."

"You went up on the mountain?"

"I was looking for the dotterel," he says. "The higher I climbed, the colder it got."

"Did you see it?"

"What can you see in the clouds?" he asks. He peers through his glasses toward the moving water between us and the ice. "Dovekie," he says. "King Eider. And look there—a Ross's Gull."

I gauge the angle and lift my glasses. Among the spikes of ice are groups of kittiwakes and larger gulls and then one small one with a pinkish chest and a thin black collar— Ross's Gull. I radio Heather and Larry and report what Eric has found.

One spring semester I had a student in my seminar in South American literature—a brilliant woman from North Carolina named Kellie. She had come to the university, she said, to be far away from the South and from the life of women there. She was coffee—that's how I thought of her—almost six feet tall, strong, dark-skinned, a smell around her, not sweet, not bitter. She had short, curly hair that looked unkempt—appearance didn't matter to her. She was fascinated by literatures that offered ideas of cooperation instead of avarice, sensitivity instead of violence, the search for meaning and joy instead of acquisition and material possessions. "Like Borges," she said in my office one afternoon. "He was a celebrity who lived a modest life in an apartment."

"He had his imagination," I said. "He lived in other worlds besides Buenos Aires."

"That's what I mean," Kellie said. "Why don't we offer our children this opportunity?"

At the end of the term, Kellie went to Ecuador to learn Spanish so she might have a new perspective on her studies. I stored her books and clothes for her—a few boxes stashed in the attic—and one evening in September she reappeared. She was not much changed, except her hair was longer and prettier. She wore shorts and a white shirt with stitched colors.

At dusk, we sat on my terrace at the edge of the marsh in

Stratham, drinking wine and watching the egrets and gulls and crows fly to roost. "I'm moving to Arizona," she said. "It's because of you."

"Me? I haven't done anything."

"You're *here*," she said. "You're alive. I've thought of you so often because you inspired me to risk."

She explained why she wanted to go to the desert — to write she had to isolate herself — and I found myself agreeing with her desire to search on her own for what she needed. She might not find answers, but often questions were better than answers.

It was dark when we finished the bottle of wine. We went inside, and Kellie embraced me, and we went upstairs and undressed. For a few minutes, an hour, maybe, the burden of everyday life was lifted from me, and I felt the moment when all was all. We slept holding each other.

After midnight, with the moon on the bed, Kellie woke me. "We should agree to have a child," she said. "A son, like Borges."

"I want to," I said.

And from this, in my mind, my son was born.

On the fourth day there's a north wind, and it turns colder. The fog isn't so thick — more wind-blown mist than heavy clouds, but, with the humidity, the wind chill is debilitating. The guides lead us through the boneyards for what seems the hundredth time, and there are no new birds. Even red-polls and longspurs are scarce. Heather proposes to take up the sea watch again, but it's so bitter cold I opt to go back to the hotel. Even Janet's riding with me on the ATV doesn't dissuade me, and I steer across the gravel bar, fighting the wind, listening to her talk about, of all things, looking for the dotterel. It's a rare breeder in northwest Alaska, a little smaller than a Killdeer, but the same plover shape. It has a noticeable white eye stripe and a white band above a chestnut belly. Because its habitat is so remote, even Heather and Larry have given up looking for it. "If there's a warmer day," Janet says, "I'm getting a permit."

I keep quiet, and we ride past the school and across the pebble track worn through the middle of town. At the hotel I downshift and let the engine die just as Eric is coming outside.

"Your mother's going to the sea watch," Janet tells him. "She says you're welcome to join her."

"Okay," he says. "Thanks."

Janet and I get off the ATV, and she goes inside.

There's an awkward moment. Eric looks at the ground, and I stare off toward Sevuokuk Mountain. "I saw you coming," he says. "I waited to come outside." He pauses. "There's nothing new at the sea watch."

"You never know what will pass by. Maybe a Bean Goose."

"I'm not going."

"I didn't think you were."

"Are you too cold to come with me?"

"Yes," I say, "but I'll get warm another time."

He raises his eyes, and I know where he means to take me. He gets on the ATV, and I climb up behind and he starts the engine. I hold my binoculars to the side and lean into his back.

We drive through town on loose stones, curve past the school, and climb the hill toward the spring where the town gets its water. There we turn right onto the muddy track above the lake. The swirling mist comes hard, and I crouch behind Eric's shoulder. The motor is too loud for talk. Even though I roll my hands into fists, my fingers are frozen inside my heavy gloves.

It takes twenty minutes to negotiate the two miles to the slough at the end of the lake, and then we bear left up the hill. The ATV coughs, bounces through rivulets of snowmelt, roars, and lurches forward. The road turns to rocks and ruts with a stream coming through. I hold tightly around Eric's middle.

Higher up, surprisingly the mist dissipates — we get above it — and we have a view of the high country and the wider island. Rocks and snow and green tundra are interspersed, and water is running everywhere. At the top of the ridge, we stop, and Eric turns off the engine.

The sound of water and wind, ceaseless motion. Mist rises from below, but where we are the sun throws down its luminous rays. Far off across the strait the white icy mountains of Siberia shoot up above the clouds. We get off the ATV, and without saying anything, Eric starts hiking up the ridgeline.

I follow twenty yards behind across the snowfields and tundra. Lichened rocks poke out. Every so often my attention is drawn by a Snow Bunting's black-and-white wings or the leap and song of a longspur. I wish the sun were warm.

After several minutes, Eric stops, and when I catch up, he says, "This is where I saw the dotterel."

"Here?"

"I didn't tell you because you'd tell others. They'd all be up here."

"We all want to see it."

"Think of the bird," Eric says.

I scan the tundra but see no dotterel. Eric climbs high-

er, as if oblivious to the cold and to whether or not I find
the bird. He scrambles over larger boulders at the base of
the mountain, disappears, reappears higher up. The farther
away Eric gets, the colder I am. I call to him, but the wind
carries my voice away.

Why has he brought me with him here, a woman twice his
age? Or is it I who's brought him, a boy half as old? Eric has
disappeared again into the rocks, and I don't know where,
and even as I sweat in my parka, I can't feel my fingers or
toes. I don't want to go on, but I don't want to go back.

I climb higher and don't go far into the rocks before I see
the coffins. They're made of old wood, weathered now, some
large, some small—three or four small ones without mark-
ings. Five. One is split apart so the black interior opens to
the light.

I hear splintering, breaking, and I find Eric behind a
boulder tearing pieces of wood apart, separating boards
nailed poorly together. He's stacking them in the small clearing. For a moment I think he's going to build a fire, but the
wood is wet and rotten and wouldn't burn. He's not piling it,
but throwing it down randomly, throwing it away.

"What are you doing?" I ask.

He stops and looks at me. His eyes are hard and sharp,
not really seeing me. "I saw the spirit bird," he says.

"The dotterel?"

He points at the splintered coffin. "It came from in here."

In the coffin a man or a woman, who is dried flesh, lies
facing upward, palms up, too. The clothes—traces of red,
brown, blue—have been eroded away.

"It's a he," Eric says. "Structure of the hips, the large
bones. And there's a knife. I thought it had to be a man from
the size of the coffin."

There's a long moment when he looks at me, and his face is twisted in such anguish I can't breathe.

"What now?" I whisper finally.

He doesn't answer but shakes his head, and in those moments, I hear the wind and water and feel the sun on my face. I understand why I'm here, what Eric needs, what every person needs in this life. Eric kneels down beside the bones and takes off his gloves and touches the fragile hand, the man's shoulder, the withered face. He rests his hand lightly on the desiccated lips, and the spirit bird rises from Eric's hands. I see it, too —misty, vaporous, insubstantial— and when he stands from the bones all I can do is close the few steps between us and put my arms around him.

# RACE

## I.

HAKIM WOKE EARLY THE MORNING OF the half-marathon—6 a.m.—the last Saturday in August, though the race didn't start until 7:30. Sarah, his renter, had to be at the Yeast-I-Can-Do at five, so she made coffee before she left, though never strong enough, and he added a spoonful of instant to the carafe. Sarah had an upstairs room—renting, for Hakim, was an experiment whose verdict was still out. The house was too big for one person, and Hakim liked having the extra money for utilities, which in a small town were expensive. He didn't mind Sarah's peculiarities. She kept an odd schedule, sometimes in bed at seven, sometimes going out with friends and staying out all night. She was tall and had wild red hair and had come from Vermont to ice climb, though it was summer when people got work and fall when rooms and apartments opened up. She had broken up with her boyfriend, with whom she'd been camping, and maybe because she was twenty-six, half as old as he was, he found himself focusing on her comings and goings more than he wished to.

Mornings except Sundays, Hakim drove his truck the three blocks to Main Street, turned on his furnace and annealing oven—it took a couple of hours for them to mount sufficient heat—and came home again for breakfast. That morning of the race, Nia was going to open the shop, though he was scheduled to be back at one for a glassblowing demo. It was almost Labor Day, and he was low on vases, Christmas bulbs, ashtrays, and other souvenirs. The opening of school was the end of the tourist season, but it was also the beginning of the doldrums. He needed to do whatever he could before then.

He sprinkled shredded wheat into a bowl, cut up a banana, and poured in half-and-half and sugar, though he felt guilty for the cream. He had on his lucky red shorts and a T-shirt that had on it a picture of his daughter, Phoebe—eight years old when the photo was made but twelve now—under which were the words I AM A GOOD FATHER. Phoebe was in Tucson with her mother, all of them two years removed from the divorce.

In between bites, Hakim tied his shoes, stretched his quads, and lifted his hands to the ceiling. On the sill of the bay window above the sink were an assortment of vases he'd made, in which he'd stuck feathers of flickers, jays, and owls that he'd picked up on trails, and a gaudy ceramic bird an ex-girlfriend—his first love—had given him years ago in a college art class. Out the window the branches of a leafy apricot tree that never blossomed hung down over the wires from the alley, and against the wall in back, hollyhocks were blooming bright pink, white, and fuchsia. A blue, cloudless sky haloed the Amphitheater Cirque above town.

Hakim wasn't going to win or place in his age group, but he'd finished two 10Ks earlier in the summer—one at 7,000 feet and with hills—and he'd run trails. The year before he'd done this same half-marathon in 2:11, but he hadn't trained a lot. His ambition for this race was to break two hours.

He punched in Phoebe's cell phone number and was surprised when she answered. "I was going to leave you a message," he said. "I thought you'd be asleep."

"I was going to call *you*," Phoebe said. "I set my alarm for seven. Good luck in the race. I know you can do it."

"I can do it," Hakim said, "but can I do it in under two hours?"

"You will blaze to victory."

"I am slow but persistent," Hakim said. "What are you doing today?"

"Mom's taking me to the Tucson Mall," Phoebe said. "Why did she have to move *here*?"

"Which is worse, fire or ice?" Hakim said.

"Both are nice and would suffice," Phoebe said. "How's the renter working out?"

"She can't make coffee," Hakim said, "but you should see her red hair."

"Maybe she's Shaun White's sister."

"I'm wearing the T-shirt you gave me. Well, I've got to run. Ha ha. I'll call you after the race."

"Good luck, Daddy."

Hakim clicked off, turned on NPR, and did knee bends. The Supreme Court, in its infantile wisdom, had decided a corporation was a person and could give money to political candidates. There was escalating turmoil in Somalia, a plane crash in Hawaii, and a downturn in the Japanese stock market, none of which affected his quest to break two hours in the half-marathon.

He felt sorry for Phoebe, but he didn't go so far as to think she'd be better off living with him. He wished there were a manual to instruct him how to do his job from a distance, but of course, he should have held onto Beth in the first place. Should he have given up his principles for hers, lived in a climate she liked, and earned more than $50,000 a year?

Race had been an issue, and background. He'd grown up in Lenexa, Kansas, where no one else had a name like Hakim or a father who was Muslim. His mother was Caucasian and his father Egyptian. He was made fun of, beaten up, and ostracized, so his childhood was fractured and unhappy. He'd learned glassblowing in a course at Grinnell, and after three years in the army, he'd come to Colorado, first to Telluride, then to Gold Hill, where he'd opened his shop. He liked the independence, the iconoclastic career, the joy of making whatever he wanted. He was sole proprietor, so he did art pieces—lamps, decanters, candlesticks—not many of which sold, and he got by selling souvenirs—vases, cups, Christmas bulbs—which allowed him to put a down payment on a house. One day Beth showed up—she and two girlfriends were climbing fourteeners in the area—and she admired his art, his gray-blue eyes, and his entrepreneurship, not necessarily in that order. A year and a half later, he was married and had a daughter.

He retied his right shoe, checked his waist pack for energy gel, Band-Aids, and peppermint candy, and looked over the course map again—start at city park, run back south into town, then a block west to the River Road, then north and downvalley to Lavely, the next town, roughly ten miles, but with side-road detours to make the distance correct—13.1 miles.

City Park was eight blocks from his house. Would walking loosen his muscles or tire him out? He elected to drive and took the Tacoma key from his chain and pondered whether he needed his driver's license to go eight blocks. He worried about not having an ID, then criticized himself for worrying. *I am a citizen. They know me here. I am an American.* He climbed the stairs and got his driver's license and tucked a twenty dollar bill into his shoe.

A crowd was assembled in the park—runners and their families, onlookers, tourists, curiosity seekers. In the line to get his race packet, he made small talk with a woman who the day before had bought eighty-five dollars worth of glass from his shop. "I love my souvenirs," she said. "You are a magician."

"The art began in Mesopotamia in two hundred B.C.E.," Hakim said. "It's painstaking work."

"Those little elf ornaments are amazing."

"Where are you from? Is this your first race?"

"Fort Worth," the woman said. "You are so lucky to live in the mountains."

At the table several volunteers were handing out packets—people Hakim knew from town meetings and events. He stepped up to Shirley Guetz.

"Name?" she said, looking straight at him.

"Bayles."

Shirley flipped through the packets. "Hakim?" she asked. She pulled his envelope. "Pin your number so people can see it." She smiled at him and said with her eyes: *Who are you? What are you doing here?*

Hakim moved away toward the ball field. People were stretching on the grass, running in place, yakking with friends. Hakim said hello to people he knew. He'd been in town fifteen years and was acquainted with business owners and elected officials, but he didn't go to bars or socialize much. He wasn't invited to dinner parties. At night he read. He was the last of a dying breed, the male reader, and though there were two book clubs in town, he hadn't been asked to join either of them.

The packet had in it his number, safety pins, a subscription card for *Running* magazine, and a race program with a disclaimer about accidents. He pinned his number 170 on his shirt under the picture of Phoebe and flipped through the program. His ad was the smallest size but had cost two hundred dollars—"Hakim's Glassworks. Art Created on the Premises"—with a picture of a vase. He didn't like the word "created," but Nia thought it spoke to their potential customers.

His training had been erratic, but thanks to Nia he'd got out twice a week for at least an hour, often longer, when Nia volunteered for overtime, though he had to keep tabs on her. She was a refugee from the music scene in Boston—"Hiding out to live a real life," she said—which suggested to Hakim she'd taken a lot of drugs. She was flighty, pretty, and frivolous, though she made an effort to belong. She'd bought a house, and, as he well knew, owning a house was as costly as owning a boat.

For training he liked running trails more than roads because he liked the solitude, and within half a mile of his shop there were four different trailheads. Beth had never understood why he wanted to run alone; she was afraid he'd get hurt and nobody would know.

"I tell you where I'm going and when I'll be back," he'd said. "We can't worry about what hasn't happened."

"That's exactly what I worry about," she said. "Why don't you run with a friend?"

"Who?" he asked. "Do you think I'd run away from you and Phoebe?"

"You might," Beth said.

He ran the Horsethief Trail to the meadow and back, the Silver Shield crossover trail to Oak Creek, the Amphitheater Loop Trail. He measured the sky, the cliffs, the shapes of the rocks, identified the solitaires, thrushes, and songbirds he saw, sometimes cranes in migration or hawks and eagles soaring on thermals high above the peaks. Occasionally he ran on the tundra, but he had to drive up one of the passes to access it, and the tundra was too open-ended. Too much freedom was not good, either.

He didn't much like races—lots of people coughing and spitting and talking—but he ran for the goodwill and to be seen as a supporter of town causes. The race cost fifty dollars to enter, and proceeds went to the senior van, the volunteer fire department, and the summer art program for children. The start was a casual, general assembly along the asphalt path around the baseball field, the anxious few who wanted to win or post a good time edging to the front. It was chilly, maybe fifty degrees. The sun was shining on Whitehouse Peak, but it hadn't yet cleared the Amphitheater Cirque to the east, and the runners were in shadow. Lamar Westbrook, head of the chamber of commerce, held a portable loudspeaker, and he thanked the various business sponsors, the volunteers who put together the packets, marked the course and manned the aid stations, the police and fire crews at the ready, and the runners who'd signed up. "Aid stations begin at mile four," Lamar said, "and there are port-a-potties every two miles. Watch out for road construction at mile seven and for cattle loose on the road. Is everyone ready?"

The crowd answered with a cheer.

"On your mark," he said, "get set, BANG."

It took a couple of seconds of jostling in the pack to get

to the starting line, where Hakim clicked his stopwatch. The group circled the baseball field and headed south. Hakim kept a slow and easy pace. He made sure his watch was moving, his shoes were tied, his number visible. The crowd spread out in front and behind over the five blocks slightly uphill, and after a few minutes the ones ahead turned west. His goal was nine minutes for the first uphill mile, then he'd relax on the downhill. He wanted to do 8:40 miles, which meant he'd finish in an hour and fifty-five minutes.

He crossed the bridge over the yellow-brown river, still laced with arsenic from last century's mines, and followed the pack up Oak Street, past a few Victorian houses and chink-log miners' cabins, and downhill along the trailer court and the city shop. His knee ached a little, the left one, but in half a mile the pain was gone. At mile three his time was 26:33.

At mile five, the road diverged from the river and ascended in a few curves through red sandstone and scrub oak into a neighborhood of trophy homes around Black Lake. Hakim followed two young women talking about giving birth. He didn't want to listen, but they kept an even pace, and the three of them loped past a few people watching from their mailboxes, with their dogs on leashes. Hakim imagined how nice it would be on a warm afternoon to sit with a gin and tonic on the deck of one of those mansions and to ponder the mountains all around.

After another mile, the road descended again to the river where ragged cottonwoods billowed out along the valley floor. Ranchers had finally realized their land was more valuable as real estate for development than as pasture, and new houses were being built in the bottomland. Some ranchland remained, though, and cattle and llamas grazed it, and even a few low-slung, shaggy yaks. The two women moved ahead, and Hakim was left with his own counsel. At mile eight, he was at one hour and five minutes and a few seconds. At an aid station there, a volunteer handed him a cup of Gatorade, and he ate a peppermint candy.

The road came out of the trees and turned left and became a gradual upslope, and he passed a woman in her rose garden, a man sawing windfall, and a kid irrigating a hay meadow. A Red-tailed Hawk soared across from one side of the valley to the other. Hakim felt a twinge in his foot, a discomfort in his shoulder, but, like the knee, nothing serious. At mile nine, he checked his watch and read 1:14:40. Was that correct? He slowed and read the numbers more clearly, 1:15. The field was spread out now, and, though no one had passed him, it was hard to gauge whether he'd slowed down. If the mile had been measured correctly, he'd done the last straightaway in 9:40.

At the top of the hill, the road bore right, and there were hay meadows on either side. The sun was high up now, and the town of Lavely spread out under the mesa to the north. He fumbled out an energy gel packet from his waist pack and oozed some into his mouth. Three-plus miles to go, but he didn't want to sprint at the finish, so he resolved to pay attention to his time in the next mile. Still, he felt a little wobbly. He slowed down, and a wave of dizziness came over him. He stopped, leaned over, and put his hands on his knees.

"Stay with us, one-seventy," a voice said. "You're doing great."

Hakim woke to moving and jostling, with the faces of two strangers, a man and a woman, leaning over him. He understood the words but not their meaning.

"You're in an ambulance," the man said, "on the way to the hospital. Do you know your name?"

"Hakim Bayles."

"Address?"

Hakim couldn't remember his address.

"You had a little trouble in the race," the woman said. "Do you remember that?"

"I was dizzy." Hakim stared past the woman's face to a bank of machines with red blips and numbers on the dials.

"You have a major friend in a high place," the man said, "but we're a ways from the hospital."

"Oxygen intake is good," the woman said. "Heart rate seventy-six, but still arrhythmic."

"What happened?" Hakim asked.

"You were dead, bro," the man said, "but now you're alive again."

Hakim drowsed and had no memory of getting to the hospital or being taken inside. He woke again in a room with curtains for walls. Nurses moved around him, came in and went out. They checked the machines he was attached to, moved the pillow under his head, measured his pulse and blood pressure. His view was of a fluorescent ceiling light and pock-marked tiles. He still had on his running shorts and socks, but no shoes, no shirt, no number.

A young man came in. "How are you feeling?" the man asked. "Good to see you awake. I'm Dr. McNally."

Hakim couldn't answer.

"You were running in a race. Do you remember that?"

"I put my hands on my knees," Hakim said. "I had twenty dollars in my shoe."

"You collapsed, and someone gave you CPR. Whoever it was knew what he was doing and did it long enough so the EMTs could get there with a defibrillator. We're about to do an angiogram. Do you know what that is?"

"I have a glassblowing shop," Hakim said. "I'm supposed to be back there by one o'clock."

"You won't make it," Dr. McNally said, "but if I were you, I'd pick a number in the lottery. This is your lucky day."

"What happened to my shirt?" Hakim asked.

"We'll get you into a gown," Dr. McNally said. "Is there anyone you'd like to notify?"

"My daughter Phoebe," Hakim said. "She's the one on my shirt."


## II.

The Thursday following his death, Hakim opened the alley door of his shop at 7 a.m., started the furnace and annealing oven, and drove home again. He had a bruise on his groin, a knot on his head where he'd struck the gravel road, and a shaved chest, but he felt all right, if a little tired. Sarah had made the same weak coffee, but he was grateful someone was there. Nia, too, had been solicitous. She'd sat with him at the hospital and talked about music in Boston, the clubs and performers—she'd played backup guitar for Alyssa Smith, and her husband was manager. When he went home Nia brought him two home-cooked meals.

Phoebe called every day, though to her he downplayed what had happened. "A blip on the screen of life," he said.

"What's the doctor say?"

"He says I can hike with you in the mountains. I'll come down there at Christmas, and we'll climb Mount Wrightson."

"Mom says she hopes you're okay."

"Of course she does," Hakim said. "She wants me to continue paying child support."

"Don't be mean, Daddy. That isn't you."

"What is me?" Hakim asked.

He was okay but not perfect. He took Plavix to keep blood clots from forming around the stent in his coronary artery, metoprolol to lower his heart rate, and an aspirin a day. The doctor said he could work if he didn't overdo it. For exercise he should walk, no running. Sex was all right if it wasn't kinky. "Sex with whom?" Hakim asked.

He still didn't know who the passerby was who'd done CPR. The first people Hakim talked to were the EMTs, but they didn't know much, only that someone must have driven by at exactly the right moment. "We were intent on getting your heart going," one of the EMTs said. "A man and his wife were there. The wife called nine-one-one. She said you had no pulse and weren't breathing. We were in Lavely."

"They were still with me when you arrived?"

"A couple of other runners had stopped, too, but we barely talked to anyone. One woman kept your windpipe clear. We were in a hurry to get the defib on you."

"And then the couple left?"

"They waited until you were in the ambulance."

"I want to thank someone," Hakim said, "as I'm thanking you. What kind of car did they have? What license plate?"

The EMT shrugged. "A van of some kind. Why don't you put an ad in the newspaper? Maybe the person will get in touch."

The newspaper had run an article about the incident— LOCAL BUSINESSMAN RISES FROM THE DEAD— but the story hadn't IDed the passersby. "A mystery couple," the reporter had called them. "Good Samaritans." Hakim thought the couple might call or stop into the shop to see how he was, not for recognition or reward but out of curiosity about the person they'd saved. But they hadn't.

Several other people he knew in town had phoned—acquaintances, most of whom wanted to know whether he'd seen a light, a tunnel to the other side, or whether his whole life had flashed before his eyes. "It wasn't your time," they said, or "God has other plans for you." Hakim felt like the butt of a joke, embarrassed for his weakness, though he was polite and thanked everyone for thinking of him.

"So there was nothing?" someone asked. "You didn't learn anything?"

"I learned how easy it was to die," Hakim said.

In his first days out of the hospital Hakim had a surge of energy. On Saturday, a week after his demise, he put in a full day at the shop, including two glassblowing demonstrations, and, after work, drove thirty-five miles to Home Depot, where he bought a belt sander, a deluxe paint scraper, three cans of Ready Patch, a dozen tubes of acrylic sealant, and a five-gallon tub of Kilz Premium. His house hadn't been painted in ten years—the blue was cracked and falling off, the white trim was worn, the slats had buckled—and he needed to do something about it.

He started on the north side, scraping and sanding and caulking, and on his breaks he walked the three blocks to Main Street to make sure Nia was paying attention to the shop. She was cheerful, which was good, and her looks were a business asset. She talked up women as well as men, though husbands, Hakim noticed, often returned after their wives had gone back to their motels. Hakim wasn't blind, either, but he ran a business, and he kept his relationship with Nia at that level.

On Saturday and most of Sunday he worked from the roof peak down to the window level. Mid-afternoon, in the midst of this drudgery, Sarah appeared at the bottom of the ladder in a tank top and shorts, her hair pushed up under a baseball cap, but springing red out the sides. "Are you sure you should be up there?" she asked.

"Dead man caulking," Hakim said. "I didn't see anyone else around to help me."

"I could work off my rent," she said.

"Are you afraid of heights?"

"I'm an ice climber, remember?"

She scaled the ladder, and Hakim had a perfect view of her breasts, though this vision wasn't a prurient thrill but rather a realization of beauty's rising toward him. Youth had everything to look forward to, nothing to regret, while he had already been dead.

They shared the plank, one on either end, scraping and, in between bouts with the belt sander, making small talk about the bakery, her climbing exploits, growing up in Vermont. During a lull in Sarah's talking about herself, she said, "How did you get the name Hakim?"

"My father wanted to honor my grandfather," Hakim said. "This was in spite of the expected prejudice."

"Would you rather be Bill or Joe?"

"The name means 'wise and insightful,'" Hakim said. "In Arabic, it's 'ruler' or 'judge.'"

"But you're not Arabic."

"I'm half New Jersey, half Canadian."

"What part of New Jersey? I was born in Trenton. My parents moved to Vermont when I was six."

"Is that where you became a climber?"

"I went to the Putney School," Sarah said. "We climbed store facades in Brattleboro. Did you know Brattleboro allowed public nudity until two thousand and seven?"

"I've never been there," Hakim said.

"We ice-climbed in the White Mountains, skied Tuckerman's Ravine. Some of the things we did were a little crazy."

The sun reached into the top of the Amphitheater Cirque and glowed pink, and for a few minutes they worked in silence. Hakim wasn't prone to nostalgia, but he couldn't help thinking he'd almost missed this moment—the stillness, the color, the air around them darkening. "I could start dinner," Hakim said. "Would you like that?"

"I'll use up this sanding belt," Sarah said. "Then I'll clean up."

A few minutes later, Hakim was in his bathroom washing sealant and Ready Patch from his hands and arms. He stripped off his work clothes and examined his body in the mirror. No one in Brattleboro would have been impressed, except maybe by the bruise on his groin. It was a foot long, dark red, turning toward black. His thin chest was shaved, though the hair would grow back. He didn't have a paunch; he was wiry, in good shape. His skin was dark, darker than white people's, but he didn't stand out as a black person or an Indian might. A few strands of gray had infiltrated his black hair, but he had to look for them. He laughed at himself for being alive, then got into the shower and wept.

That night he woke at three a.m. The house was quiet. Sarah was asleep or gone. A breeze stirred the leaves beyond the open window, and he looked over at the stack of books on his night table, then at the unmoving ceiling fan with its four paddles etched in gold and four lightbulbs haloed by patterned glass. A late truck braked down the pass and descended along Main Street three blocks away, and an owl called from the spruce above town.

He closed his eyes, but he felt anxious and displaced, there and not here. Sleep was like death, except in death there were no dreams, no waking, and he imagined the world without his being in it, as if he were behind a curtain seeing the events happening on stage, other people moving when he was still. Phoebe was in that other world.

Why had the man and his wife been passing at the very moment he fell down? Why had he not collapsed a few days before, running a trail? What combination of blood and tissue, fitness and genetics had allowed him survive? There were no rational explanations, no identifiable causes. At the same time, he couldn't believe in miracles, or god, or another power. What was he left with?

The only response to his ad in the newspaper had been a phone call from Annie Niwot, a woman racer who'd stopped to help. She'd been a quarter mile behind when he'd gone down, and she'd seen a Plymouth van come around the corner from the county road. "They must have seen what I did from closer and at a different angle," Annie said. "You leaned over and then fell to the ground without even putting your hands out. I knew something was wrong, but I was running up that hill so I couldn't get to you."

"What did they look like, the other couple?" Hakim said. "How old were they?"

"I'd say in their forties. When I got there, the man had already started CPR. You were moaning and breathing, but when he stopped, you died again."

"Again?"

"You stopped breathing," Annie Niwot said. "I guess that's death."

"How long did you hang around?" Hakim asked. "Did you finish the race?"

"When the EMTs got there, I kept going, but I wasn't after a time."

"You'd know the people if you saw them again?" Hakim asked.

"I would, but I live in Denver. I subscribe to the newspaper because I love the town, but I don't get over where you are very often."

"Come and visit," Hakim said.

"I'll tell you one thing, you are one lucky man."

"Luck," Hakim said, "what is that?"

He got up at four and, in the dark, cut daisies in the garden. He arranged them in a vase next to the coffeemaker, then went out the back door and around the house, a new superstition since he'd died. At the shop, he fired up the furnace and the oven, laid out his tools, and went out into the alley. Up and down the lane were the usual dumpsters and garbage barrels, sporadic cars parked at angles near the alley apartments, wires strung up every which way on the poles. Gray clouds were draped over the town, but he was helpless to lift them. Above the Amphitheater Cirque, the sun, still unseen, was paling the air.

He was alone for the first few hours and worked the molten glass on the blow tube into round balls, onto which, after a few moments of cooling, he rolled color. He put a ball into the furnace tank again, took it out, rolled it along the punty, and worked it with a block of cherrywood and the carbon paddle. He blew it a little more and worked it again. A woman from Memphis wanted a set of six tumblers and another man a pitcher for his wife's birthday, and Nia had badgered him twice to make them. This was the first of the glasses. He blew, rolled, worked it, heated it again, and continued the process until the glass was ready to put into the annealing oven. Then he started the next one.

Nia came in at ten and pulled open the curtain that divided the shop from the studio. She was dressed in jeans and a low-cut, short-sleeved blouse. "Are you doing demos today?" she asked.

"I might paint my house this afternoon, so don't put out the sign."

"I see you're doing the glasses."

"I finished one, and this is the second. I still have that pitcher to do."

"You look as though you haven't slept."

"Sleep takes time," Hakim said.

"My life isn't so easy, either," Nia said. "I was almost unemployed."

"I can't guarantee security," Hakim said. "If I weren't here, you'd find another job."

"But I like this one, and I can make my house payments."

"Making house payments is the purpose of life?" Hakim asked.

"Isn't it?"

"My father taught me a man's bank account was the measure of his worth, but I gave up that myth long ago."

"And what have you substituted?" Nia asked.

"Nothing."

Nia pushed the curtain back. "It's after Labor Day. Why don't we close up and go for a picnic?"

"I thought you wanted me to make these glasses for the woman from Memphis."

"Do it while I pack a lunch. We'll leave the woman a note to come back at four o'clock."

"If I'm not going to work here, I should paint my house."

"Should," Nia said. "Who says 'should'? I'll be back in an hour."

They drove up the Camp Bird Road along a clear stream. Clouds drifted among the peaks, shrouding them or letting the sun fall on the high meadows already turning brown. The road crossed through a willow thicket and a shallow stream, and, another mile up, Nia turned onto a Jeep track her Subaru could negotiate. When the terrain got too rocky, she pulled off onto a grassy spot, and they walked with the picnic basket and a blanket into an aspen glade.

"The clouds are moving down," Hakim said. "It's going to rain."

"Aren't you the pessimist?" Nia said. "Let's eat, then worry. I made avocado and cheese sandwiches."

"What kind of cheese?"

"Swiss. Is that all right? I could run back to the store."

"Swiss is acceptable," Hakim said.

Nia unpacked hard-boiled eggs, carrot sticks, Sun Chips in a plastic container, and cups of raspberry yogurt. "I wasn't sure what you liked, so I brought everything I had in my fridge."

"Thank you," Hakim said.

He spread out the blanket on the dead leaves and grass, and they sat down. Around and above them the aspen leaves were green and yellow, the tree trunks white with black antler rubs, and the view was across the basin to a ridge of granite and an uncertain sky. Below the ridge were steep meadows and dry runoff gullies that emptied into the creek below.

The weather improved, and Nia rolled up her sleeves and her pant legs to get the sun. "See," she said, "it's going to be a nice afternoon."

"It's not over yet," Hakim said. He ate a sandwich and carrots, and a cup of yogurt, then lay on the blanket, closed his eyes, and dozed.

He woke to Nia's kiss on his lips.

"What was that for?" he asked.

"You looked so peaceful," she said.

"I was, until then."

"Why don't you enjoy yourself? You must have been a person once."

Hakim said nothing.

"Do you want to hike?" Nia asked. "Let's climb to the ridge on this side. Are you able to, now that you're recovering?"

"I'm not an invalid," Hakim said. "I've been painting my house."

"But you should be careful."

"'Should,'" Hakim said.

They climbed up through the aspens, stepped over fallen trees, waded through the high grass. Hakim picked up an animal trail, and, on a long traverse, they gained altitude and came out into a meadow. "Elk have used this path," Hakim said, "though the scat isn't new."

"How do you know it's not deer?"

"Deer scat is smaller and rounder than elk."

"I learn pertinent information every day," Nia said.

"How long have you worked for me?" Hakim asked.

"A little over a year."

"And why did you want to kiss me?"

"I've wanted to before, but you were so intense. Since your incident, I don't know, you've seemed more vulnerable. I didn't mean to presume you'd like it."

"But you did presume."

"What harm could it do?"

"It depends how you define the terms." Hakim looked up the steep meadow. "What do you think? We could aim for the saddle and look out on the other side."

"How are you feeling?"

"Mentally or physically? Physically I'm okay."

"If you're uncomfortable, we can go back down."

"But maybe up there, we'll find the meaning of life," Hakim said. "It's possible."

"You mean it requires physical effort?" Nia asked. "I don't think so. I hope not."

The meadow gave way to scree, and on the loose stones each step forward caused a slide back. Hakim's strides were long, so he made better headway, but he had to be careful not to knock rocks down on Nia below. At intervals they rested. The higher they got, Hakim noticed, the more the world opened up. More peaks were visible—mountains with snow, some close beyond the opposite ridge, some blurred by distance. Clouds were strewn everywhere across the larger sky.

Nia dragged herself up to where he was. "I may not make it to the saddle," she said. "How high are we now?"

"Maybe twelve thousand feet," Hakim said. "The high peaks are fourteen."

"You go ahead." Nia sat down on the stones.

A marmot sunned itself on a rock nearby, and from the talus below, pikas squeaked their alarms. The sun faded behind the clouds, and a cool breeze slid from the saddle. At eye level, a falcon soared across and dive-bombed a hawk flying below them. The marmot took cover.

"Peregrine Falcon," Hakim said, "and a Red-tailed Hawk."

"How do you know?"

"A falcon has sharp wings and flies fast, while a hawk is larger and slower and has broad wings and a wide tail. Phoebe likes hawks."

"You know birds, too."

"I know a hawk from a falcon and most of the tundra birds."

"I wouldn't think many birds lived up here."

"Ptarmigan, rosy finches, water pipits, crows and ravens, a few raptors. Of course, in the old days, miners lived at this altitude, too. Greed motivates the strangest behavior. That's why I make Christmas ornaments and ashtrays."

"That's not greed, it's survival."

"I settle for what gets me by." Hakim got to his feet. "You lead, so we go at your pace."

They hairpinned upward in fits and starts, resting every few minutes. The last pitch was steep and over scree, and Hakim went ahead and pulled Nia up by the hand. The saddle was a low spot between two outcroppings of rock, and on the other side, to the west, they looked into Full Moon Basin, where a herd of elk was bedded down on a patch of tundra grass. The country spread out in disarray and perfection in every direction—peaks scattered across the bulging globe, shadows and blue layers of mountains, dark spruce forests, pale green meadows descending into invisible valleys below. Cloud shadows sailed across the expanse of the whole earth. A few miles to the northwest, gray rain curtained the horizon.

"If we could only take all this in," Hakim said, "we'd be rich."

"We're doing it now."

"Not for long, though. It's going to rain."

"You'll have to carry me down," Nia said.

Muted thunder sounded a few miles distant, and lightning flashed down into the high peaks.

"We'll be safer if we beat the storm," Hakim said.

"You *are* a pessimist," Nia said. "Do you always think the worst?"

That evening Hakim walked though his house as if he were a visitor living there without knowing who he was. The tables and chairs and sofa were his, the painting of the lake and the poplar trees, one of Capitol Reef at dusk, another of Taos. He had a sword his grandfather Hakim had supposedly received from *his* father after the Spanish-American War, the ceramic bird Hakim admired for its imperfect gaudiness — an egret or maybe a bird of paradise, elegantly plumed with a long tail, outstretched wings, and an elaborate crest. Its beak was open in song or in pain, Hakim couldn't tell which, though either would have been appropriate to the mystery of the unfamiliar familiar room.

For orientation, he telephoned Phoebe.

"Hello, sweetheart," he said. "I'm glad you're home."

"I'm not home," she said. "That's what's so great about cell phones. I'm in the car with Mom, and we're going to get my hair cut."

"Is the AC on?"

"Of course. You can't live here without that."

"And your hair's long?"

"Sort of. Well, you know mom. We're going to the Blue Dragon after."

"Don't eat any MSG."

"The Blue Dragon is a used-clothes store. How are you?"

"We're getting rain," he said, "so I can't paint the house.

Earlier we hiked up to a high ridge, and I thought of you because we saw a falcon chasing a hawk."

"Who's 'we'?" Phoebe asked.

"You remember Nia? She made me take the afternoon off."

"She's the pretty one in the shop," Phoebe said. "Is she your girlfriend now?"

"Not at all. How's school?"

"It's okay. My teacher is hard."

"Man or woman?"

"Woman. Mom's giving me signals. We're getting to the salon."

"A salon, is it? I'm glad my money allows you to live in luxury."

"Can I call you later?" Phoebe asked.

"You can call me anytime," Hakim said. "I hope you will."

The rain lasted an hour, and the air smelled of pine and washed brick — clean and clear — though across the backyard he counted eleven different wires. He turned the salmon on the grill and lowered the flame. He'd already made a salad with lettuce, avocado, and a few cherry tomatoes. It was still light out, but edging to dusk, and Hakim was admiring the alpenglow in the Amphitheater when Sarah appeared.

"There you are," she said.

"There's beer in the fridge," Hakim said. "We're having salmon and salad."

"I'm eating with friends," she said. "I wanted to tell you the bakery is letting me go."

"After Labor Day, everything slows down. You expected that, didn't you?"

"I haven't saved as much as I thought I would," Sarah

said, "so I'm going back to Vermont. I know I signed a lease, but my last day's Friday."

"I could pay you to help me paint the house."

"I already have a ride east," Sarah said. "I was wondering, like, can I come back when it snows?"

"I'll think about it. I may not rent the room anymore."

"Even to me?"

"Your plans might change, too."

"Can we talk more tomorrow? I could help paint when I get off from the bakery."

"If it doesn't rain," Hakim said. He turned off the grill and forked the salmon onto his plate.

The next day, Thursday, the weather turned colder. According to NPR, the high was to be in the forties. Clouds slid down into the forests and along the cliffs above town. Hakim slept later than usual, and when he came downstairs, Sarah hadn't made coffee.

He drove his truck to Main Street, opened the front door, and counted the diminished supply of vases, glasses, and Christmas ornaments. During the tourist season he had kept up with demand, but now he had to produce new merchandise for the holidays. In past years that strategy had worked, but now, after his death, ashtrays and glasses didn't concern him, and if he never made another Christmas ornament that would be soon enough. If he'd died, of course, Beth would have closed the shop, liquidated the inventory, and sold his equipment. Mac McCabe would have offered the space at an attractive lowball rent to entice a new business, and the world would have gone on as before, almost. But he hadn't died, and how could he close the shop and get by? He wouldn't have to make any more ashtrays or Christmas ornaments, but he wouldn't have a studio, either. Nia couldn't make her house payments, and he needed money, too—food, house payments, support for Phoebe.

He got coffee and a cinnamon roll at the Yeast-I-Can-Do, where, at the counter, Sarah waited on him. "Sorry about no coffee this morning," she said. "When the party wound down, it was time to come to work."

"I'll have to get used to it," Hakim said. "You weren't there before."

"I still want to ice climb," Sarah said. "I love your house."

"So do I," Hakim said. "I like the quiet."

He paid for the coffee and roll and went outside. The Amphitheater was half-hidden, but the yellow aspens gave color to the land. He had no desire to cross the street or paint his house or stand there on the corner looking up into the clouds.

The studio was warm, and Hakim sat at his work bench in his plain T-shirt. The furnace made a whooshing noise. Usually when he worked he listened to Beethoven or Mahler or to a podcast of poetry, but that day he wanted to sit and do nothing, to *choose*, but without knowing how or what. He was still sitting when Nia came in at ten. He heard her unlock the cash drawer, move her chair; he imagined her hanging her jacket on her peg by the door and changing the sign in the window from "closed" to "open."

Then she lifted the curtain. "Good morning," she said. "You're already here."

"Or not here," Hakim said. "Let's stay closed until noon. I don't want any customers. You can go home, too."

Nia hesitated. "I could dust and clean," she said, "or do the accounts for August."

"I'd rather be alone," Hakim said.

He stood up and went to the window that looked out into

the alley. Rainwater cascaded from the roof of the shed opposite and puddled in the low spots.

"Are you upset about yesterday?"

"Which part?" Hakim said.

"Any part."

"I remember what we saw from the saddle," Hakim said, "but it's already fading away." He looked over at Nia. "Or do you mean the kiss of which I wasn't aware?"

"I'll let you be," Nia said.

Hakim turned back to the window, but Nia didn't leave. He felt her watching him, and he made himself stay where he was. She came closer, though she made no sound, and put her cheek on his shoulder. "People love you, Hakim," she said, "but you have to let them."

Hakim rolled the molten glass along the bench and blew into the blowpipe. The glass expanded slowly, and the spinning motion he applied made it round. He shaped it with the cherrywood block, worked it with the carbon paddle, and tweezed an odd shape into the bottom of the glass. Then he extended the top into what looked vaguely like a head. He let the object cool, sprinkled on blue chips that embedded themselves into the glass, and put it into the furnace, where the blue chips melted into a patina. Again, he blew and shaped the object and let it cool. In three passes, the object became a bird with a tail and a beak, but it wasn't what he wanted—no wings—and he threw away what he'd done and started over. His shirt was sweat-soaked, and he wiped his forehead on his shoulder.

He repeated what he'd done before, rolling, blowing, shaping, until he had what looked vaguely like a bird again, but again it wasn't what he imagined, and he destroyed it.

How easy it was to die, but how hard it was to go back to the beginning—to years ago when he'd been free to make whatever he wanted. He didn't know another way except trial and error. What he wanted was to make a bird so Phoebe would remember him, so he would live on in her life as Hakim, the glassblower, the loner, the one with the ridiculous name meaning wise and insightful, so she would know her father, who once had been truly alive.

# LA MER DE L'OUEST

"WE ARE CONSTANTLY LEARNING." BILLY
Prioleau told me that years ago, but day to day the
education was murky, halting, and unheralded, and it
never felt like learning. In the end, looking back, we
thought we'd made progress, or at least that we'd changed,
which wasn't the same as progress. I liked to believe change
was good; it kept us alive and thinking about what we should
do next.

In the thirty years since my father moved us out here,
the island had accreted on the north and eroded on the
south. People on the north end built more houses behind the
dunes, and on the Charleston end, toward the harbor, they'd
poured cement along the edge of the island to keep erosion
at bay. In the old days, several rows of bungalows faced the
front beach, and families from Charleston and Columbia and
Spartanburg spent their summers here. By "families from
Charleston," of course I mean "white families." There were a
few houses along Middle Street, but most of the year-round
people, like my father and Purvis's family and the scattering
of black families, were back along the buggy and breezeless
marsh. In 1922 the Corps of Engineers dredged the Inland

Waterway, and the marsh became more appealing. People settled back there and put in docks, and the town built a boat landing.

My father had worked for the highway department with Billy Prioleau, who operated the causeway bridge over the waterway. My father was maintenance, but he and Billy liked to fish and almost every weekend they took out the johnboat into the creeks and harvested crabs and shrimp and oysters. Billy lived on the mainland in Mount Pleasant, which was where I went to middle school.

As people across the country became affluent, they retired and bought second homes, and developers on the island were happy to oblige demand. In the sixties, houses appeared all over, and by 1982, when I got out of law school and started my practice, my wife, Edie, and I bought a little more house than we could afford, third-row front beach—a $186,000 investment, which, twenty years earlier, my father could have bought for $30,000. Now it's worth almost a million. Charleston was fifteen miles away, over the causeway and through Mount Pleasant, like Darien to New York, except there's no train.

The buyers of the leisure island life were white: that was an observable fact. It's history. Economics was a cruel science, and the wealthy and powerful displaced the meek. I had been one of the lucky ones to get in early. Edie was still a pleasure to my eye. We had a daughter Carla, twelve, and a son Blair, who was ten and loved bones. Both were smart and willing and mostly obedient. So I shouldn't have complained about what life dealt to me, but at the same time, I felt guilty for what I had and sad for what others like Purvis didn't, and I chafed at what I saw as a misguided world.

On the morning of September 14 a black couple walked off Broad Street downtown and into my office. They were in their mid-thirties, he tall, fit, short hair, wide nose, large lips, she more like Halle Berry, thinner lips, lighter skin. They were dressed well, but their style wasn't gaudy. Each had a single ring on the marriage finger. I was at my paralegal's desk discussing the deposition I had to take in Beaufort the next day in a stock swindle case, and I overheard the black couple introduce themselves to my secretary. She fielded their question about seeing me with noncommital aplomb, and I spoke up. "Right here," I said, "Scott Atherton. Can I help you?"

"DeSean Jamison," the man said. He shook my hand. "And my wife Angie. From Atlanta."

"I recognize you," I said. "You played for the Hawks."

"Only two years. I wasn't patient enough to make a career out of riding in airplanes."

"We want to move to Charleston," Angie said.

My practice was low-key, two other lawyers and four office people, but I was the employer. I led the Jamisons into my office, which had a very cluttered desk and my degree and admission to the bar on the wall, along with a painting I liked of a sunset behind the causeway bridge. The Jamisons sat down, and I stood by the window that opened to the street.

"Angie's from Awendaw," DeSean said. "She was a broadcast journalism major at Emory, and I played ball at Georgia Tech. With my signing bonus from the Hawks I financed a couple of restaurants in Atlanta. Angie has a job here at Channel 4, and we'd like to buy a house and move back here."

"You don't need a lawyer for that."

"We like Sullivan's Island," Angie said. "We have enough money to buy and build, but we understand people might object. They might even try to discourage us."

"We picked out a lot at Station 17," DeSean said. "We thought it would be helpful to have a go-between on the purchase."

"How did you happen to come to me?" I asked.

"You were a friend of Billy and Arlene Prioleau," Angie said. "She recommended you."

I sat down at my desk and looked at the painting I saw a hundred times a day. "Billy used to work on that bridge," I said. "When my father was about to die, he told me to take care of Billy, and I did, and Billy took care of me."

"My mother's a scrubwoman," Angie said. "She and Arlene ride the same bus."

"Arlene still works at Hugeley's, same aisle. I take her to lunch every Tuesday." I leaned forward. "There's no law that says you can't buy property wherever you want."

"But it's not exactly a free country," DeSean said.

"It's a somewhat free country," I said.

"My mother still lives in my grandfather's house in Awendaw," Angie said, "and it was his father's before that. My father used to come home from the oyster shed where he worked, or from his boat, and climb up to the porch and look out toward the ocean, and he'd take himself a minute or so to breathe. Then he'd say, 'From here you can see eternity.'"

"Maybe he could from Awendaw," I said.

"We think we can see farther from Sullivan's Island," Angie said.

Since the incident six years ago with Purvis and Billy in the bridge bunker, Edie felt her life was diminished. Some of her friends backed away from her and from us as a couple, and I lost two rich clients who'd seen the fiasco reported on the news. My practice suffered in ways I couldn't guess—we can't know who doesn't show up—but I got some new clients, too. Edie interpreted my behavior as a choice I made, and it was—but not against her. Billy needed help, and I gave it. Yes, what we did, what Billy did—Purvis and I were only accomplices—was against the law and illogical and had little immediate effect, but at the time Billy thought it was right to protest what he saw as a travesty against the island. We didn't need another golf course, he said, and that afternoon he'd opened the bridge part way and blocked cars on the highway and boats in the waterway for five hours. The state police swarmed in and the coast guard and navy helicopters, all of whom Billy held off with what turned out to be an air rifle. As his lawyer and friend, I was asked to talk him down, and when I couldn't, when I saw the *joy* in what he was doing, I called up Purvis and had him bring us beer and corn dogs. A few people were inconvenienced, but no one died. The world went on, and today rich people were out there playing golf anyway by the graves of Billy and his son.

Purvis Neal was a celebrity for a few days, but because he can't talk, or hasn't since his father walked out years ago, he quickly became invisible again, hanging out as usual at the marina. That was all right, better for him. I fended off questions, too, negotiated a desk job for Billy at the highway department, and put the incident behind me. But something of it lingered in Edie. It wasn't unhappiness so much as an impatience with me or with the island. She complained more often about driving the children across the causeway to soccer games, to music lessons, to their doctors' appointments.

I was earning the living in town, so I was spared these debilitating chores. And she didn't like the school in Mount Pleasant. The standards were too low, the teachers too lax, the students unmotivated. Not that there were alternatives. The island had no middle school.

Coming up in another month was Billy Prioleau Day, and Edie's grievances escalated above the low-level hum. As she often reminded me, I was so enamored of the present that I couldn't recall birthdays, anniversaries, even holidays, but I remembered the day Billy Prioleau died. Yes, I did—November 8, three years ago. Billy's wasn't an extraordinary death like that of his son Edgar, who had disappeared into the surf, though every death is extraordinary to the loved ones. Billy died of an enlarged heart no one knew about. Arlene said he took two Aleves, went to bed early, and never woke up. The death got a tiny obit in the *Post and Courier*, but a reporter remembered the bridge incident and wrote a feature, and the upshot was Billy became a local cult hero. The first anniversary of his death we'd held random symbolic protests against polluters and developers threatening the environment, but last year it became an official event. Behind the scenes I'd put together a conservation trust, using Billy's land up-island near the golf course as the primary asset, and enough people knew about this project that I was tagged to organize the protest vigils.

Edie, in response, complained more about the broken stair to the deck, the neighbor's barking dog, and the mess under the house. She wanted me to pick up Blair after school and take her car for servicing. The morning I was going to Beaufort for the deposition she yelled at me from the kitchen that I had to pick up seafood on my way home, and Carla, who was often meditative before school, complained of a pain in her temple. "I see flashes of lights," she said, "and I feel as if I could throw up."

She lay on the sofa, and I put a cold towel over her forehead and drew the blinds so the sun wasn't so bright through the living room. When the car pool arrived, she still wasn't feeling well.

Edie was furious. She couldn't go to her yoga class or play tennis, and she'd have to see if she could get Carla in to see the doctor.

People's motives were puzzling and often incomprehensible, like my clients' in this stock swindle case. They already had a house on Kiawah Island, an apartment in a high-rise on Lake Shore Drive in Chicago, and a ski condo in Vail, but for all their money they still wanted to make a quick profit. The defendants had gone to Ivy League colleges, knew the risk they were taking with their reputations, but went ahead anyway with their scam—minor Madoffs, miniature Ponzis. Both sides, though, acted as capitalism taught them to.

Because of the down economy, I did more of the office legwork, like driving to Beaufort for this deposition. Highway 17 traversed marshes and creeks and divided in half several small towns, which, at fifty miles an hour, were blips in the road. An occasional river meandered through the lowland, the Edisto and the Ashepoo to name two. Billy had taught me to look at the living world, and driving with the windows down in my truck (air-conditioning freed the South, but I didn't like it), I was aware of egrets and herons on the mudflats, migrating ducks in the tide pools, flocks of shorebirds. Since I made this trip two weeks ago, the marsh had changed, a pale yellow replacing the stark green.

Beaufort was the second oldest city in South Carolina, a small, calmer Charleston with similar antebellum brick houses, gardens and fountains, live oaks and camellias and magnolias in the yards. Some of the houses were now inns or museums, though many were still owned by families of the original aristocracy. I was early for my appointment, so I parked in one of the old neighborhoods and wandered around, though not necessarily for the pleasure. The past was never so vibrant or good as people represented it, and to romanticize history was to recharacterize right and wrong and explain away cruelty. The houses might have shown how lives were lived in the old days, but there was an underside of suffering the tourist brochures omitted. Maybe we had become more civilized people, but only because laws forced us to be.

It was a sweet day of sun and clouds and a slither of air along the sidewalk from the unseen ocean. The flowers were gone or dying—cold ahead, but not yet upon us. Carrying my briefcase, I sauntered over the undulating bricks and now and then peered in at a garden. Cars were parked close along the narrow street, and several blocks ahead, at the opening to the square, was the white steeple of St. Mark's.

A Volvo station wagon passed traveling in my direction, blue with rust along the door, and at a stop sign the driver examined herself in the rearview mirror. She flicked something from her eyelash, rearranged her hair, pursed her lips. I was too far away to have more than a glimpse, but she looked like Jennifer Almond from Sullivan's Island. I recognized the car more than the woman. The Volvo accelerated into the next block and turned left into a driveway.

The Almonds were neighbors but not close friends and had two children in the middle school, about the same ages as Carla and Blair. They lived on the marsh in one of the big houses that overlooked the waterway, and I'd have preferred theirs to ours, or one smaller, but Edie liked the beach, the sunrise over the water, and the sound of the waves.

Lex Almond was a contractor, and in the ten years since the next island became more accessible via the new bridge, his business had grown exponentially. Lex had taken a couple of years at Auburn, and summers helped his dad in a home-repair business, but when his dad got sick, Lex quit college and ran the show. Repairs became remodels, like Purvis's studio behind his mother's place, and then new houses, and big new houses. In the course of this evolution, Lex hired college dropouts, black kids going nowhere, and women who wanted to vent their aggression with a hammer, so that now he had a cadre of skilled and unskilled labor driving around the islands in company trucks. I wanted to talk to Lex about the Jamisons. Getting a good contractor on board could help, especially one who could stand the heat when it arrived.

A couple came along the sidewalk with a cat on a leash, and when I stepped back to let them pass, the woman said, "We're birders." I was almost opposite the driveway where the Volvo turned in, and set back from the street was a three-story brick house turned into apartments. A gnarly oak sheltered the driveway, where trash cans and four cars were stacked in. Jennifer Almond emerged from her Volvo wagon. She was average height, had mid-length reddish blond hair, and wore a paisley shirt and light-colored pants. I'd always known her to be fragile, aloof, anxious. It was Lex who did the carpooling, appeared at parents' conferences, and bought wine at the superstore on the bypass. Once I ran into Jennifer on Queen Street near my office, and I was surprised how cordial she was. She complimented Blair on a role he'd had in a play, talked about Carla's tennis, and even asked about the Billy Prioleau Conservation Trust. Somehow we got onto the topic of her father, who collected old maps, and she broke down and wept right there on the sidewalk.

It was of course not my business what she was doing in Beaufort, but something about the way she had concerned herself with her appearance in the rearview mirror made me curious, and I waited to see what she did next. Another woman appeared at the side door. She looked about Jennifer's age, a little shorter, brown hair, an ex-college roommate, maybe. She smiled and clasped both of Jennifer's hands. There was nothing odd about this until they embraced and, after a long moment's gaze, shared a lingering kiss.

The opposing lawyers obfuscated and delayed, and I got the minimum of information from the deposition. When I came out, it was raining, and as I walked to my truck, I still couldn't get the sight of Jennifer Almond's kissing that woman out of my mind. I wasn't shocked or offended but entranced, the way one might have been, say, over a disappearance or the discovery of an unidentified body. It was the intensity of the moment—the embrace, the pause, the kiss—that was so vivid to me, the surge of emotion exhibited to a public of one.

On the way back to Charleston I checked my messages and found out Carla had had a migraine. She was to be watched closely. The Jamisons had called to find out if I'd delivered their offer (I had), and there was a message from Pope Gaillard saying he had something to tell me about Purvis. I listened through four other calls from volunteers helping me with the protest vigil for Billy Prioleau. This year we were planning gatherings at the navy base, because their dumping of dredge spoils was ruining a heron and egret rookery; at the highway department, which was threatening to remove centuries-old live oaks to widen Highway 61 north; and at the office of a developer who was building a retirement community next to a wetland. Edie argued we were glamorizing criminal behavior, but which behavior was criminal? The Boston Tea Party was a crime. So was Rosa Parks's getting on that bus or Billy's keeping the bridge open and blocking traffic. Did we not have an obligation to resist what we thought was evil?

In the office that afternoon I worked on other pending matters—two estates, a suit by three homeowners against a bank for questionable foreclosures, and several problems for corporate clients. I left the office at six thirty—still plenty of light—and detoured over to Station 17 for a look at the Jamisons' lot. Toward the ocean the wind had built up several rows of dunes, and crape myrtle grew thick in the swales. Beyond the trees it was another hundred yards to the beach, and I walked out on the intermittent boardwalk. Houses stretched in both directions, million-dollar babies, many of them unoccupied.

The beach was never of particular interest to me except as a way to study the physical variations of the human form, fashions or lack thereof, and the social connections of X to Y. It was free recreation, and for a few minutes I trailed along the irregular patterns of seafoam and watched young and old, men and women running, talking, exploring the tideline. Dogs were supposed to be on leash, but it was an ordinance little obeyed, and the few shorebirds—sanderlings, gulls, willets—flew and alighted and were chased again. There were a few late swimmers and windsurfers, and farther out, three cargo ships making for the Port of Charleston. I imagined eternity in the murky seahaze.

A half hour later, I drove my truck around to the back of the island to Purvis's. His mother was long dead, but I had set him up to get the rent from her house, and he lived in a separate apartment in back, in what used to be a crab shack. It was two rooms covered by a green metal roof with moss on it, three if you counted the bathroom. Purvis's Opel wagon was gone, but my johnboat was parked on its trailer, a dented metal twenty-footer I kept there for Purvis to use. He was a dockhand at the marina; it was too late to tie up boats, but he could have been in the lounge. I left a note on his door asking what was happening and reminding him of the upcoming vigil for Billy. After that I drove over to the marina lounge.

The lounge wasn't the same without Billy, but his friend Pope Gaillard was there, and the Rupert twins, and a few crabbers I recognized but didn't know. They were drinking beer from a happy-hour pitcher. Donna was behind the bar, and before I could order anything, she poured me a Jack D. "We don't see you in here much anymore, Scotty," she said.

"Life goes on," I said. "You're looking good as ever."

"But just as broke," said Donna. "On the house." She slid over my glass of whiskey.

I took the Jack Daniel's to the table and pulled in a chair next to Pope. Pope must have been nearly seventy, Billy's age when he died, and the Ruperts fifty. In five years the Ruperts had lost most of the profit they'd made selling their property up-island next to Billy's—that's where the golf course had got its land. They'd gone through cars, a sailboat, and three trips to the Bahamas, and now they were back in the marina lounge.

There was a nervous quiet when I sat down, and one of the crabbers called out for another pitcher.

"Playing any cribbage?" I asked Pope. "I got your message about Purvis."

"Purvis met a woman," Shem Rupert said. "Right here in the lounge. It's true. Ask Donna."

"Purvis isn't the meet-a-woman type," I said.

Donna brought over the pitcher of beer, set it in the middle of the table, and picked up the empty. "I saw them leave together," she said, "and Purvis hasn't been back since. That was more than three weeks ago."

"He hasn't been at work, either," Pope said.

"Do you know the woman?" I asked Donna.

"No, but her name's Shelley something from Goose Creek."

Donna went back to the bar, and I tasted the Jack Daniel's, and we men made small talk about the Falcons, the boats that had come in, the price of crabs. Then one of the crabbers said, "I hear you want to bring trouble to the island."

"Not if I can help it," I said. "What sort of trouble?"

"Negro trouble," the crabber said.

"I grew up here," I said. "There've been blacks here as long as I can remember."

"That was before," the crabber said. "This is now."

"Now we're more enlightened," I said. "How do you know about that?"

"Henry's daughter works over at the Haverfords, and she saw them walking the property. The Haverfords called the real estate person, who said you made an offer on the lot."

"They're a good couple," I said. "She works for Channel 4, and he played for the Hawks. If I turned away clients, I'd be broke."

"They can buy, and they can build," Marvin Rupert said, "but will they occupy?"

There was a deeper silence, everyone intent on drinking beer, and one of the crabbers looked at the jukebox. The others gazed out the big windows toward the boats tied up in the inlet and, beyond the trees, the sun's making its last sweep of the sky. I drank down the rest of my Jack and pushed back my chair. "You boys have a good evening."

I drove past the post office, the park, and the officers' quarters of Ft. Moultrie, in service during the Civil War, and turned at Station 14½ toward the ocean. A couple blocks down, I made a left and parked in the open space under my house, which, like all the island houses, was set up on pilings. The back-and-forth stairs led to the deck, and I tripped over the loose board Edie wanted me to nail down. On the deck I paused and walked around to the side of the house, where I could see, between other houses in front, the dark ocean and, in the channel, the moving lights of container ships.

I took some deep breaths, walked back to the door, and pushed it open.

"Is that you, Scott?" Edie called from the living room. "Where've you been?"

"Working. Did you eat already?"

"I had to feed the poor children," she said.

The kitchen had been cleaned up and was lit from the faint fluorescent glow above the stove. I opened the fridge to see what was there — Edie gave no information — and took out a dish covered in tinfoil. "Is this chicken?" I asked.

Edie came in. "It's a casserole," she said. "I had better things to do than cook a meal for someone who wasn't here."

"I should have phoned."

"Maybe if we lived in town you wouldn't have so many distractions on the way home."

"There are more distractions in town."

Edie stared at me for a few seconds, and to avoid her, I spooned casserole into a bowl and looked in the fridge for the makings of a salad. Nothing more was said.

The next Monday a settlement offer came in from the Beaufort lawyers—$600,000, which my clients refused. The wife wanted the cheaters to suffer. Greed, I argued, would lead to more expenses, but to the other lawyers I stressed that publicity would ruin the defendants' reputations, and at trial my clients would be seen as elderly victims. A jury would award more. In three days we got a new offer of $900,000, which the wife also turned down.

On that same Thursday, the Jamisons' offer on the Sullivan's Island lot was accepted—the seller was in New Hampshire and needed cash—so at my suggestion, the Jamisons drove around and inspected houses Lex Almond had built. They'd have preferred to get competitive bids, but at the same time, they wanted to avoid fanfare, and they liked what they saw. I arranged a late Friday meeting at the Crab Shack in Mount Pleasant, which was close for Lex and on my way home.

As planned, the Jamisons arrived a few minutes early, and we settled into a booth with a view over the creek where the shrimp boats were tied up. They ordered plain tonics on the rocks, and I had a Jack Daniel's. "I should tell you the word is already out on the island," I said. "The opposition is forming."

"Once people know us, it'll be all right," Angie said. "We're pretty easygoing."

"But we're not naive," DeSean says. "People feel threatened by blacks with money."

"The law is on your side," I said.

"I've been around," DeSean said. "What the law says is one thing, but what people feel in their hearts is another. We're not demanding our rights, but we won't be intimidated."

The waitress arrived with our drinks, and I gave her my credit card. "Lex once built a fifty-room hotel on the Isle of Palms, which, because of citizens' complaints and threats, no other contractor would touch. If he takes on your house, he'll be on your side."

Lex showed up a few minutes later, smiling and self-possessed. He'd showered and shaved and had on khakis and a white shirt—a man with an empire.

We shook hands. "How's Jennifer?" I asked.

"Jennifer's fine. She stays busy."

"These are the Jamisons," I said. "What can I get you?"

"A gin and tonic looks good." He nodded at Angie's glass.

Lex shook hands with the Jamisons, and there were a few minutes of small talk about Charleston, the new programming at Channel 4, and the untapped potential of Awendaw. From the tenor of the conversation, it was no surprise when Lex said, "So you want to build a house on that beautiful lot at Station 17?"

A couple of days later, the lawyers in Beaufort requested yet another meeting, and I was glad to get away from work at the office. On the way down, I did my usual scanning of the mudflats and marsh, and at one creek I spotted a bittern in the reeds, the first one I'd seen that Billy Prioleau hadn't pointed out to me. It was an odd bird the size of a heron but camouflaged by vertical brown-and-white stripes, and it held its bill and head upward, as if its neck were sore. I likened myself to it—big, but wishing I could be invisible.

In the lawyers' conference room I made the same arguments as before. "If everyone behaved as the defendants had, the negative impact on society would be unconscionable."

"So what do you think it will take?" one of the defendants' lawyers asked. "I mean, to make this go away. We agree on the principles. Why waste everyone's time?"

"One point two million," I said. "That's a guess."

"Done," the lawyer said.

I called my clients and gave them the figure, and as an inducement, I offered to lower my fee from a third to thirty percent, which would net them another $40,000. The wife said she'd think about it.

This unexpected success—it was a windfall for me, too—made feel guilty and elated at the same time, and maybe confused, and after a bite of lunch at a kiosk, I did something against my nature. Walking back to my truck, I passed the house where Jennifer Almond kissed her friend, and I went into the driveway. By the door were several names—the Stantons, Larry Monhegan, and Abby Lincoln—and I rang the bell for Abby Lincoln. No one buzzed me in, so I tried Larry Monhegan. He clicked the intercom and said hello. "Do you know Abby Lincoln?" I asked.

"Who wants to know?" he said.

He put his head out the window above, and I stepped back. I had on a tie and was holding my briefcase. "Or Jennifer Almond? I'm a friend from Charleston."

"Abby's at the Galleria on Water Street," Larry said. "Be easy on her. She's had a hard life."

Water Street ran past St. Mark's and all the way through town, and I expected an art gallery, but the Galleria was a three-level glass-and-metal mini-mall with a dozen shops. At midday the Indian restaurant, the shrimp place, and the Subway were swamped, but I asked about Abby Lincoln at a dress boutique and was directed to the top floor. I took the stairs and looked out over the hubbub of the mezzanine. Outside, a low fog had come in and muted the street.

The top floor was an eclectic mix of service offices and retail businesses—a coffee corner and sandwich shop, a travel agency, a music store. Abby Lincoln had a sewing shop, Sew and Sew, which, from across the hallway, looked to be an outlet for sewing machines, quilts of which there were several on the wall, and basic supplies. I recognized Abby—brown hair cut short—sitting in a high-backed chair, focused, like Vermeer's seamstress, on whatever she was stitching.

I wrenched a button from my coat jacket and walked over to the shop. From closer vantage, Abby was pretty in an odd way—heavy-lidded eyes too far apart, a small nose, a generous mouth uncolored. "You look lost," she said.

"Now I'm found." I set my briefcase on the counter. "Beautiful quilts." I pointed at a blue and rust one she was working on and nodded at another on the wall, hanging beside what I now saw was a framed map.

"Thank you. They aren't cheap."

"It seems an imposition to ask you to sew on a button." I opened my fist with the button.

"My minimum is twenty dollars." Abby stood up and examined my jacket. "Your wife could do this for fifty cents."

"My wife isn't here, and I have a meeting."

She took the button and, while I escaped my jacket, she searched in a drawer for the thread to match.

I stepped over to the map on the wall. "Where is this?" I asked.

"Nowhere," she said. "The first explorers in the Carolinas

thought they'd reached Asia and described a strange conti-
nent, and the mapmakers drew what they thought it looked
like. That's La Mer de l'Ouest, the last great cartographic
myth."

Abby extracted the loose threads from the jacket and
sewed the button back where it had been. I laid a twenty on
the counter.

I wasn't sure what to say next or ask, or even why I needed to, and my uneasiness was palpable. "I have one question," I said. "Jennifer Almond."

There was a pause, not long, and Abby raised her eyes.
"I've been waiting for you," she said. "How did you find me?"

"Oh, I'm not Lex," I said, "though I know him."

"You're a private detective? The torn-off button was a
ruse?"

"I'm not a detective, and I don't want to hurt anyone."

"Everyone says that," Abby said, "but people get hurt."

"A week ago I was passing along the sidewalk and saw
Jennifer turn into your driveway. I recognized her car . . ."

"She's my sister," Abby said.

I nodded slowly. "Well, that explains everything, except
why you were waiting for me."

"Do you have a name? I'll tell Jen, and she'll be amused."

"A name would make things awkward."

"They're awkward already, wouldn't you say?" Abby
pointed to the gold initials on my briefcase. "SDA. Will she
know who that is?" She put the twenty into her money drawer. "I'll tell you what. She's not my sister, but if Jen knew
you showed up here—that you knew something—she'd be
afraid. If you promise me you won't tell Lex what you think
you know, we can leave it at that. I'll know, and you'll know,
but Jennifer won't suffer."

"I'm sorry I came here," I said. "It wasn't any of my business."

"Curiosity killed the rat," Abby said.

"Did she give you that map?" I asked. "She told me once her father collected old maps."

"She doesn't want Lex to know she has it," Abby said. "It's valuable, a secret savings account. I said I'd keep it for her."

"I like it."

"Here's your jacket," Abby said. "I hope I never see you again."

Tuesday I took Arlene Prioleau to lunch, and, at my invitation, she brought along Angie Jamison's mother, Lavinia, who worked as maid in a house on the Battery. It had been a sore point with Billy that Arlene had to ride the bus, but they only had a VW Bug and Arlene, who could be as stubborn as Billy, refused to learn to drive. I reserved a booth at Hank's Seafood Restaurant, thinking Angie might join us, but she didn't, so Arlene and Lavinia sat on one side and I opposite. The booth afforded privacy but also gave the illusion that everyone else in the restaurant was like us.

"Tell me how you met," I said to Lavinia, as we folded our napkins into our laps. "Was it on the bus?"

"Yes and no," Lavinia said. She was heavyset, though light-skinned like Angie, and she smiled like a comet. "Arlene was at the bus stop there on Coleman Boulevard, and I used to watch for her because she has that sad look."

"What sad look?" Arlene asked.

"Some folks have it," Lavinia said. "I thought maybe it was because not a lot of white folks take the bus. Anyway, on this day, she wasn't at her stop, but I saw her coming along the side street carrying something . . ."

"It was a typewriter," Arlene said. "Billy wanted me to take his typewriter to the shop."

"Billy had a typewriter?" I asked.

"He was always going to write something," Arlene said. "About nature, or his land on the island, or about Edgar."

"I didn't know he had ambitions as a writer," I said.

"Whatever she was carrying, she was *struggling*," Lavinia said. "I told the driver to halt."

"The driver was white?"

"My, yes," Lavinia said, and she laughed.

"*Halt*," Arlene said. "Can you imagine?"

"He stopped and waited until Arlene got up the steps," Lavinia said. "'Thank you,' Arlene said to him. 'Don't thank me,' the driver said, 'thank *her*.' I was in the seat right there, and Arlene thanked me and sat down. That's how we met."

"She had the nicest smile," Arlene said. "We've ridden together every morning since."

The waiter came over, and Lavinia opted for crab cakes, and Arlene had a salmon salad and a vanilla milkshake. I asked about the sea trout but chose the blackened snapper. "And a martini," I said, "in honor of Billy Prioleau."

"You should have invited Edie," Arlene said.

"Carla's been having migraines, and Edie's taking her to a specialist today."

"That's your daughter?" Lavinia asked.

"She's twelve. So far we tried diet and acupuncture, but the problem may be hormonal."

"She's Edgar's age," Arlene said. She looked sideways at Lavinia. "That's why I have the sad look. Edgar was almost twelve when he died. He would be forty-one now."

"I'm sorry," Lavinia said. "What happened?"

"He drowned in the surf. Scotty was the last person to see him."

"I was eight," I said. "One minute he was there, running to the water, and the next minute he was gone."

There was a silence, and my martini arrived.

"Lavinia's daughter's buying a lot on the island," I said to Arlene. "She and her husband want to build a house."

"Tell me something I don't know," Arlene said.

"Purvis is living with a woman up in Goose Creek."

"Purvis is? What woman?"

"Her name's Shelley. I haven't met her. This is from Donna at the marina lounge."

"I can't imagine Purvis with a woman," Arlene said. "He's so shy he wouldn't say hello to a horsefly. Has he started to talk?"

"Not that I know of, but I haven't seen him."

Arlene turned to Lavinia again. "Billy and Purvis and Scott were a threesome out in the marsh. And they all got arrested up on the bridge."

"We didn't get arrested," I said. "We negotiated a deal."

"Billy used to say the best thing about Scotty was his truck."

I smiled and sipped my martini. "Because that's how we got the boat in the water."

Three young businessmen got up from the next booth, and I caught a little of their banter. One of them said, "What Gamecock football needs is a nigger tailback."

Lavinia heard this, and so did Arlene, but they pretended not to. *I* heard it, and I stood up and bumped into the boy in the pale blue suit.

"Hey," he said.

"What kind of tailback was that?" I asked.

The three of them stared at me. "You got a problem, brother?" the blue suit said.

"I have a problem with your vocabulary."

One of the other boys pushed past, as if he couldn't be bothered with me, and the one in the blue suit knocked into me for emphasis. This dismissal infuriated me, and I delivered a quick jab into his striped shirt, which doubled him over and made him vomit. He fell forward onto his hands and knees. The other two boys were on me in seconds, punching and kicking, but two waiters and several other diners were there before I got seriously hurt.

Even during a busy day at the office, usually at morning coffee, I culled out a few minutes to study old maps. The Internet had more information than I could make sense of, but a little research every day added up. Theoretical cartography apparently flourished between 1740 and 1790. It used scientific theories and little-known geographic patterns to fill in the blank spaces on earlier maps, some of which originated with Verrazano. In 1540, Verrazano had thought Pamlico Sound near the Outer Banks of North Carolina was the Great Sea of the West, and the concept, if not the location, was supported by the French, who later explored the Great Lakes, trying to find the Northwest Passage. Subsequent French maps showed La Mer de l'Ouest farther north and west.

I had no practical use for this information, but, without motive or agenda or anticipation, it was, in the indefinite future, a potential connection to Jennifer Almond. Or perhaps, burdened by my secret knowledge, it was my attempt at asking a forgiveness she didn't know was needed.

During this time, too, I established a dissolute and illegal ritual. On my drive home I stopped and bought jigger bottles of Jack Daniel's for the glove compartment. As a lawyer I was aware of the consequences, should I be caught, and as a father I was concerned about my children, but neither of these logical arguments dissuaded me. At least I waited until I passed the Piggly Wiggly, before the causeway, to open one.

When I got onto the causeway the sun spread itself low across the marsh and whispered itself into the clouds, and the lights of Charleston were coming on, shining across the harbor and through my passenger-side window. It was the same time of day Billy and Purvis and I had been in the bridge bunker holding off the assembled state troopers and navy helicopters. They wanted the highway and the boat channel opened, but I dragged out the discussion long enough to drink a lot of Sam Adams. I knew Billy was not going to stop the dump trucks or the golf course rich people wanted to build, but as the minutes unfolded, watching the sunset, I understood this was a time we, the three of us, would never get back again.

My truck clanked onto the waffled metal span of the bridge and hummed over the waterway and jolted back onto the pavement. Half a mile on, I finished the second jigger and turned right at Middle Street. That night, like others, Edie had dinner ready, and she didn't say anything about the smell of whiskey on my breath. Carla had scored well on a test, and Blair showed me the new bones he'd found on the beach. "Maybe a cat," he said. "The crabs cleaned the meat off."

Edie passed the mashed potatoes. "Tell him about your detention."

Blair lowered his head. "I had a fight at recess," he said.

"About what?"

"Someone said black people were moving to the island, and I said 'so what?'"

"Like father, like son," Edie said.

"What's that supposed to mean?"

"I heard you had lunch at Hank's Seafood."

"What happened, Daddy?" Carla asked. "What'd you do?"

"Nothing so terrible," I said. "I had a discussion with a man who still believes in the Confederacy."

"It was more than a discussion," Edie said.

There was a knock on the sliding glass door, and we all looked over and saw Purvis with his face pressed to the glass. I motioned for him to come in, but he wouldn't, so I got up and pulled the door open. "What's wrong?" I asked. "Are you all right?"

He backed off and stood askew, skinnier and taller than I was, his hair uncombed, his left hand, wounded in a shrimp boat accident, in his pocket.

"I left you a note," I said. "Did you get it? We're having a vigil for Billy on Wednesday, a week."

Purvis nodded.

"Does he want something to eat?" Edie asked from the table. "We have plenty."

Purvis shook his head, but his expression told me he had more on his mind. I went out and closed the door. We walked around the deck to the oceanside, where, beyond the houses close by, the sea was dark and the tide washed on the beach in its eternal rhythm. Purvis's face was broken into shadows from the street lamp and from the light in the living room.

"I heard you met a woman," I said. "Is it working out?"

No answer, but he wanted to tell me something he couldn't put into words.

"It's never easy," I said. "It takes the right two people."

Purvis turned from the railing, and I saw in his eyes the

ache of loss. I wanted to help, but if he wouldn't talk, how could I know what had happened or what he felt? "Why don't you come in and have dinner?" I asked.

He shook his head, and I put an arm over his shoulder, which was all I knew to do and which, of course, wasn't enough.

After several consultations, I drew up a contract between the Jamisons and Lex Almond. Lex had three other houses underway, a fourth about to start, and two more promised, so he didn't know when he could schedule the Jamisons, but once the contract was signed, it was out of my hands. I had Billy Prioleau Day to think about. The City of Dorchester had denied us a permit to protest at the Edith Mill, so we had to decide whether to proceed in defiance. Billy's spirit was the guiding principle, but the real-world consequences had to be considered.

"The company is leeching chemicals into the marsh," Janette McDermott said. "The city's getting paid off. We should go ahead and get the publicity."

"The city will stop us," Gerald Warren said. "It could get violent."

"Better yet," Janette said. "More air time."

For me our protests were to be symbolic and consciousness-raising, so it was more about the numbers who turned out than about our small successes. As a favor, the feature writer at the *Post and Courier* produced, ahead of the date, another article about Billy: "Billy Prioleau was an ordinary man who knew and loved the marsh. He had only a small stone to hurl against Goliath, the developer who was building high-end homes, a marina, and golf club on the Isle of Palms. But Billy threw his stone . . ."

The article had a picture of Billy and listed the sites where people could demonstrate their allegiance to his original rebellious act. The phone number for questions was my office, and for several weeks I paid my staff time-and-a-half.

In the middle of this preparation for Billy's day, Edie decided to visit her sister in Chapel Hill. The sister had diabetes and was not doing well. So added to my other work, I had to make breakfast and the children's lunches and drive the car pool twice. Rides home from soccer and music lessons were already arranged, but there were still several hours Edie had covered in the afternoons. Carla wasn't quite old enough to control Blair, so lacking other ideas, I called Jennifer Almond to see whether, after soccer, Blair could stay over with Teddy.

"It's no trouble," Jennifer said, "except on Thursday I have a private day for myself, and Lex takes Teddy to Summerville to see his grandfather."

"I'll figure out Thursday. This is only for a week until Edie comes back."

It was complicated in the mornings to get the children dressed and fed, worse if I was driving the car pool. Carla had lost a page of homework or Blair wanted to take a fish skeleton or couldn't locate his jacket. But necessity was a teacher.

The office was a blur. The elderly couple decided they'd accept the 1.2 million, and though they were the ones who'd delayed, they wanted the settlement nailed down right away. A flurry of emails and faxes ensued, and by mid-week everyone was drinking champagne. I had two court appearances, and every day I was on the phone with volunteers eager for confrontations I preferred to avoid. It took some doing, but each night I got out of the office to pick up Blair at six at the Almonds', where I honked and waited for him to come out. I felt uncomfortable seeing Jennifer, though she waved to me from the door.

Thursday I arrived at soccer practice early and did a few office chores by iPhone. Lex was there waiting to take Teddy to Summerville, and we chatted. He liked the Jamisons and appreciated the business I'd sent him. He hoped to build in the summer when lots of people would be around. "That will help," Lex said.

"Are you anticipating a problem?"

"I build the house," Lex said. "I don't care who sleeps in it."

Friday was the last school day before Edie returned, and I let my staff go early for the weekend, so I was a few minutes ahead of schedule at the Almonds'. Instead of honking, I parked in the crushed-shell driveway and climbed up the stairs for a view from their deck. The sun slanted in over the trees in Mount Pleasant and reflected in silver sparkles from the waterway. The tide was high and pushed the birds to high ground—herons, oystercatchers, willets—all right there on the rim of the marsh. Farther out, pelicans folded back their wings and plunged into the water. I was reminded of Billy's view from the bridge bunker—he was a master at seeing life in every form—and I was reveling in this memory when I turned around and saw Jennifer Almond at the door. She looked unprepared for anyone's arrival—no makeup, hair aswirl, an old sweatshirt and shorts. She slid the door ajar, though without invitation. "The boys are at the boat landing," she said. "I told them to be home at five."

"I'll go look for them," I said. "I didn't mean to disturb you."

"Fridays are for me what Mondays are for most people," she said. "I read about the vigil in the newspaper."

"Next Wednesday," I said, "if you can make it."

I turned, but heard the boys below and distant, laughing as they ran up the street, and something kept me there—a realization, maybe, though I wasn't sure of what. "Someday I'd like to see your old maps," I said. "I've been doing research."

"What kind of research?"

"The explorers were so much in the dark," I said. "No one had accurate information, so the mapmakers couldn't have got it right."

"At the same time, people found their way."

The boys chased one another up the stairs, and when they reached the deck, Teddy, a freckle-faced kid with Jennifer's hair, ran to Jennifer at the door. Blair got quiet and stayed by me.

On Saturday I commandeered the children to clean their rooms, while I swept sand from the kitchen floor and vacuumed dog hairs from the Oriental rugs. I even squeegeed the windows around the deck. When we finished, Blair and I walked the dog on the beach, though mostly Blair spent his time searching the high-tide line for washed-up bones. It was sunny and brisk, fall weather, and people were out with kites, dogs, and their various agendas. During the week, Edie had called several times, but, whether by chance or plan, she hadn't talked to me, until right then, when my cell phone chimed her song.

"Hey," I said.

"Hey, yourself," she said. "Where are you?"

"Blair and I are on the beach."

"I've been to colleges in the Triangle," she said. "UNC, Duke, NC State. Carla might like Duke."

"She's only twelve."

Edie hesitated. "I wanted to give you my version of our lives."

"I'm listening."

"You say you are, but is it true? You listen to what you want to hear. I'm not coming home tomorrow. I'm staying until your vigil for Billy Prioleau is over. And when I do come home, I'm looking for a house in town."

"That's not a version, it's an ultimatum."

"I don't want to be absorbed by your causes. I want the children to have the right education. And what about *my* life? Besides, you're not happy, or you wouldn't drink on your way home."

I didn't know how to answer. As a lawyer, I was aware of people's troubles but never thought much about my own.

"Aren't you going to say anything?" Edie asked.

"What do you want me to say?" I asked. I looked at Blair, fifty yards away, picking at a piece of kelp or whatever was caught in it, and I saw him in the coming years growing up without me.

In the ensuing days, my personal troubles pervaded my conversations with clients, my staff, my volunteers for the vigil, and it affected my work. I forgot to phone Arlene as I usually did to confirm our lunch, and I overlooked a deadline that, fortunately, turned out to be inconsequential. Edie had a right to be displeased about my hours and my dawdling on the way home, especially with Jack as a sidekick, and I couldn't downplay her perception of her diminished social opportunities. My fringe activities had cost her friends. But resolving to do better or be different wouldn't change her mind, and even if she wanted me to move to town with her—she hadn't mentioned divorce yet—I couldn't leave the island, where I was raised.

On Sunday I told the children their mother had delayed her return—her sister wasn't recovered—and we had a pic-

nic at Breach Inlet. It was windy and cold, and we ate in
the truck. The whitecaps swept onto the beach, and gulls
whirled through the air. On the way home we drove around
to Purvis's to take him leftovers. "It'll only take a few minutes," I said. "It's a good day to be nice to people."

"So is every other day," Carla said.

"Purvis is weird," Blair said.

"His father abandoned him when he was fourteen," I
said, "and he hurt his hand. Neither of those things was his
fault. Don't you talk that way about anyone."

Blair pouted and looked out the passenger window the
whole three miles down the island.

Purvis's Opel wagon was there, and the johnboat, too.
Carla waited in the truck, while I went to the door, and Blair
investigated the Evinrude and the spiderwebs in the boat
trailer. No one answered my knock. Purvis didn't work on
Sundays, but he could've been down the street, fishing from
the boat landing. I looked in the shed, where we stored the
fishing and crabbing gear, but it looked to be there. The
freezer was running, not nearly full, though. Blair found a
bone under a spider web, and thought a spider had eaten a
bird.

A few minutes later, we ambled back to the truck. "We
need to fill that freezer," I said. "When Billy Prioleau Day is
over and your mother gets home, I'll take you out into the
creek."

"Famous last words," Blair said. "When will you have
time?"

"I'll make time."

We crossed the yard, and I glanced toward the house
and, through the window, I saw Purvis hanging from a ceiling crossbeam.

The vigil for Billy Prioleau was supposed to be a celebration and a testament to his resolve against forces greater than he was, but Purvis's suicide changed my mood. I was in touch by cell with my committee people at every site around the county, and they reported larger-than-anticipated turnouts. That was good. The main group, the bridge-vigil folks, were meeting at the Piggly Wiggly on Coleman Boulevard because there was no parking allowed on the causeway. It was an ordinance we were going to ignore, but we wanted to take as few cars as possible. A year ago we had a half-hour silent vigil with maybe thirty people, and we didn't cause much of a disturbance, but this year we were expecting sixty or so. When I arrived at the Pig parking lot, though, two hundred people were waiting, and others had already driven out to the bridge.

"We won't be able to control that many people," I said.

"But we can't cancel," Amy, one of my volunteers, said. "What do you want to do?"

"Have the police shown up yet out there?"

Amy called someone at the bridge, and there were no police yet, but cars were parked all along the bike path.

The causeway was three miles across the marsh, with the bridge in the middle, maybe a little closer to the island. Oleanders lined both embankments, and along the bike path was an occasional palm tree that survived the hurricanes. I drove a rented van with twenty people crammed in, and we parked at the end of a lengthening line of cars, with others falling in behind us. There was to be no walking on the highway, no bad language, no violence of any kind. I'd arranged for the bridgemaster to stop vehicle traffic and let the boats through, and when the highway was quiet, I was going to deliver a short speech about Billy. But now, with so many people, I wasn't sure what would happen. I noticed Jennifer Almond in the crowd—she probably parked on the other side of the bridge and walked over—but others clamored for my attention and I couldn't say hello.

People wielded all sorts of signs—STOP THE NUKES, I LOVE BILLY P, NO MORE HOUSES. Cars slowed down, and once one car stopped, the others behind had to brake, too. Someone had brought a sign that said WORK IN PROGRESS to warn cars coming the other way, and the traffic backed up over the bridge span. In a few minutes, it was the same as that day six years ago: the bridge couldn't open with the cars on it, so the channel was blocked, and the traffic on the highway couldn't move.

"We're going to get into trouble," I said.

"So did Gandhi," Amy said. "So did Martin Luther King."

"So did Billy Prioleau," I said. "Okay, let's do it."

Amy stepped onto the bumper of a parked car and turned on the bullhorn. "Welcome," she called out, and the crowd cheered.

People in their cars shut off their motors and rolled down their windows or got out to complain or to join us.

"This is a celebration for Billy Prioleau," Amy said, "and with us today is Billy's friend, Scott Atherton, who was in the bunker with Billy that day six years ago when Billy stopped the dump trucks from getting to or from the island."

There were more cheers and whistles.

"Scott's the man who got Billy out alive."

There was applause and whistles, and Amy handed me the bullhorn.

I waited for the people to quiet down. "Billy Prioleau was my friend," I said. "He was an honorable man, devoted to the life of the marsh and to the tides that are the source of that life. Look around you. The creeks are fed by the sea, and the reeds teem with mudworms, minnows, and hermit crabs, which, in their turn are the prey for rails, egrets, foxes . . ." I stopped, lowered the bullhorn, and took a breath. "But I wasn't the only other person with Billy in the bridge bunker that day. Purvis Neal was there, too. He was in our midst but was invisible, as Billy was, until Billy stood up and said, 'I am willing to step forward.' I ask you this morning, all of you, to step forward . . ."

I went on a little longer about preserving the marsh, about the conservation trust, about Billy's grave, and Edgar's, and now Purvis's, all of whom were or would be buried on the shell mound at the end of one of the creeks. I was interrupted by sirens coming from Mount Pleasant along the free lane of the causeway, and I handed the bullhorn back to Amy, who led the crowd in singing "Blowin' in the Wind," which was appropriate because the words dissipate into the moving air.

The next Monday Edie came home from Chapel Hill, and, though she assumed her usual chores with the children, she slept in the guest room at night. She said it was temporary, but Blair immediately got into another fight at school and Carla, twice that week, had migraines.

The rest of the week went by in small enterprises. Since I already collected Purvis's rent for him, filed his taxes, and paid his bills, it was a formality to get the court to appoint me executor for his estate. Purvis had no known relatives, but published notice was required for probate, and, because of the value of his mother's property, the estate was considerable. I hoped, given Purvis's history and character, the court would eventually approve the Billy Prioleau Conservation Trust as beneficiary.

In a few days, without much hassle, Edie found a rental house she liked on Beaufain Street and wanted to move there with the children over Thanksgiving break. It was her plan to enroll Blair and Carla in Porter-Gaud at the new semester, when, presumably from sloth or malfeasance, a few other students would drop out. There hadn't been any discussion of this—"When do we discuss anything?" she asked—but it was a separation that involved a lease negotiation (I urged six months, but she wanted the security of a year) and an agreement about support. I could have contested her unilateral decision and tried to keep the children in their present school, but I considered the long-term harm such arguments could wreak upon them and, down the road, I wanted to keep open the idea of reconciliation.

One day a week before Thanksgiving, Lex Almond called and said a client had a financial problem, and since he'd already scheduled the pile driver at the Isle of Palms, he could move it most efficiently to Station 17. The framing crew could follow a few days later. "I've told the Jamisons," he said, "so can we amend the contract for date of performance?"

"I'll fax it over this afternoon," I said. "What about summer and people's being around?"

"We do what we can do," Lex said, "I want to keep my crew on the ball."

The county sheriff wasn't happy about the havoc Billy Prioleau Day had caused at the bridge or about the good publicity we got in the paper, and I heard his objection as "goddamn liberals." I proposed that next year we announce a traffic detour to the next bridge north, which would make him look as if he'd planned ahead, and I'd thank him publicly for his cooperation. "With the good press, people are going to want to do this again."

After Thanksgiving, work eased off and I stopped drinking in the truck on the way home. I liked the drive and coming home to the quiet of the island, to the dark house and my own time, to the familiar rhythm of the sea. Of course I missed Carla and Blair. Visits weren't the same as living with them day to day, but I saw the children a lot because my office on Broad was close to Beaufain. I worked out with Edie a ritual of taking them to school in the morning.

In early December one night or early morning someone torched the in-progress frame of the Jamisons' house. There were flooring and studs, no roof yet, but the Jamisons were frightened. They'd expected opposition and unpleasantness, maybe catcalls, but not damage. Angie was afraid if they ever got the house built someone would set fire to it with them inside. "I don't want to worry every night that someone will kill us," she said.

"Over time it will change," I said. We were in my office looking over their insurance coverage. "I told the island police what those crabbers said in the marina lounge. It's criminal bigotry. The chief will increase his patrols, and, if you wanted to, you could hire a watchman."

"But will we feel like prisoners?" DeSean asked.

"I talked to Lex, and he said the pilings weren't damaged. He's ready to start again. But it's your call."

"You said he'd stay with us," DeSean said. "And so are you. I think we'll try again. I want Angie to be able to see eternity."

On a Thursday in mid-December, I left the office early, picked up Blair at Porter-Gaud, and drove through Mount Pleasant out to the island. Darkness came earlier now—it was almost the shortest day of the year—so we didn't have much time. I drove to Purvis's, and we hitched the johnboat trailer to the truck, loaded the gas tanks, life preservers, nets, and crab bait from the freezer in the shed. "Put some ice in the cooler," I told Blair.

At the landing it was a hassle to winch the boat off the trailer, but Blair held the line while I drove the truck out and up to the parking lot. I lifted him into the prow and pushed the boat out, and my pants only got wet to the knees. Having the boat in the water gave me a sense of expectancy, and I recalled from my childhood how many times my father and Billy had taken me out. I wanted Blair to feel that joy, too, but I didn't say anything. He had to feel it on his own.

The Evinrude started on the second pull, and in a few minutes we were in the waterway, heading north. On the open water it was cold, and Blair put his jacket on and ducked behind the windshield and sat in my lee. I opened a Sam Adams, as we went under the bridge, I raised the beer to the bridgemaster.

For another ten minutes we traveled full-throttle north until I turned into a side creek. "This is the place," I said. "Pay attention."

"It looks the same as the last creek."

"It isn't. That's why you have to learn the landmarks. There's a mast over there from a yawl that was tossed up by Hurricane Hugo, and if you fix yourself on the antenna behind the live oak tree on the shore, you can see where we're going."

Blair looked around but didn't say anything. The creek had three wide serpentine bends, and then narrowed, and narrowed further closer to the headland. I slowed to negotiate the oyster banks and sandbars. Each turn gave a new vista of marsh, live oaks, and sky. An egret flew up like white paper, and we passed a night heron hunched over like an old man. A couple of White Ibises, with their red decurved bills, probed the mud. It was low tide, and when I was close to solid ground, I cut off the motor and drifted.

The shell mound was ahead, the crosses on top barely visible against the trees. It was too late for shrimp casting and too complicated to fish, but Blair and I tied chicken necks onto the crab lines and threw them over. The marsh wasn't pristine, not completely pure—a beer can in the mud, contrails across the sky, the sound of a boat's motoring in the waterway. A TV tower's red light blinked over causeway, and a cargo plane made a wide turn over the unseen ocean and homed in on the navy base in North Charleston twenty miles away.

If Blair was aware of these imperfections he didn't let on. I opened another beer and settled back against the boat cushions. This was what I wanted most, to let everything go—work, Edie, even Purvis and Billy—let them go. But I couldn't. They were too much with me.

After a few minutes Blair and I pulled up the crab lines, netted the dangling crabs, and shook them into the cooler. I threw the bait back in.

"You like crabs?" I asked.

"Sure," he said. "Their bones are the most intricate. Carla likes them, too, but she'll eat anything."

"Right. I know. As I remember, your mother likes them, too."

In a half hour we had a dozen, and by then the light had diminished to a pale wash on the water. The tide was coming in again. I missed Purvis in the world.

I got myself another beer. "We should go home," I said.

"We might see something else," Blair said.

"We'll come back."

I cranked the Evinrude, and we motored slowly back along the bends in the creek. It was darker, and the birds had flown to roost, and all we saw was the glimmering, shadowy world.

The waterway was a wide wet highway with the sheen of the bridge lights on its surface. Headlights of cars zoomed back and forth on the causeway. We followed the channel markers, red right returning, and in a half hour I throttled down and turned left toward the boat landing. Instead of going directly in, though, I steered past the landing and farther up the creek.

"There's the truck," Blair said. "Where are we going?"

"I have an errand to run," I said.

We cruised up the creek to the Almonds' house, lit from the inside, and I turned the johnboat so the incoming tide held against the motor. Blair was cold and huddled between my legs and didn't notice where we were. I saw one of the Almond children pass through the light from the sliding glass door, and then Jennifer appeared in the frame of the window.

Jennifer gestured with her hands and said something I couldn't have heard, and she looked out toward where the johnboat was idling in the creek. I remembered today was Thursday, her private day, and she was back from Beaufort, home again in her role as wife and mother. The complexity of her life was borne upon me with unaccountable force—was she as unhappy as Edie was, or I, or did her connection with Abby Lincoln, like my lawyering, enable the life she had here? I thought of Purvis's lonely years in his shack behind his mother's house, his father disappeared, his harmed hand, but for a month with a woman named Shelley maybe he'd known love. Jennifer Almond slid open the door and came out onto her deck—she saw the johnboat adrift in the creek—and she waved, and I waved back.

I eased forward on the throttle, and we gained headway against the tide. I imagined myself an explorer, looking not at the shapes of continents but at human needs and desires. What could I derive from a landscape so unexplored? What would I have communicated to my mapmaker? We slid past Jennifer Almond's house and on into the stretch of darkness before the landing.

# THE HOTEL GLITTER

T'S DARK AS EVA BAENA LEAVES HER apartment, but light is seeping up over the hills to the east. Her daughter, Marisa, not quite a year old, is sleeping, and Eva hates to abandon her, but what can she do? It's Tuesday, her roommate Jenny's day off—she's sleeping, too— and Eva at least doesn't have to rely on her mother, who lives across town. Eva shoulders her backpack, descends the steps from the second tier, and walks past the nursing home, the acupuncturist's office, and the gym, aiming for the fluorescent light above the Phillips 66 station on Townsend. It's August, but chilly at six thousand feet in the high desert. Eva is early, as always, afraid Ephraim will leave her, or Laszlo, or whoever's driving. In June, Sal left her—he's since moved to Denver—and every morning as she waits Eva imagines the red tail lights of Sal's truck brightening as he slowed for the stoplight three blocks away, then dimming again as he drove on. She'd had to hitchhike. It wasn't hard to get a ride because construction workers and electricians and plumbers all got going on the commute around the same time, but Eva prefers to ride with people she knows, people who won't comment on her body or grope her or ask even jokingly to pay for the ride with a blowjob.

At five after five Ephraim pulls his dented Subaru Outback to the curb. He's Egyptian, thirty, a clerk in a rug store in Mountain Village. He's already collected the others. Inez is dozing in the passenger seat; Laszlo, the Hungarian, nods; Carmen says hello. Eva gets in the back seat, and Ephraim pulls out into not much traffic.

"Where's Raffy?" Eva asks.

"Not feeling good today," Ephraim says. "I went inside and asked. Another long night."

"Is Jane okay?"

Inez opens her eyes. "She will be as soon as she gets rid of that loser."

"Raffy's young," Eva says. "He wasn't meant to lay down roof shingles with a nail gun."

"I was meant to sell rugs?" Ephraim says. "This man said I looked Persian and had a job for me. After a month in Denver, he sent me to manage this store."

"People think because I'm Mexican I can cook," Inez says.

"You get to wear the pretty white blouse," Laszlo says in his thick accent.

"They make me," Inez says. "And the push-up bra. I need these to recite the specials?"

"They think I'm Mexican, too," Eva says, "but I was born right here in Montrose."

They pass Office Depot, City Market, and the new Target, then cross the bridge over the river and are out of town into pastureland dotted with subdivisions and big houses perched on ridgetops. The sunlight expands and throws down long shadows into the arroyos. The dry hills to the west glow pink.

After a few miles, the road and the river reconverge and parallel one another through a limestone canyon. Eva settles

back and thinks of Raffy nailing shingles on the new ski condos, wasting himself on meth or booze, a lost soul. It isn't
Jane's fault. She was drawn in by Raffy's silence and his
help-me look. Eva smiles thinking of that look, or maybe she
smiles because, at the top of the canyon, the panorama of
mountain peaks is lit up by the sun.

Her mother Julieta was born in Hermosillo but crossed the
border to Tucson and got a green card, sewing for a dress
designer. Eva's father, Alvarez Baena, was an American citizen stationed at Davis-Monthan Air Force Base, and immediately after he gave his name to Eva, he flew his F-14
into the side of Mount Lemmon. Since Julieta and Alvarez
weren't married, the government paid no benefits.

Julieta moved to Phoenix, but she was frail, and the heat
diminished her. A cousin found work for her in Denver sewing for several laundries that provided that service, but after
a year, she developed palsy in her hands and took disability.
To make the check go farther, she moved with Eva to Montrose, where it was cheaper to live.

Eva grew up there and did well in school, especially in
English and science. She played the clarinet in the band and
was a not-very-good striker on the soccer team. What troubled her was her body: she drew attention from boys, even
from men. She hadn't done anything more to deserve this
than a girl who grew tall, but she didn't like the whistles and
lascivious stares and the phone calls, sometimes anonymous.

"Dress loose," her mother said. "Don't flaunt."

"I don't flaunt," Eva said.

"Be grateful," her mother said. "You've been dealt a win-
ning hand."

"What do I win?" Eva asked.

The girls were jealous and kept their distance, and most

of the boys who leered at her were daunted and shied away. Her only real friend was Rafael Trujillo, who wasn't popular at all. He was a loner, a weirdo, maybe gay. That was the consensus, because he painted pictures and lived with his mother out on Spring Creek Mesa. He was five seven, strong and wiry, quiet, a rock and ice climber. Sometimes Eva went with him—when he climbed the north face of Wetterhorn Peak or the sheer walls of the Black Canyon of the Gunnison rim-to-rim-to-rim. In winter he climbed at the Ice Park in Ouray, and she stood on the bridge over the slot canyon and watched him solo an ice falls using only crampons and an ice axe—no rope.

But Eva liked most going with him when he painted. He set his homemade easel at the Dallas Divide, or the rim of the Black Canyon, or maybe in a pasture on the mesa, and she read while he painted. They talked about climbing or traveling, if they ever had the money, or the worlds writers made up in books. Eva wanted to go to college in California and be a nurse. Raffy wanted to climb Half Dome in Yosemite, Chimborazo in Ecuador, and a nameless peak in Nepal. "But I'll have to work," he said.

"You're working now," Eva said.

"I mean, you know."

"I know."

Raffy usually did landscapes: aspens with mountains in the background or a pasture with a sky above it—subtle, never the highest mountain or the most rugged cliff. He used pale colors and painted clouds accented with differing shades of blue so Eva felt the depth and movement of air. Sometimes he painted her with a book in her hand, or beside a stream, but *doing something* like gathering berries or wading, so she was part of the larger scene.

Once on the plateau they were in an aspen glade, and the

leaves were shaking and the sun dappled the ground with shadow. "Take off your clothes," Raffy said. "I'll do a nude."

"You will not."

"The light is perfect. Are you afraid? I'm the painter. I won't hurt you."

"I wouldn't want you to show a painting like that to anyone else."

"Let's assume I wouldn't."

"What if you got famous?"

Raffy laughed.

"The answer is still no," Eva said.

It's twenty-six miles to Ridgway where Ephraim turns right onto Colorado 62. They cross the river again—smaller here and laced with arsenic from the mines above Ouray—and head along the base of the San Juans. This is as close as Eva gets anymore to wilderness: a glimpse of Ralph Lauren's property as she's traveling past—pasture, mixed aspen, scrub oak with the mountains as backdrop. They chug up and over Dallas Divide at almost nine thousand feet, where Raffy has painted a few times. There are sometimes deer or elk in the meadows, especially in the early morning, but none today.

They descend the red sandstone canyon along Leopard Creek twenty miles to Placerville, where Ephraim slows and turns left. They climb again on a narrow, twisting road beside the San Miguel River, and when they get higher, the mountains appear again—Mt. Wilson, Lone Cone, El Diente. This is the valley Telluride lies in, the ski town, the resort, now the summer playground. None of them in the Subaru can afford to live here, but if they split the gas four or five ways, they can commute. A five o'clock start in Montrose gets them to work by 6:30.

The Hotel Glitter where Eva works in the spa is only one of the big lodges in Mountain Village, each with its own jewelry shop and florist, news kiosk, barber shop, together with clothing boutiques and fancy restaurants. Between the hotels are other stores and offices, art galleries, Ephraim's rug emporium, several microbreweries, the architecture office where Laszlo is an apprentice. The Glitter is what Eva calls the hotel because everything is mirrors and glass and polished tile. The chandeliers in the lobby have thousands of facets, and the single lights along the corridors gleam like crystals. The wallpaper is cloth, dark blue, with subtle patterns of gold. The doors are mahogany. An ornate gold border decorates the ceilings.

Eva punches her time card at 6:41 and goes straight to her locker where she puts on her uniform — a white skirt and gray blouse with the hotel insignia on the breast pocket — cheerful clothes but not competitive. She pees, brushes her hair, fixes her makeup, and makes a cursory run-through of towels, robes, soaps and aloe vera lotions, shampoos and conditioners, hairbrushes, to make certain the night person has replenished supplies. This early the spa isn't busy, but Eva checks the log book. Two women have signed in. Not all the rich are idle.

The spa offers swimming, squash, racquetball, a weight room with Nautilus equipment, a climbing wall, sauna, hot tub, steam bath, massage, and juice bar. Outside are six tennis courts and a pool. The hotel guests check in through the lobby, but there are memberships, too. For \$12,000 a year, anyone from Telluride or Mountain Village can join, and some of the homes have the privilege included in the purchase price.

Eva spends the morning at the desk until Joanne, the

full-time manager, comes on. Joanne is married to a real estate broker and doesn't need the job, but she gets free privi-
leges and likes to chat with the guests. Eva collects towels
and robes, does several loads of laundry, and folds the dry
towels. On her break, she calls Jenny, but Jenny doesn't
answer, or on her cell, either. "If anything's wrong, call me,"
is the message Eva leaves.

At ten thirty, four men are playing racquetball doubles,
and the tennis courts are occupied. At the glassed-in end of
the women's locker room, there are a few tables where wom-
en congregate after their workouts to drink orange juice,
Snapple and SoBes. Mrs. Jorgensen has brought her laptop
to check email, and Mrs. Burstyn, in a robe, reads a *House
Beautiful* in the sunlight streaming through the open door to
the terrace.

Eva is collecting towels and empty glasses and bottles
when Helen Warren comes in from the tennis courts. Hel-
en's in her thirties, dressed in blue shorts and a white blouse,
and is semi-sweating, though her blond hair is frozen in an
upward swirl. "Hello, Eva," she says brightly. "How's that
baby of yours?"

"Good," Eva says. "How was the tennis?"

"I'll never get any better," Helen says, "but who cares? I
want you to bring your baby one day so I can meet her."

"I will."

"Come and sit a minute. I need to get off my feet."

Eva sits, though it makes her nervous because Joanne
could come in any moment. If Eva chats it's called loafing.

"How's your mother?" Helen asks.

"Fine. Marisa's with my roommate today, though."

"Oh, to be young," Helen says. "You can endure so much.
I remember when I was dating Gerald—this was in San

Francisco—we could stay out all night. Oh, I know it's not the same." She looks in her tennis bag, finds a twenty-dollar bill, and hands it to Eva. "I'd like a Mango Supreme, but I can't move."

Eva gets up and goes to the main desk in the lobby for change, and on her way back a man in shorts and an Izod shirt, coming at her sideways, runs his hand across her rear end. Eva glares at him, but he says, "Quiéres chingar?"

"Not with you," she says.

In the spa she puts two ones into the juice machine and delivers a Mango Supreme to Helen, who gives her the eighteen dollars in change. "There's more where that came from," Helen says.

"Thank you" sounds wrong, but Eva says it anyway and puts the money in her pocket.

In the afternoon it clouds up and rains, and there's no tennis or swimming outside, but women are in and out of the exercise room and the hot tub. Patty and Arturo give massages one after another, and Eva does several more loads of laundry. Joanne asks her to sweep the floor because the janitor has called in sick again, and Eva can't say no. At five, she's so tired she can barely walk down to Ephraim's store, and he's got a customer he can't shake. She calls Jenny.

"Everything's fine," Jenny says, "but at seven I'm going to a movie with Bart."

"Who's Bart?" Eva asks.

"If you're late, I'll leave Marisa with Sylvia."

"Please, not with her."

"I called your mother, but she didn't answer. Who else is there? Dwayne?"

"Definitely don't leave her with Dwayne," Eva says.

"Then hurry."

Ephraim usually drives home as if every extra minute he gets on the Internet is worth the risk of death, but tonight he gets behind a UPS truck and drives fifty. He's in a good mood because he sold a $48,000 Kazak. If he owned the store, he could buy a new car, but even so he can get the clutch fixed.

Inez gripes about the manager of the café who looks down her blouse. "My boobs are only for customers," she says.

"How were tips?" Laszlo asks.

"Nothing like what Ephraim made, especially if you add the driving time."

"What would you do with an extra three hours a day?" Ephraim asks.

"Sleep," Inez says.

"I'd have more time with Marisa," Eva says.

"If you didn't have Marisa, you'd have a life," Carmen says. "Such are the wages of sin."

It's almost eight when Ephraim lets Eva off at the Phillips 66 station. Eva stops in at Sylvia's apartment downstairs. Sylvia is old, and her place smells of cat spray—Eva gets it upstairs sometimes—but she's an emergency sitter, better than Dwayne, the appliance repairman. Eva thanks her and gives her ten dollars. "I have an extra TV dinner," Sylvia says, "if you're hungry."

"I have leftovers I need to use," Eva says.

Marisa cries when they leave—she likes the cats—and, as they climb the stairs, Eva points out the stars emerging from the paling sky. "The stars make pictures of animals," she says. "There's a lion, a crab, and an elk."

There's no elk, but Raffy once said there was. Elk, to Raffy, are magical animals.

Marisa doesn't understand too many words yet, but she stops crying and looks past Eva's outstretched hand. Eva can't know what her daughter sees, but she knows her voice soothes Marisa, and as soon as they get into the apartment, Eva gives Marisa a couple of wheat crackers and turns on the TV. She makes scrambled eggs and heats leftover spaghetti and Gerber's peas. She fills Marisa's dish and puts her in her highchair and feeds her eggs and peas and mashed up spaghetti. She thinks about walking over to Raffy's after Marisa is asleep. It's only five blocks. She could run over and back and stay fifteen minutes.

But after dinner Eva gives Marisa a bath and sings to her in her crib in the corner of the bedroom they share. *Want to hear a girl's patter, climb up your ladder now. It's time for you to dream away.* It only takes a couple of songs, and Marisa is asleep.

Finally Eva has a moment to herself. She calls Raffy's number, and Jane answers. "How is he?" Eva asks.

"He was in bed all morning," Jane says. "I don't know what he did in the afternoon. I was at work."

"Is he riding with us tomorrow?"

There's a pause. "How can I live this way?" Jane says. "I've tried to help him, but he has to help himself. Half the time I don't know where he is, and the other half he's lost."

"I've tried, too," Eva says.

"Try harder," Jane says.

Eva hangs up and stares at the wall where Jenny has hung a print of three people dancing in a circle as if they were happy, though Eva thinks they're only pretending. It's her fault Raffy is at risk, because a little over a year ago she went out with Milan Kleisa. That was when Raffy was in the hospital in Denver. Raffy had been climbing all winter and thought he was untouchable. That's how he talked. He'd climbed a chimney crack on Courthouse and was halfway up, putting in a screw, when a boulder above him dislodged. "I didn't have the screw all the way in," he said, "and I swung out and the screw held and the rock whizzed by without touching the rope. I swung back and caught myself."

"And here you are," Eva said. "You were lucky."

"I was good," Raffy said.

He might have been good, but a month later he fell fifty feet from a frozen waterfall and broke both his legs, his right arm, and right clavicle. For the rest of the school year he was in and out of hospitals in Montrose and Denver, which was why Eva, in a bad stretch, got talked into seeing Milan Kleisa.

She'd had her own success that spring—admission to Colorado College and Denver University, with scholarships. She wanted to major in biology and maybe study a year abroad. She might be a doctor instead of a nurse and work in Africa. Then Milan asked her out. She'd never liked Milan much, but he was *there* and Raffy wasn't, and her mother encouraged her to have fun. Milan was smart enough, but crude, a rancher's son, a hunter, a running back who boasted about being offered a football scholarship to CU. He took her to dinner and the movies, and once when his parents weren't home, invited her to the ranch. They drank beer and rode horses out to a natural hot springs up in the aspens, where Milan talked her into going in naked. He'd brought beer and bourbon, but no condoms.

The next morning at five, when Ephraim pulls to the curb, Raffy's in the car. He and Eva sit in the back seat on opposite sides of Inez. Raffy's brooding. He doesn't say anything as they pass Walmart and gain speed through the burgeoning new light.

Inez says, "I hope today isn't like yesterday."

"It will be," Laszlo says, "and no one wants to hear you bitch and moan."

"Bitching and moaning keeps me from quitting," Inez says.

"Maybe if you showed a little more skin to the manager, you'd get a raise." Carmen says.

"I'd get a *rise*," Inez says, "but I don't want to end up like Eva."

They pass into the shadow of the limestone canyon. No one says anything more.

That day is like the day before, and so is the next day and the next. Eva takes Marisa to her mother's before five a.m., and Ephraim picks Eva up there. After Marisa was born, Julieta wanted Eva to live with her in the bungalow, but Eva didn't want Julieta to have any more of Marisa's life or hers than she already did. "This isn't Mexico," says Eva.

Shame, fear, sadness—each of these had a price in rent money. Her friend Jenny felt sorry for her so she took Eva and Marisa in, though now, a few months later, the cramped life, the baby's crying, and the men Jenny has over are wearing on both of them.

Eva and Raffy ride to and from Telluride in silence with each other. They fill their days making money. On the way home Raffy smells of sweat and asphalt shingles, and he rides with his window open. There's a bruise on his arm from an unexpected tip of the ladder, a slash in his hand from a mis-angled cutting knife. At the end of the day, Eva is softer but equally exhausted. She sleeps a little on the way home: Raffy's silence is hard on her. He hasn't climbed since his fall,

and he won't again. The doctors put a plate in one leg, and
he limps, skewed sometimes one way, sometimes the other.
Jane entered the picture during his convalescence, when he
was on pain meds. She's a physical therapist. She got Raffy
off meds, but he's found substitutes on the street. Montrose
seems slow moving and apathetic, willing to let franchises
and box stores take over, but so much is hidden. What Eva
laments is that Raffy hasn't painted. Once it was what he
lived for, but now it's what he avoids.

Thursday, when Eva gets out at her mother's, she says,
"I have to drive myself tomorrow. There's a tennis tournament and party afterward, so I have a late shift." She swings
her backpack onto the sidewalk, finds her wallet, and pulls
out two tens. "This is for gas," she says, handing them to
Ephraim.

"You work Saturday?" Ephraim asks.

Eva takes another five from her wallet. "Saturday, yes.
Here's for Saturday, too."

"Your mother is a saint to stay with your kid that long,"
Carmen says.

"It's her granddaughter," Eva says.

"What time are you coming back tomorrow?" Raffy asks.
"Maybe I'll ride with you."

"The spa's open until nine," Eva says.

"I'll call you on my cell," Raffy says.


In the morning Eva takes Marisa to the park. The sun shines
through the loose clouds, and Eva carries Marisa on her back,
along with a plastic bag of accouterments—binky, snacks, a
couple of ring toys, a sweater if the sun goes under, sunblock
for if they stay longer than a half hour. She puts Marisa in
a swing, but Marisa cries. She likes the sandbox, and Eva
watches her play with a plastic container and a spoon.

A yellow Lab comes over and sniffs in the sandbox, and Marisa's scared, though she doesn't cry. Eva pats the dog. Its owner hurries up, a woman jogger.

"Come here, Aster," she says. The woman looks at Eva. "I'm sorry. He's too friendly." The woman grabs the dog's collar and pulls him away. "Aren't you Eva Baena?"

"I used to be," Eva says.

"I'm Molly Jauron. I taught you biology three years ago."

"Oh, right. You cut your hair."

"This is your baby?"

"Marisa," Eva says. "She's eight months."

Marisa lifts sand in the plastic container and dumps it out.

"She's big," Molly says. "So you're married?"

"No. You remember Milan Kleisa? He's the father."

"Milan Kleisa? Jeez."

"He's playing football at CU," Eva said. "He won't admit the baby's his, but he gave me a crappy ranch truck. What about you? You quit teaching."

"I wanted to see the Great Wall," Molly says.

"In China?"

"I know it sounds crazy," Molly says, "but one day I rolled out of bed, looked in the mirror, and said, 'You don't have to do this.' I think it was the day after I found Jeff Lee with his fingers inside Carly Nixon's pants in the lab, and he said he was doing a science experiment."

Eva laughs.

"What was *she* doing?" Molly asks. "So I quit and went to China."

"And now you're back."

"Collecting my stuff. This is my parents' dog. I'm going to Zambia to see Victoria Falls."

Aster has done a tour of the park and bounds back to the

sandbox. Molly wrestles with him and lets the dog bite her hand. Eva picks up Marisa.

"I guess I'm here forever," Eva says.

All afternoon the spa is crowded. People have come from Vail, Aspen, Steamboat Springs, even Alta and Taos, for the Ski Town Tennis Tournament. Eva wishes on this occasion she was a waitress making tips, but even so she gets an occasional ten-dollar bill handed to her for no reason.

A pretty woman, fortyish—Severin, from Aspen, her name tag says—asks Eva to come to her hotel room when she's finished working. "For mutual entertainment," Severin says.

"I'm married," Eva says.

"So am I," Severin says. "That's why I want you to visit."

Men make similar suggestions. They are intrigued by her body and are used to getting their way—buying whatever they want—but Eva wonders what she's done to make them think she might be willing. She isn't. She has Marisa to get home for and Joanne to think about. She wants to keep her job. Besides, Raffy's going to call. She carries her cell phone everywhere and checks it three times to make sure it's on.

The tennis lasts until past seven, and those who've finished are spectators fueled by alcohol from the cash bar on the terrace. There's a door to the spa, and the crowd swirls and flows and balances its drinks and shouts "hello" and "nice match" and talks business Eva doesn't understand or want to. There's a beautiful sunset—pinks and oranges in the clouds framed between the sides of the canyon—but Eva barely has time to look. She collects glasses, napkins, canapes that have fallen to the floor, mops up a spilled margarita—tidying, tidying, that's her function. She thinks of calling

Raffy, but assumes he hasn't called because he doesn't need a ride.

Joanne pitches in because there's more than Eva and Miranda and Luisa can do. Eva's not used to working so late, and she's tired and worried about her mother's putting Marisa to bed. She calls, and Marisa is already asleep.

Then Helen Warren appears from the crowd and taps Eva on the shoulder. Helen is dressed in a low-slung wraparound and has on dangly diamond earrings. "I want you to meet Gerald," she says.

Beside her is a distinguished-looking man, thirty years older than Helen, in gray slacks and a pale blue sport shirt. Gerald offers a weak hand, and Eva shakes it. "I've heard about you," he says.

"I told him you were the most beautiful woman in the spa," Helen says, "so he wanted to get acquainted."

"Did you play in the tournament?" Eva asks Gerald.

"Nothing so frivolous as tennis for me," Gerald says. "I play golf."

"I lost in the first round," Helen says. "How's that baby?"

By eight thirty the party is winding down, but dollars still float in the air. "Do as many favors as you can," Miranda says. "Drunk people are more generous." She flashes a fifty-dollar bill.

Joanne hands Eva a tray full of glasses and dirty ashtrays and asks Eva to stay another hour after nine to clean up the spa. What can Eva say but yes? She takes the tray to the kitchen, where there are no tips to be made.

A few minutes later, when Eva comes back to the spa, Joanne is on her cell phone calling security. Eva sees Raffy outside on the terrace. His hair is long and disheveled, and his face is smudged with roof tar. He has on jeans and a long-

sleeved plaid shirt, not tucked in, and right away Eva can
tell he's high on something. A couple of the guests standing
at the cash bar make way for him. Eva's too far away to hear
what's said, but the bartender, a foot taller than Raffy, shakes
his head and holds up his hands as if he's being robbed. He
means no, he can't do anything. Rules are rules.

Eva hurries past Joanne and outside to the terrace, just
as a uniformed, gray-haired security guard with a holstered
pistol comes from the hotel. Raffy isn't arguing with the bartender, but he looks sad and confused. Eva calls to him, and
he smiles. "There you are," he says.

"I thought you were going to phone me."

Raffy shrugs and appraises her. "Uniform and all," he
says.

Eva takes a twenty-dollar bill from her pocket. "Is this
what you need?" she asks.

Raffy turns to the bartender and asks for a Heineken.

The security guard arrives, along with Joanne. "Is there
a problem?" the man asks.

"He didn't have any money," the bartender says, "so I
didn't serve him."

"I do now," Raffy says.

"Do you have an ID?" the bartender asks.

"Why don't you leave peacefully, son?" the security guard
says. "Let's not have trouble."

Joanne looks at Eva. "I suggest you take your friend
home," she says. "He's not an invitee."

The word "invitee" and the way Joanne says it stuns Eva,
and for a moment she can't move or think. The long hours
and days come together in her body, the *work*, the sense of
being overwhelmed, and then she slaps Joanne across the
face.

"Whoa," Raffy says.

Joanne reels a couple of steps backward. The security guard grabs Eva's wrist and yanks her sideways, but Raffy rams his shoulder into the man's gut, and Eva pulls her arm free. She runs into the spa, crashes into a guest, and caroms away blindly. Raffy catches her in the hotel lobby.

The brakes on the Tacoma need work, and Eva uses second down Keystone Hill. On the right, her headlights illuminate red sandstone, and on the left the black void of the canyon. Raffy's in the passenger seat. It's been twenty minutes since they left the hotel, and neither of them has said more than the obvious. Raffy plays with the radio dial, but there's only static, and he turns it off.

Suddenly he laughs out loud. "Did you see her face?" he asks.

Eva laughs, too, but it's not funny. "I shouldn't have hit her."

Silence. They pass a cottonwood tree that throws darkness over the highway.

"Jane left me three days ago," Raffy says.

There's a pause.

"How's that been?" Eva asks.

"It had to happen," Raffy says. "I don't know. It's okay. It's not like—"

"We should go to Victoria Falls," Eva says.

"Victoria Falls?" Raffy says. "Where is that? What are you talking about?"

"Nothing," Eva says.

They lapse into silence, which seems to Eva the best communication. She drives toward the moon through Sawpit and Placerville, and the moon disappears behind the ridge ahead. There's no traffic. At the stop sign at the bottom of the canyon, she turns right and accelerates. She trusts the truck more on the uphill. The road winds along the cotton-woods by the creek. She's used to seeing them in daylight, and at night they're surreal—green with black shadows attached, and nothing behind them.

The moon returns, shines across the hood of the truck, and illuminates Raffy's hair with a rim of silver. She wants him to tell her more about what happened with Jane, but he's dozing, and she doesn't want to wake him. His eyes are closed, and his head is tilted against the window. How sad he looks. *Help me.* She has a glimpse of not wanting to help him, not ever seeing him again, but she doesn't decide. She wants to explain how she felt when he fell from the icefalls and broke his legs, how she fell with him that day, how she feels when she abandons Marisa every morning, how she feels *now*, but silence is the consequence of where she is. What she wants most is to spend another afternoon in an aspen glade while Raffy paints the sky. If he were to ask again if he could paint her with no clothes on, she'd say yes. She doesn't care anymore who sees.

The road levels out on the saddle, and the car hums. There are other hotels to work at, of course, and restaurants and shops. Another job will appear—a clerk in a clothes store, maybe. She'd rather work in Montrose—less money, but she'd be close to Marisa.

Ahead she's aware of something moving at the side of the road, and she takes her foot off the gas and lets the truck coast and slow down. A herd of forty or fifty elk seethe along the shoulder and out into the meadow and aspen trees near the road. Eva edges the truck forward until she's even with the elk and stops. The elk aren't afraid. She turns off the headlights and rolls down Raffy's window, and the musky scent of elk flows into the car.

Raffy wakes up. "Shit," he says, not fully there. "Where are we?"

"Right here," Eva says.

The elk mill and jostle right beside the car, mostly cows and calves, though there are two spike bulls as big as the truck. A few minutes go by. The elk amble away into the aspen trees whose leaves shimmer and waver in the moonlight. Eva reaches for Raffy's hand, and he takes hers.

"Now what?" Raffy says.

"Now what?" Eva answers.

# WHO IS DANNY PENDERGAST?

I'M NOT SURE WHEN IT FIRST HAPPENED—maybe the evening of the Other Ones Dead show in Ashland, Oregon—thousands of people, guys with electrified hair wrapped in bandannas or straight hair put in ponytails, wearing T-shirts with Jerry on them, or shirtless with tattoos of peace symbols and body paintings, shorts unbuttoned with one-eyed snakes hanging out, *unreal*, and chicks, in all manner of getups or non-getups (getdowns?), their eyes like comic book XXX's, barefoot a lot of them, their breasts swinging and their hair all sweaty as they danced. I'm talking about *2002*, one of the rare palindromic years. The Other Ones were left over from the Grateful Dead, and Jerry Garcia had already been gone seven years.

I wasn't on drugs, but I was on the fringe—always have been. Dusty had gone to find a friend—yeah, like among the multitudes?—and I knew I wouldn't see her again until next week. I was cruising, not for a woman, but in my head, poking my brain into this little cove and that narrow inlet, sailing sometimes full spinnaker downwind. The band, such as it was without Jerry, was between sets, and there wasn't a lot to focus on except a sea of ugly body parts and the sun sinking casually into hazy farmland. Maybe that's when it came to me.

Or, I don't know, it could have been weeks before that,

when the sun actually *was* going down into the *real* sea. This was in Mendocino, and I was with three guys about my age, who'd rented a motel room to watch the Super Bowl. They were college students from Eugene, and I was hitching from Seattle to Tucson. They said I could sleep on their floor. Before the game—I didn't know who was playing—we'd been on the beach, the sun falling into the blue horizon, and I was listening to their juvenile bullshit about alcohol and blowjobs, as if they had any clue. The sun was flattening like a deflating basketball, as it will at the end of ex-eternal time, but none of it—the war in Iraq and W's *re*election and alignment of sun, moon, and stars—made much sense to me. I was relaxed, letting go, glimpsing the end of things, which idea had nothing whatsoever to do with the sensation I felt, which was disjointed, illogical, and irrelevant to the sunset or even to its colors—no drugs, remember, I don't do those—red, pink, and sweet lavender. I was in tune with body, mind, and emotion, these being the essence of reality.

It could have happened then.

Or maybe it was at the trailer in Sabino Canyon, where I was surrounded by saguaros and agaves and chollas, when the summer heat was tempered by clouds and rain, thunderstorms that brought me to my knees more than once. On the day I'm thinking of, after I'd been to Seattle and had come back, I'd run up the dry arroyo at six in the evening, and thunder was booming behind Mount Lemmon. Shoes and shorts, that was all I had on. Temperature in the eighties. Sand gave way under my feet, one step forward, a half step back. I was sweating. A bolt of lightning stabbed down into the saguaro hillside not more than a hundred yards away, and water—a wall of brown—frothed toward me. It hadn't even rained where I was.

Could it have been then?

You may have the impression I'm a scruffy, long-haired, fitness freak, but I own my own home in a gated community (no mortgage) and am the CEO of Darwin Enterprises that makes terrariums, bird houses, and specialty habitats for small animals—we do a lot for hamsters and gerbils and even ferrets, and we stock a wide variety of cage troughs, eyedroppers, and hummingbird feeders. Name a cage or a feeder, and we have it. My office is on East Speedway, and I was thinking about when it happened because I'd just come from my counseling appointment, and Tiffany, the counselor, thought I should go back to the beginning.

You'd think I'd remember exactly when the beginning was, but that's the weird thing. It was a sensation, no, a *knowledge* (more than belief, less than reality) that came over me at odd moments, like a meteor's falling through the night sky, *bzzzzt*, and then gone, or a sparrow that flits across the highway when you're driving seventy-five. Did I see it? That's how it was, unpredictable, and it used to be a second, no more. Now it lasts longer—a minute, two minutes. It's hard to say how long, exactly, memory being what it is.

Okay, okay, I know, so what is *it*, right? "It" is a pronoun, referring to another thing, the referent. This "it" has to do with a farm, to an experience on a farm, *the* farm, where this "it" occurred, being two hundred and forty acres in Georgia. I can't change the facts—Georgia. I was twelve, eleven, maybe, and still subservient to my parents. I went where they went. I was the victim of their orders and whims. They told me what to do. If I had charted my own deviant course—smoking in the hayloft or questionable grades or stealing from Walmart, say—they'd withhold their love. Even if they hadn't known I'd done anything to punish me for, they made me feel guilty for unknown transgressions.

This was *northern* Georgia, and on this day in fall I had been instructed to get the eggs from the henhouse. I know, today, with Jerry dead, and the sun falling into the ocean west of Mendocino (and rising somewhere else), it sounds pioneerish to collect eggs from a henhouse, but they were my parents. It was foggy. Cold air at night had collided with the warmed-up land from the day before, and as I walked across the yard, still sleepy, as the sun oozed blood through the ground fog, I heard a sound off in the not-too-distant distance—primordial, eerie, not a wolf's howl or an owl's hooting, but a more strident screech. I knew what the sound was, but because of the fog I couldn't tell where it came from. I carried the egg pail past the henhouse and ventured up the grassy hill behind. The hill had been there yesterday and the day before that, but today, *that day*, I wasn't so sure. I heard the sound again and stopped, surrounded by mystery.

I knew of tractor accidents, poor crops, and the price of soybeans, but I still believed mongooses screamed outside my bedroom window at night, and I thought tigers lived in our county. I was in the fourth grade, or fifth, at Trenton Elementary, and there were UFOs, space aliens, atom bombs, moon flights, earthquakes, guns, six professional sports, and women without clothes. I had *seen* these. I wasn't sure, though, what was on the other side of that hill.

The persistence of the unknown, the supernaturalness of time—these were at work. What I *expected* to see, judging from the sound, was, in fact, *exactly what I did see*—a shape shrouded by mist rising from the far side of the hill, taking clarity from proximity—an animal. It stopped when it saw me—I *suppose* it stopped for that reason, but how would I know? The shape said, "Eee-Aww"—it was a donkey. That's the "it" I've been getting to: At certain moments, without foreseeable antecedents and for an undetermined duration, I am a donkey.

It's not what you'd wish for yourself. Not suave. Not kosher. Not romantic. As I said, at first it was only a flash of recognition—*Fuck, I'm a donkey!* and then I'm *me*, Danny Pendergast. At the Others Ones show it wasn't too serious. So what if, for a split second, I was a donkey? I fit right in. And the other time, say, scrambling away from a flash flood? What difference did it make? *Poof*, things were back to normal.

But then, this: I was in the Super Walmart on Speedway, walking down one of the hardware aisles, checking out the Skil-saws and power drills on my way to the paint department to find a shade of peach to use in my bedroom. Peach would make a statement of emotional readiness for a relationship. I crossed into the main aisle when, *blammo*, I was a donkey. I know, preposterous. Hard to explain. My hands were still hands, not hooves, and my ears were still the same little flesh-and-gristle protuberances and not furry, floppy flyswatters. People didn't scream or run. But I was not a human being who thought he was a donkey. I wasn't a donkey that thought it was a human being, like Mr. Ed, the talking horse, or those song-and-dance cartoon fish in a Disney movie. I was overwhelmed by smells and sounds, by colors. I felt hot. I felt surging alarm. I was hungry and thirsty. I was a *donkey*. I dropped down on my hands and knees and brayed.

Whether that was a *shazam* or not I don't know, but I snapped out of it and was Danny again. I was on my hands and knees, looking up at the Wal-martyrs who were backing away and detouring around me as if I'd yelled, "Jesus is the Devil." I scrambled to my feet and stood there stunned, but I *remembered* being what I'd been. I remembered what it felt like to see shapes and colors and have no words. How is that possible? Well, how possible is it to be a donkey?

Luisa was one of the onlookers. She had the day off from the Desert Museum where she was a guide and translator for Spanish speakers, and she was shopping for towels and washcloths. Dark skin, light brown, almost bronzy eyes, and teeth that needed an overhaul, but I wasn't choosy. Ugly worked both ways. She was humming "Take Me Out to the Ball Game," so I asked whether she was a Diamondbacks fan.

"What do you care?" she asked.

"Gonzo's my favorite," I said.

"They traded him years ago," she said.

"Good pitching," I said. "Schilling and Randy Johnson."

"They're long gone, too," she said. "You have a cell phone? Let's go to a game."

On my way home, having remembered being a donkey, I thought I needed therapy and, you know how it is, I made an appointment but didn't go. My symptoms didn't return. Six months went by without any donkey experiences. During that time, Darwin Enterprises launched a new line of fortified birdseed and added to its catalog a fragrant hardwood dowel small rodents could hone their teeth on. I bought the rights to a hypnotic comfort tape for small dogs so they wouldn't yap at night, useful also for sleepless hamsters and gerbils, and I saw Luisa. I admit I hadn't dated much. Okay, I was thirty-one and never had actual sex. Sad. Women think I'm silly. I've got super-blond hair, one upper incisor, the right, that's bigger than the left, ears the size of walnuts. A woman at Prescott College said my eyes were from outer space. Big. At least they're both the same shade of blue. But appearance-challenged people have sex. Some of them get married and populate the planet with weirdos. My parents, for instance, had Daisy and me. (Daisy has the same incisor, the same mantis eyes.)

I've had occasional girlfriends. In Ashland there was Dusty, who, before she wrecked it, borrowed my car a lot. In Seattle I went out with Fast-Food Frieda, who weighed two hundred pounds and was partially blind, and in Tucson, here, I saw Sun and Moon, two sisters I met at a small-business seminar who were revving up a head store about the same time I was starting Darwin. I held hands with both of them in their apartment when we were watching *Blade Runner*, but they got busted and moved to Flagstaff.

So, Luisa. She lived in the barrio, and we went to three baseball games and to dinner twice. She already had a green card, but she liked me anyway. She showed me around the Desert Museum, and one afternoon we drove up Mount Lemmon through the fire-ravaged ex-forest and had pie at the café. Things were cozy. We embraced a few times and kissed once, eyes closed, teeth gnashing. One night we were sitting across from each other in a booth at the China Garden—red pagodas and golden dragons on the walls. She'd ordered sweet-and-sour chicken, and I was getting moo goo gai pan. We were waiting for the miso soup and egg rolls, and Luisa was reading from the place mat about 1977, when she was born, the Year of the Snake. "Wise and intense," she said, "with a tendency toward physical beauty."

"You have it," I said, "or you want it?"

"I want it," she said and looked up at me. "What year are you?"

What Luisa must have seen was Danny Pendergast, straw roof, big blue eyes, good teeth except for the unbalanced incisors. She didn't scream. I'd have remembered a scream. What *I* saw was a face without a name, red and gold on the walls—nothing I could put into words. I had no words. Luisa was smiling at me and expecting me to respond: That's what I interpreted afterward—sounds coming from her lips, a quizzical look. *Is something wrong?* she might have asked.

She went off to the ladies' room, while I made snuffling sounds and bared my teeth. When she came back, I was Danny Pendergast again.

That was the event that made me do something. I couldn't be driving my Cherokee on the interstate and turn into a donkey. What cop or victim's relatives or judge would understand a donkey was at the wheel? What if I was a donkey for five or ten minutes? The next morning I made another appointment with the therapist.

Then I called my sister, Daisy, at her office in Bethesda, where she was a travel planner. "You're the family archivist," I said. "Are there aberrant genes in our past?"

"J-E-A-N-S or G-E-N-E-S?" she asked. "Are you talking about tough pants or deoxyribonucleic acid? Have you been drinking?"

"I don't use drugs," I said. "Are we related to any bizarre Mammalia?"

"On Mama's side there was a skunk and a couple of weasels," Daisy said. "One of Mama's brothers did prison time. On Daddy's side there were lots of black sheep. Listen, Danny, I can't talk now. I'm arranging a golf package for the spiritual advisor to a congressman. Why are you asking me this?"

"Never you mind," I said. "I was wondering about equine types. They might be pretty far back."

"Shit," Daisy said. "Growing up you were selfish, devious, and lazy. Are you wondering why you're a jackass?"

"I was not lazy," I said. "I was lonely."

"If you have a question about your genetic makeup, call Mama and Daddy."

My secretary, William, came to the door and pointed at

his watch to remind me I had a meeting. I nodded. He handed me a sheaf of papers.

"Do you have weird dreams?" I asked Daisy.

"Talk to Mama," Daisy said, and she hung up.


Naturally, I thought of possible explanations for donkeyism—this on the way to the Tanque Verde Mall for my
shrink appointment. I was being punished for unremembered incidents when I'd given my mother shit for moving
the family from the farm in Georgia to Tucson, from Tucson
to Orlando, back to Tucson, and finally to Bethesda. (My
poor father.) Was becoming a donkey linked to thoughts of
avarice, lust, and antipolitical correctness we're all prone to?
Was I being tested like Job about my loyalty to God? What
god? Anyway, what god would bother to test me, Danny
Pendergast?

Maybe donkeyness was a wacked-out disease, like el-
ephantiasis or gout. Maybe a capillary in my brain was
clogged, the exact one that *prevented* donkeyism. Or I had an
extra synapse that *created* it. Maybe the absence of sex had
dammed up my testosterone, and this surplus, after a point,
manifested itself in donkeyness. But then, wouldn't there be
thousands of people braying in the streets?

Or stress might be a variable. Darwin was larger than
small business, smaller than big business. It was middle
business—more successful by each order for gerbil trough,
hummingbird feeder, and parakeet cage. Early on, I had cut
my employees in on profits, which happened to go up and
up, but should I now expand and hire more people, perhaps
reducing the employee benefits? Should the company move
to a larger building? In the short term, that would cut into
net profit. Should I sell the whole operation?

Of course, theories were just that, theories, some less plausible than others. Not much to go on. I was a pretty average Danny. I paid my parking tickets, my utility bills, and my taxes. So why me? And why a donkey? Why not a hawk, say, to see from up high or a hummingbird flitting from a bougainvillea blossom to a prickly pear flower, or an owl to probe the darkness? Or a wolverine, the most savage mammal, a bear so powerful it had no predator, a pronghorn antelope, fleet afoot? Why a donkey? Of all the equines— horse, zebra, pony, etc.—the donkey was the least graceful, neither wild nor cute, in a word, boring. *Pathetic.* Donkeys were laden with prospectors' provisions and ore from the mine. Donkeys carried tourists down the Bright Angel Trail to the bottom of the Grand Canyon.

I didn't choose to be a donkey. That was merely what I became.

Tiffany Ferraro was a fuzzy-haired blonde, my age, with perfect teeth, lots of zits, and six dangly bracelets on her left wrist. A tattoo was partially visible under an errant strap of her pink top. She started with the usual questions—Did I have insurance? Was this an emergency? Was I in pain?

"We're talking metamorphosis," I said. "Not a cockroach, not Jeannie turning into a genie, or a phoenix, either. A donkey."

Tiffany laughed. The windows on the third-floor walk-up were open. A car horn honked.

I launched into the family drama of my sister's usurping the attention—her record in high school, teen pregnancy, marriage, lost baby, divorce, remarriage, redivorce, while I was ignored, etc. I told her about my parents' dragging us to Tucson to Orlando and back to Tucson, and to Bethesda to be near the Republican administration. I stayed in Arizona and went to Prescott College, where I majored in business and fine arts.

"Fine arts?" Tiffany said, as if this were the first good detail she'd heard.

"Painting," I said. "I painted hamburgers. Cheeseburgers deluxe, onion, pickle, relish. Bacon burgers. Mushroom burgers. All different colors and shapes. It was design genre, icon art."

"You didn't pursue it?"

"It wasn't escaping," I said. "Ha ha. Serious artists laughed at me, so now I run a multi-million-dollar company that makes custom-designed cages and feeders for birds and small mammals."

Tiffany took some notes, jangled her bracelets. "And sex?"

"I was seeing someone before I turned into a donkey."

"Let's get back to that."

I told Tiffany about the incident on the farm, the incident in the Super Walmart, the time in the Chinese restaurant.

"Sounds like traumatic reversal," Tiffany said. "You go back to the morning on the farm and put yourself in the donkey's place."

"But what triggers the episodes now?"

"That's what we'll try to figure out," Tiffany said. "What about the woman?"

"Luisa," I said. "I haven't called her since she knew me as a donkey."

"We'll talk about that next time."

In the interim between then and the next time, I made adjustments. I rode the bus to work. I slipped into my office surreptitiously through the terrace door and spoke to William and other employees via email or over the intercom. I ate a box lunch in my office. For dinner, instead of picking up a bite to go at Greasy Tony's or sitting down in an Applebee's or Western Sizzlin', I went to Wild Oats (I know, I know!) and bought *food*—cauliflower, broccoli, red-leaf lettuce, fish, chicken, etc.

At home I stuck close to the TV and watched old movies I got through Netflix. I didn't wander the neighborhood or play tennis, even when the woman next door, who sunbathed nude, asked me to fill in at doubles. I didn't swim at the neighborhood pool. What if I were swimming laps and became a donkey?

When Daisy said to call Mama and Daddy, she didn't mean on the telephone. She meant I should channel them. She meant communicating with the dead. And I confess I thought of it. The threat of donkeydom so skewed my life that I was desperate, but when wounds were cauterized, why cut them open again? There was an off chance my old antagonisms, festering for years, were coming to the surface in fits and starts, and I didn't want to go there.

Here's what happened: I was in Prescott College doing hamburger art. Prescott is in the high desert, pinyon/juniper country, clean air, no drugs. (I knew some people who did drugs.) College was a luxury I'd never imagined—a four-year vacation to focus intently on the void that lay ahead. But I had to take courses. Which ones would be of use in a culture that shunned the intellect, sullied its own habitat, and prayed to money? It was no accident the bank was next to the church. One group of subjects made sense: economics, finance, and accounting. If I were going to negotiate the terrain of the nether world, I might as well have a map. On the other hand, I was spiritual and wanted to be close to trees, animals, and birds. I considered forestry and environmental studies, ornithology. I chose art.

Let me backtrack slightly. All my life I'd doodled in the margins of textbooks, library books, notebooks, a cartoonist with a satirical eye, but also a realist. I could draw a house that looked like *that* house, a mountain like *that* mountain, a person like *that* person. But I liked doodling. I was good at it.

One spring day I was late and raced into art class to find everyone immersed in a silly still life, an arrangement of hats and vases and flowers. I happened to have come from Burger King, so I painted my hamburger — the Whopper — ketchup, mustard, mayo, lettuce, underripe fauxmato, pickle, sugary bun, a slab of grilled meat — good colors, but with a health value somewhere in the minus numbers. I slapped paint on my art board. A Whopper in midair, a couple of trees behind, a cow hastily rendered, a five-dollar bill floating into the distance.

Even before I finished this painting, I envisioned other hamburgers, hamburgers a la Magritte, "This is not a hamburger," a Picasso, "The Blue Hamburger," Warhol's "Iconburger." I saw realistic hamburgers, collageburgers, abstract hamburgers, impressionistic hamburgers. I might use gouache, oil, paper, cardboard, metal, or combinations. In the space of a three-hour studio class (the professor hadn't critiqued my work yet), my outlook on the future changed from the prison of finance to the helium balloon of art.

So how did my parents die? I'm getting to that, "that" being the referent for "the story." At Prescott I spent my last two years cooking up hamburgers on my easel, and after graduation I had a van full of paintings. Almost, but not quite, as I was pulling away from my crummy apartment toward oblivion—where would this have been?—a gallery in Spokane called me on my cell. They had seen a Magritte-burger on my website. Could I send slides of other work?

I did better than that. I drove straight to Spokane.

There followed a flicker of fame and a period of wandering. I had a tan Chevy, no windows—Van Go—in which I slept and schlepped. I started in Spokane and hit galleries in Yakima, Seattle, and Tacoma. People bought my paintings. I collected money and horsed around. The gallery in Spokane wanted more, and it was clear if I were going to make a career of art, I had to fry up more burgers, slather on mayo, juice up a few tomatoes.

Enter my parents. They hadn't heard from me since before graduation, and they hadn't made it to Prescott for the ritual of passage. They wanted to know where I was. I had sent Daisy a postcard from Spokane and one from Portland, terse notes like, "Having a great time," and "I'm alive!" and one from Ashland that said, "Gone to the Other side." Unbeknownst to me, this card prompted my parents to conclude I needed rescue. They hadn't given me two minutes of attention in years, but now they had to save me. They flew to Seattle, rented a Ford Pinto, and, near Grants Pass, Oregon, hit a patch of ice and crashed into a bridge abutment.

My parents were buried at the Baldwin-Fairchild Cemetery in Orlando, and I continued my plunge to obscurity. By then I'd rented the trailer in Sabino Canyon and was living on snared rabbits and lettuce scrounged from the back of Quiznos. A few dollars dribbled in from dogsitting and three nights a week as busboy at Captain Sam's.

The dogsitting was for a debarked Pomeranian named Papillon and a beagle, MacArthur, whose family went to Colorado to escape the heat. One afternoon, as the dogs staked their territories in the backyard, I got into a conversation over the fence with Mrs. Frannie Wells, who complained about the inadequacy of her canary cage and its feeding trough. "Why don't they make a feeder the bird controls?" she asked. "What if I wanted to go away for a few days? Why should I pay someone like you to watch Rodolfo?"

That night I invented a bar attached to a spring that Rodolfo could tap on and get a measured amount of food. Mrs. Wells paid me ten dollars, and Darwin Enterprises was launched. That same day, when I checked my mail, I learned from Daisy that my parents were in the grave.

A few weeks went by in relative quiet, no conversions to a donkey. I rode the bus. I ate fish and salads. At Darwin, I contracted with a company in Burkina Faso to manufacture bamboo bird cages, transferred our accounting to Nesleski & Daughters, and had William update our computer program for filling orders. Then Purina offered to buy the company for eighteen million dollars. Not a bad investment for a spring and piece of wood for Mrs. Wells's bird cage. But if I took the money, what would I do with myself? Did I want to be put out to pasture so young? Ha Ha, a donkey of leisure. Purina gave me a thirty-day window to decide.

One evening not long after receiving this offer, I was sitting on my patio in shorts and a T-shirt, no shoes, drinking a SoBe Lava Lizard and staring at Mount Lemmon's nubbly trees and serrated outcroppings that were in the last orange sun, when I heard the irritating tinkling chimes of my doorbell. I ignored it. It rang again. The garage door was closed, the lights were off in the house. It had to be a neighbor, because the community was gated. Maybe the nude sunbather. The chimes rang a third time, and I padded into the house.

Through the peephole I saw, not the neighbor, but Luisa's

overlarge mouth crammed with yellowing teeth, her eyes bulging, her scraggly black hair flying every which way. A sudden gust of love blew over me, and I opened the door.

"Where have you been?" she asked in a tone that suggested I hadn't paid child support.

"There's a gate," I said. "How did you get in?"

"You kissed me once," Luisa said. "Do you know what that means? Don't think you can apologize. I've been worried about you and that funny little act you put on when I was reading about the Year of the Snake."

"I've been indisposed."

"I thought you were honest."

I gazed at Luisa with curiosity and lust. The distortions through the peephole moments before had coalesced into soft lips, limpid eyes, hair the color of ink. We kissed and swooned to the floor. In a flurry of gyrations, our clothes disappeared, and, for the first time, I found myself about to engage in the supposedly pleasurable act that had caused so much misery in the world. And yet, I paused. Even as I said, "This will be for fun, right?" she was saying, "Yes, yes." But if she were so affected by a kiss . . .

But it was too late. She moved forward, I moved forward. Within a few seconds I sensed the impending crisis, the stored-up energy bubbling to the surface. Luisa's "I love you," floated in the sweaty air.

And then I turned into a donkey.

Early the next morning, in response to my previous evening's panicked message, I got a callback from Shrink Tiffany. "What's up?" she asked.

"There's been a breakthrough," I said, "no pun intended. Can I see you right now?"

"It's six-thirty in the morning," Tiffany said. "Give me a hint."

"I was a different donkey," I said.

"I charge double for overtime," she said.

At seven-thirty I was sitting in a green leather chair watching Tiffany pick at an irksome blackhead that looked like a groundhog taking a peek out of its hole.

"So," Tiffany said, "you haven't seen me in three weeks, and now there's an emergency."

"I was coping," I said. "I was eating right, avoiding traffic, and I got an eighteen-million-dollar buyout offer from Purina."

"Events have been in motion," Tiffany said.

"Then Luisa showed up."

"Oohh," Tiffany said, as if she knew what was next. "¿Qué paso?"

"I had to decide what to do with the rest of my life."

"And you chose to become a donkey?"

"It happened."

"Did you take the eighteen million?" Tiffany asked, oozing the nasty zit.

"I have another week to decide," I said, "but with the conspiracy of so many variables, and then to confront—"

"Evil?" Tiffany asked.

"Love," I said.

"Define your terms."

"Everything was exactly in alignment, precise balance, perfect pitch, in the zone—the body, the mind, and the emotions were all simultaneously turned to high. That's where I was last night."

"When you were Danny Pendergast or when you were Donkey Danny?"

"Who is Danny Pendergast?" I said. "That's the question that occurred to me in the most intimate moment with Luisa."

"Did Luisa know you were a donkey?"

"Not till afterward. At the time she thought I was just weird."

"And how do you know you were a different donkey?"

"The ears. The ears . . . I heard things."

"Like what? What did you hear?"

"And the nose. I smelled things."

"You're not being specific."

"You had to have been there."

"How long were you . . . your other self?"

"Minutes that seemed like hours, and hours that seemed like minutes."

"To the donkey you?"

"Luisa said it was ten minutes tops. I refused to go for a walk around the neighborhood. I was recalcitrant. I drooled a little, and I made funny sounds. I remember that."

"Memory's a gift and a curse," Tiffany said.

"Being a donkey full-time would be easy," I said. "No skin cancer, no elevated cholesterol, no high blood pressure."

"No doctor's bills," Tiffany said.

"But no pain, no gain," I said. "I'd miss worrying about money, the work I do, and the anguish of romance."

"How did you leave it with Luisa?" Tiffany asked.

"I didn't leave it with her. I took it with me."

"If I were with a man who was drooling and making funny sounds, I don't know what I'd do," Tiffany said. There was a silence, and she dabbed at her zit with a Kleenex. "How can I help you further?"

"Do you know any channelers?" I asked.

That evening I found myself taking the bus west on Speedway. It was nine p.m. by the Wells Fargo clock downtown, and the dark outlines of the Rincons drew a jagged line across the paling sky. I got off at Park and walked south.

I'd not slept much the night before, having made love, turned into a donkey, and lost Luisa again. My appointment at Tiffany's had been early, and I'd worked a full, dull day at Darwin. I'd half-decided to sell the company, but hadn't talked to any employees yet. I found the adobe house I was looking for—shutters, chipped corners, and a crumbling stoop that led into a dirt yard. At the sidewalk was a neatly lettered sign: Yolanda's Palm Readings, Tarot, Listen to the Dead. No Solicitors.

I paused at the gate and pondered where I was in the cosmic sense. My parents were dead, my sister worked for neo-Christian right-wingers, and my therapist had done nothing except despoil her complexion. Luisa had abandoned me in my hour of neediness. True, in the economic realm, I had a paid-for house, a Jeep Cherokee, and the assets of Darwin Enterprises, but what did any of that mean? In my spiritual life I was alone and on the edge of a black hole. What choice did I have but to open the falling-off gate in front of me?

I did that and climbed to the stoop. The door opened of its own volition, but I wasn't fooled by the motion detector. I entered a boudoir with chiffon draped from the ceiling. The effect was of a spider web. The room smelled of incense with a hint of burnt chicken. In a moment, a young man appeared in jeans and a T-shirt that said, Long Live the Mutants. "You here to see Yolanda?" he asked.

"Is she available?"

"She's always available," he said. "You want a cup of tea?"

"I don't do drugs."

"A wise choice. What about hot cocoa?"

"Are you experienced with mutants?" I asked.

"It's a punk band," he said. "Are you here for the palm read or the full treatment?"

"I want to talk to my parents."

"You need permission?" he asked. He laughed at his own joke. Then he pointed to a daybed with a paisley spread on it. "Lie down there."

"I want to meet Yolanda first," I said.

The man disappeared behind a tall Oriental screen with storks on it. On the walls were photos of what I presumed to be family members, dead or alive, heart-shaped stones with COURAGE and RISK etched on them, lots of dresser scarves on the bureaus and tables with unlighted candles. There was no way I was going to lie down on that bed.

A beaded curtain separated, and a woman emerged. She had a shrunken and shriveled face, silver hair, wattles under her chin and on the backs of her bare arms—eighty if she were a day. She had no dangly earrings, no bracelets, no garish makeup or head scarf. (No zits, either.) She wore shorts and a thin sleeveless shirt. Behind the swaying curtain I glimpsed a startling, iridescent blackness.

"Who died?" she asked, and she went about lighting the candles with a mechanical grill igniter.

"Are you Yolanda?" I asked.

"I'm Mary," she said. "Shall we settle the financial arrangements?"

"I spoke to Yolanda on the phone."

"Oh, I doubt that," Mary said. She lit the last tall candle. "Are you a timid flyer?"

"Do you mean do I believe in this nonsense? Do you have a license?"

"Yolanda is the mediary," she said. "I know about these things since I already have one foot in the grave." She held out her hand to me, but I backed away as if it were a high-tension wire. "You understand I don't give a shit whether you communicate with your parents or not."

I hesitated and pulled out my wallet and handed her a one-hundred-dollar bill.

"Tell me more about them," she said.

"My parents were middle-class Americans who voted for the Bush leaguers. They came to find me in Oregon and hit a patch of ice."

"Together? If they died together, they'll be easier to find."

"Are they lost?"

"There are many dead," Mary said. She motioned toward the bed. "Shall we lie down? That's how we get in touch with Yolanda."

A few minutes later I was lying down, blindfolded, beside an eighty-year-old woman. She was toward the wall and held my left hand in her right and extended her left through a hole in the wall into the startling blackness.

Mary had warned me it might take a little time to find my parents, that on the whole the dead were an uncommunicative lot. They were dreamy and carefree and busy.

"Busy doing what?" I asked.

"They move around," Mary said.

I lifted my blindfold and saw the burning candles. "Where are they that they need to move around?"

Mary's eyes were closed. "It's not like our pedestrian idea of heaven and hell," she said. "Where they are is more like an amusement park—noisy, lots of rides that don't go anywhere, confusing. Some people are scared and some think it's thrilling."

"My father will be scared," I said.

On the bus on the way over I'd formulated questions to

ask my parents, especially my father—why he'd moved from the farm, why he'd loved my mother, what his state of mind was when I was conceived—but if he were riding a roller coaster, I wouldn't get much of an answer.

Almost as soon as I lay down, I felt dozy, and I think I slept for a minute. When I woke, Mary was still in the same position. "Have you got hold of Yolanda?" I asked.

"You couldn't tell?"

"I didn't hear anything."

"It's not hearing," Mary said. "It's energy flow."

"I didn't feel anything. And how would she know what they look like? They were cremated."

Mary sat up. "All I know is she couldn't find them this time. Can you come back tomorrow?"

I went back four times, and, riding the bus, more questions came to me. If they were so intent on finding me in Oregon, why hadn't my parents shown up for my college graduation? Did love change for a child after, say, the age of ten? Why had they given Daisy five thousand dollars when she turned eighteen and not me?

Lying on that daybed with Mary, I anticipated an energy force that would crackle across the synapses of my brain, but what occurred was disappointment. Mary kept her arm through the hole in the wall, and once in a while I sensed her slide away into the nether world between me and them, as if she were searching the darkness for Yolanda. But nothing happened. After each session, at diminished cost for increasing failure, I took the long bus ride home exhausted and empty-headed.

Twice that week I turned into a donkey—short interludes of panic and debilitating terror at being in the human world.

One time I was ravenous and snarfled in the tiny patch of lawn I kept watered beside my house. The other time I was on the bus going to work, but I don't think anyone else knew Eeyore was riding in the back.

The second time, arriving at work, I had the sense I wouldn't become a donkey again right away so I assembled the employees to discuss the Purina offer. We agreed to hold out for thirty million, and we could all retire.

Afterward, I went off again to Yolanda's. The candles were burning. Incense drifted among the chiffon curtains. Mary held my hand. Then, out of the darkness, I felt something like pinpricks, a series of meaningless blips—static on a radio or snow on a TV screen. I can't describe exactly what they were because there were no words or pictures, but it gave me a premonition, the way, without reason, you feel *on this day* something good (or bad) will happen. The blips or pinpricks gradually spaced out, and I stood at the edge of a calm pool of water watching stones being thrown into it. The rings from the stones radiated outward, one after another, in perfect concentric clarity, but as more stones were tossed in, the rings intersected, the water became roily and turbulent. Mary squeezed my hand.

My mother was there, not in pictures nor in an explicit vision, but in a swirl in my imagination. She was contained in a high-pitched, wheedling voice. She garbled like a squawk box and made no sense at all.

I nudged Mary.

Mary nudged back.

"I can't understand her."

"Shhh." Mary scraped her fingernails across my sweaty palm.

I listened, thinking of Yolanda traipsing around among

the dead, tapping on peoples' shoulders. Where was my father? Even before I was born he'd lived on the farm in Georgia, running that tractor back and forth, back and forth across the red hills, worrying about the weather, the fertilizer, the harvest of soybeans, tomatoes, and carrots. My mother was no bargain. She was a flinty nagger, and he must have agreed to retire in Tucson to keep her quiet. Doing her bidding never worked. As soon as they were settled into their townhouse—I remember the swimming pool and a green-and-white lounge chair my father sank into in complete exhaustion—she was at him again to move to Orlando. The desert heat evaporated the fluid from her eyes. He must have protested, but it didn't do any good.

No wonder, once they had moved two or three times, my father wanted to look for me. I'm sure he thought my mother wouldn't go along.

My mother kept up her screechy rant for several minutes, until I said, "Where's my father? He should be here." I pulled off my blindfold, and light poured into my face.

Then the static resumed, the picture darkened, and Mary let go of my hand. "Aren't you ashamed of yourself," she asked, "treating your mother like that?"

"She wasn't *saying* anything."

"She told you plenty," Mary said.

I got up, disoriented. I blew out the candles next to the bed and bolted through the door, and outside I staggered to the sidewalk. It was dusk, and lights were coming on in the neighborhood, scattering through the palm fronds. Across the street in the park, kids were swinging, climbing on the jungle gym, and careening down a metal slide alongside the homeless women and drug dealers. I crossed over and called Daisy on my cell.

"I'm working," Daisy said. "I have to provide a blood-of-the-lamb feast for a thousand evangelical Christians who have a meeting with the president tomorrow."

"I took your advice and called the folks."

"And?"

"Mom garbled her words. Dad wasn't there."

"That's the family dynamic," Daisy said. "What did you expect?"

"I expected answers."

"That would take a miracle," Daisy said, "which is what I have to conjure up for tomorrow at the Feast of the Blood of the Lamb." She slammed down the phone.

My mother's diatribe and Daisy's hanging up on me made me wander, and it occurred to me Luisa lived not too far from where I was—over a few streets and down a block or two. We had been to this park once, on the other side, so I knew where I was.

I skirted the palm trees and detoured into a clamorous street where discordant music was playing from several different doorways. Kids were running from house to house and across the street, shouting at each other. I walked deeper into the barrio, but nobody paid any attention to me. Then something new—there always is: I felt in advance, in the next moment, I was going to turn into a donkey. Should I sit down on the sidewalk? Slip into the alley coming up on my left? Turn back to the park? I had never anticipated the change before, had never known it was coming, and I was disconcerted.

A mockingbird sang from a low adobe wall beside me, and I stopped, totally in limbo. I felt the air, smelled the carne cooking. Bougainvillea shimmered against a wall, and a woman's voice cooed from a doorway singing "Still Waters Run Deep." Any second I'd be a donkey. Then other donkeys appeared nearby—one crossing the street, another one dropping a package on the sidewalk, a small donkey jumping rope and not doing a very good job of it. I was still Danny, though, full of human talents and frailties, but also not Danny, keenly aware.

I could live the rest of my days not *as* a donkey, but anticipating becoming one. That's what I wanted, betweenness, heightened senses, but brainpower. I could accept a fate of uncertainty, not knowing the moment I'd be donkey or Danny. Wasn't it true everyone endured such uncertainty because, come on, which of us isn't a donkey?

I felt better immediately, more *human*, if that's possible.

Luisa's place was in the next block, beyond the corner laundromat, where a donkey was struggling to get the door open. I walked on, neither donkey nor Danny, sensing the imminence of donkeyness, but not yet the reality. I was seeing things from a middle ground, as if I possessed the animal sense of smell and hearing, but with a human perspective that made me aware of the sweetness of the mockingbird's song and its fading as I walked farther away. I sensed the texture of the air, the brilliant blue of the sky.

Three houses down was a corner grocery, and I stopped again. Luisa was passing along the opposite sidewalk carrying vegetables in a net bag. She was watching the people coming toward her, as if curious about them, admiring them, as she was when she'd seen me that first afternoon in Walmart. In her appreciation of what was around her, she saw me across the street and paused. There was such kindness on her face I couldn't help but think she understood and was at last seeing me, Danny, the real me, embracing all and everything.

# THE MAN AT QUITOBAQUITO

THE CIRRUS ARE SHRINKING BUT STILL white, high above the desert. The thicket darkens. The sun has fallen through the leaves of the single cottonwood at the pond, and the water is blue-gray and rose from the reflection of the sky. Near the slough the air is muggy, but the quiet is what makes me uneasy. As Ellen and I follow the animal path around the water, I'm conscious of the pall that rises from the silence. A towhee's scratching among dead leaves is the only sound.

We're twenty miles from paved road, thirty from Lukeville, though from where we are we can see the Mexican border. The treeless rocky sierra, which from Lukeville seems so smooth in the distance, is forbidding now—jagged, serrated, holding long into the evening the blank heat of the day. So long as it is level, we hold hands, but when we climb away from the pond, the trail peters out, and we separate to choose our own paths through the rocks and saguaros and tangled mesquite. Each of us knows the place from years before—the ledge where flowing water has polished a smooth granite slab.

I lag behind, carrying the cooler, thinking of the food and cold beer. My maroon and white truck parked a quarter mile from the pond recedes as we climb, and once above the thicket, the Abra Plain stretches out toward the border. I scan the brush and the aprons of the bajadas for animals. Coyotes, fox, badgers, deer, sometimes a javelina, drink from this spring at Quitobaquito. But now nothing moves.

Ellen, home for a visit, she says, though Lukeville was never home to her. Her father had once been head of the local Customs and Immigration Office, and she had merely passed time there during two years of high school. Her first night back, lying together in bed in the room above the store, she told me how it had been for her. "You were quiet," she said. "That's why I cared for you."

"And not for lack of choice?"

"I have always thought of you," she said, turning toward me. She kissed me as though to prove what she said was true.

"And I of you."

She eased away and propped her weight on her elbow. I listened to the insects droning in the darkness. "What do you do here?" she asked.

"I read."

"And work?"

"Yes, I work."

"What are you waiting for?"

I shook my head not understanding her question.

"You must be waiting for something. Everyone is waiting. I waited to get married, then I waited for the divorce. I waited to move from El Paso when my father was there. I waited to see you."

I smiled and felt the smile linger at the corner of my mouth. "I have only run the store."

"Oh, yes," she said, "the *store*."

I had been raised in the store. Lukeville was a border crossing, a town of three hundred, a place of transition. My mother spent her years remembering what travelers needed when the seasons changed, what they would have forgotten when they went to Mexico. The store stocked cans of food, dry goods, flashlights, gloves, tire repair kits, drinking water, medical supplies, shoes, hardware. We catered, too, to the townspeople, and my father died behind the counter measuring out for Pepe Sanchez's aunt a pound of coffee, which, when he fell, spilled across his body like dried blood. They traded off the hours, my mother and father, then my mother and I, until she died, too.

"What is wrong with the store?" I asked.

Ellen and I made love fiercely at first, then gently, as we had long ago, and she slept with her head on my shoulder and her bare leg across mine. But I woke early in the heat, thinking, staring at the broken fan on the ceiling. There were flies, thrashers singing beyond the open window, and trucks just crossed from Mexico probing the incline on the outskirts of town.

A warm wind flows from the mountains, and I pause and watch a Red-tailed Hawk on a thermal. The bird tilts its wings slightly or spreads its tail, but these are the only movements it needs to keep astride the invisible currents of air.

Ellen is far ahead of me, already nearing the ledge. Her white blouse stands out against the rocks and the gray-green mesquite on the hill behind her. She weaves behind a giant organ pipe, then reappears—jeans, white blouse, blond hair loose. We've dispensed with the past. She has told me about the breakup of her marriage, about her cars and clothes, houses, pets, travels to Dallas, Denver, and Santa Fe. Her husband had an affair; she had discovered it after the divorce, and the bitterness had not been exorcized. She spent a time drinking, then stopped. Now she wants to move forward again; she feels she is young enough to resurrect her life.

"You, too," she said one night at dinner.

"So it's religious?"

"I don't know. I never prayed for the forgiveness of sins."

"A sin in itself."

"What sins had I committed? With you? Was I to ask forgiveness for that? It wasn't the love that was wrong, but later the absence of love."

I stop to rest and put down the cooler. March, and still hot, even in the evening. The land absorbs the sun and keeps the heat. I wonder whether the sun could erode these rocky hills, whether the particles of light, like tiny grains the size of atoms, could in eons without rain break apart the rugged ridges of the Ajo and Puerto Blanco. Water and wind: yes, the gently sloping bajadas spiked with organ pipes and saguaros are the remains of mountains already washed from higher up. And the sand in the gullies is carried down by winter rains. But if it never rained, could not the sun wear away the hills just as it rots the leaves of creosote and paloverde once their waxy leaves have lost their moisture, just as it now bleaches the bones of the dead?

The hawk breaks from its still flight and wheels backward in midair toward the desert to the south. I open the cooler and take out fruit, ham, hard-boiled eggs, mayonnaise, to find a beer in the melting ice at the bottom. I snap open the beer and drink.

From my new angle on the hill, the reflection on the pond has changed to a darker blue, the color of the higher sky. The single cottonwood has shifted, too, and the pond is quiet, the birds still in cover. I can't see anything in the impenetrable brush.

Ellen pulls herself over the last few yards on hands and knees and gains the ledge. She stands against the black pockets of the ridge where shards of pink light remain and waves to me. "Hey, you!" she calls. She unbuttons her blouse, rocks her hips from side to side, and holds the corners of the blouse at her waist so it flaps like white wings. I smile at her brazenness, knowing what she asks is so simple.

I'm sweating when I reach the ledge, and I put the cooler down and catch my breath. The Quitobaquito hills are in blue shade, and the distant Ajos are pink-orange and black with the ascending line of the earth's shadow. The cirrus have dissipated, and soon only the moon that rises over the mountains will be in the light of the sun. I take off my shirt and sit down to take off my boots. The smooth stone is still warm to the touch.

Ellen edges closer. "What would you like?" she asks.

I don't answer.

"This?"

She touches me, as though she wants me to understand she is the same as before, the same as she'll always be. She kisses me, then moves away to slip off her jeans and the blouse which flutters at her shoulders. She stands for a moment in profile, her face bearing into the warm breeze, her hair clear of her face. Against the darkening rock her body shines.

Then beneath us a rock dislodges and clatters down the hillside. I sit up quickly and pull Ellen beside me.

"There's no one," she says.

"Quiet." I tighten my grip on her arm, lean forward.

Three deer—two does and a buck—pick their way down the rocky slope toward the spring. Another stone rolls, snaps on rocks and brush, and bounces to the bottom of the draw.

"Do they know we're here?" Ellen whispers.

"No, the wind is wrong."

But the buck stops. The does browse the thin grass on the hillside, but the buck's ears are upright, and he gazes toward the dark slough below.

"Maybe a coyote," Ellen says.

I shake my head. "If it were a coyote, the birds would still sing."

Ellen looks over the edge. "You think someone's there?"

The buck snorts, still staring at the swarthy tangle of brush beside the pond, and I follow his gaze. It is still light enough to make out shapes in the open—the bulk of a saguaro, the thin spires of an organ pipe, the blue-gray light of the pond.

"There," Ellen says, as though I haven't seen.

A solitary figure emerges from the thicket. He is rail-thin, bald, dressed in a ragged sweater and dark pants. A ridge of black hair curls above his ears. He is intent on some object, though his body hides it. He bends low to the ground.

Ellen retreats from the edge of the rock and pulls on her blouse. "Do you think he's been watching?" she asks.

As if hearing Ellen's voice, the man turns toward us.

"Is he Mexican?" she asks. "Maybe he's come across the border."

"Maybe," I say. But he doesn't look Mexican.

Ellen lies down on the rock and slides into her jeans, then stands and turns her back to snap them and to button her blouse. "Maybe he's escaped," she says. "Maybe he's wanted."

The buck snorts again and jumps away, leading the does into the draw. The deer crack more rocks as they spring across the scree, but sensing no pursuit, they slow again, and the buck stops to test the air.

The man lays a bedroll on the ground, puts something on it, then rolls the bedroll and tucks it under his arm like a newspaper. The sweater hangs on his bony shoulders. For a moment, with his bald head held awkwardly, he gazes at the moon, which threads through the cirrus drifts, and then, as if deciding there is enough light, he starts along the path and begins to climb the hill.

"We could run," Ellen says.

"In the dark?"

"It's better than sitting here."

"There are snakes."

"We can split up and go for the truck," she says. "He can't follow both of us."

I check the truck far below us. "Who takes the keys?"

I lift another beer from the cooler, thinking it ironic Ellen is afraid. I'm the one with shadows. I want the cans stacked neatly on the shelves, the books piled carefully on the desk. I keep my dirty clothes in the bathtub and put sugar in the salt shaker. Between two and three in the afternoon, I order what I need from the supplier in Tucson.

The moon spins through the thinning clouds, but the sun's last breath on the horizon gives a little light. The man climbs unsteadily, with stick-like strides. His trousers swish, and the bedroll under his arm makes him list to one side, but he does not measure his progress against us. Instead, he follows the sounds the deer make skirting the draw.

He stops and rerolls his blanket, then climbs the last few steps to the smooth rock. An unkempt black beard swirls over his jaw. Beneath his heavy eyebrows, his eyes glitter like a coyote's. For a moment he considers the empty beer cans, the cooler, my boots on the rock. I know this man. He comes from a city where steam rises from manholes and horns split the air, where he sits in cafeterias and draws stares as he walks the streets. Or he comes from the farm belt, the smell of manure acrid where he sleeps. Crops roll by in rows of optical illusion, like the crosses of soldiers' graves, and he searches the gravel roads and freeways for aluminum cans. Or he comes from the mountains where snow sifts around the loose panes of his windows and his breath rises in the icy air. He watches the Jeeps and Hummers pass and hears the young men shout. I know he has sunk to the desert at Quitobaquito for water and shade. He sleeps on the ground in his thin bed roll and rises with the dawn. He hunts deer and rabbits and eats the meat of snakes. He has scavenged mesquite, peyote, and the fruits of cactus, and he has endured without the notion of shame.

He can harm us — perhaps he has a knife or a gun in his bedroll — but something beyond my fear makes me pause. He stares at Ellen who moves behind me into my lee, then at my boots. He lays his bedroll on the ledge, searches among the folds, and pulls out a ragged leather shoe. The sole is rotten, and the stitches are torn away from the leather so the sole flops open like a slack mouth. The broken laces have been tied and retied into knots. With one eye on us, he measures his worn shoe against the sole of one of my boots.

Ellen moves from my shadow. "Stop," she says.

The man crouches, fingers arced on the stone, and glares. I don't move.

The man puts my boots on his bedroll and leaves the leather shoe on the stone.

"You're going to let him steal?" Ellen asks me.

He has no knife or gun. I could rush him and knock him from the rock, send him a few feet down the hill and he would scurry away. But I wait and watch. He pulls the cooler over and rummages through the food. He takes out cheese, ham, hard-boiled eggs and assembles what he wants on his bedroll—boots, food, my shirt—then folds the bedroll like a sack and lifts it to his shoulder.

The moon makes him a specter on the edge of the rock. Yet, I don't let him go. I hold him with my eyes, knowing when he leaves he'll leave forever. I dig into my pocket for the key to the truck. "Here," I say, holding out the key, "take this."

Ellen cries out when the headlights of the truck sweep across the dark thicket and turn onto the gravel road toward Lukeville. She screams and clambers down the rocky slope toward the spring. The deer bound away into the darkness.

For a while I lie on the warm rock and stare at the stars. We're told the stars move, that in millions of years the constellations will have changed shapes, and new configurations will emerge. I am comforted only by soaking the warmth of the rock into my body. We choose, and we choose to stay the same, until we choose to change.

Ellen is miles ahead when I start along the road. The Ajos and Puerto Blancos are coal black against the sky. The moon obliterates the stars, and the cold breeze is brittle on my bare skin. I imagine Ellen striding resolutely along the dusty track, not looking back to see whether or not I have followed. I think of her standing naked on the rock with the wind in her face, offering herself, but taunting me—whether to make me realize what I could have or to show me what I will be without.

Miles, hours. My feet ache and blister. I scan the tan gravel for snakes. The moon becomes smaller as it curves past the zenith, but I still make out Ellen's footprints in the roadway. Clouds have disappeared into the colder night air. It is silent around me as I walk, though now and then, amid the silhouettes of greasewood and saguaros, I hear the skirmishes of animals in the darkness.

# SEEING DESIRABLE THINGS

Not exalting the gifted prevents quarreling . . .
Not seeing desirable things prevents confusion
of the heart.

*Tao Te Ching*

THE EVENTS THAT LED TO MY SECLUSION
on Ocracoke Island began a little more than four months
ago at a weekend family reunion in Panama City. During the weeks earlier, in May, I'd had orders for custom
cabinets, a dining room set with six chairs, and a bureau
of cherrywood, and I was finishing two of my own table
designs I wanted to get into a furniture gallery in Atlanta.
Wood is irrational and can't be rushed, so when the reunion
occurred (if that's what it was), I was more impatient than
usual. That's what Emma said. "You weren't yourself, Allen," she said. "Think back on it in that light."

We had differing views of what happened, or at least
of the aftermath, and this created a strain between us that
remained through the ensuing weeks. Emma insisted on a
resolution because she didn't like the past looming over the
future, but it was my family, not hers. Family was special to
her, *critical*, she said. She had two sisters in Dunwoody she
was close to and parents she adored. But how could a resolution be achieved? A crossword has an answer to be filled
in, and a Sudoku or Kakuro can be figured out by logic, but
the circumstances with my family had missing pieces, ques-

tions I couldn't answer no matter how many times I replayed the events. It was a mystery such as a man might feel if his wife went out to get her hair cut and never came home. One might search among the details of the past and still not arrive at a reason for the disappearance.

I'd driven up to the Outer Banks from Atlanta on Monday because Emma thought I might sort things out better alone, without the pressure of work, without a telephone (though a cell phone is hard to escape), in an environment separate from my woodworking shop, away from her, though she was coming up on the weekend. It was a clear September day, and the forty-minute ferry ride made me feel as if I were separating myself from trouble. Islands can do that, even though it's an illusion.

Ocracoke was ten miles long and a mile wide, an expanse of sand and dunegrass and a few wind-skewered trees bordering on Pamlico Sound and, on the other side, the vast Atlantic. I had traded a pair of end tables for the use of a friend's white clapboard cottage, well-maintained, though it was drafty and not meant for winter habitation. I had brought warm clothes, because at any time of year the sea can make a place cold. A live oak in the yard absorbed the light from the front of the house, but I had a view along the street and two blocks down to the masts of sailboats in Silver Lake Harbor.

It was a short walk to the village center, but I preferred the beach or the spit that extended on the landward side into the sound. In the evenings I liked to walk there with my binoculars because birds were flying to their roosts, and the light ebbed into the salt-air haze. The lesser world of birds seemed simple compared to human beings' interactions, but anything looked at closely became complex. The

Sanderling on the beach followed the tide in and out searching for grubs and minutiae the water brought to it, but what synapses were in its brain that allowed it to know one thing from another? How did its eyes work, its olfactory sense, its hearing? How did it know of danger? A single bird has myriad feathers for different purposes—soft breast feathers for warmth, tail feathers for balance, tertials and the stronger primaries for flight. (And each species has specialized requirements—think of a hummingbird or an owl.) Where did the bird nest? How did it know where to go in winter, when to leave, how to navigate? I contemplated such things when the low sun made the light magical across the water.

It was to divide my father's possessions that we had assembled at the old house in Panama City. My father was a lawyer (I hate to say it) and a Southern gentleman, though not of the do-gooder stripe. He wore a suit and tie and white shirt every day—not a blue shirt or a pale yellow one, but a white shirt with long sleeves. He didn't question why. Elemental justice got lip service, but he was more concerned with his bank account, and he used his position in the community to get an edge on the competition. The word of a piece of real estate's coming on the market reached him before the public, and he used whatever loopholes he could in the tax and zoning laws to maximize his profit. He knew when other people were having a hard time, and he took advantage of their vulnerabilities.

At home he was a calm tyrant. If he wanted quiet, there was silence. If he wanted biscuits and gravy, these appeared. If he wanted the lawn mowed, it had better be done before he got home. My mother made excuses for his angry moods— how hard he worked, how tired he was, and how well he provided — because she found it easier to accept the regimen than to argue. While he showed my mother deference, even respect, he also ignored her.

For all his seriousness, though, my father played catch with Roger and me — baseball or football — and took us fishing, even Rita, sometimes in the ponds of people who owned plantations, sometimes on a friend's boat in St. Andrews Bay. Each session of catch or fishing had a lesson: hold the ball with your fingers on the seams, twirl the shrimp net so the weights can operate the way gravity intended, cast your line high and far. We should know the neighborhood and the creeks and the bay, and though there was a wider world, he didn't want any of us to go too far into it.

In addition to the house, my father left my mother with a lifetime of accumulated furniture, Oriental rugs, Indian pottery, sculptures and paintings, first edition books, shotguns and hunting rifles, linens, jewelry, two closets full of clothes, and a lion's head from a safari in Botswana. To divvy up these goods was our primary task for the weekend (hence "reunion" was a suspect word). Roger, my younger sister Rita, and I had never got along particularly well with one another. Rita was a nutritionist for the same school district in Fort Walton Beach in which her husband Garrett taught fifth grade. She was high-strung, bossy, and emotional. Rather than blame my father for neglect, she took it out on Garrett, and to a lesser extent on Roger and me. Roger, the oldest, lived in Tallahassee and was divorced, neither of which was a crime, but indicative, nevertheless. He was an anesthesiologist, which gave him money and license — so he thought. He collected art pottery, coins, stamps, horse sculptures, Indian friendship bowls — you name it, he collected it. This would have been tolerable, except he did it at garage sales, where the owners of the items he wanted didn't know what they had. He was my father all over again.

Not that my own history was anything to hold up as virtue, as Emma frequently reminded me. I had been third in my high school class but had dropped out of the University of the South and enlisted in the U.S. Army, which, luckily for me, sent me to New Mexico instead of Iraq. I'd played lead guitar in several bands, worked as a bird researcher in the Apalachicola National Forest, and then built houses with Habitat for Humanity. I constructed the cabinets that no one else wanted to and discovered I was good at meticulous work with my hands. As an experiment I built a table and four chairs and sold them for $600, so I built more. I liked the perfect miter, the dovetailing of joints in a drawer, the lathed dowel that fit precisely into drilled holes. My father, by his silence, before and after his death, labeled all my endeavors insufficient.

Emma was a chemistry professor at Emory and desired order. She had bought one of my bookcases at a gallery and called me to build a matching table and chair. One thing became another—she wanted a handmade bed, etc.—and we cooked meals together at her house. She liked my productivity, she said, and when I moved in she insisted on converting her garage into a woodworking shop.

It was dusk when Emma and I arrived in Panama City, a Friday evening. The house was white with green trim, a ramshackle Victorian too big for my mother, and she intended to sell it and move to a condo in Destin. There had been email talk among us children about assisted-living, but she had many times made clear her adamant opposition. "I have money," she said, "and I won't be demoted."

Lights were on inside, and through a leafy sycamore I

pointed up to a shuttered room on the second floor. "My room's in the gable on the left," I said.

"I know, Allen," Emma said. "I've been here before, remember? You used to climb in the tree and had a fort and found bird nests. Are you that nervous?"

"Maybe," I said. "I'll take some deep breaths."

Rita must have seen the headlights, because she came out the side door into the driveway. "There you are," she said, as if to confirm our existence. "How was the drive?"

"Tiring."

"Your drive was nothing compared to being here for three hours with mother and Roger."

"Is Garrett here?" Emma asked.

"Unfortunately," Rita said.

Roger was in the kitchen at his laptop, checking his action on eBay. "It's the Michelangelo of Wood," he said. He rose and hugged Emma and threatened me with an embrace, too.

"Tu ti siedi," I said.

He embraced me anyway. "How's the groove in the tongue?" he asked.

"I'm making a living."

"But you're not paying rent," he said.

"How's life at the hospital?" I asked.

"I put people under," Roger said. "I like that part. It's what to do with all that money that's got me hot and troubled."

"Where's Mom?" I asked.

"She and Garrett are sorting books," Rita said. "And, so you know, Mom wants to keep the first editions."

"That's her prerogative," I said.

"I wanted the Mark Twain," Rita said.

"All things come to those who wait," Roger said.

We left our bags in the dining room and went into the library. Garrett was up on a ladder pulling books from a shelf, while my mother stood poised over several half-empty cardboard boxes to receive them. Since I'd seen her at the funeral, she looked older, frailer, and maybe wiser. Her hair was dyed yellow, and she wore a T-shirt and shorts.

"Philosophy," Garrett said and handed down three heavy tomes, which my mother set into a box.

"Hello, Emma, dear," my mother said. "Allen, you're looking thin. Have you lost weight?"

"I've been running," I said.

"Running from what?" Garrett asked.

"Exercise is work," my mother said. "We're all here now. Let's go to dinner at the Boatyard. Your father's paying."

Nothing much stands out from the chitchat that night. As usual I was quiet. Twice Roger was on his cell phone with potential buyers for a couple of sculptures, and Rita let Garrett talk about the Little League team he was coaching. Mother and Emma had a minor set-to over the upcoming senate race, but my mother had the last word. "I'm glad you don't vote in Florida," she said.

In the morning I walked around the outside of the house and made notes on maintenance issues my mother should attend to before listing the property—the porch needed to be jacked up and leveled, a few pieces of gingerbread trim wanted repair, two upstairs windows were rotting. When I came inside, Rita and Emma were frying bacon and whisking eggs for French toast. My mother had assembled cheese and onions and an orange pepper for an omelet she was planning to make.

"Slice this," my mother said, handing me the pepper. "You don't like peppers, but Roger does."

"If Roger wants pepper, let him slice it."

"You like onions, and Roger doesn't."

"I'll stick with French toast," I said.

Nevertheless, I sliced the pepper, while Rita organized the silverware and napkins, poured milk into a pitcher, and set out glasses. We ate in the dining room, though Roger didn't come down until we were almost finished. "Salt air's soporific," he said. "Pass the omelet, please, and praise the Lord. I'm playing tennis at ten."

There was much to be done before we could divide the goods, but Roger played tennis anyway. My mother hadn't done any sorting or throwing away because she didn't know what we'd want, and it was physical labor, which she avoided if she could. That morning, without Roger, we went through books, linens, tools, rugs, and art. My mother reserved a few books, miniature paintings, and sculptures for herself, but there was still much to haggle over, disagree about, and regret losing.

Before that weekend I'd of course anticipated the problems of dividing my father's possessions because my family had a weird history about the worth of objects. My mother lamented over how much a car repair cost, how much groceries were, how little my father gave her to run the household, so money was important; but these daily issues had nothing to do with *things*. We had an uncle, my father's brother in Charlottesville, who, whenever we visited, showed us his personal museum and regaled us with how much he'd paid for a sculpture or a painting or a book and how much it had increased in value. I suppose this had a trickle-down effect. When my father made a tuition payment or gave a gift, each

of us made a mental calculation about fairness—was it fair
Roger got to go to Vanderbilt and Rita to FSU? Rita didn't
think so. My father gave Roger a new Jeep, and I got the
family's decrepit Dodge. Was that okay? For graduation,
Roger got a new computer, Rita got a four-day trip to Can-
cun, and I, who didn't graduate, got nothing.

The ground rules for the division of stuff were simple: for
whatever item we selected, we'd be charged the appraised
value in our father's estate. If, say, I wanted a bird sculpture,
I'd have to pay $400 for it, and the same if Rita wanted a
violin worth $1,000, or if Roger wanted a Seminole friend-
ship bowl worth $800. At the end, there'd be an accounting,
and cash would be paid by one of us to the others. How
much one got depended on how much one wanted to pay,
which led, naturally, to the rich getting richer, namely Roger,
though, at the end, because I wanted less, I stood to make
some cash.

This was where personalities came in and brought to the
fore our respective histories with one another. Rita had gone
to college with the intention of finding Garrett, or a husband
like him—that's what she'd been expected to do—and she'd
been testy about this ever since. Why should a woman not
be expected to reach as high as a man? Roger had known
early on he wanted to be a doctor and to practice in Tallahassee, which he'd done. Except for a few visits home at
the holidays (I'd brought Emma the previous Christmas),
we didn't socialize—though we didn't anti-socialize either.
Rita and Garrett led a different life around the school in Fort
Walton Beach, and Roger was enmeshed in his buying and
selling. I'd happened to be in Tallahassee once for a meeting
of regional bird researchers, and on the weekend Roger took
me to garage sales. He planned his itinerary from newspaper

ads and was up at dawn, an early bird with predatory zeal. We arrived at a rundown house in West Tallahassee, where a family was putting its goods on folding tables set up on a decaying cement driveway. No one else had arrived, and within minutes Roger offered the woman $15 for two unremarkable Indian pots marked $25 each, and as we drove away, Roger was ecstatic. "She got rid of her junk," he said, "and I got two Sacco pots worth $400 apiece. Who's not happy?" At the next house, Roger assembled a painting, a couple of baskets, and a wooden box with a clasp, and made a lowball offer of $50 for all of it, which was accepted. "You collect baskets?" I asked. "No," he said, "but I can sell them for three times what I paid. The painting will fetch three hundred, and the box is from England. I can get two hundred for that."

"I thought garage sales were a way for people to redistribute things they didn't need," I said.

"You mean, like sharing?" Roger asked. "Get a life, Allen. This is capitalism in action. Furniture dealers, art people, antique store owners—they all go to garage sales."

"But don't you feel guilty?"

"Let the seller beware," he said.

As kids we'd done our usual bartering—Park Place for two red properties, six comic books for a magic ring, etc.; I wasn't aware of Roger's taking advantage of Rita or me, but after I saw him manipulate people at garage sales, I dredged up the episode of the penny. When I was nine or ten Roger persuaded me to trade one of the pennies in my penny board for a baseball glove. The mitt was almost new, and I needed one for Little League. The penny was a 1914 D I'd found in a sack full of coins my uncle had given me. I knew it was more valuable than most of the others, but Roger understood economics—over time the penny would appreciate, while in a year or two the glove would be worn out and discarded.

That afternoon we started with the items appraised in the estate at under five hundred dollars, and, by agreement, drew straws (Rita won) to see who would choose first. Garrett and Emma were consultants and advisors. Garrett wanted one of my father's hunting rifles, so Rita took it for him, and Emma liked a hat box that belonged to my father's mother, so I selected that. Roger got two shotguns and four sets of old stirrups. I ended up with, among other things, most of my father's tools, three German steins, and several linen tablecloths Emma liked. Since the items weren't particularly valuable and roughly equivalent, there was no accounting.

The accounting began for the next group—items worth five hundred dollars to two thousand. This group included most of my father's paintings, sculptures, and Indian artifacts—baskets, pots, jars, beadwork that Roger had his eye on. I took two paintings—a boat in a harbor and another of a hill and a distant horizon—but I wanted to conserve my capital. The less I took early on, the more I'd have in reserve, and in the next group was a painting I wanted.

During this more-or-less friendly couple of hours, Rita brought up a question about theory: "We know the estate appraisals are low," she said, "but when Roger takes most of these things, Allen and I suffer."

"Suffer how?" Roger asked. "At the end I'll give you a check, which is almost as good as money."

"We don't know the market out there. If you buy an Indian pot for six hundred dollars, you pay Allen and me two hundred each. If you sell it for twelve hundred dollars, you get all the profit, and Allen and I get nothing."

"*If* I sell it," Roger said. "And what if I sold it for three hundred? I'd lose money. There's also overhead—time, advertising, and all that. I take all the risk."

"You have a booth in an antique mall," Garrett said. "If Rita and Allen paid you 15 percent, they'd still come out ahead."

"The gin's talking," Roger said. "If you and Rita want to buy things, do what I do."

"Are you saying Garrett is drinking?" Rita asked.

"Let's move on," my mother said, "or we'll never finish."

I don't know whether Garrett was drinking. He was married to Rita, which would have been a contributing factor. He got up several times to use the bathroom, and once I heard ice being handled in the kitchen. I mention this only because of the way Roger deflected the discussion.

Right after that, we embarked on dividing the high-end items—ten pieces in all, including a globe-shaped Tiffany table lamp my father had bought in New York, five friendship bowls of the Caddo and Seminole tribes, a hand-lettered and hand-illustrated account of the Spanish exploration of the Florida Panhandle, which I knew Rita coveted, two bronze horses by a contemporary of Remington, and a painting my grandfather had picked up in the Philippines when he'd worked there during a cholera outbreak in 1947.

The painting was what I wanted. It was of a young woman dressed in a peasant skirt and white blouse, carrying a basket of grain, with a background of a pink and yellow sunset. As a teenager I mooned over the girl and had often lain on my parents' bed when they weren't there, gazing at her on the opposite wall. The girl was radiant, fresh, her expression joyful, as if she were hearing a lover's voice calling to her. Her body was ample and strong. To me she was the embodiment of unqualified hope.

Rita and Garrett and my mother were on the sofa, Roger in my father's recliner, though not reclined, Emma in a wingback chair, and I on the floor in front of her. It was dusk, and no one had turned on the lights yet, so darkness threatened the room. Before we started, there was banter about selling the house we'd grown up in, about my father, and the unpleasantness of a few minutes before dissipated. Rita asked my mother why she wasn't taking the Tiffany lamp we all thought she loved. "Didn't Daddy buy it for you?" she said.

"He did," my mother said. "That's why I'm not taking it."

"You don't want to be reminded of him?" I asked.

"It goes deeper than that," my mother said. "I suppose I could sell it, but I thought one of you might like it."

"I would," Rita said, "but not for six thousand dollars."

"It's worth twenty," Roger said. "We could put it up at auction in New York and split the proceeds four ways."

"Now he's Mr. Generosity," Rita said. "Look, we know what we want, don't we? There's no point in drawing straws since Roger wants everything. The only thing I care about is *The History of the Florida Panhandle.*"

"Take it," I said.

"Wait a minute," Emma said. "Roger gets a vote."

"I wasn't denying him one," I said.

"No objection," Roger said. "You all know I collect Indian bowls, so I'm partial to them."

"And you're a horse fancier," Rita said. "You'll want the two statues, too. Fine, so Allen gets the painting."

"I'd be glad to have the painting," I said.

"But I like the painting, too," Roger said.

This is the moment I try to recapture—the tone of voice, the glances around the room, the unspoken intentions. Roger hadn't spoken any louder than before, and I'd detected no eagerness in his voice. Had he looked at my mother, or at Emma, who had seemed, a moment before, to take his side against Rita? My own gaze had been on the painting, and when I turned to Roger, he was looking at the Oriental rug on the floor.

"You're getting seven other things," Rita said. "Allen should get something."

"Allen doesn't care about the seven other things," Roger said. "I'm not saying I should get the painting, but I should have a chance at it. We should flip a coin."

I was stunned.

"For Christ's sake, Roger," Rita said. "It's a painting from the Philippines worth five thousand dollars."

"This is between Allen and me," Roger said. "It's not your affair."

"Why can't you ever be generous?"

"I told you I'd sell the lamp," Roger said. "You said that was generous."

"You gave Rita the history book," Garrett said. "Why can't you give Allen the painting?"

Rita got up from the sofa and left the room, and I heard ice tumbling into a glass in the kitchen.

"Have some more gin," Roger called.

My mother rose, too—her expression was pained—and I made the mistake of turning around to Emma. From her look, she perhaps thought I was asking her what I should do, but I wasn't. I couldn't tell whether she sided with Rita in her anger or with Roger's apparent rationality.

Roger turned back to me. "Do you not see my point? If I lose a coin toss, I lose. That's all right."

"I'm not flipping a coin," I said.

Roger sighed. "Then I guess we're finished," he said. "I'll figure out what I owe you and Miss Congeniality out in the kitchen, and we'll keep the painting in limbo."

I thought my mother might intercede and take the painting herself, or at least comment on Rita's behavior, but she said nothing.

The next morning Roger left a settling-out statement on the dining room table, along with checks to Rita and me. Rita and Garrett had already driven back to Fort Walton Beach the night before. They'd refused to spend another night in the same house with Roger. Emma and I packed up before my mother came down, though we waited to say goodbye. Nothing was mentioned about the night before. We discussed how hot it was for May.

Driving back to Atlanta, Emma was silent, as if she were critical of what had happened, and for several days afterward we existed in a state of uneasy avoidance of one another. Given my work schedule, not talking was fine with me. I had the cherrywood bureau to deliver on deadline. But then one day I looked up from a miter cut, and Emma was in the open garage door. I turned off the saw and lifted my goggles.

"Why didn't you flip the coin?" she asked.

I paused to let the question sink in, because I understood the words were deeper than their superficial meaning.

"Roger had a valid argument," she said. "You didn't want any of the other items. If they hadn't existed, there would have been only the painting, and you'd have flipped the coin."

"Why did he give Rita the one thing she wanted?"

"Politics. Diplomacy. Good will. Who knows? Maybe it was the only thing he didn't want."

"Are you taking his side?"

"Of course not, but you're letting this drag on. What he did before, what he does at garage sales, isn't relevant to what he does with his family."

"And so you think I should give in to him?"

"Is it giving in? Or are you mimicking Roger by being greedy?"

"I don't want to talk about it," I said. I flicked on the saw again and slid down my goggles, but I knew that wasn't the end of the argument.

In the days after the reunion I heard twice from Rita, once via an email in which she said she backed me 100 percent. ("Don't let that bastard screw you over.") And once she sent me a check for $3,070, "for the history book and the several pieces of jewelry Mom threw in, for which his lordship figured I owed you." In a P.S. she said she expected a check from me "for a third of $5,000, when good conquers evil."

There were a few calls to and from my mother, in which she informed me of her lunches with friends, a sailing excursion she'd made with neighbors to Crooked Island, and the progress on the condo in Destin. "This living alone isn't easy," she said. "But it has its advantages, too."

"Are you dating?"

"The men I know are not my type," she said. "And men in general are a hopeless lot."

"You have two sons."

"Which is neither recompense nor solace," she said. "You don't know what I went through with your father."

"That's why you're not taking the gifts he gave you?"

"My place is only twelve hundred square feet. I won't have room for the past."

"But you could take the painting with you," I said.

"I'll keep it here until I move," she said. "That's your deadline."

"Have you talked to Roger?"

"He's not said anything to me," she said. "I know you think Roger has a lot already, but . . ."

"I loved that woman," I said. "It's hard to give her up."

"It's a painting, Allen, not a person."

"Tell that to Roger," I said.

My first days on Ocracoke I made little progress. I ran on the beach, drank coffee at the café in town, and watched boats arrive and leave from the marina. I cooked shrimp and bluefish, made my own slaw, and drank beer. I called Emma, but for the most part we steered clear of the elephant in the room. Once she asked if I were doing anything about the situation, and I said I was running on the beach and looking for birds. "Maybe you'll be impetuous," she said. "You might say, 'Why not?' and call your brother."

"And what would I say to him?"

"That would be up to you," Emma said.

"Are you still planning to come up on Friday?" I asked.

"I have the reservation, but I have to get back to Norfolk Monday afternoon so I can fly back and teach my Tuesday lab."

"Did you see Mauna Kea erupted?" I asked.

"I thought you didn't have television."

"There's Internet at the café," I said. "And with a phone, I'm not all that isolated from the world."

"Don't change the subject."

"We can talk about whatever you like."

"Since when?" Emma asked. "You avoid talking."

That Friday morning in the dark I was wakened by the wind. It had changed direction and was blowing from the north. The temperature in the house had dropped notice-able degrees. A shutter banged, and I found the eye-bolt had pulled loose, so I went out with a hammer and a nail. The live oak was thrashing above me, and sand was blowing across the yard, and I felt as if I were in the howling throes of death—poetic, yes, but even so, light was seeping up from the sea. I nailed the shutter closed.

It struck me that in such a gale the ferry might not run or Emma's flight to Norfolk could be delayed, but these were straws to grasp at. My response to her pressure was resis-tance, whether rational or not, and I found myself dealing with more than the painting. At first I thought Emma saw not flipping a coin as stubbornness and irrationality. (She was a scientist, after all.) But now I believed she saw me as fearful and weak.

Over the course of the day the wind died off, though birds still stayed low in the bushes. A few gulls and terns patterned the air, but not many boats went out. I watched a yawl come in from the north, sailing without its mizzen or jib, and the captain brought her in perilously close to the breakwater. Out beyond the harbor, the sea was angry.

Emma's arrival loomed, and at four thirty that afternoon I goaded myself into calling my mother. She was on her way to a cocktail party at the Allesandros'. "I know Opa got the painting in the Philippines," I said. "He and Nana were there during a cholera outbreak. But what else can you tell me about it?"

"Your grandfather went to explore for minerals," my mother said. "Oma found the painting. Or rather, she commissioned it. Really, Allen, I can't talk now."

"Emma's arriving in a few hours," I said. "I want to demonstrate I've been doing my homework."

My mother sighed. "Oma was a nurse, and during the outbreak she met this man, Amorsolo, in a village. She liked his sunsets and asked him to paint her one, which he agreed to do if he could put in his niece."

"And why was the painting appraised at five thousand dollars?"

"I was surprised it was that high," my mother said, "but one doesn't question the appraiser. Roger was here, you know."

"Do you know why Roger wants the painting?"

"Why don't you let go of this, Allen? It's not worth the torture."

"Maybe it is," I said.

"No, I don't know why Roger wants it. Perhaps, like you, he was enamored of the woman."

"I still am," I said.

"One doesn't get over feelings," my mother said. "You have to live with them."

"Thank you," I said. "Have a good time at your party."

An hour later Emma called from Norfolk. Her plane had landed, but the storm had shut down the computers at the rental car desk and they were backed up. "They're promising me a car by six," she said. "How long is the drive?"

"You might make the nine o'clock ferry," I said. "Would you rather stay in Norfolk?"

There was a pause. "What's in Norfolk?" she asked. "This might not be a simple weekend, Allen. We have to talk."

"I called my mother," I said. "She gave me more information about the painting."

"Is there anything new?"

"Call me when you get to the ferry." I said. "I can meet you."

"You gave me a map," Emma said. "I'm not helpless."

We hung up, and I sat for a long moment and looked around the room at the white wicker furniture, the cheerful pastels on the walls, the coming darkness beyond the window. I had bought fresh crab for dinner, but now Emma wasn't going to be there, and I felt forlorn and anxious, so I put on a windbreaker and walked into the village.

It was Friday, and despite the storm's passing through, people had come over from the mainland so the village was more crowded than usual. I read the menus at the Fiddler Crab and the Café Atlantic, and farther along, browsed in a bookstore. Then I stopped at Cyber World, and, on a whim, went in and Googled the painter Amorsolo.

I was surprised when several entries appeared, and I clicked on Wikipedia. Fernando Amorsolo was the most famous painter from the Philippines, and his paintings of young women in rural settings were collected worldwide. In 2007 a sale at Christie's brought $77,000, and one in 2009 was a record $89,000. Several paintings were exhibited, and the styles and colors—exotic pinks and lavenders—resembled those in my father's painting that, for years, had hung in my parents' bedroom.

I clicked off and pushed my chair back and took a long deep breath.

It was dusk, and the tide was out. I walked on the spit, with the lingering clouds, colors spread out in a wide band of pinks, reds, and oranges that were, in turn, reflected from the choppy swells in the sound. Gulls and terns strove southward in silhouette, and scattered herons, egrets, and ibis crisscrossed in the air on their way to their different roosts on the mainland. A few ducks, black in the paling light, flew low across the water.

What was it that inspired people to deceive? Was it the money Roger was after? He had plenty already. Was it the thrill of arranging the details and experiencing the tension of being at the edge? Any of us could have got on the Internet and found out about Amorsolo, either now or later on. That was probably what Roger had done, or he had bargained with the appraiser. Was I being unfair? I had no proof Roger knew the value of the painting in advance, and had I confronted him, he'd have denied prior knowledge and claim to be maligned. But his behavior at garage sales and the incident with the penny spoke to me—he was so confident of his superiority and other people's ignorance.

The wind diminished, and after a few minutes I stopped and faced west into the colors of the sky. Everything was different now. Even were I to draw straws and win, I couldn't afford the painting, and if I agreed to sell it at auction, like the Tiffany lamp, I'd have only money in return, not the image of the young woman, which was what I wanted from the start. Telling Emma what I'd learned about the painting wouldn't matter, either. She might see Roger in a different light, but her sense of who I was or had been wouldn't be altered—and I was in love with the woman in the painting. That was why this wouldn't be "a simple weekend." She saw my family as damaged, and it was. How could I—or Rita—be friends with a brother who had played us for fools?

Darkness came down around me, and across the sound lights flickered on the mainland. Stars looked as if they were flying in the wind, though, of course, the movement was in the air. Birds, those complex creatures, were at rest now in their roosts and in the dunes, and, far to the north, the lights of the ferry delved across the waves.

# THE GRACELESS AGE

These days are fast, nothing lasts,
in this graceless age.

*Bon Jovi*

ANSON HEMPKIN BELIEVED IN JESUS
Christ, and every night, while Faye put the kids to bed,
he got down on his knees and prayed to the plastic
statue on top of his television. He prayed his roofing
company would prosper, the weather would be good, and
Enrique and Pablo would show up for work. He prayed the
city council would grant a variance for the megahouse on
the bluff, the roof for which he had a contingent contract.
He prayed for his children's welfare and Faye's, and that
she would lose weight. He prayed he wouldn't get caught
marking up shingles and tar, charging transport fees he'd
have had to pay anyway, and taking questionable tax write-
offs. He prayed the NRA would protect his right to own
the 30.06 Remington in the den and the .38 Special he kept
loaded in the pantry.

Anson considered himself a semi-outlaw, though he
knew this was the New West, Cheyenne, Wyoming, to be
exact, where there were building inspectors, tax auditors,
and sheriff's deputies. While he was praying, the TV was on,
though the sound was muted, and images of exotic women
on *Desperate Housewives* flickered on the screen. He hadn't
yet bought a plasma set so the Jesus statue had a promi-
nent place among the photographs of the children, Gary and

*186*

Lynette, now eight and ten, propped up in their kid-made frames.

It was a Wednesday evening, eight thirty, and Faye was rumbling down the plush-carpeted stairs. Anson rose from his knees, settled into the recliner, and changed the channel to *Dancing with the Stars*. "Hey, sweetheart," he said. "Your show is on."

Faye stood in the doorway in her blue robe. Her hair was washed and wet, her face devoid of the usual streaks and blurs of makeup. "Gary's worried about the bears," she said. "Will you talk to him?"

"It's hard to tell whether these people are dancing or fucking," Anson said. "I hate that."

"Lynette's asleep. Don't wake her."

"I put the lid on the trash can." Anson said. "What's he want me to do, pick all the plums?"

Faye sat down on the sofa. "They're dancing," she said. "Reassure him. Tell him there aren't any bears."

Anson went to the kitchen, got a Coors from the fridge, and pffted it open. The backyard beyond the window was dark, but in the ring of gray TV light fracturing through the sliding door, he didn't see any bears. There were Faye's beloved flowers—he never knew what kind—and beyond them the clothesline, Gary's bike, and the two plum trees with almost-ripe fruit. Far in back was the fence, courtesy of a garage-roof-for-a-fence trade with Randy, the handyman next door. If the bears wanted the plums, a fence with Home Depot slats wouldn't stop them.

Anson climbed the stairs and set his beer on the top step. Gary's room was to the right. "You in here?" Anson asked into the darkness.

"Duh," Gary said.

"Your mother said you were having a problem."

"I'm all right."

"You want a glass of water?"

"I was thinking about the bears," Gary said.

"Those big ferocious critters? Don't you worry. They're going to hibernate pretty soon, and we won't see them till spring."

"But they haven't hibernated yet."

"No, right now they're eating as much as they can, so if they find a couple of careless kids wandering in the neighborhood—"

"Dad, come on."

"You're not careless, Gary, except when you leave your bike out."

"I don't want bears in the yard," Gary said.

"I looked," Anson said. "There isn't a single one, not yet. And bears don't eat bikes, so you're lucky there."

"Why do you always tease?" Gary asked.

"Never say always," Anson said. "If the bears got into the yard and ate a few plums, what does that hurt? Nothing and nobody."

"What if they get into the garage? The garage door doesn't work. They could get into the garage and then into the house."

"There isn't any food in the garage, but I'll tell you what. I'll close the garage door. Will that work for you? And we can pray to Jesus the bears don't get into the house by the back door. Have you prayed to Jesus?"

"I did already."

"Then what do you say we call it a night? You have school tomorrow."

Anson slid out of the door and closed it not-quite, recovered his beer, and treaded down the stairs. Music was rising from the den, and at the bottom of the stairs Anson paused and drank a long gulp from his can, two long gulps. "Honey, I'm going over to Imre's to shoot pool."

There was no answer.

"You hear me, sweetheart?"

"I thought you were going to do those mailings for the church."

"They aren't due out till Friday."

"Don't stay late," Faye said. "I have to be at the office at seven, so you have to get the kids off."

"If you need me, call," Anson said.

Again no answer, and Anson was out the side door into the garage. He backed his truck out, his baby, a Dodge Ram with "A-1 Roofing—We Can Top That" painted on the doors—and let it idle while he yanked down the garage door. "Jesus, spare me," he said. "Don't say I never did my kids any favors."

It was a drought year, and berries and roots were scarce, so bears had come down out of the Medicine Bow Forest right into the suburbs of Cheyenne. They marauded trash cans mostly and an occasional dumpster and ate the fruit of whatever trees were handy. Several people in Anson's neighborhood had complained to the sheriff, who put the onus to do something on the Game and Fish Department. But what could the government do about the bears' food supply? The previous Sunday even the pastor of Anson's church on the corner had reminded the parishioners that some of God's creatures could be dangerous. "Cover your trash," the preacher said, "and deliver us from evil."

Of course, not everyone went to church. The neighborhood where Anson lived—Prairie View—was a sixty-year-old subdivision east of Cheyenne, cheap houses, declining values, but with watering the fruit trees had grown up—apple, plum, apricot, cherry—and this year they were producing a bumper crop. Anson backed out of his driveway and made a circuit around the block and down the alley, but he didn't encounter any bears.

He came back around on Orion, passed his own house, and drove to the main exit from the Prairie View, where there was a branch bank on one corner and a church on the other. Instead of turning onto the highway, he made a right into the church parking lot and gunned the Dodge around back where, the summer before, he'd found a naked couple going at it full-tilt-boogie on the hood of a Subaru. No such luck tonight, though. It was too chilly. He wheeled around and, as he passed the front of the church, pointed his index finger at the Jesus above the door. "Stay with me, old buddy," Anson said, and he squealed the truck out onto the highway.

Imre lived a mile down in the Lazy J Trailer Court, and Anson turned in there, passed the office, and more or less obeyed the ten-mile-an-hour speed limit to Imre's double-wide. Imre wasn't home, but in case Faye asked, Anson made a few observations. Sybil, in the turquoise single-wide, had her lights on, there was an ATV and a Ski-Doo parked by the trailer opposite, and there were no cavorting bears.

From the trailer park, it was four miles to town, and the halo of lights glowed above the horizon. Anson imagined the shimmering strips of intersecting Interstates 80 and 25, the exit at College, the industrial park where his business was, and beyond that the bars and strip clubs where outlaws and foreigners and college kids were making their best efforts to sin.

There were other places to play pool—the Crazy Eight, Joe Q's, and Jacking the Box, to name three, but Anson had lost interest in pool. Not that he'd planned anything else particular, not that he *ever* planned what he was going to do next. Outlaws calculated their opportunities on the spur of the moment, and Anson was restless and ready to do whatever presented itself. Fortunately, the banks were closed; unfortunately, the bars were open.

Anson had never been much in the looks department and didn't have surplus dollars, either, so to get attention he had to improvise. He could tell a joke or do card tricks, and he could recite the lyrics of every single Willie Nelson song, but women didn't give a shit about Willie anymore, even in Cheyenne. Not that he made a habit of flirting. He didn't like rejection. Sure, now and then he threw money at a college football bet or a local poker tournament or he wasted a twenty on bingo at the Elks, but mostly he was an okay provider. He didn't mind going out with Faye, either—he didn't actively avoid it—but going out with his wife wasn't the same as going out alone, like tonight, when he had the imaginary freedom he pretended he wanted.

He drove along darkened pastureland sprinkled with pole lights and onto the strip where he cruised by a couple of bars looking for pickup trucks he recognized—Imre's, say, or Lannie Metzger's. Lannie was in his church, was recently divorced, and had the same Dodge Ram, though it was green instead of maroon. It was Wednesday, though, and not many folks would be out on a Wednesday, except the bears.

Faye woke at 1:17 on the red numbers, and Anson was not in bed. That wasn't like him. He was usually home by eleven, midnight if he went out with Imre on a Saturday, but it was Wednesday, or Thursday now. She sat up. *That bastard* was her first thought.

She got up, found her cell phone, and padded to the bathroom. She sat, peed, and punched in Anson's number. Of course the slimeball wasn't going to answer. She had Imre's number in her contact list, too, and she pressed that next.

"Yeah, what?" Imre said when he answered, none too pleased.

"Where is he?" Faye asked.

"Who?"

"He said he was going to your house to play pool."

"I got rid of my table three months ago," Imre said. "Too much riffraff. Come on, Faye, I have to work tomorrow."

"So do I. So does Anson."

"I was in Joe Q's tonight, and he wasn't there. Besides, if I knew where he was, I couldn't tell you. You know that."

"Shithead," Faye said. "Thanks for nothing."

"Up yours."

Faye closed her phone and flushed the toilet and then heard grunting noises in the backyard. She went to the window but couldn't see anything. The city was supposed to have put lights in the alley, but it hadn't, and the yard was dark. She opened the window, and the sounds stopped.

She checked on the children, a peek in. Lynette was sleeping on her back and snoring, and Gary, bless his heart, was askew in his bed with the covers twisted in his hands. Faye reorganized him, and he stirred. "It's snowing," he said.

"It's not snowing, sweetheart," Faye said. "Everything is okay."

Gary sat up. "What's today?"

"Technically it's Thursday. You have school in a few hours." Faye laid him back on his pillow and sang a couple of verses of "Mammas Don't Let Your Babies Grow Up to Be Cowboys."

"I saw the end," Gary said.

"The end of what?"

"I'm glad it's Thursday."

"Go to sleep, darling," Faye said.

"Where's Daddy?"

She patted him and sang another verse, and when he didn't stir, she went downstairs and got the .38 Special from behind the canisters on the pantry shelf. Then she turned on the light over the patio, slid open the glass door, and looked out into the yard. The plum tree came alive, the leaves and fruit shaking like the fever, and two pairs of eyes shone from the darkness—raccoons. Faye went outside, and the animals flailed out of the leaves, and in thirty seconds, they'd skedaddled over the fence and were gone.

Faye went back inside and pondered which bars Anson might be at. They all closed at two. She wasn't worried about other women, really. Not Anson. He was all bullshit and no action—though it unnerved her to think she could be mistaken. Who else to call—Lannie Metzger, the sheriff, the state patrol, the hospital? She was more worried about tomorrow—her lack of sleep, his not getting the children to school, not to mention the money they'd lose if he didn't work.

It had been her goal, not Anson's, to get married. Twelve years ago, she'd been working in the one-woman office of Allied Energy, typing up field reports and filing documents with government agencies. Most of the men were geologists, field engineers, or greasers, many of them married to women out of state. They hadn't minded a bathroom fuck once in a while—she hadn't either—but her long-term prospects with any of them was zero or minus zero. Beyond work, her parents' church threatened to absorb her life, which was why a little sin here and there was a good thing, reminding her she was alive and had other work besides being a missionary. One day Allied contracted for a new building for its equipment, and Anson was doing the roof—a simple tar job. He was there every day for two weeks, punctual, a roofer, but who cared, if he had a paycheck? Six months later they were married, and she was pregnant with Lynette.

Now she had more or less what she wanted—a house, a flower garden, and two children she adored most of the time, though Lynette could be a little bitch, and Gary was a weenie. Anson came home smelling like shingles and tar paper, beer and sweat, depending on the season, but at least he came home and was a churchgoer, though she was suspect sometimes about his devotion to the Lord. During hymns he sang loudest, and he prayed loudest, too, as if he were adamant about being a better person, which meant he wasn't good enough to start with.

She sat in the living room and thumbed through the Bible without being able to put her mind to a particular passage that applied—repent, the sinner? The parable of the lost soul? The wanderer in the desert? She was in the midst of this pondering when the phone in the kitchen rang. It was 1:52 a.m.

She and Anson used cell phones, and the land line never rang except for the children's calls. She had to get up to answer. "Faye Hempkin?" the voice said.

"Where is he?" Faye asked. "That bastard, is he dead?"

"This is Deputy Reichel over at the sheriff's office," the man said. "No, he isn't dead. You are listed in his wallet as the contact person."

"He's in the hospital, is that it? God, with the insurance and all, that's worse."

"He's not in the hospital," Deputy Reichel said. "Will you let me finish? He's all right. We have him down here at the jail. He wants you to post bail. Will you do that?"

"Post bail for what? What'd he do?"

"He was arrested in a sting," the deputy said. "For soliciting."

"Soliciting what?" Faye asked. "I'll bet he wasn't handing out church literature."

"No, ma'am." There was a pause on the line, and the deputy coughed. "I don't know if you want to hear the details. Are you two still married?"

"With two kids," Faye said.

"You know what a glory hole is?" the deputy asked.

Faye didn't say anything for a moment. "No, I don't want to post bail."

"That's fine," the deputy said. "Don't blame you a bit. Leastways you know where he is."

"Tell that asshole to get in touch with Jesus," Faye said, and she hung up.

She eased herself down on one of the kitchen barstools. The world of Anson's unknown whereabouts that had a moment before been uncertain became, now, in its new certainty, much more scary. "We'll have to move," Faye said aloud. "How can we stay here? How can *I* stay here?" She slammed her fist on the counter. "My husband is a pervert." She lifted her head and eyed her reflection in the sliding glass door to the terrace. Her hair was a mess. Her robe was open and exposed a fattish thigh. "Tucson," she said. "Tucson is warm, but would it be good for the children? I sure as hell don't want to move to Nebraska."

"Mom?" Lynette called from top of the stairs.

"The fucker," Faye said. Then louder, "The fucker." It was a long way from Cheyenne to Tucson.

Lynette called again.

"What, sweetheart?"

"I hear something outside. I think it's bears."

*Will Jesus desert me in my hour of need?* Anson thought. *Faye will kill me.*

He was standing in his cell when the deputy came back and told him Faye wasn't going to post bail. "You can call a bondsman in the morning," the deputy said. "Now don't you feel bad?"

Anson blamed himself, naturally, but it wasn't all his fault. He'd stopped first at the Crazy Eight and then at Pedro's Tex-Mex on Third Street, where he'd ordered a tequila shot and a Modelo and talked with a couple of Hispanic dudes at the bar, who, it turned out, knew Enrique and Pablo. The last of the dinner guests were leaving, but the bar was picking up, and Anson stayed an hour. Coming out, it was ten thirty, time to go home, but when he got behind the wheel of the Ram, the truck turned the wrong way, right, toward the air force base. The Golden Triangle was out that way, past the city limits, alongside the used cars lots, oil and gas supply companies, and the AG Equipment dealers. Even as he drove into the parking lot and saw the neon yellow triangle, he felt himself sliding toward sin.

There were maybe a dozen cars and trucks in front, mostly beat-up ones, though there were a few newer SUVs—lawyers liked this place, too. He parked at the far end of the line where the name on the side of his truck would be less obvious, though how many customers in the Golden Triangle would hire a roofer? He'd been there before, not that often, and he'd not been particularly entertained or enticed or satisfied, whichever applied. So why was he there again? He couldn't answer the question. He was *aware*, and if he was aware, why hadn't he gone home?

Inside it was dark except for the stage where a blond woman in a red dress was dancing to Dire Straits. A waitress in panties and bra asked if she could help him find a table, though there were plenty of them empty. "How much help can I need?" Anson said. "I'll sit at the bar."

"I'm Tammy," the woman said. "Let me know . . . whatever."

"I'm married," Anson said.

"So am I," Tammy said.

Anson ordered a gin and tonic and laid down his last ten-dollar bill, though for emergencies he kept a fifty folded up inside a picture of Lynette and Gary in his wallet.

The bartender was a bruiser, hired, no doubt, precisely for his capacity to bruise. "First one's free," the bartender said. He set down the gin and tonic. "And it's Wednesday."

"What happens Thursday?" Anson asked.

"Depends. You from here?"

"Here, meaning the planet? Maybe, sometimes."

"Here being Cheyenne."

"Home of the outlaws," Anson said, "and the Frontier Days Stampede and Rodeo."

"Cheers," said the bartender. He drank from a glass hidden behind the bar.

Anson figured the bartender's drink wasn't alcohol, but camaraderie was a way to get customers to drink faster, and the second drink wasn't free. Anson downed half the gin and tonic in one gulp, then swivelled his stool toward the stage. The woman in red was no longer in red, but was strutting in a frilly pink teddy, now and then bending over, front side or back, toward the men in the first row of tables. The bending elicited the predictable oohs and exhortations. Another linebacker type, maybe the bartender's brother, was stationed near the stage to make sure order was maintained.

Anson paid ten dollars for a second gin and tonic and carried it to the middle of the tables farthest from the stage. Another woman had succeeded the blond in red—a brunette this time in top hat and tails. The music was "New York, New York." It was already toward midnight, and Faye would be in bed asleep, but all the same Anson felt her disapproval, not so much for where he was or that he was late, but because he wasn't home, that he was out *wherever*, even at Imre's, while she'd been left behind to manage. On the other hand, he hadn't chosen to be a husband and father, not consciously, anyway, and not voluntarily. If one person wanted something a lot and the other person was indifferent or even slightly negative, who won out?

Anson thought of himself as Cole Younger—ruthless, greedy, willing to do anything. He wanted to get the money and run, but at the same time he didn't have the right attitude, whatever the attitude was. He hadn't made up his mind about that, but he didn't want to hurt anyone. He was already in trouble, though, and he saw how things were going—he'd break the fifty-dollar bill for another gin and tonic, maybe two, and watch the women take their clothes off. Then what? He rummaged in his pocket for his cell phone and turned it off, but he knew that wouldn't solve anything.

The woman on stage threw her top hat into the crowd and took off the tuxedo coat, and underneath was a false-fronted shirt, bare in the back, and she danced back and forth in front of the whoopers and yelpers, all of whom were leaning forward. But what was the joy in being close enough to touch but not touching? Anson, to his own surprise, finished his gin, got up, and walked out.

After midnight. There was nowhere else to go but home. He had to sleep. Tomorrow was another day of putting on tar paper, ice-and-snow shield, and nailing shingles. More of the same, less of what he wanted, whatever that was. He had a couple of potential clients to see, too—Melanie Brooks, for one, who might be able to get her insurance to pay for a new roof, and the Fort Cheyenne Museum, which wanted someone to do maintenance, which was both tricky and lucrative.

He wandered out to his pickup in no hurry, when a semi whooshed past on the highway and headed north into the darkness. The red tail lights disappeared past the seventy-five-mile-per-hour sign, and Anson pondered how different that trucker's life was from his own. That driver was loose on the road at midnight, eighty miles an hour, free as the nameless trappers and explorers, who were the real outlaws, living in places that hadn't been named yet. Anson got into the Ram and, barreling out of the parking lot, turned north.

The semi had already vanished, but there was only one highway. He accelerated to seventy, then to eighty, eighty-five. He had no reason to head to Casper or Billings or Canada, but it felt good anyway. The gin was streaming into his heart. His mind was racing. The headlights splayed out over barren grassland, delved into darkness, *created* darkness between the land and the sky. A few miles up the road, a bright burst of neon appeared, and Anson slowed to read the sign. Adult Store. CDs, Books, Toys. He braked and swerved in.

To turn around, really—and his lights swung across a low-slung ranch house converted to a business enterprise. A single sedan was parked outside. Anson got curious and parked in back. He'd seen this place written up in the newspaper—problems with the First Amendment or county zoning, or protests from church groups, or background checks of the owners. Whatever the issues, the place was open now.

The solid new door had bars on it and was lit by a sixty-watt pigtail bulb. Anson pushed the door open and inside two movies were advertised on a stand, *Sinlight* and *Flesh Flood*, and there was a bookcase of CDs, a magazine rack with *Hustler*, *Muff Diver*, and others, all wrapped in plastic, and several padlocked glass cases with vibrators, dildos, strap-ons, harnesses, and other paraphernalia Anson couldn't identify. The several doors to other parts of the building were closed, though some had numbers on them. Anson hadn't heard a customer bell when he entered, but his arrival must have alerted someone in back, because he heard shuffling and, seconds after, a man appeared, a tattooed weasely guy in a too-tight T-shirt from Gold's Gym. "Yo," the man said. "You need something?"

"Doesn't everyone?" Anson said.

"I mean, you know."

Anson browsed the magazines, looked more closely at the harnesses and dildos, but couldn't imagine Faye would be interested. And the church wouldn't approve, either. There were whips and feathers—a feather with a leather strap attached was called The Energizer and cost $19.95. "What are the numbered doors?" Anson asked.

"Depends," the man said. "Movies, etcetera. What are you looking to do?"

"Not movies," Anson said. "Can I look in?"

"Be my guest. You got to pay before anything happens."

Anson opened door number two. A forty-inch TV was perched on a wall platform, a fake-leather recliner facing it, and a coat rack on the wall, along with a roll of paper towels. Anson backed out and looked in number four, which had no TV, but rather a six-inch hole in the wall, duct-taped in a star to smooth the rough edges. "Hello," a woman's voice said from the other side of the hole.

"Hey," Anson said. The hole was covered with a cloth on the far side.

"Forty dollar for blowjob," the woman said, "thirty for hand."

She had a foreign accent, Serbian, maybe, or one of those new Russian countries Anson wasn't sure existed. "No, thanks," he said. "I have to get home."

"For you, five dollar off," the woman said.

Anson pursed his lips. It was late, and he was tired, but there he was, and what difference would it make to anyone else? Faye never gave him a blowjob, and already he was saving 12.5 percent. Besides, what about the poor woman behind the wall? She had bills to pay like everyone else.

He dug into his wallet and found the fifty between the two school photos of Gary and Lynette. It wasn't exactly an emergency, but it was close enough.

Faye had heard Lynette calling from the top of the stairs and had shouted up at her, "Go back to bed." She hadn't moved from the kitchen stool. *What would the neighbors think, the people at work, the parents of the kids in Lynette's and Gary's classes?* But she was hurt, too, as well as angry. The list of what she needed to do had got longer—hire a mover, harvest bulbs, transplant bleeding hearts, find a safe neighborhood in Tucson, where there weren't perverts or bears.

Then Lynette appeared on the stairs in her pajamas with Steven Tyler's big lips on the chest. "Where's Daddy?"

"Daddy's not home tonight."

"I think I hear bears."

"They're raccoons," Faye said. "They woke me up, too."

"Is Daddy all right?"

"Daddy's busy, sweetheart. He's not coming home."

"Busy doing what?"

"Hunting," Faye said. "He went hunting." She roused herself and walked over to the sliding glass door. "I'm going to bed now, too."

"Hunting what?" Lynette asked.

"You know men, sweetheart. They get up early in the cold and shoot at ducks and geese. He might be gone a few days."

Lynette came all the way down to the kitchen. "He didn't say anything about hunting."

"That's another lesson to learn. Men don't communicate. They don't tell you beforehand what they're going to do, and later they ask forgiveness."

"What do you have the pistol for?" Lynette asked.

"I didn't know what was outside," Faye said. "Now go on upstairs . . ."

In the yard there was a loud crack and a thump, as if someone had thrown the grill or maybe a minicar.

"That doesn't sound like a raccoon," Lynette said.

Faye turned on the patio light again, and through the glass door, they saw a bear cub on the grass, right beneath the fence, where a couple of slats had been broken off at the tops.

"It's a bear cub," Lynette said.

"Hush, now."

"Where there's a cub there's a mother bear close by," Lynette said. "We learned that in school."

"Shut up, Lynette," Faye said. "He'll climb out again."

The bear cub looked at the fence, then at the house, not even dazed, and ambled over to one of the plum trees. He stretched up, grasped a limb, and bent the plums down so he could rip off a half-dozen at once. A few seconds later, two more fence slats shattered, and a paw reached through. Then three more slats were splintered, and the mother bear broke through into the yard.

"Well, shit," Lynette said. "Let's call the police."

"That's not a word a Christian girl should use," Faye said. "I want you back upstairs *now*. And don't wake Gary."

"I'm awake," Gary said. He padded down the stairs. "Are we about to die?"

"There's a cub and a she-bear in the yard," Lynette said. "They're vicious."

"Are they grizzlies?" Gary asked. "We're food."

"They're black bears," Faye said. "We had bears in Sheridan where I grew up, and they're more afraid of us than we are of them."

Gary stayed back from the door. "They're desperate," he said. "Daddy said they can come right through the glass."

"Daddy's not here," Lynette said. "He's hunting."

"I'm handling this," Faye said, "and I want you two upstairs. I mean it."

Faye escorted them up to their rooms and threatened grounding and losses of allowances. "If I tell you to, I want you to lock yourselves in the bathroom. Lynette, you be sure to take Gary with you. Do you understand?"

"Yes," Lynette said. "What are you going to do?"

"Keep watch," Faye said. "They're only going to eat the plums, but I'll be down there to protect the house."

"I want Daddy," Gary said.

"Get over that idea," Faye said. "What did Daddy ever do for you?"

When Faye came downstairs again, the mother bear had taken the cub's place at the plum tree with the most fruit, and the cub had gone over to the tree by Randy's yard. She knew from a horror movie that bears had bad eyesight, and she turned the light off, then on again, off and on, to see whether the bears might be scared off, but they barely seemed to notice. The mother bear was on her hind legs and bent the higher limbs with the biggest plums down to her mouth, sometimes breaking the limbs.

Faye didn't want to kill anything, of course, unless it was Anson. Why would a man put his dick through a hole in a wall for a few seconds of anonymous pleasure? Was it thrill? Necessity? Proof of something? She supposed a man who'd never had sex might do such a thing—think of the priests!— but that wasn't Anson. Not quite anyway. Maybe she hadn't done her duty on that score, but she had priorities, too, limitations, *standards*. Hadn't he thought of the consequences? The governor of South Carolina, the senator from Nevada, the governor of New York, Tiger Woods, that religious guy in Colorado—schmucks, all of them. What were these men thinking?

Maybe ten minutes had gone by while the bears ravaged the plum trees and scarfed down as many plums as they could. Then the mother bear got down on all fours and looked toward the house. A rivet of fear snapped into Faye's heart, and she backed away from the glass. She, of course, couldn't know what the bear saw or smelled—food, Faye assumed—and she didn't know what to do. Lock the door. She did that. The mother bear came toward the terrace, but about halfway there, the scent of something else attracted her, and she veered toward the flowers. She dug in the ground and lifted out the daffodils and irises and chewed on them.

That was when Faye picked up the pistol. "Oh, no, you don't," she shouted. Faye unlocked the door and slid the glass back the glass.

"What is it, Mom?" Gary called from the middle of the stairs.

Faye ran out into the yard waving the pistol and screaming.

The next day was overcast, and to the west clouds scudded over the low hills. Anson had called a bondsman, who'd got him out of jail and, for an extra twenty, agreed to take him to his truck. "Can they do that?" Anson asked as soon as they were out of earshot of the justice complex. "Can they lure you in and then arrest you like that?"

"I ain't a legal beagle," the bondsman said. "You're lucky I got enough gas to get you out there."

"See, this semi, he was doing eighty—"

"Save it for the judge," the bondsman said.

In daylight, the area beyond the air force base looked worse—used-car lots with pennants flapping from wires and miles of cars, stacks of cinder blocks, yards of garden ceramics. The Golden Triangle was on the right, a washed out ver-

sion of what Anson had seen the night before, like a roller
coaster shut down the morning after. The sign was visible
but unlit, and there were no cars out front.

They drove another two or three miles through open
grassland to the adult store—the sign appeared thirty feet
above the horizon. His truck was still there, more visible
from the highway than Anson would have liked—A1 Roofing. The bondsman did a U-ey beside it, and before Anson's
feet hit the ground, the guy accelerated and the passenger
door slammed closed on its own.

Usually Anson took Gary and Lynette to school on his
way to wherever he was working, and it was only eight, but
if he showed up at the house, he was afraid Faye would have
his .38 Special ready and waiting. He stopped at Cuppa Joe,
bought a grande, and drove across town to the Baldwins'.
The house was a fusty Victorian with a roofline that went
six different directions. He had underbid the job, partly to
keep Enrique and Pablo employed and partly because he
thought he could get the Baldwins to pay for extra flashing
and ice-and-snow shield, for which he could overcharge. He
had two other jobs underway, too, Millicent Karsh's bungalow and the Panozzo Education Foundation. Once supplies
were on site, it was hard for an owner to change roof con-
tractors, so the trick was to string out multiple jobs without
damaging anyone's furniture, famous art, or business papers
and still get word-of-mouth advertising. Per contract, Anson
left the time element vague, because, as he said, "You never
know when it's going to rain."

In fact, it looked as if it were going to rain that day, and,
when he got to the Baldwins' house, he didn't see any sign
of Enrique's Mercury. The scaffolding was in place from the
day before, the dumpster still full of wooden shingles and the

worn-out asphalt ones, the ladders laid alongside the house. A blue tarp was spread over a section of the roof. It was a pain in the ass to work alone—getting the tarp off, for example, and schlepping rolls of tar paper and ice-and-snow shield from the lawn, where the delivery truck had left them, to the ladder, and up the ladder to the scaffolding, and from there to the roof. He'd have to measure alone and cut the tar paper with an X-Acto knife and lay it down before the wind wrapped it around his legs. There was some skill involved; it wasn't plumbing.

He hoisted the ladder, extended it, and leaned it against the eave. Getting the tarp off was a matter of untying the grommets, but the tie-downs were far enough apart he had to move the ladder three times, and invariably the tarp got hung up on a nail or a corner of the scaffolding. He wasted a half hour, then spent another hour cutting and stapling down tar paper.

At eleven, Enrique showed up on foot. "The Mercury not start." Enrique said. "Es muy frio."

"*Frio* or not," Anson said, "we start at eight thirty. I'll get more *frio* before it gets more *calor.* Where's Pablo?"

"He fixing the car."

"Bring up that roll of ice-and-snow shield," Anson said. "It's going to rain."

They worked until twelve thirty, when the rain started, then spent twenty minutes getting the tarp back on. By then, the rain had slacked again, and they stood under the eaves gazing up at the clouds. "What's it going to do?" Anson said. "Why doesn't God make up his fucking mind?"

"What about *los osos*?" Enrique asked. "You see them?"

"What are you talking about?" Anson asked. "What *osos*?"

"I hear from the radio *esta día*, there are bears in the neighborhood. They have crashed into a house."

"I didn't see any bears," Anson said. "What house?"

"One was killed."

"A bear or a person?"

"*No se. No comprendo.*"

Anson looked up at the darkening sky. "Let's go have lunch," he said, "and see what the fuck happens this afternoon."

Anson dropped Enrique off at his hovel in west Cheyenne and headed downtown. He'd missed the radio news, but at a Safeway he bought a *Tribune-Eagle* and leafed through it over the hood of his truck. On page three was an article about bears in the city—several incidents out Happy Jack Road, one on the air force base, another near Lion's Park. No one was injured, at least so the article said. He couldn't find any mention of Prairie View, though it wasn't right in town, either, and if an incident had happened late, it wouldn't be in the paper.

It was twenty minutes across town to the College Drive exit, and time dragged like a suitcase. He missed every traffic light and had to wait while an eighty-year-old woman in an orange poncho crossed at a stop sign. Beyond the box stores, it started to rain hard.

The windshield wipers smeared dirt back and forth, and the rain swept over the yellow pastures on either side. The alfalfa fields were green, and the countryside was dotted with grain silos, oil rigs, and storage buildings of various dimensions. The rain was shit for farmers who needed to get their hay cut and baled. It was shit for him, too. He'd *prom-*

*ised* the museum two days ago he'd be there yesterday, and
Millicent Karsh was already mad at him. Besides, when they
didn't work, they didn't get paid.

He passed the Lazy J and, a mile down, turned left at
the church. Jesus stood in front in a blue robe, his hand
raised in benediction. "Thanks for nothing, pal," Anson said.
He sped past and turned left on Orion. His house was the
third one on the right, a greenish pastel with asbestos tile.
At least it was still standing, and the roof didn't leak. Those
were positives. The garage door was closed, so he couldn't
tell whether Faye was home or not, but why would she be?
She had a job. On the other hand, given the news she'd gotten from the deputy, she might have called in sick.

He passed the house, turned right at the next intersection, and right again into the alley. Ahead, about where his
house was, the alley was blocked by a pickup truck—Randy's maroon Tacoma. Randy was a liberal in all the bad con-
notations of the word—long hair, peace tattoo, and foreign
truck, a goofy guy, but tolerable, except he had a bumper
sticker that said, "Make Love Not Guns." Anson parked
nose to nose with the Tacoma.

Randy was in Anson's yard with a cordless drill in his
hand and was unscrewing screws from a broken fence slat.
Anson idled the Ram and got out. "Looks like a tornado
touched down," he said. "What's going on?"

"Bears," Randy said. "They did a number on your fence."

A dozen slats were broken, and in the yard the plum trees
were mangled, too—branches hanging down and littering
the lawn. Beyond the two trees, though, the house looked to
be intact.

"Everybody okay?" Anson asked.

"Depends on your definition," Randy said. He lowered the drill and gave Anson the once-over. "Faye asked me to do this because she said you weren't living here anymore."

"I was only gone one night," Anson said. "I'm back."

"I don't want to get mixed up in anything between you two," Randy said. "I'm doing this for Faye."

"A new fence won't keep out the bears," Anson said.

"Faye killed one of them," Randy said. "That one won't be back. Game and Fish took the cub."

"Killed it? Faye killed a bear?"

"She came out firing, with a pistol no less. She woke up the whole neighborhood. It was wild. The sheriff was here, a bunch of deputies, the Game and Fish people. This was in the middle of the night. I don't think the sheriff cleared out until about four." Randy unscrewed a screw, the broken slat fell off, and he tossed the slat toward his truck. "It's against the law to fire a pistol in the city limits."

"You're allowed to protect your property," Anson said. "That's a basic right."

"The bear was in her flowers," Randy said.

Anson's phone vibrated in his jeans' pocket, and he looked at the number—Faye's. "A-1 Roofing," he said. "We can top that."

"What are you doing in my yard?"

"I heard about the bears," Anson said.

"Go away."

Anson stepped back into the alley. "You shot a bear with my pistol," he said. "Good for you."

"I might use it again."

Randy carried a few more of the broken slats to his truck and tossed them into the bed. "I can finish this later," he said.

"I'll come back."

Anson looked toward the house. The curtain was pulled across the sliding glass door, and in the window upstairs—their room—the venetian blind was down. "Where are you, Faye? I can't see you."

"Go away," Faye said, "and stay away. I hate you."

Randy got into his truck and backed down the alley to his own garage. Anson put his foot on his back tire and pulled himself up into the bed of his truck. "I live here," he said. "I didn't do anything. That's the truth."

"That's why I got a call from the jail?"

"I had a few drinks and stopped at the Golden Triangle," Anson said. "Then I was on my way home when a semi zoomed past. The next thing I knew I was following him north, see, and I came to this place to turn around. There was a light on . . . I don't remember exactly. There's good and evil, darkness and light—same as ever—but now you have more freedom. Drugs, airplanes, cars, television stations, booze, money. You name it, it's all part of the same thing."

"Satan led you there? Is that what you're saying?"

"It wasn't Satan. It was Jesus. Jesus wanted me to see how easy it was to sin. He wanted to see if I could avoid temptation."

"But you didn't."

"We don't know that," Anson said. "I was tempted, yes. But they arrested me before anything happened." Anson climbed up onto the roof of the cab and knelt down. "Can you see me, Faye? I'm kneeling on the cab of the truck."

"I see you," Faye said. "I hope they put you behind bars."

Anson looked up into the gray sky and adjusted the

phone. A burst of sunlight shot down through the clouds. "Jesus, I see that a moment of weakness is all it takes. One moment when I wasn't vigilant—"

"Stop the bullshit," Faye said.

"Even if Faye can't forgive me . . ."

Anson glanced over at the house and saw the curtain move at the sliding glass door. Faye slid the door open and stepped out into the yard with the .38 in her hand. She walked past the grill, picked up a couple of broken branches from the plum tree, and examined the half-eaten plums. Then she looked up toward the alley.

Anson was kneeling on the cab of the Ram. There they were, one kneeling, one holding the branch of the plum tree, a man and woman caught in a dilemma, intimate strangers.

# THE PATH OF THE LEFT HAND

MYRON DIDN'T KNOW WHERE THE IDEA came from. It wasn't born of desire or need, but more from wondering about what he hadn't done, like laying bricks or wiring a house or living on the coast of Maine. Was he missing an experience that might have enriched him? How would he know? He'd been married to Julia for thirty-three years, lived in Globe for twenty-six of them, and had two daughters who'd graduated from Arizona State—one, like Myron, a pharmacist who lived in Tucson, and the other an elementary art school teacher in Fresno, cohabiting with her boyfriend. Myron could point to no reason for his thoughts, if "thoughts" was the right word, no incident in his recent past that explained his malaise, if that's what it was. There had been a couple of small incidents in college and pharmacy school more than thirty years ago, but how could these be relevant now?

No specific person had engendered this feeling, no one who'd come into the pharmacy, say, or who was in his and Julia's social group; certainly not his friend, Jed, he hunted quail with, or Arnie Leitz, his tennis partner—no one Myron had seen in a magazine or anyone he imagined. Nothing Julia had done or not done had incited him. Their lives meshed. They were early risers, exercised regularly, and while he was at work, she oversaw the hospice volunteers and worked part-time in The Eyes Have It, the local bookstore. They engaged physically about once a week, and she complimented him on his zeal, his strength and gentleness, his concern for her feelings. Their bodies were compatible—hers slim and toned from lifelong yoga and running, and his from the rowing machine in the basement and Nautilus at the gym, not to mention the tennis. He took an aspirin once a day (vitamins were useless) and had a good appetite. Julia cooked chicken and fish. They ate out at the club occasionally and ordered light. He was satisfied in his work and still in love.

There was nothing, either, Myron could have interpreted from his parents' histories. His father had been in the air force, and they'd moved a lot when Myron was growing up—Maryland, Colorado Springs for a stint at the Academy, San Diego, and Tucson at Monthan Air Force Base. His mother was a nurse and found work anywhere. His parents' relationship was cordial—that was Myron's interpretation. They didn't argue, but they weren't particularly affectionate either. His father had died three years before, and his mother moved to a townhouse in Casa Grande.

As he was growing up, Myron felt ignored, but he was all right with that. He got good grades, played football and tennis, and, when he was a senior in high school, his father gave him a Camaro, which made life easier. He'd done a chemistry degree at AU and pharmacy school at Oregon State. He had no brothers or sisters to evaluate or to compare himself to.

That October, Myron dallied after work, not in a bar or on the Internet, but in the back of his store, going over what needed to be stocked, rearranging shelves that were already orderly, and labeling medicines with bigger letters. He read trade publications, though he knew from the drug reps and distributors most of what they contained, and he walked through the outer store to check on the greeting cards, sunglasses, watches, magazines, and snacks that made up for what the supermarkets and Walmart had taken away from the pharmacy. Sometimes he sat at the marble-topped soda fountain, where Susan, his assistant, made malts and shakes and cherry phosphates. He sold tourist items, too—T-shirts, maps, pamphlets on the history of the Globe mines, and guidebooks and checklists of the surrounding desert plants and birds.

Often he walked around town. By 6:00 the heat was not so oppressive, and it was pleasant outside. Because of the mines, Globe had never paid much attention to itself aesthetically, but now there was a new art center, and several downtown restoration projects were underway. Myron had served two terms on the city council and prided himself on getting grant money for civic improvements. Being seen walking was good advertising, and he was friendly, so it surprised him on these evening excursions that he had to make himself wave to people he knew and to stop and talk to the older people who were his best customers. He felt as if his social skills were atrophied, though, at the same time, he had a keener private sense of the world around him. He was aware the barber's pole at Hair Today Gone Tomorrow was stopped, that Fern Adams had added another flamingo to her lawn and a butterfly to the side of her house, that Ali Kazak, going into the post office, had on a clean white shirt. When Myron paused at Larry Medwick's café window, he not only saw the tables and chairs inside, the patrons, the waitress, Mitzi, talking to Tim Price, but also a reflection in the glass, a double of himself filled with longing.

One evening when he came home, Julia was in the

kitchen cutting yellow squash into rings. She had rice in the steamer, chicken marinating, and a glass of Cabernet on the counter. The strap of her sundress was down over one shoulder, and sweat beaded on her forehead. "Were you at the club?" she asked without looking up.

"I was in town."

She stopped cutting. "What's going on, Myron? I saw you."

Myron set down his briefcase. "You saw me where?"

"In the city park."

"There's no law against being in the park."

"I was over to see Mildred. She broke her hip. And I was on my way to the grocery."

"I know she broke her hip. I delivered her pain meds. What's this about?"

"You were staring up into the trees."

Myron got a wineglass from the cupboard and poured a glass from the bottle Julia had opened. "I don't see the problem."

"I honked and called to you, and you even turned around, but you didn't see me."

"I'm sorry."

"You looked far away," Julia said. "Remote. Demented. Or maybe enthralled with your own thoughts."

"I've been noticing things," Myron said. "The trees, the clouds, the brickwork on City Hall. Maybe it's stress. Maybe it's age."

"Maybe it's someone else," Julia said. "That's what I thought."

"There's no one else," Myron said.

"You've never made me worry before," Julia said. "I don't want to start now."

The next week, Myron changed his schedule. Susan would work afternoons on staggered days so he had more free time, and Myron gave her a raise to accommodate him. Susan had a weird life anyway, with an Alzheimer's father and a boyfriend on swing shift at the mine. "If Julia comes in," Myron said, "tell her you have no idea where I am."

"Which will be true," Susan said.

"I'm not doing anything devious," Myron said. "I need time to think."

Myron drove to Roosevelt Lake, and another time to the overlook above the Salt River Canyon, and once to Dudleyville, where he waded in the San Pedro River. Several times he visited the Boyce Thompson Arboretum, which was along a section of Queen Creek thirty miles west of Globe on the other side of the Pimal Mountains. It was Upper Sonoran Desert—palo verde, ocotillo, agave, varietal cacti, acacias, creosote, mesquite, and hackberry, along with a collection of other desert plants from around the world.

Myron was a supporter, benefactor, and occasional volunteer at the arboretum, and he and Julia often drove out on a Sunday morning and walked the trails. But in fall, there weren't many flowers. Myron sat in the Demonstration Garden, feeling the light fade, smelling the subtle scents, listening to the solitary cadences of overwintering thrushes and sparrows. There were shadows in the arroyos, soft variations of green, and the murmur of the creek over stones.

Julia rarely phoned him at the pharmacy, but during these days she called his cell several times and asked where he was and what he was doing. She used the pretext of an errand—"Can you pick up mushrooms from the market," or "Do you want to go to the Schwabs' this Saturday?" On

Thursdays, after her work at the bookstore, she stopped by the store.

One night in bed reading, Julia turned from her book. "You're quieter than usual."

"I'm frequently quiet," Myron said.

"It's a different quiet," she said. "This is silence. Why are you taking the afternoons off?"

"I don't take all of them. I wanted time to myself. Why are you checking up on me? I've been a couple of times to the arboretum. I've told you where I was."

"I'm worried," Julia said. "Right now, it's as if you aren't here."

"I'm reading," Myron said. "It's a dark book by Sotomayor. You think someone else is in bed with you?"

"No, I recognize you," Julia said, "but what's going through your mind?"

"Nothing but the words on the page."

"Do you think people change?" Julia asked.

"They can," Myron said. "Most people don't."

"I don't want you to change too much," Julia said.

In his early twenties, Myron wanted to prove he could be alone. No one asked him to, no one instructed him how, no one made him, but he'd felt a lack in himself he thought needed to be addressed. He took long walks in the Catalinas and Rincons, explored the Santa Claritas and Organ Pipe Cactus National Monument. He carried his sleeping bag to spend the night out under the stars—once on the summit of Mount Wrightson, once at the spring at Quitobaquito, and another time on a slab of sandstone in Aravaipa Canyon. Separated from the crowd he felt fulfilled, satisfied but also uncertain about fitting in. In Corvallis, at pharmacy school, he bought a one-man tent and hiked into the Drift Creek Wilderness. He climbed Mount Jefferson. He spent a long weekend in the back country at Three Sisters. His friends didn't understand his wanting to be in remote places by himself, but Myron felt it was the right thing to do. He found a fritillary emerging from its chrysalis, a coyote's den with puppies, a small owl calling from a few feet above him. At Cape Lookout, fog came in at twilight, and he felt himself, body and soul, fade into the gray air.

One rainy right, he was walking home and telling this to a woman he'd met in their yoga class. She was a senior, majoring in literature. "I could have sat in my room or gone to a bar," he said, "but then I'd have been lonely. I'm not lonely in wilderness."

"What were you?"

"Solitary. There's a difference."

"I hear what you're saying, but if you need solace and courage, maybe you're too isolated to start with."

"I hope to solve that over time."

"Maybe I can help," the woman said. "Take me with you."

"But I wouldn't be alone then, would I?"

"Maybe you don't want to be."

The next time he went into the wild, he took the woman with him. Her name was Julia.

Globe wasn't cold in winter, but there were months of less light and more darkness. In other years he'd played tennis, hiked in the mountains, and increased his minutes on the stair-step machine, but that December and January he responded as if he were in a state of dormancy, like the fish in Queen Creek that lowered their body temperatures or the snakes that stayed in burrows for days at a time. He rarely went to the gym or the club. He watched television dramas and read English sea novels, and, when Julia offered to host a party or they were invited somewhere, he begged off.

"Do you want to talk about it?" Julia asked.

"I might if I knew what to say."

"Start with the beginning."

"When was that?"

"Start with now," Julia said. "Are you depressed? How do you feel this minute? Why don't you want to go to the Miltons' barbecue?"

"I'm not sad. I haven't been drinking. Frieda Milton irritates me with her chatter about her wonderful children."

"Do you want a divorce?"

"What are you talking about? No, I don't want a divorce. I love you."

"But you're not with me," Julia said. "Maybe love isn't enough."

"Why isn't it? It is for everyone else."

"You tell me, Myron. You have to make choices."

"I am making choices," Myron said. "I'm not going to waste my time on Saturday listening to Frieda Milton talk about her children."

The incidents Myron remembered from his past had occurred so long ago he wouldn't have thought of them at all if he hadn't had reason to. In his senior year at Arizona, while his roommate was on spring break in Puerto Peñasco, Myron had to finish a chem project, and he'd come home late one night from the lab. The phone-message light was blinking red, and he pressed the button on his way to the shower. He took off his shirt in the hallway and listened to his mother's voice. "Myron, we're hoping you can get to Lake

Powell this weekend. Dad's taking the boat, and you could waterski. I'm going to make that chili you like so much. Let us know." The machine clicked and whirred, and another voice came on: "Hey, Myron," a man said, "I want to suck on you. Meet me at Greasy Tony's tomorrow night at ten. I know who you are."

Myron ran across the room and snapped off the machine. He hadn't recognized the voice, but he played the message again to be sure. Then he erased it. He didn't go to Greasy Tony's but spent the weekend waterskiing at Lake Powell.

Then, a few years later toward the end of pharmacy school, early in his married days, Myron applied for an apprenticeship in Lake Oswego. The owner, Larry Theisman, had invited him for an interview, and Myron left Corvallis at two—it was eighty miles—with the idea of being back to pick up Julia from her shift at the library. Theisman's practice was a one-man operation, pretty much what Myron had envisioned for himself, though he'd have preferred to be in Arizona. Theisman was in his sixties, soft-spoken, graying hair receding from his temples. He wanted the neighborhood taken care of by a good man. A pharmacy was a service. He'd train Myron for a year, then let him assume the practice at a sacrifice buyout. Box stores hadn't taken over the economy in Lake Oswego yet, and the income from a sole proprietorship would be enough for Myron to reduce his school debt and make payments on the practice.

Theisman's offer was so generous Myron felt he couldn't refuse the subsequent dinner invitation, and he'd left a message at the library for Julia to get another ride home. He might be as late as eleven. The restaurant was a tasteful fern bar. Theisman ordered Manhattans and complimented Myron on his seriousness of purpose, his good academic record, his calm demeanor. They chatted about Lake Oswego and some of the characters in the neighborhood. When the waitress returned, Myron chose halibut in a cream sauce, and Theisman ordered rib eye, medium rare, and another round of Manhattans.

After dinner Theisman wanted brandy. "You don't have to drive back," Theisman said. "You can stay at my place."

"Thanks," Myron said, "but my wife's expecting me. I should have coffee."

"Coffee with brandy," Theisman told the waitress.

At nine thirty, when he stood up from the table, Myron felt tipsy. They'd driven over in Theisman's Mercedes, and, walking out to the parking lot, Theisman took Myron's arm. They passed from the light of the parking lot into the shadow of the building, and Theisman recited a poem, "Intimations," which Myron found odd but sweet. Theisman unlocked the passenger door, embraced Myron, and kissed him on the mouth.

Myron pushed Theisman away. "What are you doing?" Myron yelled. "Are you crazy? This was my future."

The exchanges Myron had with Julia were evasive and ephemeral—he admitted that—but since he had no intent or plan to do anything, how could he be culpable? He made an effort to be more upbeat and sociable. He worked out at the gym, played tennis, and as a concession often stayed for a martini afterward with Arnie Leitz or with Julia, if she had a yoga class. Julia relaxed. She asked Myron if he'd consent to an Ides of February party, and Myron willingly grilled chicken for twenty friends, though his double did the cooking while he, Myron, was elsewhere. He was still aware of the smallest things.

A week after the Ides party, he put an ad online in the MSN personals:

### CURIOUS MAN SEEKS SAME

50s married professional, healthy, 6'0," 175, non-smoker, wishes to explore the unknown with like-minded person of similar background. Must be discreet.

For the next three days, Myron dared not look at his emails. When he did, he had fifteen replies. Some he wouldn't have answered anyway—from men who were too eager ("Just let me try you . . ."), or too experienced ("Are you top or bottom?"), or too illiterate ("I've never laid with no man"). But he found a few messages intriguing.

> I'm a college professor, divorced for eight years, and only in the last year have I thought of trying this, whatever it is. I'll tell you up front I'm not into kissing. How about a drink somewhere? I used to be a bourbon man, but for me now it's white wine.

> Married five years, 34, legal assistant, don't drink or smoke, slender, a river kayaker, though it's hard to find rivers in Arizona. Well, the Colorado. My wife would kill me if she knew I even looked at this ad, much less answered it.

> Dear Curious Man,
> You have more courage than I do, but here I am answering. I'm 54, married, three children. Curiosity is more powerful than evil, but is this evil? Do you think so?
>
> Scared to Death

Putting in the ad was an act of intent, but responding to messages was further incrimination. Still, the scenario puzzled him. If he were interested in men, why hadn't be been attracted to Jed at the club, whom he'd known fifteen years and seen naked a hundred times? Or Nigel, the Brit, who worked for Sunshine Mining, who was homesick and lost? Or Arnie Leitz, tall and good looking, who always gave Myron a hug at the end of their tennis matches? The saving grace, Myron supposed, was he was unknown to any of the respondents. He was invisible, anonymous, so he was not yet guilty.

Guilty of what? Myron didn't even know what he wanted. He had no desire to kiss a man, and he wasn't interested in top or bottom. He wanted to know *more*, but he wasn't sure what that meant.

Everyone lived without doing what he wanted. So what if he wanted to see Nepal or a barren-ground grizzly bear in the Brooks Range or what it was like to live in Los Angeles? He could live with those unfulfilled desires. He was happily married. Why change what already worked? Besides, he had his children to think about, and his pharmacy practice, his reputation, and his peace of mind. What if he suffered guilt afterward? Or if he liked what happened and wanted more?

But what about *once*, only once, try it, whatever "it" was, and get it over with. Knowledge was superior to ignorance. He hated waffling. Do it! Do it! Do it and find out. Don't do it! Don't be a fool. No, do it! What was wrong with being a fool once in your life? And negative consequences accrued only if he were found out.

Myron signed up to go to the American Pharmacy Association's convention in Phoenix, in late February, though he had not been to a national convention in fifteen years. "It's close by," he said to Julia the evening he signed up, "I might as well keep up with the crowd."

"Is there a crowd in Globe?" she asked.

"You know what I mean."

Julia was mollified by Myron's return to regular afternoons at the pharmacy, his signing up for golf lessons, and his coming home earlier in the evenings. She didn't say anything about his having two or sometimes three glasses of wine instead of one. The days were lengthening again, and Myron rototilled the garden, rebuilt a rock wall adjacent to the neighbor's, and cleaned up trash in the alley, though he stayed up later in the evening, checking the sports scores on the Internet — so he said.

On a Thursday, after visiting his mother in Casa Grande, Myron met the professor at a bar in Mesa. Myron had on shorts and a polo shirt, but the professor wore slacks and a coat and tie. He'd driven over from the community college where he taught political science. He had a beard, which, right off, made Myron uneasy. They each ordered a glass of wine, red for Myron, white for the professor, who refused to give his name.

"But here we are in person," Myron said, "right in front of one another."

The professor looked around. "I don't want to know you."

"Have you done this before?" Myron asked.

"A couple of times. Don't ask so many questions."

"You're way ahead of me," Myron said. "What am I supposed to do, be silent?"

"Look," the professor said, "this isn't going to work for me."

He got up and left even before the wine arrived.

The thirty-four-year-old with the wife who'd kill him didn't reply to Myron's suggestion to meet, so Myron tried Scared to Death, whose message had mentioned evil. Scared to Death wrote back the following day. He was an ex-CPA, a Suns fan, and played the piano. He and his wife bought and sold coins and stamps on eBay, more as a hobby than as a business. He was a little older than Myron, five ten and overweight by a few pounds, but not ungainly, apolitical and open-minded. His wife wanted to move somewhere that had seasons — Minnesota, maybe. She was a nurse.

"My mother was a nurse," Myron wrote back. "I'm a pharmacist in a small town — I'd prefer not to say which one. My father was in the air force, and we moved around. I admired my mother for being adaptive."

"I've never touched a man," Scared said. "This is all new to me." The man provided a cell phone number and told Myron to call if he got to Scottsdale. "Maybe we could meet for coffee."

The day before the convention, Myron called Scared to Death from a pay phone in front of the Globe Mall. "It's the C Man," Myron said.

"Good to hear from you," Scared said.

"Are you at work?"

"I'm at the piano." The man played a few notes in the background. "Where are you? I can talk. My wife isn't here."

"I'm driving to Phoenix tomorrow," Myron said. "I could meet you in Scottsdale at ten."

"Ten a.m.," the man said. "I can do that. There's a Starbucks at the Fashion Mall."

"I'll wear a blue button-down shirt," Myron said. "I have brown hair."

"I'll have on a red shirt," Scared said. "Red for danger."

Scared laughed, and Myron did, too, but nervously.

The next day, Susan agreed to open the store, so Myron didn't have to go in. Myron was up early. "The arboretum's on the way," he said. "I thought I'd work on the trails for an hour."

"Will you be home for dinner?" Julia asked.

"I don't want to go to the convention in the first place," Myron said. "Yes, I'll be home for dinner."

"Is there anything special you'd like? Shrimp? Scallops?"

"Halibut," Myron said.

The arboretum was closed when he arrived at 7:30, but Myron knew a way in around behind the caretakers' sheds. He saw in the Cactus Garden amid saguaros, agaves, ocotillo, and cholla. The morning was cool, and Myron was aware of the pale sky's deepening to azure. The air warmed up. He heard songs of birds. He could, of course, change his mind. He didn't have to have meet Scared to Death for coffee. He could go directly to the convention. And if he did meet the man, a plan was only what might happen, not what would happen.

People came along the path, and Myron stood up. The arboretum opened at eight—it was a little after—and Myron walked back along the creek. Insects were caught in the sunlight above a shallow pool, a dozen blue butterflies basked around a puddle, and a falcon flew across the hillside covered with saguaros and mesquite. He noticed a bird foraging under a berry bush, a robin in shape and habits, the way it perked its head up, but not one Myron recognized. It had a pale breast and a rusty back—a foreign robin, a bird out of place, a different species. He heard the voices of a group entering the garden.

The Scottsdale Fashion Mall was easy to find, and so was
Starbucks, right on a corner. Inside, no one had a red shirt
on. There were a couple of women chatting over lattés, a fif-
tyish man reading a book, another man doing a Sudoku puz-
zle. Myron ordered regular coffee and laid his jacket over
a chair by the window. From an unkempt *Arizona Republic*
lying nearby he extracted the sports page.

When he picked up his coffee, though, he was too nervous to read. A young couple came in and sat down at the
next table, and while the woman went to order, the man set
up chess pieces on a wooden board. Three college women
came in and ordered skinnies to go. Then, at five after ten,
a Toyota minivan pulled up outside in the handicapped
space, a woman driving. The man in the passenger seat had
on sunglasses and a red shirt. The woman got out, no more
handicapped than Myron was, put the car keys in her purse,
and came around to the passenger side. She was pudgy, but
nicely dressed in a pantsuit. The man opened his door, and
the woman helped him out. He tucked in his shirt, and the
woman handed him his cane, and turned toward the Starbucks.

The woman entered first and led the man to the counter to order. Then she looked around, waved to Myron, and
came straight over. "Are you the one?" she asked. "You have
on a blue shirt."

Myron stood up. "I don't know," he said. "I . . ."

"Curious Man," the woman said, "the one Terrell's been
emailing? He's quite excited by this."

"Who are you?" Myron asked.

"I'm Tilly."

Terrell had got his coffee and made his way toward them,

tapping with his cane against the chair legs. Tilly got him settled into the seat across from Myron. "I'm going to leave you two," she said. "I'll check back in an hour. If you're both here or Terrell is by himself, that's fine. If not, I'll see him later at the house." She whispered something in Terrell's ear, and he smiled.

"My wife said you're a nice man," Terrell said.

Myron sat down, stunned.

Tilly went out, crossed in front of the window, and got into the van. She waved to Myron, though Terrell couldn't see her. Myron was silent.

"So, well, now," Terrell said, "I'm Terrell."

"That's what your wife said."

"My wife and I have no secrets," Terrell said. "She has to read my emails and answer them, so how could I be deceitful? I said I was interested in finding out about a man, and she said fine, if I wanted to, do it. 'Go ahead, honey,' she said."

"Just like that?"

"We're not getting any younger," Terrell said, "or any wiser, that's for sure. How's the coffee? What they say about Starbucks may be true, but the coffee isn't bad."

"I don't drink much coffee," Myron said.

"Neither do I, but once in a while I'll take a whiff."

Terrell smiled again. The smile was genuine, Myron thought. Terrell was pleased to be there. His whole body seemed pleased. He was gray-haired, neatly dressed, and sturdy. He had a strong-looking face, handsome, if that mattered. Myron assumed Terrell didn't care what he looked like.

"So what are you thinking, C Man? Tell me the truth."

Myron didn't know how to answer.

"Things could be worse," Terrell said. "I'm not black. At least I don't think I'm black." Terrell laughed.

Silence.

"Not that black is bad," Terrell said. "You didn't think that was funny?"

"I did," Myron said. "No, you're not black. But, well . . . I had other ideas."

"I bet they didn't include a blind man," Terrell said.

Terrell's expression was expectant, and Myron felt he had to fill the void. "I went to the arboretum this morning," he said.

"I've been to the arboretum," Terrell said. "It must have been nippy out there."

"I wore a jacket," Myron said. "It was peaceful in the Cactus Garden. And then, coming out, I saw an unusual robin. Do you know what a robin is?"

"I'm blind, not ignorant," Terrell said. "I know what a robin is."

"This one had a rusty back," Myron said.

"And you took it as a sign? Is that what you mean? What was it a sign of?"

"I don't know. It made me think of being different in an ordinary place."

"Is this wrong?" Terrell said. "Is that what you're asking? Is there a should and a shouldn't?"

"Isn't there?"

Terrell laughed. "You tell me what you want to do, C Man. We can sit here and talk about the water shortage in the desert. Pretty soon we're going to have to pipe water down here from Alaska. Or we could discuss our children. My two boys are in college in California, and my daughter is married to a linguistics professor."

"One of my daughters is a pharmacist," Myron said.

Terrell sipped his coffee. "My house is a few blocks away," he said. "You heard my wife. She's going shopping."

"Wouldn't it seem strange to you, you know, being in your own house?"

"It's cheaper than a motel. But you have to decide. It's going to take two of us."

Myron drank his coffee, which had cooled off now.

"I'm scared, too," Terrell said. "But we got to this point."

"All right," Myron said, "let's go one step farther. We can always change our minds."

"Until after the fact," Terrell said, "if we get that far."

Terrell knew the names of streets—Arcturus, Sirius, Aldebaron—though he'd never seen the signs. "Navigating by the stars," he said. "Turn right at the next street. That's Deneb."

"Nice neighborhood," Myron said.

"The average house is three-hundred thousand," Terrell said. "So how's the pharmacy business?"

"It'd be better without the competition from Walmart," Myron said. "What are you retired from?"

"I was CFO of a dot-com in Modesto," Terrell said. "I knew the bust was coming, and I got out rich, or relatively so."

"And now you deal in coins and stamps."

"Coins, stamps, and postcards from around the world," Terrell said. "The street coming up is Rigel. That's a first-magnitude star in Orion. Turn left there. My house is the fifth one on the right, the two-story green ranch house. Three eighty-two."

Myron turned left and drove by pastel houses set on

large lots. A row of palm trees lined the street on both sides. Most of the houses had xeriscaping, but some had lawns and shrubs. The green ranch house was large, but not ostentatious. It had a flat roof, dark green shutters on the plate glass window in front, pebbles instead of grass. Terrell extracted a remote from his pocket and aimed it at the two-car garage. "Tilly thinks of everything," he said. "You can pull right into the empty space."

"If it's okay, I'd rather park at the curb."

"Easier getaway," Terrell said. "Sure, suit yourself. I want you to be comfortable."

Myron steered to the curb and turned off the engine.

Terrell opened the passenger door and set his cane on the sidewalk. "I don't have a key to the front door. I'll go through the garage and let you in. Don't leave yet."

"I won't leave," Myron said.

Terrell tapped up the incline toward the open garage, while Myron looked out the open driver's-side window at the beige house across the street. It had a lawn and a green hedge and a red-tiled roof, and on either side were adobe privacy walls. He heard the splash of someone's diving into a swimming pool. "Alaska, here we come," Myron said.

He got out and faced Terrell's house. What occurred to him was, *no one I know knows where I am.* He liked the feeling, but it frightened him, too. It was like being alone in the Huachuca Mountains or the Drift Creek Wilderness. But he imagined being found dead in Terrell's house. Julia and the children wouldn't understand what he was doing in a blind man's house in Scottsdale.

Terrell opened the door and looked out. "Are you all right, C Man?"

"Just thinking," Myron said, and he walked up the flag-stone walk to the door.

"Home is where the heart is," Terrell said. "Welcome."

Myron stepped inside a sparsely furnished living room that was spacious and wild with light. The sun poured through the plate-glass window and shone from the edges of a glass table and shimmered from the waxed oak floor. On the walls were line drawings of plumpish women by Juan Velasquez Diaz, six in all. In the doorways irregular lengths of strung beads glittered and sparkled, and dust motes were alive in the air.

"You're nervous, I can tell," Terrell said. "You want a drink? I can make martinis."

"It's eleven in the morning," Myron said.

"It's five o'clock somewhere," Terrell said. "Come on. It'll take the edge off."

Myron shrugged.

"I can't see you," Terrell said, "so I take silence as yes."

"Sure," Myron said. "Why not?"

Terrell led the way to the kitchen at the back of the house, and from a cupboard got out Tanqueray, vermouth, and a shaker. He found two scalloped martini glasses, ice, and even knew where in the fridge the olives were. "You're a pharmacist," he said, "so you probably know this, but the old alchemists used to think the left hand had a path the right hand didn't know. The left hand was sinister—'sinistra,' from the Latin—and so what the left hand was up to was evil." With his left hand, he unscrewed the lid of the olive jar, plucked out an olive, and put one into each glass. He poured the gin and vermouth into the shaker, shook it, and poured the glasses to the brim.

"How do you know where the brim is?" Myron asked.

"Sound," Terrell said. "And practice."

"The alchemists were the forerunners of pharmacy," Myron said.

"And bartending," Terrell said. He lifted Myron's glass toward him without spilling. "Do you want to sit in the living room?"

Myron took the glass in two hands. "All right."

"First a toast," Terrell said. He raised his glass and held it out toward Myron. "To us, explorers of the universe."

Myron touched Terrell's glass and sipped, and the heat of the gin descended to his stomach.

Terrell negotiated the doorways and the strings of beads and found the bright room. Myron followed. "You take the chair," Terrell said. "I like the sofa." He sat down at an angle on the end toward the window and put one leg up across the cushions. "So tell me, what gave you the courage to place your ad?"

Myron remained standing. "I wondered whether I was missing something," he said, "though I don't know what."

"Are you about to leave?" Terrell asked. "Don't you want to sit down?"

Myron sat in the chair and took another sip of his martini.

"Beethoven was left-handed," Terrell said. "So were Michelangelo and Leonardo da Vinci."

"I didn't know that."

"Were they evil? What's evil? How would we define what evil is?"

"The law defines some things as evil," Myron said, "like robbery and murder and incest. Religions have their opinions, too."

"What you're worried about is your wife," Terrell said.

"She wouldn't approve of your being here."

"My wife thinks I'm at a convention," Myron said.

"Doesn't she want you to discover anything new?"

Myron drank his martini. "Let's say she doesn't want me to venture too far beyond the ordinary."

"But you're happy with her?"

"Yes, absolutely. We've had a good life together."

"Are you wondering if you're gay?"

"No, I'm not gay. We hear about things, we read, we have our own histories—I don't mean to be vague. At a point in our lives we realize we're running out of time to see the places we haven't been and to do the things we wonder about."

Terrell turned toward the window. "I look at that light," he said. "I know across the street is a beige house with a tile roof, maroon colored. There are three windows with shutters matching the roof. Tilly told me that, sure, but I can see it in my mind. What I can't imagine, though, is movement. I can't see the gardeners out there, or the clouds, if there are any, floating in the sky. People think a blind person's other senses are better, you know, to compensate, and maybe they are. But that's why I wanted to meet a man. I wanted to feel, smell, taste, *listen* to a man's sighs. It'd be different. Do you understand what I'm saying?"

"I think so," Myron said, "but I'm right-handed."

Terrell laughed. "Good," he said. "You're not evil. I didn't think you were." He shifted his leg to the floor and sat up straight. "So what's next? My wife has a limited tolerance for shopping."

Myron was silent.

"You want a reprieve to use the bathroom? Reflect a little? It's down the hall on the right."

"That would be good," Myron said.

"No pressure, but what room do you want to use? Not this one. There's too much light. The bedrooms upstairs are too cozy. Take my word for it. Tilly likes frills. There's a sofa in the den. What about that—the den of iniquity?"

"The den, okay," Myron said. He stood up.

"The den is at the end of the hall. I'll meet you there. I won't start without you."

Myron carried his martini to the hallway looked over the display of photographs of Terrell's children when they were small, at graduations, on hikes in the mountains. There was a wedding picture, too—younger versions of Terrell and the woman Myron had seen in the coffee shop. He found the bathroom and set his glass on the sink counter. He urinated, flushed, and ran his hands under warm water. In the mirror above the sink was a middle-aged man, six feet tall, slender. He looked familiar, but he wasn't the man of twenty years ago, or ten, not even the person he'd been yesterday. Myron dried his hands and held them up in front of him. In the mirror the left looked like the right, and the right like the left.

Outside the door was a shuffling sound and then a soft knock on the door. "You still in there?" Terrell asked. "You didn't bolt?"

"Still here," Myron said.

"Take your time. Be certain."

"Thanks."

"No pressure," Terrell said.

The footsteps diminished. Myron took a breath. He unbuttoned his shirt and ran his hand down between his legs. He wasn't hard, but he felt a stir, a real possibility. Then he heard the piano, the notes muted by the walls and the closed door. Terrell was playing "As Time Goes By," and Myron hummed along. Was he the nice man Tilly said he was? Or should he leave? Terrell wouldn't know where to find him, of course. He was still anonymous. All he had to do was turn left out the door and run for his car, but would he? Myron smiled at the double in the mirror, drank the rest of his martini, and ate the olive.

He opened the door and stepped into the darker hallway. To the left was the bright living room, and to the right, at the end of the hall, was an open door with a softer light emanating from it. Terrell was singing, "You must remember this, a kiss is just a kiss, a sigh is just a sigh . . ." and Myron lifted his hands and turned them back and forth in the competing angles of light.

# LA GARZA DEL SOL

THERE WERE TWO OLD GRINGOS AT THE bar with two young Costa Rican women in short dresses, and the bartender was pouring shots of Wild Turkey for five, thinking, I suppose, he was in on the action. The taller gringo stood between the barstools where the women sat. He was lanky, tan, gray hair in a ponytail, and he wore a blue flowered Hawaiian shirt, shorts, and sandals. The other was balding, paunchier, and had on a tan safari shirt. The bartender was young, also American, though now and then he threw in Spanish words when he made jokes to the women.

I had gone into Quepos to buy groceries, and on the way back the bus had broken down. It was mid-October, eight o'clock at night, and raining hard. The rain had started about noon, and it was like no other rain I'd ever seen, even in Tacoma—warm rain, more from the air than from clouds. I had my backpack with the three plastic bags in it—bread, dorado, pollo, bananas, and Orangina. I'd ducked into the bar out of the deluge, already wet to the skin, while the others on the bus walked home.

Except for the gringos and the women and me, the bar was deserted. It was called Billy's and was connected to the Hotel Mirador del Pacifico higher up on the hill. It was open-air, with tables under a metal roof covered with palm fronds. A metal roller shutter was pulled down over the liquor at night.

In the States, these gringos would have been living in a trailer court, but in Costa Rica, they lived "la pura vida." They brought down their gas-guzzler cars, bought cheap beach property, and threw their money around. That's what the women were assuming, anyway. Why else be with them? I ordered an Imperial and sat at a table off to one side. The rain roared on the roof.

Normally I'd have paid no attention to any of them. I'd have read my book or studied my thesis notes, but because of the rain I hadn't brought my notes, and my book, an archaeological history of Central America called *Empire of Light*, was in a plastic bag under the groceries at the bottom of my pack. Besides, in a few minutes I had to walk up to the Mono Azul because exactly at nine Gwen was calling.

Something struck me about the taller gringo. He reminded me of someone I knew—a professor in college, maybe, or an aging movie actor. And the women were worth watching in their own right. They were dark-haired, in their twenties, with figures they were proud of, or at least displayed to advantage. One had a round face with short hair crimped with silver clips. She wore a thin red and white sundress. The other had a more angular face, long hair loose down her back; she wore a white blouse over a short black skirt. She was flirtier with both the gringos and the bartender, and a few times, she even looked at me, sitting off in the shadows.

I was a dweeb, a nerd, a geek, though my personality wasn't visible to anyone in a foreign country. I'd grown up sheltered by my mother, who taught junior high school in Gig Harbor, and by my father, a geek himself, who worked for the Gates conglomerate. I'd graduated a year early from high school, finished a bio degree at the University of Washington, and was now in graduate school in ornithology at Cornell. I did word games in my head—I, in, pin, pine, opine, opined—timed myself on the *New York Times* daily and Sunday puzzles (my record for Sunday was 18:10), and answered the chess and bridge challenges. I'd spent the last two weeks at the natural history museum in San José, then moved down to Quepos because a friend was letting me use his house to write in.

The women and the gringos talked about nothing much—the rain, going dancing later, where to eat in town. The shorter gringo kept grabbing the hand of the woman in the sundress, and she kept pulling it away, so I gathered they weren't familiars, not yet anyway. The women sipped their shots, but the men tipped theirs back, and the bartender uncapped the bottle for refills.

"What about him?" the woman in the white blouse asked suddenly. She looked over at me. "He's an American, isn't he?"

"We aren't paying for everyone," the tall gringo said.

"Está empapado," the woman said. "He can have mine."

"I'll give him one on the house," the bartender said. He poured another shot glass full.

The woman picked it up and brought it over. "You need this," she said. "No es una buena noche para acampar."

"Tienes razón," I said, "pero he alquilado una casita."

"¿Donde?"

"Sobre la colina."

"You speak good Spanish," she said, and she sat down. "I was in Houston two years. Houston's like San José, but without the mountains."

"Hey, Marty," the tall gringo called over, "who's buying the drinks?"

"I'm coming," the woman said. She turned back to me. "¿Tienes trabajo aquí?"

"Sí, estoy investigando algo."

"¿Comoqué?"

The gringo walked halfway from the bar, and the woman stood and put out her hand. "I'm Marta," she said. "Disfruta la lluvia."

"Bren," I said. "Thanks."

I thought this odd, but maybe not so odd. I looked pathetic, alone in the rain, a nobody. With someone else buying the drinks, she could afford to be nice.

For a few minutes I watched the rain pour off the palm leaves. There weren't many cars, and when one passed, the tires hissed and the headlights delved through the rain, darkness swallowing the wake. I stared at the shot of Wild Turkey. I wasn't a drinker. A beer or two was my limit, but Marta had got this drink at some cost, and I sipped it once, twice. It tasted like fire. Then, following the gringos' lead, I drank it down in one gulp and slugged my beer.

"Why don't you have a jukebox or something?" the woman in the sundress asked. "You ought to have live music to draw a crowd."

"In tourist season, there's a band on Saturday night," the tall gringo said.

"We're tourists," the woman said.

"A jukebox rusts," the bartender said, "but I have a guitar."

"There you are," the short gringo said. "Live music."

The bartender disappeared behind the bar and came back with a beaten-up f-hole Gibson. He strummed a few chords and tuned the strings, smiling with a toothy half-grin, as if this were what he'd been waiting for on a slow night. "What do you want to hear?" he asked. "Don Henley? Stephen Stills?"

I took this opportunity and stood up and came into the light. "Donde esta el baño?" I asked.

The taller gringo pointed toward the walkway to the hotel, and I crossed behind them and climbed the steps. The bathrooms were in the empty lobby of the hotel, where a light shone from behind the unmanned desk.

I used the john and came out again and found the tall gringo standing in the breezeway smoking a cigarette. "Want a hit?" he asked.

"No, thanks."

"What's your story?" he asked.

"My story is I stopped in here out of the rain."

"That's all?"

"That's it," I said. "That's the only story I know."

"It better be." He took another draw on the cigarette and went into the bathroom.

Back in the bar, the bartender was singing:

> *I've been lonely, I've got the blues*
> *Don't know how love happens, I paid my dues*

At my table, there was another shot of bourbon beside a fresh beer. I looked at Marta and the woman in the sundress and the short gringo sitting at the bar. They were listening to the music.

With the rain coming down, it was hard to hear the guitar or the words. No one looked at me. Then the tall gringo came back, and I drank down the shot, grabbed my pack and the full bottle of Imperial, and stepped out into the rain.

A German was on the pay phone at the Mono Azul. I was soaked again walking from Billy's, but except for wet underwear and soggy bread, I didn't mind. The *pavo* and beer had settled in. I stepped around under the eave of the Mono Azul and drank the Imperial, and when I came back, the phone was free. For a few minutes I stood under an awning and waited for it to ring. I'd have called Gwen, but she was visiting friends in New York City, and I wasn't sure where she was. She was my *soul mate*—that was her term. She was a fellow grad student from Cape May, New Jersey, a pelagic bird expert, which was why she was at Cornell.

She was my first lover. Twenty-five was late to start at love, but I had never fit in with my academic peers. To them, having no sexual history was a joke, like playing the oboe or studying chemistry, but to me it was ordinary. And anyway, sex was not the rapture I'd been led to expect. Neither Gwen nor I was expert, and no doubt anxiety and inexperience inhibited our pleasure. It felt good; it was unusual, but not transforming or particularly exciting. At least knowing what it was freed Gwen and me from ridicule.

The phone never rang—maybe she'd tried when it was occupied—but why didn't she call back? I walked on up the hill. Now and then I passed a house or a pole light at a bus stop, or a car came shooting by, but mostly it was so dark I could only tell I was on the road by the feel of the pavement. It was eerie walking that way, almost blind, in the rain.

Finally the lights from the Escuela Patricia glinted ahead, and I saw water running down the asphalt in silver layers. I turned into the muddy road and sloshed through puddles. My casita was next to the school, and at the door I felt around for the lock and fitted my key. I turned on the light and shed my pack and my wet clothes at the door and carried the pack into the kitchen. I kept thinking of the scene in Billy's Bar — those women with those men, how I'd stumbled in on something sinister. I still felt the bourbon running through me.

The house was one large room with the kitchen, a bathroom, and one bedroom. The windows were barred, with screens but no glass. On the Pacific slope it was never cooler than sixty. I dried myself with a towel, put away the pollo, and, without getting dressed, fried the dorado in olive oil. I made a salad and ate looking over my thesis notes. Ants, las hormigas, made a line across the tile floor.

The next two days the rain kept me indoors. The farmer's house below my casita was invisible, and the offshore islands were hidden by low clouds. Even the singing from next door at the language school was drowned out by the noise of the rain on the tin roof. I made good progress on my thesis.

My subject was *Eurypga helias*, *la garza del sol*, the Sunbittern, a bird I'd first heard about in college in a Spanish elective on the myths of pre-Columbian civilizations. Even more than the quetzal, this bird was a symbol of the primal authority of spiritual nature. Why this bird was so elected no one knew, except that, among the birds of the tropical Americas, the family *Eurypgidae* was unique, the only other marginally close relatives in the world being two small families, the trumpeters and seriemas in South America, and the Kagu in New Caledonia. The image of the Sunbittern appeared on ornamented shafts of the Miquiori Indians in the neotropics, in the tomb of the shaman Initupsi, and in many temples throughout Central America. My own interest in the bird was enhanced by its presence in Spanish-speaking countries, language being, like music, an enrichment. I thought of my thesis as a way to improve my Spanish as well as to satisfy a curiosity in ancient history and archaeology. The texts and epigraphs in the Museo de Historia Natural were in Spanish, and my reading skills and specialized vocabulary had improved, though I felt in some measure, being alone, my conversational Spanish had withered. Anyway I was within a week or so of finishing the groundwork and research, and my last two weeks in Costa Rica were already arranged with the Organization for Tropical Studies to search for this elusive bird in the jungle streams in the Caribbean uplands above Las Horquetas.

Midweek around noon — I'd lost track of the days — the rain abated. The clouds lifted dramatically, and the sea appeared as a smooth arc of blue-gray that widened and gathered into specific form. The coastal rocks I hadn't seen in days emerged; a solitary fishing boat crossed the bay in the rising mist. The sun came out, and the orange-flowered guarumo tree in front of the terrace swarmed with tanagers, honeycreepers, and euphonias.

I took my notes and my laptop outside and worked for an hour at my camp table. Then, just before two, when the heat was mounting, a shadow passed at the corner of my eye. A woman in jeans and a blue T-shirt appeared at the edge of the terrace. At first I thought she was looking for the escuela, but then I recognized her from the bar, Marta's friend with the short black hair. With her sandal she slid a drowned scorpion off the tile and came toward me.

"¿Te acuerdas de mí?" she asked, her tone neither flirting nor friendly.

"Sí, claro. De Billy's Bar."

"Exacto," she said. "I want your help."

"¿Qué pasó?"

"Fue tú culpa," she said.

"My fault? How could anything be my fault?"

"You were there," she said. "You are also American."

"I can't help that."

"It took me three days to find you," she said. "I asked the bus drivers that drive past the Mirador del Pacifico. I described you—a gringo with short brown hair—and one of them remembered you got off at the school." She paused and looked out at the ocean. "You must have money."

"A friend is letting me use his house," I said. "Sit down."

She looked at me. "Because of you, he beat her up," she said. "Marta's in the hospital."

Marta and Carilena worked at one of the big hotels farther down toward the park at Manuel Antonio, and they'd met the gringos at a beach bar. There'd been talk of drugs. If the women would go out with them for a while, the gringos were going to give them cocaine. That was the idea of the get-together at Billy's.

But there the drinking had started, and things turned ugly, but I didn't see how I was involved. I didn't know the gringos. I didn't know Marta or Carilena, either. Marta had got me free shots of bourbon I didn't want and had sat with me for five minutes. That was my connection. Of course I could understand how they might blame Americans for the burger franchises in San José, the cars and TVs, and exclusive development of their beaches, but I personally hadn't done anything. I was an ornithologist, respectful of private property, devoted to the preservation of the cloud forest, and careful, even, about my Spanish. What did they want from me?

Money.

Carilena had a Festiva, and she drove me to the hospital, which was out by the airport on the road to Dominical. My idea of hospitals came from TV and the movies, and this place was nothing like what I imagined. It was a low-slung cement building with five spokes radiating from the center. When we arrived, an empty ambulance was at the curb, with a dozen people gathered around it for no reason I could see. We went into the reception and down an open-air walkway into the women's wing.

Families passed by, talking and crying. Sweat, bleach, and salt air were the smells. Carilena paused in front of one of the doors. "Let me make her look good," she said. "I'll call you in."

She pushed open the door and went in, and I waited. Out the window I watched a small plane descend for a landing at the airport, though from my perspective it looked as if it were going to crash into palm trees. It disappeared, and then Carilena came out.

"Está listá," she said. "She wants to see you. Dile que es bonita."

"I shouldn't be here really."

"Y dile que sí."

"Yes about what?"

Carilena didn't answer. She held open the door.

Marta was at the window looking out into a nearby pasture where cows were grazing. A Laughing Falcon, beige with a black mask, was sitting on the snag of a dead tree. Beyond the field was jungle and the gradually ascending foothills of the Talamancas obscured at the top by clouds.

"¿Qué ves?" I asked.

"Nada." She turned to me. Her arm was in a sling, and her face was puffed up and black-and-blue on one side. "I broke my arm when I fell down."

"¿Te duele?"

"Sólo en la cabeza," she said.

"You look all right."

"I can't write," she said. "At the hotel I wrote letters and took down information. I'll be in the cast six weeks."

I didn't know what to say, so I kept quiet.

"My mother kicked me out long ago," Marta said, "and Carilena lives at home with her brothers. I can't stay there. You could help me. Carilena says you have a place."

"Only for a few more days," I said. "And I'm writing. I need quiet."

"I won't bother you."

"I have a girlfriend in the States."

"Wouldn't she want you to help someone in trouble?"

Out the window the Laughing Falcon lifted from the snag and receded toward the mountains. "Maybe she would," I said.

That was the wrong thing to say. I had already agreed.

The next day Carilena brought Marta over with her clothes and her radio and a small suitcase of jewelry and hair curlers and shampoo. Her clothes weren't enough to fill the closet, so I left my shirts hanging. The rest of my things from the bureau I put into a banana box. The sofa was too short to sleep on, but I'd brought camping gear to be in the field, so the prospect of sleeping on the floor for a few days wasn't particularly daunting. It was the loss of privacy I dreaded: having to be dressed in the house, closing the bathroom door, worrying about making noise early in the morning. My only consolation was that I would be gone in a week.

That afternoon from the phone at the Mono Azul I reached Gwen at her apartment in Ithaca. She'd been back three days and was working long hours in the library so she could take the time, when I was finished, to look for birds in Panama. "How's the thesis going?" she asked. "Are you making progress?"

"I've run into a snag," I said. I watched a Rufous-tailed Hummingbird probe the blossoms of a magenta waterfall of bougainvillea across the road.

"What sort of snag?"

"I can explain, but it's not what it sounds like. A woman's staying with me." I paused a moment. "She needed help."

There was silence on Gwen's side. Then she said, "Bren, lots of people need help."

"I'm sleeping on the living-room floor," I said.

"Why tell me this?" she asked. "You could have told me after I got down there."

"It's happening now. I wanted to be honest."

"You'd rather hurt me now than later? What am I supposed to think about this, that you're doing this woman a favor?"

"If it weren't innocent—"

"—then you wouldn't have told me? That's honesty?"

"You were in New York with friends. Look, I've already figured out how to get to Panama . . ."

"I'll think about it," Gwen said, and she hung up.

The first morning Marta slept until ten, made coffee, and sat on the terrace where I was typing on my laptop. I hadn't slept well on the floor, and though Marta didn't say much, I was tired and irritable. How could I not be aware of her presence? She read magazines, paged with one hand through a few of my books, then changed into a skimpy red and yellow bathing suit and sat on the corner of the terrace where there was midmorning sun.

I went inside and worked, but even then she disturbed me. She was idling in the sun, taking advantage of me. And she'd flirted with me at Billy's Bar. I wasn't oblivious to a pretty woman of questionable character in my house. At the same time, I was determined to ignore her, and I did for most of an hour. I wrote several paragraphs about the Tchiti chief, Gauru, who in the fourteenth century used the Sunbittern in his rituals for speaking with the gods.

Then Marta strolled through the room on her way to the bathroom. She didn't look at me or say anything, but it was impossible not to watch her. I heard the toilet flush and the shower come on. I imagined her naked ten steps away.

In the afternoon, Carilena came over from the hotel and gave Marta the news on everyone there. I went for a walk up to the Barba Rosa and called the Organizacion de Etudios Tropicales at La Selva to inquire whether I might come a few days earlier than planned. They had no vacancies. Then I called Gwen again, and her answering machine came on. I had a beer at the bar.

So it went the next few days. The weather stayed sunny; my work suffered. Then on a day of nameless days, I woke early. For some reason, I'd slept better, and I got up early to revise a transition chapter important to connecting the ancient symbols of the Sunbittern with the present day. I was conscious of the clink of a pan on the stove, my cup's rattling, even the drip of the hot water going through the coffee filter. I took my coffee outside.

As I did every morning, I scanned for birds. There were the usual Golden-hooded Tanagers, kiskadees, grassquits, anis, and ground doves. A flock of Red-lored Parrots flew over, and several vultures waited in the distant trees for the sun to warm the thermals.

Marta appeared in the doorway barelegged in a long white shirt. "What do you see?"

"I didn't mean to wake you," I said.

"You think I'm lazy, but I'm not."

"How's the arm?" I asked.

"It wakes me up in the night." She came over to where I was. "Show me something."

"What do you want to see?"

"Something new."

I was surprised. "New depends on what you've seen before," I said. I pointed at the guarumo tree and handed her the binoculars. "There's blue moving among the leaves. See if you can find it."

She looked through the glasses and adjusted the focus. "It's blue with black on its back and across its eye. Uno pájaro bonito."

"Blue Dacnis," I said. "It eats seeds and fruits and the nectar of flowers. Es muy común."

"A bird so pretty can't be common," she said. After a minute she lowered the glasses. "What are you writing about all the time?"

"La garza del sol," I said. "*Eurypga helias*."

"It lives here?"

"Higher up in the foothills."

"What's it look like?"

"It's roughly the size and shape of an egret, but it's pale brown, with a long orange-yellow bill, orange legs, a slender neck. Its head is black with white stripes, but its most striking fieldmark is the wings. When it flies, there's a pattern of chestnut, yellow, black, and white that flashes to the eye like the sun."

"Have you seen it?"

"I've studied its history and read accounts of its habitat. Seeing one isn't required for what I'm doing, but I'm spending my last two weeks in Costa Rica over by Horquetas."

Marta was quiet for a moment. "Do you want me to go with you?"

"Would you want to camp in a rainforest with a broken arm?"

"I've never camped," she said. "I've never spent a night outside. I could cook for you, and we could speak Spanish the whole time."

"I don't think so."

"¿Pero no definitivemente?"

"Sí, lo se. Quiero ser sólo."

"You should say, 'estar sólo,'" she said.

"Quiero estar sólo," I said. "I want to go alone."

Later that morning, I took my laptop to the café up the street, and when I came back in the afternoon Marta wasn't there. Her clothes were still in the closet, so she hadn't moved out. I worried a little when she didn't show up at dinnertime; I made pollo con arroz and a salad and ate on the terrace while the sun fell into the sea beyond the spit formed by the Rio Arboles. It was peaceful to watch the reds and oranges dissipate and darkness take over.

Was she coming back or not? Maybe she was in another bar with other men. I cleaned up the kitchen and was tempted to sleep in my own bed, but in not knowing it was easier to sleep on the floor. Even in absence, she impinged on my life.

Around midnight, I heard the click of the lock, footsteps, the bathroom used. Moonlight came in through the screened windows. The bed in the other room gave under her weight. Then she got up again and pulled back the curtains to let more of the breeze in. Again the bed sighed.

The moonlight was bright, and I lay awake for several minutes listening to insects chirring. Then something landed on my sheet, an object fallen. I felt movement, and I sat up quickly. A scorpion three inches long had dropped from the light fixture above me and was crawling across my thigh. I yanked the sheet and jumped up and flicked on the overhead light. Another scorpion was about to fall. "Jesus Christ," I said. "What next?"

Marta came out in a T-shirt, just as the second scorpion dropped onto my bed. "They like ceilings," she said. She got the broom and swept the two scorpions outside and off the terrace. "I'm hungry," she said. "Can I eat something?"

"There's cereal," I said. "And heuvos and leftover chicken."

She stared at me, and I realized I had on only a pair of blue underwear. I didn't care. Marta opened the refrigerator and got out eggs and chicken.

"Didn't you eat?"

"Desde la manana, no."

"You should take better care of yourself."

"Lo tomaré en cuenta."

I went outside and sat down on the terrace. My body calmed. The ocean was black with a wedge of silver running across it, and stars and clouds flew overhead.

Marta stood in the doorway.

"Carilena said you were getting drugs from those men," I said.

"That's over," Marta said. "I don't have any money. Anyway, I have an appointment for a job in San José."

Then for a few minutes we didn't speak, but I was conscious of her pale silhouette and the looming silence. There was a texture to our closeness, the visible and the invisible, presence and the absence that existed in every moment. The longer the silence lasted, the closer we were.

Marta went back inside and cooked the eggs. I waited for several minutes. The night was altered by the memory of our recent silence, and I watched the sea change with the moonlight and the moving clouds.

The clouds covered the moon, and I went inside. The room was darker than before, the window a rectangle discernible only from the light of the escuela, the vertical bars stark upon it. I crossed to the bedroom. Marta was in bed, her body outlined by the sheet, her cast propped on the next pillow. I hovered in the doorway.

"It's all right," Marta said. "I understand about scorpions." She lifted the sheet with her good arm and let me slide into the bed beside her.

A week later, Marta and I hiked from La Selva into Braulio Carrillo National Park. She was as eager as I, more eager perhaps, because she had never spent a night in the jungle, never a night outside. She carried a pack and a sleeping bag she'd borrowed from a friend in San José. I had my own backpack with the food and the tent.

Though it wasn't raining yet, clouds were low over the Cordillera Central. We passed along the Río Puerto Viejo for three or four kilometers, then climbed up a tributary into the forest. I'd been advised there was good habitat for the

Sunbittern along the Cala Nuboso higher up. One had been seen there the previous spring.

As we walked, trogons called from the glades, and we heard the snapping wings of manikins and the clear whistle of the nightingale-thrush. The trail was little used, and I cut away vines and elephant fronds with a machete. Several times we worked our way around seeps or springs. We proceeded this way for most of the morning, and then it rained.

We took shelter under a banyan tree canted over the trail and rested on our packs. Rain in the rainforest was water on leaves, drops sliding, rivulets cascading and roaring. The air was gray and misty. For more than an hour there was no letup, and finally I set up the dome tent on a flat spot. In five minutes in the open, I was soaked through. I crammed the gear inside, helped Marta under the flap, then took off my clothes and left them hanging on a branch. Marta laughed at me as I danced naked in the rain before I ducked inside and dried off with a clean T-shirt.

Marta took a cigarette from a plastic bag. "¿Has probado esto?" she asked.

She lit the cigarette, drew in, and handed it to me. The sharp tang of marijuana filled the tent.

"No, gracias," I said.

"We aren't going anywhere for a while. Go ahead. Try it."

I took the cigarette and puffed.

"Hold the smoke in your lungs."

I took another puff, held it, and coughed. And again.

"Mejor," she said.

I took another hit.

"Don't do the whole thing," she said. "I only have two."

She took a hit, and I did another, and in a few minutes the

tent was filled with smoke, and we were laughing and hugging and listening to the rain beat down.

"¿Qué mas no has probado?" she asked.

My geekiness diminished. It rained all afternoon, and all the next day, and we did everything two people can do in a tent in the rain, at least if one of them has a cast on her arm. We read, we made love in ways I'd never imagined, we slept, we talked in Spanish, we laughed. Marta cooked rice and beans over a one-burner stove, and we ate the canned chicken and canned tuna we'd brought for just such an occasion.

On the third day, I put on my still-wet clothes and left Marta in the tent and went to scout the territory of the Cala Nuboso. Marta would wait and read. The stream was high, but clear—a rainforest is used to rain. I made a cursory inventory of plants, took samples of creek water, examined under rocks and shore debris for insects the bird might feed on. I sat on the bank, hidden, but with a vantage point upstream and down. Rain seethed on the moving water.

The Sunbittern didn't appear, but after half an hour Marta came up the trail in her red poncho. She didn't see me, and I was curious to see what she'd do alone in such a place. Her expression was alert, but as she got closer she seemed apprehensive. She called out to me, but I didn't answer.

She slid down the embankment to the stream and waded out to the sandbar where birds' tracks were woven in intricate pattern. From there she had a view of the stream flowing toward her and away, the towering trees, and whatever distance the clouds allowed. A hummingbird, a Crowned Woodnymph, appeared at her poncho for a second before the bird skimmed away. That relaxed her: her eyes, her whole body were more at ease. And I saw her differently, too—not the city dweller who needed entertainment, but instead a geek of the wild, no different from me. The rain fell across my image of her and, in my imagination, created a new person.

In the night the rain stopped. The silence woke Marta, and her waking woke me. We listened to water falling from leaves onto other leaves, onto the tent, into puddles on the trail. After a while Marta's breathing evened out, and I put my arm over her and slept again.

We had planned to go out to La Selva in the morning, Marta to catch the bus to San José, and I to get supplies in Puerto Viejo. But, because the rain had stopped, we hiked back up the trail to see the Sunbittern.

Without the rain, the place was different. A shimmer of sunlight broke through the gray and illuminated various greens along the stream and made shadows in the higher trees. The current of the Cala Nuboso riffled over the rocks and around the sandbar in varying rhythms of light. We hid in the brush along the bank, and I expected at any moment to see the bird emerge from around the bend upstream, picking its way among the stones, feeding on larva and crayfish. If we were lucky, it would fly so we might glimpse the patterned emblem on its wings. But we spent two hours in silence, listening to the calls of other birds freed by the pause in the rain. To see a bird and to know it are different, and the longer we waited, the more I understood the absence of a thing. The absence made the presence real, created around the true thing its beauty and its myth.

In the afternoon we retreated. We left the tent where it was because I would return for another few days—I had other chances to see the bird. But I packed up Marta's sleeping bag and her clothes. Depending on what happened in

San José, she might or might not come back. Going out, we didn't hurry on the trail; we watched butterflies and a huge praying mantis; we listened to birds and saw a Song Wren in the shadow of an elephant frond. We stopped and talked — each moment of her presence a part of the long absence I would carry with me. That was how we chose to have it. We knew it would be dark before we came out of the rainforest.

# JOAN OF DREAMS

THE WINDROWER LURCHED LEFT, AND Joan raised the cutting bar to slide over what she knew was the unseen mound of a gopher hole under the dry alfalfa. The earth in the dark shadow was damp still from rain days before, and the windrower veered sharply until Joan caught the wheel and brought it back. She imagined the gophers underground, frightened—as she had once been as a child when a jet fighter flew overhead so close the ground shook—scurrying away from the new light the cut hay shed on them, down into their burrows into blackness, into damp earth, into the smell in their lungs, wishing they could descend farther, deeper, where there was no tunnel for light to follow.

Joan lowered the cutting bar again. Behind her in the wake, the uneven row of cut hay had an angle, like a sudden jolt of lightning through music on the radio. The engine of the windrower resumed its steady roar and, above that, the clicking of the metal teeth and the slapping of the canvas conveyors that carried the cut hay to the center where it slid away under the wheels of the windrower, and some kind of music in the air like cool wind, like voices moving among the particles of dust and pollen and insects and bits of alfalfa thrown up from the reel. Sometimes Joan thought the music was the alfalfa singing as it rolled under the reel; sometimes she thought it was the wind whirling through the stems and leaves, which leaned in on one another. But that morning it was the voices of the dead sighing under the ground, the whispers of bones echoing a language she did not understand, except the sorrow of it and the longing.

She had wakened that morning early, hearing the wind through the loose window glass and under the eaves, moaning, begging, lifting her from the bed. She was the wind and the sound, whatever form it took—a dove's lowing from the cottonwood outside or a sparrow's long slow sweet whistle. Ray had always waked her with his singing in the kitchen, the bacon frying, the dishes clattering as, careless, he whistled to himself as the light seeped in over the Lakota, and she lay in the cool bed wondering why he had left her for the work he needed to do. That morning he had called her with another voice, with the month of June, with the alfalfa growing too heavy, waiting and ready, the sun rising.

She had done two perimeter cuts to give the windrower space to turn around at the ends of the rows, and now three rows north and south. She raised the cutting bar at the end of a row, turned the windrower sharply in front of the irrigation ditch, and turned again, lowered the cutting bar at the edge of the high alfalfa. The belt slapped, the metal teeth clacked, the high hay lay down, the quick descent into windrows of gathered hay that trailed behind her. Joan glanced into the sun, then drew with her eyes the line between the mesa and the sky. This line was flat, too, not unlike the lines of hay she had already left on the ground, though to the west, the mesa dropped off into a gentle swale and disappeared into the trees along the river.

She dreamed she had a broken leg, a heavy white cast

with Ray's signature on the plaster in thirty or forty places. A broken leg didn't matter to what she was doing: she could raise and lower the header with the toe of her left foot, and the gears were hand levers. To drive the tractor or to shift the four-wheeler, to ride Pecos Bill, to turn over in bed— each of those tasks took such close attention, such strength of muscle and bone and perfect resolve that she had to prepare herself like a Zen master who could walk on burning coals. She sat in the windrower seat feeling the heaviness of her leg, the withering of her flesh under the cast. She readied herself for the time she would have to step down to free the conveyor, which from time to time got clogged with alfalfa, or to get the gasoline canister from the pickup to fill the windrower tank.

In the fifth row the cutting bar caught a stone, jerked it from the ground and up into the reel of the windrower where the wooden slats slapped it higher into the air. The stone dropped and was struck again by the next revolving slat, and instantly Joan remembered the rattlesnake Ray had run over last summer. It had been sliced nearly in half by the cutting bar, then thrown into Ray's lap in the seat where she was sitting now. Ray had caught the snake in his gloved hand, knowing exactly what he had hold of, he said, but unable to do anything but gaze into the snake's eyes. It was hurt badly, the red flesh spilling out where the metal teeth had cut it. Ray had watched the remainder of it coil around his hand, the jaws open, and he had suffered its bite as the least he could do for it.

But the stone was too heavy to be thrown high, and it fell away and rolled under the windrower. Joan stopped the reel to see whether any of the wooden slats were damaged, and then, letting the engine idle, got down from the seat, braced herself on one tire and stepped to the plate, without any sign of a broken leg, and to the ground where she picked up the stone and carried it slowly toward the ditch so the baler wouldn't run over it.

She dreamed herself as the stone she carried, having come from a volcano as fire, and having been once, eons before, a part of a cliff under the sea. She waited inside the granite until the sea fell away and then the lake, until the sun shone and the glaciers wove their way down through the land, tearing the cliff around her, and rolling her down among the other stones, rounding their edges and hers to the smoothness of her body. She stopped at the ditch and threw the stone into the weeds.

Across the field, beyond the windrower, the green billows of the cottonwoods obscured part of the pale brown butte. A hawk skimmed left to right in front of the rocks, discernible to her eye only as movement—the Red-tail that had a nest upstream in the trees. She imagined its call in the air, though she couldn't hear it for the idling engine, how it cried that sharp note echoing on the cliff, heard in its call Ray's whisper before he died when he had lain under the heavy body of the pickup and could not speak words. He'd looked at her and said everything the hawk cried out hunting along the butte and scanning the river bottom.

To feel Ray's voice everywhere in the world had made her body spare, the muscles taut, breath shallow. She knew by heart the work she had to do—feeding the horses, mowing the lawn around the house, the dishes and the cooking, the garden, the haycutting and baling and stacking and selling. But doing things by heart was not her way. She dreamed the hawk touched her skin with its wings, tore her flesh with its beak. Ray's body had done that to hers without any sound at all except their hard breathing under the blue light of stars.

The rows of hay stretched across the field—ten, twelve, fourteen. The sun claimed more of the sky. Joan put her hat on—the one Ray had worn sometimes when he visited his mother—a clean, yellow University of Montana cap with a visor and a grizzly on the front. The sun warmed her back, burned through her thin shirt. She took off her shirt and stuffed it under her seat so the sun could burn her back and the tips of her breasts. She was the sun, on fire with its desolate consumption of itself. She burned herself in a thousand sleepless nights, and in so many words she had never spoken. For what else could she have given Ray but such words when she was so tired she couldn't move to touch him? She did not know her own strength, or care, warming the earth and urging the alfalfa to grow tall, but with equal ignorance, blistering the stones, drying the pond from which the ditch flowed, letting the darkness fall.

Her breasts ached with the sun when she drove north, and her back burned heading south: the rows of hay lying in pale green stubble were lines on a blank page, a sheet of music unwritten, parallel bars of a cell, each row assembling gradually, and more to cut, a field whose dimensions she had forgotten—how many rows? Fifty, a hundred, a hundred thousand?—at least that many in a lifetime of cutting this field and the lower meadow three times a summer for as many years as she had to grieve after Ray.

She thought of herself as blind, driving the windrower back and forth across the field by the feel of it, staying in the grooves where the irrigation water ran, by measuring and keeping to the angle of the sun, by feeling the echo of the engine from the cliff across the river. She closed her eyes and estimated how many minutes it took to run one row, maintaining speed and rpm's by touch and sound, the sun on her eyelids, the whirring of the canvas conveyors and the alfalfa breaking underneath her.

The minutes expanded: she lost cadence. The windrower sputtered and stopped, and she opened her eyes. For a moment the stillness astonished her. The cutting bar was silent. The conveyor filled with hay had ceased moving. Then she heard the wind through the high alfalfa and the gurgling of water in the ditch. The water was not running onto the field, of course, but straight from the reservoir along the edge of the meadow and under the road at the far end of the field and past the next meadow she had to cut tomorrow. Joan dismounted from the windrower to fetch the canister of gasoline, but once on the ground she felt the heat caught among the stems of the cut hay, listened to the flowing water. She dreamed she was water possessed of memory of where it had come from, where she had been once in her mother's frail body, on her father's lap as he drove his tractor down the gravel road to a town distant and hazy now. She seeped into the ground, rose to the air as clouds, fell as rain. Ray lifted her in his cupped hands to drink. Or she stayed in the stream to the river, down the river to the bigger river and more silent, rose again to the clouds, perhaps to another place, but always here again over eons to this alfalfa field, this ditch, this body of hers.

She leaned against the wheel of the windrower, its rough tread against her bare skin, her face shaded by Ray's yellow cap. She heard the water and the wind and the hawk's cry, listened to Ray's sighing against her neck, felt his hands touch her breasts, felt his fingers in her mouth, wet, then sliding down her stomach to unbutton her jeans and delve lower until her dreams taught her the lesson that was never the same.

The truck was parked at the bend in the gravel road where she had begun to cut the hay. She got into the cab and drove the lane to the row where the windrower was stopped, then turned into the field running parallel to the shallow grooves where the water had run. Ray had been killed in that same pickup when it had slid on the gumbo and pitched askew into the river bottom. He'd got out and tried to push it back to level, but instead had only rocked it so it toppled over further and pinned him. She'd been up at the house watching the rain, hearing the crackling on the tin roof and the water falling over the eaves and wondering where Ray was in such lightning and thunder, until she had gone out on the four-wheeler to look for him, and found him in the gray light, in drizzle, having died all those hours without her.

She drove the pickup to the windrower, hoisted the canister to the seat, leaned the nozzle into the empty tank. She thought of herself in a faraway city where everything worked—the electricity, the telephone, the traffic lights, the elevators, the automobiles, the computers—all organized, as Ray had said, by people who wanted it to be the way it was.

She finished pouring the gasoline and got back into the seat. The engine whirred and caught. Joan lowered the cutting bar to the ground. She did a row, then another. The sun slanted away. She put on her shirt. Every row of cut hay had to be retraced by the baler, then the bales carried with the tractor to the hay pen and stacked for the feedlot truck. With the money she would make, she'd get through the winter and she'd have hay for the cattle so she could do the same the next year and the next.

Ahead of her the deep alfalfa swirled and thrashed, and suddenly a buffy hen pheasant fought clear of the cover and burst into the air. The hen swerved over the windrows and beyond the road where she sailed down into the weeds. Joan stopped and lifted the reel, watched the mown hay shuffle on the conveyors to the center, the flightless pheasant chicks cut and bleeding, dropping from sight under the windrower.

Joan pulled to reverse and backed away a few feet, then idled the engine and got down. The chicks had been shredded, dead or maimed. Two of them crawled away. One bird's wings had been torn off, and its eyes were glazed in shock. What Joan imagined the bird saw was the near earth so bright with sun, the blue sky paling. She picked up the bird, righted it in her open palm, and shaded its eyes with her other hand. The life which seconds before had been merely the joy of hunger and warmth was now an assemblage of useless feathers and bones and blood and flesh drying in the air.

Joan cut hay till dark, till the clouds dissipated in the cooling sky, and the trees along the river turned gray-black, till the blue darkened overhead, the earth's green became colorless and without depth, till the cliff lost its patterned shadows and turned black. She dreamed herself the hay meadow, the roots holding the soil, the air and water and sun merging in her leaves and growing stems. She was the gophers burrowing deeper, the pheasants in cover in the uncut high alfalfa, the hawk's shadow gone without trace, the intricate darkness, the sighs the wind made calling.

# THE BEAUTIFUL LIGHT

THE ECONOMIC SLOWDOWN CAUSED by George W. Bush's arrogance, incompetence, and malfeasance threw Glenna Wolski's work schedule at Olson's Saab into turmoil. People weren't buying cars, but they weren't maintaining the ones they had, either, and Randy, the service manager, had let two mechanics go and restructured the others' time. Fred and Alvin liked four-day weeks; Geoff wanted overtime; LaTrell and Leviticus preferred eight-hour days with a half-hour for lunch. Larry and Glenna didn't care. According to Randy's estimate of customer satisfaction and employee efficiency, Larry was the best service technician, but Glenna was up there close, which, as the only woman, gave her bargaining power, if she'd cared to use it. But she'd had other things on her mind. Her parents had died within four months of each other — her mother in a bicycle accident in May and her father of grief in September, and over the winter in Seattle it had rained seventy-two days out of a hundred.

She worried certainty in her hours might lead to boredom and further grieving, so she didn't know what to ask for. She was in Randy's office and ran a teaser comb through her frizz. "What about sporadic days?" she said. "You know, here and there, now and then, every once in a while."

"You mean, come in when you want?" Randy asked.

"Take off when I want, maybe one day a week."

"I'm willing to work with you," Randy said, "but I need to plan."

"Plan for randomness," Glenna said. "I will, too."

She'd worked at Olson's on Aurora for four years, lived in a one-bedroom in Eastlake, not far from I-5. A high-school friend, Vicky, lived two floors above. In the neighborhood, Mr. Kang, the grocer, knew Glenna liked halibut, broccoli, and red-leaf lettuce, that she drank 1-percent milk, mango juice, and occasionally Dr Pepper, that her apartment had plumbing issues because every few weeks she bought Drano. Janet, the counter person at Bean There, knew her because every day on her way to work Glenna ordered a regular and a cranberry muffin. Her check from Olson's was deposited automatically at Wells Fargo, and the tellers knew her because she came in Mondays and drew out cash. Her father had told her using cash made it harder to spend.

Mostly Glenna hung out with Jimmer, though she didn't consider Jimmer a boyfriend. They'd met standing in parallel lines at Bean There. Jimmer was tall and lanky and had on jeans, a rust-colored pullover, and a black knit cap. That day, he was going to take his driver's test.

"Aren't you a little old?" Glenna had asked.

"When I was twelve, I drove on the farm," Jimmer said, "but I never got a license. Is twenty-seven old?"

"Why bother now?"

"My mother's eyesight is wasted, and she needs me to run errands in her Dodge."

"So you live with your mother?"

"No, I have an apartment in the University District. What about you?"

"I'm a service tech at Olson's Saab. Dodges are crap cars."

"I'm not responsible for my mother's lack of taste. What do you think I do?"

Glenna looked at him. He had blue eyes, teeth that had been fixed, a shock of threshed wheat sticking out from his cap. For a young man his face was weathered, and he had creases around his eyes from looking into glare. "What's your name?" she asked.

"Jimmer Zimmer," he said. "James, really, but you can't escape a nickname."

"You're a fisherman," she said. "Maybe a river runner or a fugitive from justice."

"I'm a chef," he said. "I grew up on a farm near Sedro-Woolley, but my father had liver problems so we sold the farm machines and moved to Green Lake. He died, but my mother still lives there."

"Green Lake is fancy-dancy."

"The combines, windrowers, and tractors were worth a lot. My parents kept the land but bought a house here."

"Last year my parents died within four months of each other," Glenna said.

They arrived at the counter at the same time, and each of them ordered a large regular. "And a cranberry muffin," Jimmer said.

He called her that afternoon at Olson's, told her he'd passed his driving test, and asked if she wanted to go sea kayaking.

Jimmer was not a chef, but a sous chef in training at Saint Pierre's downtown. He'd dropped out of UW, was good-natured but not too savvy about cars, and loved the outdoors. They made a list of things to do together when the rain stopped—climb Mount Rainier, paddle from La Push

to Lake Ozette, run the Seattle Marathon. Glenna wanted
to swim the Strait of Juan de Fuca.

"I'd have to learn to swim," Jimmer said.

"Go outside," said Glenna. "You can learn in the street."

The rain didn't stop. Seattle's usual was forty inches a
year, but that winter the papers wrote stories about it, and
people made the usual jokes about building arks and carrying life preservers to work. Glenna and Jimmer made love
more often. Glenna liked sex well enough, though not always for the pleasure. Since her parents' deaths, she'd felt
weightless and lost, and being held down by another body
made her feel secure, as if she were going *nowhere*.

Her father had written ad copy, dabbled in journalism,
and been hired on with Boeing to work on their newsletter.
For his last twenty years he'd been miserable. At home, as
solace, he worked on Saabs, and around Tukwila, Renton,
and Kent, he was known as the man to see. For her sixteenth
birthday he gave her a blue Saab 96 V4 he'd found frozen up
in a garage in Ashland, Oregon.

They'd worked on it together, with Rachmaninoff on the
Bose. They rebuilt the carburetor and ignition system, over-
hauled the transmission, and replaced the rack-and-pinion
steering. Mostly her father looked over her shoulder, and if
she made a misstep or needed a seventeen-millimeter wrench
or wanted help, like for lining up the gearbox shaft, he was
there. He loved the Russian composers.

She read, but she'd never applied to college—what for?
She wanted to make money, and Olson's sent her to Saab
technicians' school in Santa Barbara. After that, for the first
couple of years, she lived at home, but when Vicky told her
of a vacancy in her building, why not? Be independent.
That's how she was raised.

After her father died, she sold the house in Tukwila because she couldn't see herself as a landlady, and bought a two-acre parcel of unimproved land on Lopez Island. Sooner rather than later, she wanted to build a cabin. And do what? That was the question.

For several weeks it rained on her random days off, and she didn't know what to do with herself. It was cold. Jimmer was working. The only friend around was Vicky, who'd been laid off from the Gap and was taking unemployment. "I'm thinking of moving," Vicky said. "California's too expensive, but maybe Hawaii. I know that's *more* expensive, but at least it's an island."

"It's several islands," Glenna said. She was standing at Vicky's window watching the rain fall between their apartment building and the next one over.

"Todd's on the Big Island," Vicky said. "He says he can get me work at a hotel in Kona."

"Being a maid?"

"At least I'd be there instead of here."

"Is that a philosophy?"

"Do *you* have a philosophy?"

"I have a job. I don't need a philosophy."

"Excuse me, but I don't see your life as an example."

"It isn't yet," Glenna said. "I'm working on it."

"I want to do something new," Vicky said.

"This conversation isn't helping," Glenna said. "I need some air."

Glenna went downstairs, put on her orange poncho, and walked up the hill to Eastlake. Rain obscured her perspective of the street—the buildings in both directions faded into gray—but she saw a bus coming from the south. She crossed the street and, without looking at the destination, got on it. It was a little after eleven a.m.

Not many people were riding the bus at that hour—eight or nine lonely souls—nor, in the rain, were many people out on the sidewalks. The bus passed fast-food franchises, apartment buildings, shops, a mattress outlet. At a hardware store, Glenna saw a woman in a maroon beret standing under the awning holding an umbrella that had been blown apart. She must have been a tourist—no one in Seattle carried an umbrella—and her expression was anguished, as if a terrible catastrophe had befallen her. Glenna pulled the cord for the next stop and got off the bus at the middle door.

She doubled back, and when she reached the hardware store, the woman in the beret was getting into a Chevy Nova. Glenna stood under the awning, pondered being unable to help, and wept.

The rain let up a bit, and she walked along the shops, looking in windows. At a pet store she saw colorful lovebirds and parakeets, several turtles, a gray cat. Farther on was a sushi bar with Japanese words on the glass, then a used bookstore and a shop for big sizes.

At Green Lake a mist hung in the trees, and water dripped from the leaves. The lake held the aftermath of long rain, a hesitant, vulnerable sheen, as if it were waiting, though a lake couldn't wait for anything. A few people walked on the path, some with dogs on leashes, a man with a pet ferret, a woman with a lovebird on her shoulder. A woman talking aloud to herself strolled past. Glenna had no idea what to make of this spectacle of people with their differing gaits, expressions, clothes, languages. One Asian man was running backward across the grass, and a homeless couple was sheltered under a piece of cardboard.

Not counting Randy, there were a dozen male service techs at Olson's. Glenna put on her coveralls in the same locker room as the men, and, except for Geoff, everyone was respectful. Randy called her "little woman," but he didn't intend to demean: he was from Texas. When he talked to anyone else about her, he called her *Gleena* — "Gleena's our best female technician," he liked to say.

The work was pretty standard. That particular day she had the seven o'clock early bird service with LaTrell and Alvin. She took in two 900s, one of them needing a new timing belt and major tune, and Alvin asked her a few questions about drive trains. Geoff showed up at nine and did his usual sashay past her station. "What're you hoping for later on?" he asked.

"Nothing to do with you," she said.

"Call me if you change your mind," Geoff said.

"Don't hold your bad breath."

It was a long morning. Because of the rain, she ate lunch in the employees' lounge with LaTrell and Larry, but when Geoff came in with his Domino's pizza, she got up.

"I was going to share," Geoff said.

"I don't like pizza."

"It's un-American not to like pizza."

"I'm Polish," Glenna said.

The afternoon dragged, too. She had a 900S and a vintage Sonett, which she loved working on, but she felt an odd restlessness from her bus excursion of the day before. All those people — she felt as if she'd been in a foreign country.

She worked a half-day on Saturday, and on Sunday she had breakfast with Jimmer at his mother's. The mother was visiting her sister in Spokane, and Jimmer was staying in the house to oversee a kitchen remodel. It was a mansion, Glenna thought—twelve rooms, four gables, and a turret. "You mean, someday you'll inherit this?" Glenna said. "It's another strike against you."

"I didn't know I was up to bat," Jimmer said.

"I plan on a simple life, with risk."

Glenna took the following Wednesday off. She bought her regular coffee at Bean There and intended to sit and read at a window seat—her version of luxury because she'd been a reader all her life. But the seats were taken, so she bought a cranberry muffin and walked up to Eastlake. It was misty, but not actively pouring rain, and she took the first bus that appeared, the #8 via Capitol Hill.

She had no reason to go to Capitol Hill, but within a few minutes of being on the bus, she felt, in an odd way, calm and at ease. She wasn't the Saab technician the grocer knew or the woman who drew out a hundred in cash at the bank every Monday. She was a stranger unknown to everyone else.

Buildings went by, and traffic clotted the street. At a grassy park Glenna saw a woman in a smock and a straw hat bending toward a canvas on an easel, and Glenna got off at the next stop. Why not? Who would know? The park overlooked the sound and the Space Needle, though these landmarks were obscured by clouds, and Glenna walked down the path and stood at a respectful distance from the painter. The woman was in her fifties and wore a red scarf under the hat. A parasol was attached to her easel.

The trees in the painting were larger than they should have been, the Space Needle smaller. The dog in the foreground looked like a horse. The sound should have been farther away, but it was difficult to judge because it was barely visible through the real mist. Anyway, there was no reason the woman had to see what Glenna saw, and painting wasn't like fixing a Saab, where other people relied on her expertise.

After a few minutes, the woman turned around. "Are you an artist?"

"No, I'm not anything," Glenna said. "Am I bothering you?"

"I'm finding painting so much more difficult than I thought it would be."

"Everything is."

The woman applied an odd blue to the sky in the painting. "This is a nice neighborhood," she said. "I moved here from Yakima when my husband decided to live with the neighbor's wife."

"I live on Lopez Island," Glenna said.

The woman daubed on an even lighter shade of blue, wishful thinking maybe, and didn't reply. Over several minutes the sky in the painting became bluer still.

"I have to meet some friends," Glenna said, and she backed away. "Good luck with your painting."

"It's not supposed to involve luck," the woman said.

Clouds were rising from Bainbridge Island, and the Fremont Bridge coalesced and faded. A patch of blue appeared through the mist. A strange aura, made up of light pouring through the swirling clouds, created a world Glenna didn't know. She walked into the neighborhood near the park and paused in front of a barbershop. A man getting a haircut was gesticulating to the barber, and the barber cutting his hair waited, poised with the scissors. The scene appeared to be pantomime, though real words were being spoken. Words were merely sounds human voices made in order to communicate inexact meanings. What did "luck" mean, for example? Glenna wondered. Nothing. And what about the lies Glenna had told—she wasn't meeting friends and didn't live on Lopez Island. These words were merely conveniences so the painter might not be offended by Glenna's retreat.

Glenna stopped at a bookstore a little farther on and read the titles in the window display—*The Last Horizon, By the Way of Dispossession, The Unremembered Dream*. What did such words signify, except as hints to other words? After the bookstore, the windows were filled with guitars, jewelry, cell phones, pictures of houses and condos, ski equipment, high-heeled boots, bicycles, cameras, posters of Ecuador and Costa Rica, lingerie, tires—none of which Glenna planned to purchase, though she went back to the travel agency and found out a round-trip ticket to Kona cost $846.

At another intersection down the hill, a priest was holding an American flag and waving a sign that said AID FOR RWANDA, though RWANDA was crossed out and HAITI written above. The man was soliciting money from cars stopped at the light. At a dress store in the middle of the next block, Glenna made the mistake of gazing into the window while a salesclerk was lolling in the doorway. "Want to try something on?" the woman asked.

"I don't have any occasion to wear a dress," Glenna said.

"Make one," the woman said. "There's no harm in seeing what you'd look like."

Glenna found herself in the dressing room taking off her jeans and shirt and running shoes and putting on a yellow sleeveless dress with white flowers embroidered around the neckline. She hadn't worn a dress since her high school prom five years ago, and the woman she saw in the mirror wasn't who she imagined she was now, but, nevertheless, there she was. Glenna pulled out the barrette in her hair and let the wild frizz loose around her shoulders.

Not that she was dissatisfied with what she saw. Her legs were solid; her body was proportioned reasonably. Her nose was too small, and her ears protruded, but that was what ears did. Her eyes were competent, active, Polish blue. But appearances were as deceiving as words. LaTrell or Alvin or Randy didn't notice what she looked like, and Jimmer never said anything one way or the other. She was a Saab technician, apartment dweller, movie fan, reader, orphan, wishful thinker. How could her physical appearance be related to these?

And was she a wishful thinker? What did she wish for or think about? The idea implied she was unhappy or that she wanted something else, a change, or *more*. Her parents had died; yes, that was sad. Vicky might move to Hawaii. Jimmer wasn't the love of her life. But she liked her job, her freedom, her land on Lopez Island. She supposed it was wishful thinking to want a cabin there someday.

That evening Glenna showed up at Jimmer's mother's house unannounced. Jimmer was on a ladder painting the foyer beige. The radio was tuned to a country music station.

"I thought you were overseeing the kitchen remodel," Glenna said.

"My mother left a to-do list. Do you like this color? My mother picked it out."

"I want you to get undressed."

"Now? In case you hadn't noticed, I'm on a ladder with a paint roller."

"Are you saying you won't?"

"What about mood? What about ambiance?"

"Change the radio station."

Jimmer sighed and put down the roller. "What about romance? You've been thinking about this, and I haven't."

"We don't have to mess up the sheets in the bedroom," Glenna said. "I was thinking of the floor or the sofa." She kicked off her shoes and walked into the living room. There was an oriental rug, a coffee table with knickknacks, several cushy chairs. Through the portico was a long dining-room table with six chairs set around it and three candles in a row. "The dining room table will be perfect."

Jimmer climbed down from the ladder and followed. "What's this about?" he asked. "You want to make love on the dining room table? My mother would have a fit."

"She'll only know if you tell her," Glenna said. She pulled out one of the chairs and set her backpack on it. "Are you with me or against me? Take off your shirt."

Jimmer pulled his beige-splattered T-shirt over his head and unlaced his tennis shoes. "I think we should talk about this."

Glenna unbuttoned her shirt and took off her bra and overalls, then reached into her pack, got out a length of cord and a pair of scissors. "I want you to tie me up," she said. "I want to feel vulnerable."

"I'm *not* tying you up," Jimmer said.

"I don't want you to hurt me. Thrill is the operative word." She lay across the table and stretched out her arms.

"This doesn't make sense," Jimmer said.

"Stop whining," Glenna said, "and get busy."

Jimmer looped the cord around one of Glenna's wrists and pulled it around the table leg. "I used to know knots," he said, "but I've forgotten."

He lashed one end of the cord to the radiator and the other to the sideboard, so Glenna could raise her legs but couldn't move them together. "When we make love it's always in the dark," Glenna said. "You only see me going to and from the bathroom."

"That's not true."

"Look at me now." She felt his gaze, and her desire was underway, her body's wish.

"This isn't so exciting as you imagine," he said. "I mean, in theory, I'm okay with it, but you look like a specimen on a slide."

"That's not funny."

"I like the dark," Jimmer said.

"If you're not going to take off the rest of your clothes, then untie me," Glenna said. "Now I feel embarrassed."

"I'm sorry," Jimmer said. "How could I ever eat at this table again?"

A few days later Glenna took the first bus that appeared from the fog—the #2 Madrona Park via East Union. It was a little before ten, and, though she had her choice of seats, she made her way to the back, where a man was strumming a guitar and humming or singing, she couldn't tell which. He had short brown hair recently washed and wore an oxford shirt and a raincoat loose around his shoulders. Glenna sat in the seat catercorner. Outside, there were squeaking brakes, shouts, honking horns. Glenna couldn't pick out individual words. The man experimented with chords, stopped, started again, and sang a few words—off-key, she could hear that much.

When the driver announced Madison Street, the guitar player got up and hurried along the aisle to the door. Glenna followed him down the stairs to the sidewalk, where the bus left them in a cloud of exhaust.

"Do you play in a café," Glenna asked, "or in a night-club?"

The man smiled. "You're kidding, right?"

"But you love to play."

"I play because, once in a while, I hear a perfect note."

"Only one?"

The man put the guitar over his shoulder and started walking, and Glenna kept astride.

"Timing," the man said. "Little by little emotion accumulates, and then the note appears."

"That sounds like the lucky chimpanzee at the typewriter," Glenna said. "It's possible for him to type *Hamlet*, but it's not plausible."

"The one note doesn't happen very often."

"You want to get coffee?" Glenna asked. "I'll buy."

"I'm on my way to work," the man said, "and I have two girlfriends already."

Glenna stopped on the sidewalk, and the man continued toward Lake Washington. People went by—spitters, wheezers, yakkers, people carrying bags, magazines, manila folders, purses, backpacks, newspapers. Cars whizzed by, garbage trucks, meter police, cabs. A Sunrise Seafood truck beeped as it backed up to a fish market. Down the street was a boarded-up Blockbuster, the Uptown Florist, Disc-Go-Round, a movie theater. Dozens of wires crossed overhead. Glenna liked being anonymous, but at the same time, she wasn't invisible. She occupied a place in the world.

An old man approached, pulling a white dog on a leash, and he stopped in front of a flower shop to look at bouquets in the window. Glenna patted the dog, a fluffy chow-type.

"Would you watch him a minute?" the man asked. "I want to buy flowers for my wife."

Glenna took the leash, and the man went into the florist's. She could have walked off with the dog, but what then? She scratched the dog's throat. "Would you come with me?" she asked. Jimmer liked dogs, but she wasn't speaking to Jimmer, and dogs weren't allowed in her building. She'd have to move to a place that accepted pets. Or she could move to Lopez Island. But what about work? The man came out of the shop holding a bunch of calla lilies. "Flowers are the cheapest therapy," he said.

"Nice dog," Glenna said.

She descended toward the lake visible in the vee between the buildings. The hills beyond the water were shrouded in mist. Mercer Island was there, but not there. She paused at a coffee shop where a crowd was gathered—people sitting at tables and standing against walls—watching a man on a tiny stage. She moved into the doorway. The man at a microphone was reciting a poem about Cape Cod in summer— "the boats were like popsicles and the people were spongy muffins." Everyone had such serious expressions that Glenna laughed.

The man stepped down, and a woman moved from the counter to the stage. She was part-Asian—whitish skin, wide-open black eyes, short black hair with bangs, though an elastic tipped the rest of her hair upward like a geyser. She wore a short skirt and a loose pink blouse. Glenna liked the woman's looks and sympathized with her: in her hands she held a trembling piece of paper. She faced the mike. "Tropicbird," she said and looked up at Glenna in the doorway. She read: "What wind or current brings this bird so far off course that for the first time it encounters cold? / Such a feat makes me desire to visit a land I have never seen / where the moon erodes rock and the sun hides what's obvious / But what do I do with the heavy burden of love, gathered over the years / like stones spread out on my floor? / You and I live on this pale island, the sea as our limit, the sky as our aim / though we are without the wings to dream."

The woman glanced again at Glenna and lowered her eyes. There was quick, polite applause.

"Who is that?" Glenna asked the woman beside her.

"Helen somebody," the woman said. "She has the stationery store down the street."

Glenna waited through two more poems, one about machines being the souls of ants and the other about a man carrying a sailboat into his apartment, and, during the second poem, she noticed Helen Somebody slipping out through the back of the coffee shop.

Pen & Ink was two blocks down on the left side, next to an insurance agency. The window display showed a selection of leather-bound notebooks, one opened to a line of calligraphy that said, "Be open to the world." A curtain was pulled across the door, and a sign inside said, BACK AT. . . . The arrow on the clock face pointed to 12:30.

Glenna walked to the lake and watched boats motor in and out of the marina. Two seaplanes took off and one landed. In an hour she was back at the stationery store, right when the woman turned the key in the lock.

"I saw you at the reading," the woman said. "You were worried about me."

Glenna stepped inside. The interior smelled like incense and paper and was narrow from front to back, darker as one moved away from the window. The woman pulled the curtain from the door, and more light flooded in. On the counter were racks of greeting cards, postcards of Seattle, old-fashioned black-and-white pictures of Einstein, Edison, Rita Hayworth, Lincoln, JFK. One card showed a man tossing into the air a piece of paper that turned into a bird, another a woman floating above the clouds, another still of a woman sleeping between the pages of an open book.

"I liked your poem," Glenna said. "Do you always write about birds?"

"Not always, but birds measure the health of the planet."

"Then the news isn't good," Glenna said. "I see mostly pigeons."

"You don't look closely enough," the woman said.

"I don't know much about birds," Glenna said. "They fly. They have feathers."

"On the contrary, you know a lot," the woman said. "You know an owl from a hummingbird, a gull from a heron."

"I suppose so."

"I'm Helen, by the way. Did you want to look around?"

"I'm Glenna," Glenna said. "I was admiring those notebooks in the window."

"Are you a writer?"

"I've never written anything," Glenna said. "Do you own this business?"

"More or less. It was my husband's parents', and I send them a percentage of the profits. They let me live upstairs."

"Where's your husband?"

"In Nairobi with the UN. But he's not my husband anymore. I tell people that so they won't bother me." Helen led the way to the window. "The notebooks range from three dollars to three hundred, depending on the cover, the quality of the binding, and the kind of paper."

Helen took out several, including an expensive-looking

white one, and laid them on the counter. Glenna opened one, then another, and looked through the empty pages.

"Will you carry it in a purse or in a backpack, or maybe in a pocket? Use determines the size you want. If you're new at this, you might not want to make a big investment." Helen brought out several pens—streamlined silver ones, name-brands like Parker and Paper Mate, and a quill calligraphy set. "I have tea brewing in back," she said. "Would you like some?"

"That would be nice," Glenna said.

"Bring the notebooks to look over."

Glenna carried several notebooks of different sizes and followed Helen's steps along the linoleum. Helen's legs were slender, her movements smooth and easy. Along the wall were toner cartridges and ink for printers, and toward the back, where it was darkest, was a vestibule and a kitchen-ette with a half-sized refrigerator, and a bookcase on which a blue teapot was already steaming. Opposite the bookcase was a table with papers spread out on it—pages marked and corrected in red, with arrows, scribbles, and lines crossed out—and beside the table a staircase led upward.

"Are you a teacher?" Glenna asked.

"Those are poems," Helen said. She poured tea into the mugs and handed one to Glenna. "Cream or sugar? It's there on the shelf." Helen turned on the lamp above the table. "So we can have light on the subject."

Glenna opened a package of sugar and emptied it into her mug.

"The problem is they're never finished. The one I read today—does it need more structure? Should it be longer? Is it too ephemeral? Will the reader know what 'the heavy bur-den of love' means? It takes all my strength to go to the café every week, but I go to remind myself I'm writing for other people. Otherwise, I'd languish here all day in the back of the store trying to find the beautiful light."

Glenna blew on the edge of her mug and sipped the tea. "When did your husband leave?" she asked. "I mean, your nonhusband."

"Over a year ago, but it takes time to make adjustments. Are you married?"

Glenna displayed her ringless left hand. "I've never believed that's all there is in life, but I'm not sure what else to think, either. Maybe keeping a journal will help."

"I wrote in a journal for a long time," Helen said, "but it was more like obsessing over what I was already upset about. I started writing poems instead." She stacked the papers on the table. "Sit down, if you'd like to. What do you do? I mean, for money."

"I fix Saabs. It's steady work and good benefits."

"Then you can do whatever you want."

"I could if I had time."

Helen took a spindled cigarette from her shirt pocket and held it up. "Do you want to try some of this?"

Glenna peered at the joint. "Is that marijuana? I've never smoked."

"Does that mean yes or no? To me it's salvation."

"I could do it once."

The door opened at the front of the store, and the chime over the bookcase rang.

"Now they arrive," Helen said, "right when the story is getting good."

"I'll buy this," Glenna said. She held up the white notebook with the gold-leaf border. "I want to spend enough to be sure I'll use it."

"I'll donate a pen," Helen said. "You'll have to come back and try the doobie."

"Anybody home?" the customer called from up front.

"We are," Helen said.

Glenna followed Helen up to the register, where Glenna paid for the notebook and got a free pen.

"I've given notice to Mr. Latimer," Vicky said on her cell. "If you want my apartment, you should call him."

"I'm walking down from Eastlake," Glenna said. "I'll be there in a minute."

"If it ever stopped raining, you'd have a view of Lake Union and the Olympic range."

"Dream on," Glenna said. "But thank you. So you've decided to move?"

"Hawaii has what's known as sunshine," Vicky said. "I see you on the sidewalk. What's in the bag?"

"Nothing you'd care about."

"Do you have beer?" Vicky asked. "I want to celebrate."

"I think one or two."

"I'll meet you at your door."

Vicky was there when Glenna climbed the stairs to the second floor. She pressed the key into the lock, and Vicky pushed the door open. A gray light shone through the windows on the street side and fell on a poster of a Saab Sonett III. The first thing Glenna did was tear the poster from the wall.

"It was my father's poster," Glenna said, "not mine."

"What will you put up there instead?"

"Nothing. Whatever I want. Poems, maybe."

Vicky opened the fridge. "Corona's good. You want one?"

"You know, Vicky, I understand you think it's a celebration, your deciding to move, but I'd like to write in my journal now."

"Is that what's in the bag? Go ahead. What are you going to write?"

"I don't know—why people suffer and move to Hawaii. I need to be alone."

Vicky pried off the bottle cap and took a swig. "So do you want my apartment or not?"

"I might, if Mr. Latimer fixes the elevator," Glenna said. "Take the beer with you."

"Well, good luck with your journal," Vicky said. "I hope you're very happy together."


Glenna worked the early bird on Friday, got off at three, and drove the eighty miles to Anacortes, where she left her car at the terminal and rode the ferry to Lopez Island. She'd brought along her tent and her bike—Lopez was a good place to cycle because it was timberland and farms and had very little traffic. She stood at the nose of the ferry and watched the gulls and dark birds on the water. The sky was lead, and the islands rose from the sea and mist like behemoth whales.

Lopez was fifteen miles long, four wide, and her property was inland, almost in the center of the island. She had two acres of hemlocks and pines bordered by roads on two sides and pastureland on the other two. Across the swale, on a rise, was a neighbor's farmhouse and outbuildings. She pitched her tent at the edge of the field, dug a fire pit, and scavenged tinder and wood from the forest. She'd brought wurst, salmon, salad fixings, two beers, an air mattress, a sleeping bag, and her iPhone. What else did she need? She took out her white notebook with the gold border.

She'd already written a few things about the man running backward, the fake priest, the painter, and the guitar player, though she couldn't phrase things as she thought them. Her vocabulary was pretty good from reading, but she couldn't translate her feelings. She wanted to write more about colors, weather, moods, and movements, but she figured it was a process, what she had to learn. That evening she wrote of the clouds racing across the pasture, the weak sun, the whines and croaks of crows, the clearing sky, and the stealth of darkness coming down over her land.

Glenna struck a match, and, after a few tries, the pine needles caught, and then the twigs and branches arranged like a tepee, and, when these burned to coals, she laid in a piece of salmon wrapped in foil. She drank the two beers. The sky, she thought, was already opening to tomorrow. When had she last seen the moon lift up in the sky and sail through dispersing clouds?

In the morning the sun slid over the meadow and lit up the dew in the grass and the top of the fog that hung in the swale. She dressed in the open and rode her bike to Shark Reef, a mile away. She saw crows, gulls, and small birds flying across the road. At the trailhead she locked her bike in the rack and walked through the woodland. Moss hung from the trees, and the high canopy was slitted with starlike spaces where the sun shone through. Even in the middle of the forest there were birds—a wren, a thrush with spots on its breast, a big woodpecker.

Near the coast, the trees diminished, and a broader light spread through the woodland. The shoreline was rocky, and directly across the water, maybe a mile, was San Juan Island. To the southwest, on the other side of the Strait of Juan de Fuca, were the Olympics, with snow still on the peaks. A couple of nearby houses were perched over the water, but the trail led the other way to an overlook, where a tidal bore coursed between the shore and the outlying rocks. Seals lounged on the boulders, and gulls roosted beside them. Picking its way along the edge of the rocks was a black bird with an orange bill, and, in the bore, a few colorful sea ducks rode the current.

Glenna zipped her windbreaker, put her hand in her pockets, and found her phone. Helen's number was easy enough to find, and she punched it in and listened to it ring.

"Pen and Ink," Helen said.

"I have a bird question," Glenna said.

"Glenna? I'm glad you called."

"I'm on Lopez Island, and I'm looking at a black bird with an orange bill. It's on a rock near the shore."

"Crow-sized?"

"It's not a crow."

"Black Oystercatcher," Helen said. "It's a funny name because oysters don't need to be caught, but its bill is sturdy enough to open the shells."

"There's a pretty duck, too. It's pale blue and rusty and white."

"That's a Harlequin male," Helen said. "They live along the shore and in rivers."

"I've been to this place before," Glenna said, "and I've probably seen these birds, but I never noticed them. If you were here, I'd learn the names."

Helen paused on the line. "Is there another question here?"

"On the other hand, without names, the birds are more mysterious," Glenna said. "I guess it's a long drive for you to get up here. There's a seaplane from Lake Union to Fisherman Bay . . ."

"I can't now," Helen said. "Will you call me another time?"

On Monday Glenna departed from her usual routine and bought a medium French roast with cream and a glazed doughnut at Sal's Espresso on Queen Anne Avenue and drove to work on back streets. She arrived at Olson's at 7:50 and went directly to the locker room and put on her coveralls. She was looking in the mirror, getting her frizz-mop into a bandanna and under her cap, when Geoff came in.

"Hey, beautiful," he said. "Do you see what I see?"

"Be glad you don't have hair like this," Glenna said.

Geoff put his satchel on the bench and unbuttoned his shirt. "You look different," he said. "You must have got laid."

"Grow up, Geoff," Glenna said. "Get some help."

"I want it from you," he said. He unzipped his pants and pulled out his penis. "You could have this anytime you want."

Glenna jammed her hair under the cap and bolted to the door.

"Don't be in such a hurry," Geoff said. "You haven't tried it yet."

Glenna barged into the garage where Alvin had pulled a 900 into Glenna's work bay. Randy was walking across the floor with the paperwork. "The Jamesons are driving to California this afternoon," Randy said. "What do you think, little woman? Can you get this out by . . . ?" Randy paused. "What's wrong?"

"Geoff is wrong." Glenna picked up a three-foot pry bar from her work bench. "I'll be back in a minute."

"Is there trouble?"

"I can manage. But when I finish, Geoff may need medical assistance."

"Whoa down, Gleena," Randy said. "Hold on there."

She strode toward the locker room, Randy and Alvin in pursuit. LaTrell, whose bay was nearest, was bent over into an engine with the hood open, but he straightened up and wiped grease from his hands. "Is there going to be an event?" he asked.

Glenna threw open the locker-room door. Geoff was sitting on the bench, still half naked. "Change your mind?" he asked.

"Yes," Glenna said. She whammed the pry bar on the bench.

Geoff jumped up. "Jesus Christ, darling, don't take things so personal."

Glenna swung the pry bar into the row of metal lockers and dented a couple of them. Randy and Alvin stepped into the room, then LaTrell and Larry. "Either he goes or I do," Glenna said.

"The bitch is hysterical," Geoff said. "I didn't do anything."

"Gleena, let's you and me go to my office," Randy said. "And, Geoff, put on some clothes. Take the day off."

Glenna snapped the bar on the bench again. "He does tune-ups and oil changes because he's incompetent at everything else," Glenna said. "He only works here because his uncle's named Olson." She turned toward Randy. "If this asshole stays, I'm not ever coming into this fucking locker room again or fixing another Saab. You choose, Randy. Right now."

"I'll talk to Olson," Randy said.

"That's a waffle," Glenna said, "but it's a choice." She pounded on the bench another time and tossed the pry bar into the light fixture, which shattered and rained down glass.

For the next few days Glenna took random buses that came from either direction along Eastlake Avenue. If she went downtown, she transferred to any bus, and one day she ended up at SeaTac, where she watched planes take off and land, toured the news shops and gift stores and fast-food nooks. She sat for a while and wrote in her journal. Another day she found herself in a Somali neighborhood and standing in a strip mall on Highway 99 not far from where she grew up. She ate lamb and hummus at a restaurant whose name she couldn't read. Once, at the university, she wandered the halls, the student center, and the library.

On a Friday she helped Vicky carry her possessions—mostly clothes, dishes, and pans—from her apartment down to a U-Haul, which Vicky was going to unload at her parents' house. Mr. Latimer had agreed to her early departure because Vicky was forfeiting her deposit, and another renter, not Glenna, had signed on for an increased monthly rent. Goodbye was goodbye, and Vicky was gone to Hawaii.

The following Wednesday at 11:30 a.m., Glenna stood across the street from the coffee shop that hosted Poetry Before Noon. It was gray: the clouds were breaking up or coalescing, but Glenna couldn't tell which. Helen hadn't shown up yet, but Glenna recognized some of the people from two weeks before. She preferred to stay distant—there was nothing worse than bad poetry—but she watched from across the street while a couple of people read. A little before noon, Helen came up the sidewalk. Her stride was graceful, but she looked preoccupied—she glanced at a sheet of paper, up at the clouds, down again. Glenna crossed the street.

"Hello," Glenna said. "You have a new poem."

"I wished you'd be here," Helen said, "but I know you work."

"I quit my job," Glenna said. "I've been exploring."

"So have I," Helen said and held up the page with words on it.

They edged into the crowded doorway of the coffee shop and listened to a poem about dumpsters and another about the war in Tibet. "Do you have to sign in?" Glenna asked.

"I could read to you instead," Helen said. "That would be the same to me, even better."

"I'd like that. Where?"

"Let's go to the park, or there's a schoolyard a couple of blocks from here."

They passed several apartment buildings, a shoe store, a restaurant called Luigi's. Glenna explained about quitting her job, her bus trips, her journal writing. Down a block and over two was an elementary school with a fenced-in playground with benches beyond the perimeter fence so parents could watch their children.

"How's this?" Helen said. "It's open but private. We won't be here long."

They sat on a bench near the gate and for a few moments watched gulls skim over the low buildings and across the gray sky.

"What's your poem about?" Glenna asked.

"I don't know what it's about," Helen said. "I only wrote it." She lifted the paper, then closed her eyes. "The Long Valley," she said.

"I don't think anymore things will be the same / We've moved the furniture, eaten our meals, argued in the night. / The tight-lipped distance that defined for you what was and was not is as much a mirage as love. / The long valley threaded with a river of glacial silt—rain blows in invisible birds. / The unseen mountains are home to me now. / Neither of us sustained the least of our promises, but my longing is still around me in the air."

They sat a while, and Glenna let the words sink down. She felt from Helen's longing her own taking shape, solace composed of time and weather and earth and air. "We all have shortcomings," Helen said. "There's no use trying to escape."

"I don't know whether I'm ready," Glenna said.

"How can you find out? There's so much to learn, don't you think?"

The sun drifted in and out of the clouds, the gulls appeared and disappeared, and the light moved over the island, which was, in the mist, neither land nor sky. Then children emerged from a half dozen doors, shouting and running out.

Helen stood up, and Glenna did, too, and Helen took her arm.

# MY CRAZY FATHER

Salvation is the right to disappear for good.
*Albert Camus*

THE PAINTING CLASS STARTED SATURDAY morning at ten and lasted until Gabriella decided she'd had enough. Gaby Schiavoni was my father's friend from the past, not a lover, with whom he stayed when he visited my half-sisters, Ottie, who was ten, and Sal, who was seven. I'd graduated from Haverford the previous June and wanted to travel in Asia, but was saddled with student loans. My parents weren't about to let me escape earning a living (or paying off my debt), so I'd taken the straw my stepmother Charlotte waved at me—she'd get me to Berkeley if I'd au pair for Ottie and Sal. Charlotte and I had always got along—women stuff, closer to the same age, etc.—and California was closer to Asia and coincided with my half-baked, half-broiled idea to get a corporation to send me abroad.

There were five students in Gaby's art class, and they came to her living quarters in the warehouse co-op at the corner of 45th and Horton, not far from the 80, which ran beside Oakland Bay. Mr. Leyritz had left for a funeral in San Rafael, and so that left DeSean, the young black dude in a beret; Mrs. Murphy in a print dress—she was seventy-three; a fortyish investment banker named Gordon, who was thinking of changing careers; and Ottie. Gaby said I could participate at no charge, but I preferred to keep my lack of talent a secret.

Gaby's studio was in the corner of the building and had hundreds of tiny windows along both intersecting streets. A few of the windows were broken and some had cardboard taped in them, but they provided good light, even on a gray day in October when it was about to rain. Gaby prebirthed my father by fifteen years. She was five feet tall, had black hair and black eyebrows, and was one hundred and twenty pounds of anguish. She worried because her paintings didn't sell; she fretted because she had no man in her bed, or woman, if she wanted that. She never knew how she'd pay her rent. She was too poor to do anything about her neuroses, so it was The Vicious Cycle.

It was evident Gaby had not much of a social life—one sofa, a twenty-year-old TV, and bookcases in which she stored her dozens of sketch books. Several tables, made of wooden doors thrown across sawhorses, held her brushes, papers, paints, and unpaid bills. Her kitchen was built into one corner; her bathroom was four-by-four, shower included, and had a blanket pulled across the door. The light-switch plate was an image of Michelangelo's *David*, with David's penis as the on-and-off. She also had a lava lamp and an aquarium with tetras and guppies. Anyone who got her entertainment from a lava lamp and a fish tank was socially zip.

My father had known her as a fac brat in Santa Cruz, when he was a grad student and still married to *my* mother, not Ottie and Sal's. She was painting even then, and now her paintings covered most of the wall space and leaned four deep under the windows and in the entry hallway. She reinterpreted classical themes for the modern world—the Seven Deadly Sins were women in a ladies' room lounge; a guest at a party, who'd put her fur coat on the bed, snooped into the hostess's jewelry box and released Pandora's ills into the world; ethereal muses wafted around the head of an artist at her computer, the artist dressed in Gaby's art uniform—green pants, red-and-white striped blouse, and black cap. The work was well executed, but done in caricatures no one wanted to display in a house with antique furniture, crystal, and Oriental rugs. She was working right then on an enormous canvas of Cleopatra in front of a Roman frieze, Marc Antony waiting in a stretch limo for Cleo to decide what to wear.

The class started with a few charcoal exercises on plain paper—big circles, cylinders, pyramids—and then went through a series of breathing techniques pioneered by Henri Vivante, the French stylist. I was reading a novel set in Bangladesh, waiting for my father and Sal, because Sal and I were going to spend the morning in San Francisco. He'd taken Sal to get her coffee at Peet's.

After the breathing, the students either worked on their own projects or painted the still life Gaby had arranged—a straw hat, a vase with two slender twigs of rose hips, and a pair of red ballet slippers. The week before, DeSean had begun a painting of two jazzsters dancing with their arms around each other, and though the colors were good, something was wrong with the legs (too long) and arms (too short). Mrs. Murphy was doing a self-portrait, though the woman in the painting didn't look anything like her. "Oh, shit," she kept saying, and she tugged at the bra strap visible on her shoulder. Ottie and Gordon were doing the still life; Ottie's was a tad better.

"So you knew my father in Santa Cruz?" I asked Gaby, when she passed me after counseling DeSean.

"My mother was an art professor," Gaby said, "and now and then your father came into the student gallery where I worked. He was pretty unhappy."

"My mother's specialty is creating unhappiness."

"She had money," Gaby said, "and because of that, he couldn't make his own decisions."

"Charlotte was a decision," I said. "So were Ottie and Sal, though he might deny that."

"There are worse things than children," Gaby said. "Of course, he wasn't happy with Charlotte, either. The only person your father gets along with is Milo. I'm surprised he didn't bring her along."

"A dog is not a person," I said.

"You know what I mean."

I loved my father, really I did, but his life was random events. I never knew what woman he was with or why. He had a PhD in history, but in real life he was a repairman — the Stone Trust, Thomas Stone, proprietor. He fixed disposals, washing machines, roof leaks, computers and printers — everything except cars (though he could have, but he didn't want to trek to parts stores). Anyone within thirty miles of Placitas, New Mexico, knew him and his yellow Lab. He'd been married first to Hedda (three years), then to my mother (ten years, two children), then to Charlotte (five, two more). His priorities were to support Ottie and Sal, pay for his mortgage, buy Milo treats, and chase birds. Whatever money was left, he gave to my brother Pax and me, but trickle-down never worked. I admit he wrote Pax and me snail-mail letters every week, which was an indication of something, maybe love, but still. . . .

The buzzer rang, and I let my father and Sal in. Sal carried a backpack and a to-go from Peet's, and my father his camera. "We got held up by a knife-wielding crazy man," Sal said. "He stole Daddy's time."

"And my money," my father said. "You won't have an inheritance."

"Did you guys know Dad wants to be a rock star?" Sal asked.

"You're fifty-three, Daddy," Ottie said. "There's already Steven Tyler and Mick Jagger. And we're not 'guys.'"

"He can aspire to new ideas," Gaby said, "and he has an excellent voice."

"La," my father sang. "La la la." He stopped and grinned, the madman genius. "I aspire to long hair," he said. He snapped several pictures of Gaby up on her stepladder, painting a blue patch in the far right corner of the sky.

Sal wandered over to the table where Ottie was confronting the red slippers. "Can I do that?" she asked.

"'May I,'" Ottie said.

"You may," my father said, "if it's all right with Gaby."

"You're late," I said. "I thought Sal and I were going into the city to explore the Japanese Gardens."

But I knew my own desires and expectations were irrelevant. What Sal wanted to happen happened. She had a broad face and glasses, and had a sweet, helpless look that made people cater to her whims, including my father and Gaby. In due deference, Gaby got Sal's watercolors ready, while Sal wandered around the studio looking at the fish, the collection of ceramic giraffes, the miniature fruits spread around in the bookcases.

Of course she found the bathroom light switch. "Why is he naked?" she asked.

"That's David," my father said. "He was a curveballer for the Cubs."

"David slew Goliath," Ottie said. "Everyone knows that."

"Slew," my father said, "what kind of word is that?"

"The watercolors are here, Sal," Gaby said. "Anytime you're ready."

My father distracted Sal by pointing to a folk artist's depiction of the Virgin Mary done on tin. "Look at this," he said. "In the old days, because the church had all the money, artists had to make pictures of Jesus and Mary and the angels."

"I like angels," Sal said.

"So do I," my father said, "but would you rely on one to transport your soul?"

"What are the options?" Sal asked.

The doorbell chimed "Für Elise," and Gaby looked up from showing Gordon the difference between daubing and stroking. "Can someone get that?" she said. "Mr. Leyritz said he might come back."

Sal ran down the hallway, stuffed on either side with paintings, and opened the door.

"Oh, are you in Gaby's class?" said a woman in a high-pitched, breathless voice.

"I'm a visitor," Sal said. "Who are you?"

"Come in, Alice," Gaby called.

Alice of the high-pitched, breathless voice came around the corner into the kitchen. In college I'd seen every sort of tattoo, studded body part, and color of hair, but I'd never seen anyone like Alice. Alice was white. Not her skin—she wasn't an albino, though she was pale—but her hair was white, her eyebrows were white, her teeth were white. She wore white lipstick, a long-sleeved white shirt, baggy white pants, white sneakers.

"I need someone to help me move Lyndon," she said. "I thought a couple of your students could use a break."

"Where are you moving him?" Gaby asked.

"To Carmel. My truck is out back."

"Who's Lyndon?" Ottie asked.

"He's a sculpture," Alice said. "Very heavy."

I imagined the *Pietà*, the *David*, of course, the slaves emerging from rock.

My father put down the tin Virgin Mary. "I'll help."

DeSean and Gordon felt obliged to join in, and Ottie crumpled her drawing. "I hate this," she said. "I'm coming."

"So am I," Sal said.

I stirred myself from lethargy.

The warehouse Gaby lived in was divided by hallways with floors of burnished cement. The walls were decorated with Native American totems, peace symbols, and directional arrows to various artists' studios. Alice led us down one hallway, then another, made a left, and stopped in front of— guess—a white door, into which she fitted a key.

Her space was smaller than Gaby's, but open from floor-to-ceiling, and light plummeted down from a half dozen sky-lights thirty feet above to a forest of white marble or bronze trees—pines, elms, bonzais, cedars, aspens. Name it, there was a tree. Linden, I understood, was a tree, not a person.

"He's this one," Alice said, pointing to a leafy sculpture in the middle of the forest.

It took five of us to clear a space and two jacks to hoist Linden onto a rolling cart and to schlep him through the hallways to the back door. Alice's white Tacoma was parked there with the tailgate already down. The problem was how to get Linden up into the bed. The jacks had limited range, but they got Linden up a few feet. Alice and Ottie climbed into the truck bed and steadied the leaves, while Sal held the branches away from the tailgate, and the rest of us heaved from the bottom. With our effort, Linden cleared the tailgate, and my father and Alice wrestled him to the center, where they tied the trunk to the grommets in each corner.

As they did this, it began to rain, and the rest of us retreated under the awning. Water cascaded from the roof, and puddles formed in the parking lot. DeSean and Gordon wanted to go back to their lesson, so Ottie and Sal and I went back, too. There was no reason to watch them tie knots in the rain.

I got a drink of juice, and Ottie went to the bathroom, but Sal made a beeline for the painting table. She climbed up on a stool, and, kneeling, mixed water and paint. In five minutes she did the straw hat, the rose hips, and the red ballet slippers, and her rendition was pretty good, an accident, maybe, but carefree and natural.

My father came in twenty minutes later. Mrs. Murphy was in tears about her self-portrait. I was listening to Lester Bear on my headset, and Ottie was reading Harry Potter. Sal watched one of Gaby's lava lamps bubble up a big red blob.

That evening my father roasted two chickens, mashed ten potatoes with garlic, and made a salad of red-leaf lettuce, fauxmatoes (as he called those engineered red things), avocados, and orange peppers. Four other people came from the co-op—two painters, a print artist who made his own paper, and a composer of atonal music. Alice All-White was in Carmel. The adults, of whom I considered myself one, drank Chardonnay, which my father also provided.

The talk was about how little money was available for art in a country where 1 percent of the people controlled 95 percent of the wealth, what Emeryville would become if BART built a new station on San Pablo, and the price of gasoline, which was heading up from four dollars a gallon. Once, in response to a rhetorical question, my father expounded like an alchemist about how computers worked. "They're like novels," he said, "but a computer program has to be absolutely 100 percent perfect or it won't run, while in a novel . . ." He wrote something down and passed it around—"u cn undrstd sntnces evn w/o pnctutn and w/ mny lttrs mssng."

After everyone else had gone, Gaby invited us to stay the night—she had a futon and blankets—instead of going back to Charlotte's. "It'll be like camping indoors," she said.

"Do you have marshmallows?" Sal asked.

"Home is twenty minutes away," I said. "I want a bed."

I lost the vote but as compensation was awarded the hide-a-bed. My father horsed a futon out from behind a few paintings and brought in the air mattress he kept in his Jeep. There was a weird period of settling down, because the light from the street shone through all those tiny windows and the fish tank gave off a blue glow. Gaby told us about a hummingbird that had come through a broken window once and had flown around her studio. She'd finally caught it in a butterfly net she'd borrowed from Alice. My father sang "Summertime" and "All La Glory" in a sweet tenor—really, he could sing—and the girls went to sleep. Gaby climbed to her loft, and my father read a while in the kitchen. But I stayed awake, my mind scattering from here to there like the car headlights across the ceiling. My life was going nowhere fast, but what could I do with Chinese and Mandarin? Translation, maybe. I could offer to work a month at a corporation gratis to see whether I fit in, or foreign embassies might have suggestions. I was thinking all this when my father got up from his chair and crept to Gaby's front door.

The next morning, Sunday, my father commandeered us to go to Point Reyes to look for birds. His Jeep wasn't big enough, so we took Gabriella's Artmobile, a four-door blue Mercury, 1992, painted in orange swirls and with the message "NEED ART?" Her phone number was stenciled in yellow on both sides. We chugged across the Oakland Bay Bridge, passed through the Presidio, and crossed the Golden Gate Bridge to Marin County. It was slow going through the towns, but toward the coast the traffic eased. The farms were lush green, and the air smelled of the sea. Sal rattled on about the cows and horses, and even Ottie put her book down to look out the window at the eucalyptus trees and the sea far away.

"This is what we need," Gaby said. "This is real life."

"What else is there?" Sal asked.

"Art," Gaby said, "but art doesn't pay."

"Neither does being a middle child," Sal said.

"You aren't a middle child," said Ottie.

"I will be if Mom gets pregnant."

"She won't," I said. "She's learned her lesson from you two."

The beach was breezy, but we had brought windbreakers and fleece jackets. We took off our shoes at the edge of the dunes, and my father dared us to put a toe in the cold water, but no one had the courage. He chased down Sal, lifted her into the air, and threatened to throw her into the surf, but of course he didn't, and Sal ran away shrieking. Ottie explored the tideline for shells and dead fish, while Gaby caught up with me, carrying the picnic basket and a blanket. "Why do people bring blankets to the beach?" I asked.

"Rituals are important," Gaby said.

"This family has no rituals."

"Nonsense, your father sang you songs last night. You said he wrote you letters every week."

I looked over at my father, who was gazing seaward. He had an exhausted, sleepless look on his face, and I imagined he was searching for seabirds or wondering how far out he could swim before he drowned. Or he was thinking of Alice All-White.

That my father had sneaked out the night before to meet Alice All-White (who else?) didn't shock me so much as his secrecy about it. I mean, we knew he drove a dented, rusty Jeep with dog hairs and bacterial experiments, and he carried around a jumble of pry bars, come-alongs, dollies, and assorted pieces of metal. His fingernails were chewed to the nubbins, he shaved erratically and got a haircut every two years. He and Milo hiked together in the Sandias or in the arroyo behind his house, but he revealed nothing about what he saw or discovered or felt. He was witty. We expected him to do crazy things so why did he have to be silent?

"Let him alone," Gaby said. "He's figuring out who he is."

"He has four children," I said. "It's about time."

In my father's defense, and by comparison, my own clothes came from thrift stores or trades with college friends, and I'd removed a nose stud I got too old to wear. My hair was short so it wasn't trouble in the morning, and I wore only a tinge of eyeshadow and lipstick—no disguise. I read novels by young women like Arundati Roy and Jhumpa Lahiri and feared abandonment, so I wanted to go to Asia to feel I was abandoning someone else. That was my theory.

I spread out the blanket and rummaged through the picnic basket for a Diet Coke. Sal was walking back toward us, and Ottie approached my father with a piece of driftwood worn smooth by the sea. "It's an albatross," she said.

"Or a boomerang," he said.

"You can take it to Milo."

"I'd like to," my father said, "but Milo's dead."

Ottie stared at my father. "Milo died?"

"Who died?" Sal asked, coming up.

"Why didn't you tell us?"

My father looked back toward the water. "I think I'll walk up to that stream," he said. "Birds like fresh water. I saw a godwit up there." He handed Ottie the piece of driftwood and walked away.

We were dumbfounded. No one knew what to say, except Sal. "Dad has had Milo longer than he's had us," she said. "I'll bet he misses her."

We turned toward Gaby. "You're father's going to be a while," she said. "We should eat."

The girls sat down on the blanket, and I unwrapped a turkey sandwich and gave each of them half. There were cheese slices, machine-made carrots, hard-boiled eggs, and cans of mango and apricot juice. Ottie and Sal nestled in beside me out of the wind, and I felt useful. We played Guess, and we guessed how far it was to Hawaii, the life span of the sea lions whose heads popped up in the swells, the number of grains of sand on the beach. But we were aware of my father, who was walking farther and farther away in the sea mist.

Monday my father took Ottie and Sal to school, and I had two interviews in the city, one with headhunters from Beijing and another at Bank of America. The Beijing entourage—four men—wanted an economics expert, preferably a man, but the bank was more positive. The woman there suggested I make foreign contacts working stateside. "English is the international language of business," she said. "Mandarin is good PR, but you need experience."

"Catch-22," I said. "I need experience, but you won't hire me because I haven't got any."

"You have ambition," the woman said. "I'll write up the interview, and we can see where we go from there."

I hadn't expected immediate glory, but I hadn't anticipated rejection, either, and, riding the BART, I wasn't in a good mood. Charlotte was seeing a client in Walnut Creek, and I had to pick up the girls, so I got off in North Berkeley and took a bus down University.

The first thing Sal said was, "Where's our ride?"

"No ride," I said. "We're hiking home."

"You mean *walk*?" Sal asked. "Where's Daddy?"

"Daddy's not here," I said. "You have to deal with me."

"Can we go for coffee?"

"No coffee," I said.

We walked twenty blocks, and Sal looked in every dress shop and tattoo parlor, every hair salon and bank, and Ottie didn't complain because she was reading like a zombie. We made one stop for frozen yogurt. At home I forbade the girls computer games, email, and cell phones until they finished their homework.

I liked Charlotte, but she was a lousy housekeeper, and I hadn't signed on for being the maid. There were dishes from a dinner party the previous Friday, two breakfast plates (hmmm) with dried eggs on them, magazines and dirty clothes scattered in the family room, and a plant that had been tipped over on the rug. Outside in the backyard were broken wind chimes, a croquet mallet and three wickets, garden tools, and several sodden books. A hammock dangled from one hook on the overgrown lawn.

As a token gesture I cleaned up the kitchen, but at five I was meeting a college acquaintance Edison for a beer, and at six my father was picking up the girls to meet Gaby and me at a Thai restaurant on College Street. I got Ottie and Sal to take early baths, and they both wanted to put on dresses as a surprise.

"Daddy's a slob," Ottie said, "and we want to express our sympathy for Milo."

"To be a slob you have to work at it more than he does," I said. "I'd say he was casual."

"He'll still be surprised," Sal said.

"Can you two get through an hour by yourselves?" I asked.

"I can," Ottie said, "because I know how to read. I don't know about Sal."

Edison had the personality of a self-defrosting refrigerator, but he'd been in one of my Mandarin classes and knew someone in Fresno who imported carvings and rugs from Hong Kong. But all he could talk about was tennis—the Asian women were improving, Julia Goerges was the prettiest player, and serve-and-volley was going the way of the wooden racquet. He asked me to a movie on Saturday, but I declined and was glad when he dropped me off at the restaurant.

Sabuy Sabuy was at the weird-angle intersection of College and Broadway across the street from the art institute. It had six or seven tables indoors and about as many on a patio separated from the street noise by a vertical stick fence. It

was a mild evening, so I ordered a Tsingtao and sat outside
and read the menu.

Gaby arrived a few minutes later, wearing a red T-shirt
over a pair of shorts, not a good combination. "Sorry I'm
late," she said. "Where is everyone?"

"You know Dad."

"I was going to ride over with him. I thought he'd come
back to my place for a shower."

"How's the painting coming?" I asked.

"Never-ending. If I had love or money, art would be easier."

"At least you have work you care about."

My cell phone did its dance, and Charlotte's number appeared. "Daddy hasn't come," Ottie said. "Sal's crying. What
should we do? I called his cell, and he didn't answer."

"And your mother isn't there?"

"I called her, but she's not coming back till nine."

"We can pick them up," Gaby said. "It's not that far down
College."

"Mom said this has happened before," Ottie said. "Daddy's disappeared."

My father didn't show up for dinner that night, nor did he
return to Gaby's or appear the next morning when he was
supposed to take the girls to school. Apparently Charlotte
had experienced my father's unexplained absences when
they were married. "I used to think he'd had a heart attack
or was in an accident, and the first few times I called hospitals and the police. They knew nothing. After a week or
so, he materialized out of thin air, without an explanation or
excuse. One time he said he'd wanted to be alone for a while.
'Fine,' I said. 'Be alone.' And we got divorced.'"

"Ouch," I said. "But I don't blame you."

"The rest of us have to go on with our lives," Charlotte said.

She dropped the girls off at school, and I went to Peet's for a latté and emailed Edison's importer friend in Fresno about his business plans. I called Bank of America (not home) and my mother in Boca Raton, who bragged about her new beau, Laurentius, and what a good golfer he was. I could tell she'd been drinking, though in Florida it was only two in the afternoon.

After that, I drove to Gaby's co-op, followed a delivery-man inside, and knocked on Alice All-White's door. I was surprised when I heard her high-pitched, breathless voice on the other side. "I'm working," she said. "Who is it?"

"Erin Stone," I said. "I'm looking for my father. I thought he might be with you."

The door cracked open, and Alice's white hair and white eyebrows appeared in the vertical space. "He's not with me."

"Would you know where he is?"

Alice opened the door to four inches. She had on white clothes and white lipstick, and her hands and face were covered in white dust. "He came here," she said. "I'll tell you that. I couldn't turn him away. I thought he was in trouble."

"When was this?"

"And I like your father. He asks questions and listens to answers, and he never once asked me about my fetish for white."

"White is weird," I said.

"I have to live with myself," she said.

She left the door and dusted chips and flakes from her white apron. I pushed the door open.

"He was here yesterday and said he had something to

tell me. I met him for coffee in the lounge. It would be hard to reconstruct the conversation. He was tired. There were long silences. I was barely awake, because the night before we'd stayed up late. He told me about going to Point Reyes with all of you, and he gestured a lot with his hands. I got as much from his expressions as I did from his words." She paused and looked over. "Why me? Am I the seatmate on the airplane?"

"You thought he was troubled?"

"He put forward an idea like 'How should one live?' and then retreated from it — 'What does it matter how one lives?' He asked me to visit him in New Mexico, then he said, 'No, you wouldn't do that.' He explained about the light and shadows outside his back door, how, sometimes at evening the light was so beautiful he felt it was running in his blood. 'I have nowhere to put the light,' he said, 'and then it's gone.'"

"Did he say anything about his dog?"

"He didn't mention a dog. He didn't tell me anything about his plans."

"No date to a movie? No concert in the city? I don't mean to be cynical."

"No," Alice said. "Nothing. I haven't seen him again."

"Thanks," I said. "I appreciate your time."

"We have so little of it in this world," Alice said. "That's what your father was saying."

I backed out into the hallway and called my father's cell again. He didn't answer, so I went over to Gaby's. Her door was open, and she was up on her stepladder painting Roman numerals on the frieze with such concentration I thought she didn't hear me come in, but she finished the numeral C and looked down at me. "What have you found out?" she asked.

"Alice saw him yesterday," I said, "but it's been over twenty-four hours."

"He'll come back," Gaby said. "His clothes are here. Do you want to call the police? You can use my phone."

"Charlotte said not to bother."

But I dialed a few numbers. I was put on hold, I got recordings, I got static. The people I talked to didn't know anything. Around Berkeley there were a lot of hospitals and towns with their own police departments. He could have gone into any bar, or into the city, or driven north across the San Rafael Bridge. I wasted an hour and gave up. "I have to fetch Ottie and Sal from school," I said.

"If you're at loose ends, bring the girls here," Gaby said. "Ottie is a serious sweetheart, and that Sal, she has talent."

"Thanks for being his friend."

"I'm your friend, too," Gaby said. "Get a job and stick around."


I turned off University onto Sixth, but there was no place to park, so I left Charlotte's Prism in a church lot three blocks away and walked back. The leaves were turning, maybe from acid rain, and they littered the sidewalk with a grimy brown. What should I tell the girls about their father? When people were sad, they did strange things, or he couldn't help wanting to be by himself? It wasn't their fault. That was the main message to get across.

Ottie was at the school gate, but she didn't know where Sal was. "We were supposed to meet at the fountain," Ottie said, "but she's unreliable."

"Like father, like daughter," I said. "We're the exceptions."

The guard assured us Sal hadn't gone out, and we asked

around in the playground. A few kids had seen her but didn't know where she'd gone. We asked Ms. Jenkins, Sal's third-grade teacher, who'd been worried about her, too. "She wasn't herself all day," Ms. Jenkins said. "I asked what was wrong, but she wouldn't talk about it. Something was going on."

"Family issues," I said.

We checked in the closets, the girls' room, the gym. I asked whether there was an art room, and Ottie led me to a room above the library, and, sure enough, we found Sal sketching on a big pad clamped to an easel. Light shone in from an angled bank of windows.

"You were supposed to meet me at the fountain," Ottie said.

"I wanted to draw," Sal said.

"There are promises and *rules*," Ottie said. "You can draw at home."

"I like it here. It's a studio like Alice's."

She was drawing trees—big ones, little ones, ones with leaves and ones without. One tree looked like Linden—a trunk, tapered limbs, smaller branches and twigs, imperfect leaves, but, for the size of the tree, evenly proportioned. "I thought about trees all day," Sal said. "Trees make oxygen, which is what we breathe."

"We have to go," Ottie said. "The man at the gate is waiting."

"Okay," she said, and she put down her pencil. "But I want to take this drawing for Daddy."

Gaby's neighborhood was mostly warehouses, though a giant medical research facility was expanding around the co-op, and there was new construction, dust and noise. The old

PacTel building, now a furniture showcase, had noble sculptures along the skyline. We turned at 42nd Street, and right away I saw my father's truck parked at the curb in front of Gaby's co-op.

When we got closer, we saw him sitting on the front stoop, looking up at the clouds, though who knows what he was seeing? He was unshaven, and his T-shirt with a bird on it was stained with dirt and grass. He was looking at pictures on his camera.

"Daddy!" Sal said, and she clicked open the door.

"Wait till we stop," Ottie said.

I slid in behind his truck, and Sal scrambled out of the car in a flurry of arms and legs. My father stood up and caught her in her headlong dash. "Where *were* you?" she asked. "We were worried."

"I went after a bird," he said.

Ottie and I got out more slowly. "Where were you, really?" Ottie asked.

"I heard a Baikal Teal was in Oregon," he said. "It's a rare and beautiful duck. So I drove up there."

"Ottie was mad," Sal said. "How did you know this duck was wherever Oregon is?"

My father put Sal back down on the sidewalk, and there was a long silence. His shoulders slumped forward. Then he looked up with tears in his eyes. "No," he said, "I didn't drive to Oregon." He took a breath. "I was there the other night to pick you up for dinner. Ottie was on the porch reading, all dressed up, you looked beautiful, and Sal was in the yard twirling around, and her dress was flying up. I cruised past, and you didn't see me. I thought what if I weren't here? What if I were dead?"

"But you aren't dead," Ottie said.

"I wondered how you'd get along, what would happen to you? Do you understand? I wanted to know that after I'm gone, you'll be all right."

"We wouldn't be," Sal said.

"But here you are safe and sound. You didn't need me. Your mother and Erin watched out for you."

Right then Alice came to the door. I guess my father had buzzed her to let him in, and she was surprised to see all of us scattered there on the sidewalk. "Oh," she said, "the happy family."

"I painted your tree," Sal said. "Do you want to see?"

Sal didn't wait for an answer, but ran to the car and got it.

Okay. The tree was good. Better than ordinary, especially for a seven-year-old who drank coffee. Brilliant, maybe. I knew that. Ottie knew that, which was why she frowned when Sal showed the tree to Alice and our father.

"It's beautiful," Alice said in her squeaky high voice. "It's extraordinary."

"Great," my father said. "I like it."

"We came to see Gaby," Ottie said.

"Gaby isn't here," my father said. "I rang her first. I need a shower."

"I have a key to Gaby's," Alice said.

I stepped forward. "Does this have to do with Milo?" I asked.

My father looked at me as if I'd slapped him.

"Milo," I said. "You wonder how Ottie and Sal will get along without you. You must wonder how you'll get along without Milo. Do you think we don't know how lonely you are?"

There was a silence that lasted too long, and then my father did something I'd never seen him do, never imagined of him—he got onto his knees on the sidewalk and he cried.

I was stunned. Alice All-White stepped back. Ottie went over and put her head on his shoulder. Sal touched him on his head, and so did I.

My father wanted to drive to César Chávez Park to watch the sunset. We all went, Gaby, too, and with our encouragement, even Alice. We piled into the Artmobile, and Gaby drove side streets to University, turned left, and crossed the interstate. The park was mostly grass hills along the bay. To the west the skyscrapers of San Francisco loomed through the sea haze, and to the north was the Golden Gate Bridge and the uplift of the Marin Headland and Mount Tamalpais. People were walking here and there, and kids were flying kites. We drove around the cove to the pier, which spider-legged out toward the horizon.

The pier was crowded with fishermen, mothers with kids in strollers, couples of all stripes and genders. Alice had never been to the pier, but she and Gaby walked arm in arm and talked to each other. My father had his binoculars around his neck and stopped to look at birds. Sal wanted to look at the gulls perched on the pilings.

"They're right there," Ottie said. "You can see them without binoculars."

"I want to see them *close*," Sal said.

"There's a loon," my father said. He pointed to a bird sitting low on the water. "Check it out."

Ottie stood at the rail and raised the glasses. "'Loon' is a funny word," she said. "He dived under."

Sal made a lunge for the binoculars, but my father held her off. "Loons feed underwater," he said, "He'll come up again."

Sal went off in a huff, but I waited for a turn to see the loon. The bird surfaced, and through the glasses I saw it was in gray winter plumage—nothing special.

"Five species of loons occur in California," my father said.

Alice thought the bird was beautiful—low in the water, efficient, the perfect shape.

I followed after Sal, who was a few hundred yards down the pier watching a Vietnamese fisherman reel in something, while his wife readied a net. They spoke in arguing tones, though I had no idea what they said, and I dragged Sal by the hand to the end of the pier, which was a fence with a sign.

"You can't act like that," I said. "Don't be so spoiled."

"I thought you were going to Asia," Sal said.

"Not right away. Maybe not ever. That's irrelevant to your behavior."

"I wish you'd go tomorrow."

"You do not."

Beyond the metal fence were cement pilings still in the water where the pier had once extended farther out into the bay. On the water, sailboats canted to the breeze, and several fishing boats chugged through the waves. The Golden Gate Bridge looped across the space where the sun was settling into clouds. Gulls, close and far away, whirled through the air.

"He never sat down with us," Sal said. "That day at the beach we should have known he was sad."

"And what would he have said?" I asked.

"That he loved us, of course," Sal said. "And then we could have said we loved him."

"That would have been wise," I said. "But we know he loves us, and, anyway, we're stuck with him. Children can't divorce."

"He's stuck with us," Sal said.

We walked back and checked the fishermen's buckets for what they'd caught. Now and then we stopped along the railing to look at the gulls, each of which was beautiful in its own way. Sal clambered up onto the bottom rail and flapped her arms pretending to fly.

Farther down the pier, my father was pointing into the distance, explaining to Ottie something he saw, or so I imagined. Ottie was looking through the binoculars, and Gaby and Alice had moved off by themselves. This was the world I was living in now, I thought—my family fractured, my stepsisters confused, my future in jeopardy, my father the troubled soul. I missed my brother Pax. But what mattered was being needed. I could postpone Asia to help Charlotte. I could be around Ottie and Sal and every so often fend off my crazy father, who loved us and the world.

# ACKNOWLEDGMENTS

The following stories first appeared in magazines:

"Alba" in the *Atlantic Monthly*; "The Spirit Bird" in the *Virginia Quarterly Review*; "Race" in the *Missouri Review*; "La Mer de l'Ouest," in the *Georgia Review*; "The Hotel Glitter" in *Shenandoah;* "Who Is Danny Pendergast?" in the *Antioch Review*; "The Man at Quitobaquito" in the *Southern Review*; "Seeing Desirable Things" in the *Sewanee Review*; "The Graceless Age" in the *Gettysburg Review*; "The Path of the Left Hand" in the *Missouri Review*; "La Garza del Sol" in the *Sewanee Review*; "Joan of Dreams" in the *Virginia Quarterly Review*; and "The Beautiful Light" in the *Southern Review*.